> ### *"Come at me again, I'm going to hurt you," he growled low.*

Collecting herself and her thoughts, Jax considered her current tactics. They weren't working. She was strong. He was stronger. She eyed him covertly from beneath her long, dark lashes. Power radiated off him in waves. He reminded her of a big, sleek, predatory panther. From his stylishly cut jet-black hair, his arresting face and full, mocking lips to his impeccable black suit and the way it hung effortlessly from his big, muscular body down to his custom black-leather Italian shoes, she didn't miss a thing. Most especially the harsh glint of his unusual blue eyes.

She nodded, mentally shifting gears, then pushed off the wall.

In total op mode, Jax slowly stalked her nemesis. She smiled slightly. His eyes burned with anger, but he couldn't hide the heat flickering behind them. She shook her head and was rewarded with his gaze raking her from her naturally thick mahogany-colored hair to her fitted black turtleneck to her short black-leather skirt down to the tips of her black, thigh-high stiletto jack-boots that clicked on the hardwood floor.

She stopped two steps from him, planted her feet wide, and set her hands on her hips. "What if I like it to hurt?"

KARIN HARLOW

ENEMY LOVER

POCKET STAR BOOKS

New York   London   Toronto   Sydney

Pocket Star Books
A Division of Simon & Schuster, Inc.
1230 Avenue of the Americas
New York, NY 10020

This book is a work of fiction. Names, characters, places, and incidents either are products of the author's imagination or are used fictitiously. Any resemblance to actual events or locales or persons, living or dead, is entirely coincidental.

First Pocket Star Books paperback edition June 2010

POCKET STAR BOOKS and colophon are registered trademarks of Simon & Schuster, Inc.

For information about special discounts for bulk purchases, please contact Simon & Schuster Special Sales at 1-866-506-1949 or business@simonandschuster.com.

The Simon & Schuster Speakers Bureau can bring authors to your live event. For more information or to book an event contact the Simon & Schuster Speakers Bureau at 1-866-248-3049 or visit our website at www.simonspeakers.com.

Cover design by Lisa Litwack, art by Gene Molica

Manufactured in the United States of America

10 9 8 7 6 5 4 3 2 1

ISBN 978-1-4391-0982-3
ISBN 978-1-4391-7796-9 (ebook)

ACKNOWLEDGMENTS

Once again, my thanks to Kimberly Whalen for her expertise, guidance, and also for being there when I need her most. To my editor Lauren McKenna: I aspire to become your dream writer and therefore save your editorial hand from permanent disfigurement. In the meantime, thank you for being the best and hardest working editor in New York.

To Captain Barry Barber of the Baltimore County Police Department, and godfather to my youngest son, thank you for dealing with those you-know-who's down at Central-you-know-where.

To my home girls! Jos, Tawny, Syl, and Sharon. Ladies, you keep me real. Thank you for that. To the real Jax Cassidy, for such a cool name!

And last but not least, to my husband, Gary, for his never faltering patience and willingness to help me with everything from the little questions to the big scenes and for fixing all those last-minute dinners when the muse was so damn hot my keyboard was smokin'! Thank you for all the pots of your special coffee and calmly dealing with me when I morphed into the writer from hell. And for allowing me to wake you in the middle of the night after you were asleep for hours because I was just coming to bed and had to tell you how many words I wrote. And finally, thank you for all the errand runs, grocery runs and for getting me dark chocolate when I needed it most.

I love you.

ONE

{

January
Baltimore City Courthouse
Sally port prisoner transfer section

Irony was one fickle, messed-up bitch, Angela thought. A year and a half ago she was the fair-haired darling of Charm City. Baltimore's hottest get-the-hell-out-of-my-way-I'm-going-to-the-top cop. Today, in the icy rain that bit at her skin like shotgun spray, two female deputies escorted her, hobbled and cuffed, clad in prison orange, from her courthouse holding cell into the sally port.

The anger she'd kept tamped down since her assault, subsequent arrest, and trial—even when that asshole prosecutor had twisted the facts and her sergeant had trashed her on the witness stand—finally erupted. Yeah, she'd made it too damn easy for them. It was a given there was no honor among the criminals she'd spent most of her adult life putting behind bars. You never trusted them. Never turned your back and never gave them an opportunity to do you. Never had she thought her squad would betray her in such a vicious, public way as they had. If you couldn't trust your partner, who the hell could you trust?

How the hell had she let this happen? She hadn't let

this happen. Her squad had sold her out. And what had happened afterward? She clenched her jaw, grinding her teeth. She was only human, and, in the end, justice had been served. The price? Her freedom.

Involuntarily, she jerked against the hands grasping her biceps and shivered as a harsh jag of frigid air slapped her in the face. She was going away for life with no chance of parole for at least two decades. Mild hysteria began to seep into her pores. Soon, it would sink deeper into her muscles, then her bones and her organs, before it ate her up. Her chest rose and fell in quick, harsh puffs. She felt like she was walking a gangplank, the shark-infested waters below swirling, churning—waiting.

Angela expelled a long breath into the cold air and watched it curl, then disappear when another harsh blast of air caught it, immediately turning it into nothingness. She refused to become nothing. She was tough. She could handle prison, even though she wasn't going to get the preferential treatment she had received in the Women's Detention Center here in the city. She was a trained professional. It was the damn cell, that eight-by-eight space that caused her more concern than a shank-carrying inmate who wanted some fresh meat for the night. Ange hated small spaces. As a little girl, her cousin had locked her in an old refrigerator in the abandoned field behind her house. She'd panicked, her screams for help unheard. She'd woken up in the arms of a policeman. He'd smiled and told her she was going to be OK. She'd known then what she wanted to be when she grew up.

Now she was going to prison and probably never coming out. She was glad her mother had died before

Angela had been sentenced. Her dad? Long gone. He didn't matter. How could he, when she and her mom had never mattered to him?

Angela balked, the muscles in her arms and neck tightening. The guards yanked her along, and this time she offered no resistance, not even when she heard a bus engine roar to life. Inhaling the cold air deeply into the warmth of her lungs, she exhaled it slowly, refusing to watch it disappear without a trace.

She blinked against the shards of rain, wanting, despite the foul weather, to stand in it rather then step on that bus. The bus to Jessup. The bus to the Maryland Correctional Institution for Women. The bus to hell.

Angela shook her head, forcing herself not to focus on what was ahead of her. But as one thought hijacked another, she came full circle, thinking what a cluster fuck her life had become. And there wasn't a damn thing she could do to change it. Not now. Not ever.

"Giacomelli, I hope you have some friends over at Jessup. If you don't, make some fast," Deputy Alvarez said as she steered Angela toward the bus. "Those girls in Jessup are gonna want a piece of you the minute they find out you're in the house."

Angela's head snapped back and she looked Alvarez straight in the eye, nearly tripping in the short shackles. Alvarez tightened her grip, as did the other guard. "They'll have to get to me first," Angela said. And she knew they would. Eventually.

"I can't believe I'm hauling you off for murder one, Giacomelli," Alvarez rambled. "I thought you were a lot smarter than that."

"Yeah, well, walk a mile in my shoes."

Alvarez shook her head and *tsk*ed *tsk*ed like Angela was some kid who'd gotten caught with her hand in the cookie jar.

"Fuck you, Alvarez."

Smyth, the other guard, grunted and tightened her grip on Angela's arm. "You think that mouth of yours is going to keep the boogeyman away?" Smyth shook her head. Pity radiated from her deep hazel eyes. "I'm scared for you, Giacomelli."

"Don't waste the energy, Smyth." Angela threw her shoulders back, commanding herself to show no fear. Where she was going, the predators fed on fear. When word got out who she was and what she'd done, she'd be an instant target. And even though she'd be housed away from the general populace, they could still get to her. And she'd be ready.

She'd get no help from her ex-colleagues. Not after all the dirt that had come out during the trial. They were funny that way. Back in the day, when cops had been allowed to be cops and not PC pansies, the blue shield had protected its own even at a cost to the rank and file. Now? Every prick in the department walked the PC line. The thugs ruled the streets and the cops were screwed, with their hands tied behind their backs.

Just as she'd been totally screwed by that pimp, human trafficker, and all-around piece of shit, Carlos Montes. And her backup? Nowhere to be found. They *should* have been there, but they hadn't been. When she'd gone after her sergeant and her partner for answers, they'd had none. And then the shit had really hit the fan. There was no love lost between ex-cop, now convicted felon Angela Giacomelli and BCPD.

Angela let out a long, pensive breath as a sudden wave of guilt, laced with self-directed anger, washed over her. Not for what she'd done. Not because she'd made it easy for them to send her to prison for the rest of her life. But that in the end, she had let down her mom, the only person who had loved her unconditionally. It was her only regret in life.

"C'mon," Alvarez grumbled, yanking her along. Angela ignored her, keeping her steps deliberately slow, almost casual. She'd get on the damn bus when she got there: in her time. The guard leveled her black eyes on Angela and paused in her step, causing the other guard to yank her forward as if she'd been a rope in a tug-of-war. "You're not my only prisoner, and just because you used to wear a uniform doesn't give you special treatment."

"Where's the love, Juanita?"

"I got no love for felons."

Angela smirked. "Yeah? What if that slimeball Montes sold your little girl to the highest bidder?"

Juanita shook her head, refusing to answer. But Angela saw the fury spark in her dark eyes. Alvarez could act like a holy roller, but in the end, she'd do what she had to do, badge or not. Just like Angela had.

"Don't tell me when he skipped away free as a bird you'd be OK with that."

"God will be his ultimate judge."

"God works too slow for me."

"He might work slow, but His vengeance is mighty. You'll have lots of time to read all about Him where you're going."

"Great, can't wait," Angela muttered as she was pushed toward the correctional officer standing like a

brick wall in front of the open doors to the prison transport. She met his piercing eyes, staring back unwaveringly. She took exception to the calculating glare in his
eyes. "You have something to say to me, Officer?" Angela
challenged.

A slow half smile twisted his lips. He towered over
her five-foot-five-inch frame. Not many men intimi-
dated her, but this one? Maybe. Just a little. He was
broad and muscular, and there was something primal
about him that made her very aware she was a woman.
He looked around to make sure no one of significance
was watching and leaned a little toward her. "What if I
do?" he taunted.

"Get me out of this hardware and I'll teach you to
keep that mouth of yours shut."

"End it, Giacomelli," Alvarez said, pushing her forward. Angela stumbled, the hobble giving her barely a
six-inch step, and slammed into the wall of the guard's
chest. He grabbed her shoulders to steady her. She jerked
out of his grasp and hissed.

"Don't touch me!"

Doing the opposite, he spun her around and slammed
her, face-first, against the side of the bus. Pressing his
big body against her, his fist bore into the small of her
back. Angela gritted her teeth and closed her eyes, suddenly feeling suffocated and weak at the knees. Since her
assault, she could not stand to be touched by anyone,
especially a man.

"You have no rights, prisoner," he softly said against
her ear. "I'm bigger and badder than you, so you decide
now how you want this to go down."

"Let. Go. Of. Me," she ground out.

"Are you going to play nice?"

"Let go and find out."

He chuckled, but damned if he didn't back off, yanking her with him. He spun her back around. Angela caught the surprised look on Alvarez's and Smyth's faces. While an unruly prisoner was often at the mercy of the guards, this type of conduct was what lawsuits were made of. Yet they did nothing to stop the guard's behavior. She glanced at them with a sneer, then looked up at the brute. "So you get off roughing up helpless women?"

He threw his head back and laughed in genuine humor. "There is nothing helpless about you."

Angela eyed him angrily. She never could stand being the brunt of someone's humor, however innocently intended. One of her many character flaws.

Alvarez handed him the file folder she had been carrying. "Inmate 24-417-9327, Giacomelli, Angela, Celeste. She's all yours, Officer"—she squinted at his name tag and looked back up at him—"Brinks. You're new."

"I'm filling in for Horner." He took the file and grabbed Angela by the arm, his fingers biting deep and hard, forbidding resistance.

"Prick," she hissed and preceded him up the narrow steps she could barely climb, the shackle chain was so short. She glared at the driver sitting in his cage and took umbrage at the soft shove Officer Brinks gave her, pushing her to the back of the bus.

Great. Right next to his cage at the very back of the box.

Once she was seated and locked down, Brinks stalked back to the front of the bus, where he brought in another prisoner, locking her in before going for another. By the time he was done, six other women were up front, while Angela got the preferred seating in the back.

She looked up and squinted against the struggling ray of sun that filtered through the gray clouds. She lowered her gaze and looked out the window to the concrete sally port. She'd stood in it many times, watching shackled criminals file into this very bus like cattle. Animals being hauled off to the big house. Off to do time for their crime. Too many of them came back, only to repeat the process. No lesson learned.

She would never know if it would be the same for her. It didn't matter that she'd be up for parole in twenty. Her gut told her: Once she stepped through the prison gate, she wasn't coming out.

She pushed back into the stiff, torn cushion. The panic that had seized her earlier began to snake up from her belly. She swallowed hard and took deep cleansing breaths. The bus smelled like piss and shit, and there was no air circulating. A short, harsh wave of nausea rolled through her. Her stomach tightened and a dry heave spasmed. Her back clenched in pain from the tightness and she tried to puke, but nothing, not even bile, came up. Closing her eyes, Angela hung her head between her knees, trying to get her bearings. She took a deep breath. The stench of the bus was too much.

She jerked up and fought another heave, but this time she did puke. She spit the yellow bile onto the floor next to a dried loogey. Turning her head, she wiped her mouth on the shoulder of her jumpsuit. Angela caught the contemptuous stare of one of the prisoners seated several rows ahead on her left. The woman spit, then grinned, showing off her four teeth. She made a smacking sound, then slurped, eyeing Angela up and down. "I haven't had fresh meat like you in a long time."

"I hope you like a little AIDS and a few cankers to go with it," Angela said, staring down the Amazon.

Brinks coughed beside her where he was messing around with his equipment.

"Welcome to the club, sweet cheeks," the woman said.

"Shut up and turn around, Wolinski," Brinks bit off.

The woman shot him a glare and turned, but not before she blew Angela a kiss.

"Stay out of my business," Angela said to the guard.

He looked up from stowing away the files on each prisoner in a metal box in his cage. His deep green eyes glittered in amusement. "You're going to need a friend where you're going. You might want to think twice about being nice to me."

Angela scowled, warning him off. "I don't play well with others. Leave me alone."

He ignored her and walked toward the front of the bus.

Closing her eyes, Angela leaned her head back on the hard headrest and took in several deep breaths, trying to get a handle on herself. She was scared. There, she'd admitted it, scared shitless actually, and no one, not one single person, gave a damn about where she was headed.

She kept her eyes closed when the automatic-locking, heavy-gauge metal door closed around the driver. The hiss of the air release from the bus doors, followed by the heavy cling of it locking them all in, jarred her drawn nerves.

This was it.

No more jail. No more court. No more, nothing. She was going away. To Prison. Angela wondered if she'd survive.

Heavy footsteps thudded toward her. Officer Friendly. The whoosh of air his body disturbed as he walked past her into his own cage brushed across her cheeks. His clean, citrusy scent was welcome in the dank stink of the bus. She kept her eyes closed. The sound of the jump seat creaking with his weight sitting upon it, followed by the lock and load click of his shotgun, triggered another wave of nausea. *Fuck.*

"All secure," he miked to the driver.

Over the bus radio, the driver said, "Transport fifty-two, 10-49 Jessup Women's Facility with seven on board, starting mileage, 24,766."

"10-4, T-fifty-two, starting 24,766 at 1517 hours," Dispatch cleared.

The bus lurched forward and so did Angela's life.

TWO

The bus slammed to an abrupt halt. Angela's eyes flew open, and immediately her intuition told her something was wrong. She jerked her head back and craned her neck, staring at Brinks through narrowed eyes. He grinned.

Sonofabitch!

"What the hell are you doing?" she quietly demanded.

"What's the problem?" Brinks miked to the driver as he looked over his shoulder behind the bus. Angela craned her neck farther around, straining her muscles to look in the same direction. A black panel van idled several feet behind them. Brinks gave a shallow nod to the van's driver and received the same gesture in return. Then he turned back, giving the bus driver all of his attention.

Scenarios careened in Angela's brain. A breakout? Hostages? She looked up at the driver. His head moved back and forth as he leaned forward over the steering wheel in an attempt to see what was causing the delay. Angela scooted as far to the edge of her seat as she could. A new fear treaded disruptively across her tightly held composure. She did not want to die. *Keep your cool, Ange.*

"Looks like a backup ahead. Traffic's at a standstill," the bus driver miked back.

Angela and Brinks turned at the sound of the van door opening behind them. Brinks gave the all clear sign to the two men who emerged from the van, completely blacked out head to toe.

"What the hell's going on?" Giacomelli hoarsely demanded. Brinks ignored her and set the shotgun down butt first against the rear emergency door. With all eyes forward except hers, he pulled up his right pant leg and grabbed a small canister strapped there.

Angela watched in shock and awe as he pulled it out with his right hand and, with his left, pulled the pin.

"Bomb!" Angela screamed to get the driver's attention. The driver jerked around in his seat, his eyes on Brinks, who remained unflappable. Brinks unlocked the security door and rolled the bomb down the aisle to the main passenger area. Angela shoved her head between her knees and braced for impact. Just as it exploded with a bang and she realized she hadn't caught any shrapnel, she popped up in her seat, only to be stayed by her shackles. Frustrated by her inability to react, she glanced at the cage. Brinks turned, pulled down the back of the jump seat, and extracted a hidden gas mask, which he quickly placed over his face. The hiss of the released noxious gas infiltrated her senses. Ignoring the screams of the passengers and the driver's frantic calls, Brinks turned to Angela. Dreadful realization grabbed hold of her and would not let go. *She* was the target. Holy hell, her face would be splattered on every post office wall from here to California.

"Who the hell are you?" she demanded as she was overcome with a fit of coughs.

He grinned under the mask and said, "If I told you, I'd have to kill you."

Wildly, Angela scanned the perimeter of the bus. The driver was down and she could see only the slumped shoulders of the other passengers. Brinks opened the rear emergency door, where the two masked men now stood. After opening the security door to his cage, he entered the passenger compartment as smoke billowed out the open door. He hurried toward Angela, who tried holding her breath to stave off the fumes of the sleeping gas. The dark hole of unconsciousness shimmered on the fringes of her mind. As Brinks bent to unshackle her, Angela was powerless to stop him. Her last conscious thought was of him slinging her limp body over his hard shoulder.

Slowly, consciousness filtered into Angela's muddled brain. Her head pounded, her back screamed in pain, and her mouth was desert dry. She could barely draw in a deep breath without feeling smothered. Slowly, her senses returned. She was sitting, but her body felt heavy and stiff, as if it had been in the same position too long. Her chin rested against her chest, but as she tried to raise it, it wobbled. Her head bobbed back down.

Although her eyes fluttered open to see, everything was black.

What the hell?

Lifting her arms and shifting her weight, she realized she was still shackled and cuffed. Her head pounded and her aching body strained against the steel handcuffs.

In one bright sunburst of clarity, Angela realized she

was hooded and sitting upright in a chair. A chair she was tied to!

Her last conscious thoughts came crashing down around her. The transport, that guard, Bricker—*Brinks!* The bus stopping, the sleeping gas, then . . . nothing. Until now. Where the hell was she?

She caught her breath, the fabric of the hood sucking into her mouth. She spit it out, wrestled her rising panic down, and listened.

Silence.

The air around her was heavy, but alive. She could feel life forces surrounding her, watching, listening, and waiting. She lifted her head once again, and this time she was able to maintain her position. Her vision was now clearing but still in the dark. "Take this goddamn bag off my head," she demanded.

"I told you she had a foul mouth."

Brinks.

"Fuck you, Brinks. Is your dick so small you have to hood your next victim?"

Several amused snorts swirled around her.

"I see, you have friends with small dicks too." She strained against the chains. "Go on, get it over with," she challenged. Even as she said the words, she tried not to imagine what a rabbit would feel like when a pack of pit bulls tore it apart. She squeezed her eyes shut and knew she could not emotionally handle another assault, especially a gang rape. "Just do it," she whispered, steeling herself.

"You're in a secure place and among friendlies," Brinks levelly said.

Her head snapped back, and she smirked under the

hood. "*Friendlies* don't bag and tie one another up unless they're both into the same kinky shit, and frankly, boys, I'm not feeling wet between the legs, so what the hell's going on?"

"You have an impressive service record, Officer Giacomelli," a deep voice said from the two o'clock position. "Two unit citations, several commendations and a nomination for the Medal of Valor."

"What of it?" Angela challenged.

"Then there are the three officer-involved shootings and the seven IAs. You've been busy for just eight years on the job. How is it, Officer, that you have three fatal shootings in the last three years when most career officers never pull their service weapons?"

"Three *righteous* shootings of deadbeat scumbags that left me no choice, that's how." She leaned forward so that the rope tied around her chest bit into her breast. She didn't wince but pressed harder. The pain diffused her fear. "Since we both know so much about my career, let's skip the flattery. Who are you, what do you want, and where the *hell* am I?"

"All in good time," the deep voice responded. He paused for nearly a full minute before he continued. "You seem to have a problem with authority." The soft click of fingers on a keyboard preceded his next words. "I see that although you're qualified and your test scores are quite high, you've been passed over twice for promotion. A notation in your file states, 'Officer Giacomelli has strong leadership qualities so long as she's the one leading. She fails to take directives when she disagrees with the direction ordered.'"

Angela shrugged. The reasons didn't matter now.

"Are you simply contrary for the hell of it, or is there a just cause in your mind for failure to follow a superior's orders?"

"I'm not following an asshole to hell just because he's got the rank." She sat back, glad for the relief. "Can we dispense with the ancient history lesson and get this bag off my head?"

"Your file indicates a hot temper."

"Free me, dismiss your looky-loos and I'll be happy to show you just how hot." Several of those looky-loos laughed aloud. "I hear the rest of you. Go fuck yourselves."

"A piece of work, that Montes business," another deep voice said, this one from behind her.

Angela twisted in the chair but was hampered by the bindings. She turned back to the one that seemed to know so much about her. "Is that what this is all about? I thought I was going to Jessup, not Gitmo."

"You're in neither," the first voice said. "You're a smart cop, Giacomelli. Why did you let yourself get caught?"

"Poor planning?" she shot back.

"Indeed. Had you been a little more precise after you executed Carlos Montes, chances are you would be on the streets of Baltimore City as we speak."

"Yeah, but I'm not, so let's get to the reason you invited me to your little party. Are you going to kill me? Get to it if you are."

"We have no intention of causing you any bodily harm, Officer Giacomelli," the voice behind her said.

She turned slightly to direct her comeback to him personally. "If you check your notes there, Einstein, you'll see I got fired. That means I'm no longer a cop, so cut the 'officer' crap."

"How would you like to be returned to your peace officer status?" he softly asked.

Stunned by his question, Angela sat silent for a long minute. What the hell was this? Some form of torture? Pretend to give the prisoner everything, then snatch it away and make them willing to give up anything to have it? Problem was, she had nothing they wanted. "People in hell would probably like ice water, and they're more likely to get it than I am of returning to BCPD."

"I didn't say anything about Baltimore City PD. How would you like an opportunity to continue putting bad people, very bad people, away? A chance to work for the law but just slightly outside of it? On the fringe, so to speak."

She was done as a cop. She'd lost all faith in that brotherhood. If she was going to go at anything, it would have to be alone, no outside or inside interference, and even on her terms, she wasn't sure she had it in her. She was too fucked up. She didn't want to be a part of anyone's personal tragedies anymore. She needed time to heal herself, otherwise how the hell could she help a victim? But the flip side was, numb was good—it kept her emotions out of the equation, and it made life a hell of a lot easier. And what they were offering was a hell of a lot more appealing than an eight-by-eight-foot cell at Jessup. "I'm listening."

The scrape of a chair moving backward and the soft rustle of fabric as the man behind her stood alerted her. She could smell him. Clean and spicy. The soft swish of his leather-soled shoes as he walked around her gave her his position. She followed him with the turn of her head. When he stopped directly in front of her, she could feel his body heat. She tilted her head back and looked directly up at him, wishing she could see him through the dark fabric.

"You have two choices, Angela Giacomelli: We can return you to face your sentence and a very small cell to call your own for the next twenty plus years, or you can come to work for us. Your record and conviction would still stand, and at any time you could be made to serve out that sentence. Any time you get out of line, disobey an order or find yourself in any other kind of trouble, it's fuck-you-very-much and you're on your way."

"What the hell kind of deal is that? I get to be your slave or else?"

"It's a deal that gives you back your freedom, or most of it, anyway. It's a deal that gets you out of your cell and allows you to continue working for the right reasons and the right people. It's a deal that in thirty seconds will be taken off the table. It's a free country, Officer, but not always a just one."

"I'm a fugitive in the eyes of the law! Where would I live? How would I make a living? How the hell can I do anything if I'm constantly looking over my shoulder for a damn marshall?"

"Let's not sweat the small stuff, Officer. Our organization does not make any move unless it is completely vetted. Yes, in the eyes of the law you are a fugitive, a fugitive who broke out with the help of some friends, a fugitive who on paper can easily appear to be deceased. A hazard of her escape, if you will." He paused, then said,

"You now have fifteen seconds to accept or reject my offer."

The room fell deadly quiet, and as each second ticked off, Angela's heart thumped with it. She could feel every eye in the room on her, waiting, wanting her to throw her lot in with them. And why not? What the hell did she have to lose? And while she knew it couldn't be this simple, because nothing in her life ever was, she nodded and said, "I'm in. Now take this fucking bag off my head!"

THREE

{

The first person she saw was Brinks. He no longer wore the correction officer uniform; now he was casually clad in dark slacks and a gray pullover sweater. He stood to the right of her, looking at her as if he couldn't decide whether she disgusted him or he should feel sorry for her. When she cast her gaze around the room, her nerves tightened, and she drew herself up. The others, all men, all devoid of emotion, all big, all looking like the definition of badass, nine in total, sat behind a huge round table watching her. And just like Brinks, they were the silent, hard-ass type with an air of arrogance that she wanted to slap off their handsome faces.

She felt like an organism under a microscope the way she was surrounded by all of them. Her, alone on a chair, inside a huge round table, them on the other side facing her. Only Brinks, who stood to the right side of her, was remotely aligned with her. Her heart thudded like a steam engine in her chest. But although they were all tough-as-steel looking, and could squeeze the life out of her with one hand, she didn't feel threatened. She looked past them to several black flat-screen monitors that covered three of the four walls. In her peripheral vision, she could see more. Along the right-hand wall, shiny black floor-to-ceiling cabinets. Above the oversized windowless metal door, painted in stark black, the symbol of the mythical phoenix. Who were these guys?

"What is this, the modern-day version of the Knights of the Round Table?" She laughed at the absurdity of it. But she was the only person in the room who found humor in her jibe. The men sat stone-faced, intently watching her.

"Officer Giacomelli." The deep voice got louder as its source came from behind her, walking the periphery of the table until he stood across from her, the table between them. He stood with his hands behind his back, rigid and ominous, dressed in black from head to toe. The button-down shirt and black slacks did nothing to hide the muscles beneath. Her gaze dipped to the floor and she could just see his size 14s peeking at her from beneath the table. When her gaze traveled back up to his face, she found it hard and unyielding. Angela's eyes widened. Brinks was big and he was bad, but this guy, he was . . . her skin shivered. His frosty blue eyes gave no hint of emotion. He was, she decided at that moment, as dead inside as she was.

He echoed her thoughts. "You are, for all intents and purposes, dead." His last word was a death knell that smashed the inside of her brain, splattering everything she knew and understood to a pulp. She was in way over her head, but there was no way in hell she was going to show any of these guys a hint of weakness. She'd go down with a fight they'd all remember.

She stiffened her spine and narrowed her eyes threateningly. "What's that supposed to mean?"

"Forget where you grew up, forget your roots, forget

you ever knew a woman named Angela Celeste Giaco-melli."

"You expect me to just take all of this at face value? Like you're doing me some kind of favor? Who are you? *What* are you asking me to be a part of?"

"As you were informed, we are friendlies. A covert organization that can and does cross the line to go as deep into the dark side as needed to achieve mission success. A covert op that handpicks its operatives, erases them, then, with a new identity, turns them loose."

The hair on the back of Angela's neck spiked. "A covert op that breaks the law in the name of upholding the law?"

Frosty eyes smiled and nodded. "More or less."

"And I'm just supposed to go along with the program?"

"That or Brinks will escort you to Jessup."

Angela pushed back into the hard metal of the chair and contemplated the offer as it stood. A chance for freedom, to a degree, but on their terms. And what if she didn't like their terms?

"From the moment of your extraction, all your previous identifying data have been reissued. Blood type, fingerprints, DNA," the man in black said.

"How?"

"We have long arms and deep-rooted connections all over the world. We can, with one fell stroke on a keyboard, erase anything and anyone."

"But I existed!"

"And so you still do, but with altered information."

"Are you implying that the fingerprints on file in every system that houses them including DMV are not mine?"

He nodded.

Angela swallowed hard. Who were these guys? And why her?

"When you are fully indoctrinated, you'll be apprised of the full scope of our capabilities. Get familiar with Jax Cassidy, which is your new name—"

"Are you kidding me!" She struggled against the rope. While Brinks fought a smile, so did a few of the other jerks circling her. The man before her, however, did not so much as blink.

"Call her Cuddles," one of the guys taunted.

Brinks's green eyes glittered. "How about something sweet, like her vocabulary."

She moved to kick him away, but her legs were bound to the damn chair. "If I'm going to play, I want a name I like."

"This isn't a game. It's my rules or you go back to your old life," the dark-haired iceman softly said.

Angela—she refused to think of herself as Jax—narrowed her eyes and leaned forward. "Listen, before we go any further here, why don't you put it all out on the table. I reserve the right to change my mind."

"Too late. You have seen and heard too much. I'd have to kill you, or worse . . ." The man in black moved to stand behind the empty chair in front of her.

"Who are you?" she demanded.

The one in charge smiled slightly, and it wasn't really a smile, more like a token I-guess-I-should-throw-you-a-bone-if-I-want-compliance sneer. "To the outside world I'm known as Mr. Black." He looked around the room to the men surrounding her. "Here, on the inside, I'm known as Godfather."

Angela sucked in a sharp breath. She'd be damned if she'd call him Godfather. That title was one of fondness and respect. She felt neither for the man who held her life in his hands. Mr. Black nodded to Brinks. "Unlock her."

Brinks stepped forward and eyed her cryptically. "Promise not to bite me?"

"Oh, trust me, a bite from me is the least of your worries."

He pulled a key from his pants pocket and dangled it from his fingers. "Promise?"

Angela shook her head, exhaled, then relaxed back against the stiff metal. "Just do it."

As he deftly unlocked each lock, Angela watched his every move. She stiffened when he got too close. He looked at her and said, "I won't touch you, and if I do it's by mistake, so don't freak out."

Once freed of the chains and manacles, she stretched out her arms and groaned. When she straightened her legs, she hissed in a sharp breath. Bunched muscles tightened harder at their sudden freedom. She arched her back and stood, rubbing her chafed wrists.

"Sit down. Before we proceed, there are a few matters to get clear," Mr. Black said.

Angela nodded, no longer up to verbal sparring. What she wanted was food, a shower and a comfortable bed. She sat.

"You are a victim and survivor of rape, battery and betrayal by your department. As such, before you are released for active duty here, you will have to be cleared by one of our medical personnel. That means therapy—"

Angela bristled. No way! Shaking her head, she moved to stand.

"Sit down!" the boss boomed. Hands fisted, he leaned down on the table in front of her. "You are unstable, and as such you are no good to me or any member of this team. Lives are at stake, Jax, including yours. Now knock that chip off your shoulder and get with the program!" He stood to his full towering height. "When you are medically cleared and fit for duty, we'll meet again."

"I changed my mind, Attila. Jessup has a cell with my name on it."

He cracked a snide smile, and Angela felt a shiver of apprehension shimmy up her spine. Slowly he nodded. She looked to Brinks for help, but he, like the others, stared unwaveringly at her. "That can be arranged. But before you return, this is how it would play out for you: We dress you up and shoot you up, then leave you doped out in District Attorney Judd Pulaski's place." Angela stiffened at the mention of her ex-boyfriend. Mr. Black nodded knowingly and continued, "When your ex finds you, he'll have you arrested for B&E, you'll go back to prison for your original crime, plus the added charges of absconding, drug possession and B&E. I'm sure we can come up with a few others as well. And you can kiss any chance of parole good-bye." He leaned closer. "And while you're in Jessup? We'll make sure you get good-night kisses from all of the inmates."

Potent fury erupted deep inside of her and she spewed. "How do you think life will be for you wannabe Lancelots when I tell the authorities exactly what happened to me?" she threatened.

Deep chuckles reverberated off the walls. Angela

stiffened to steel. They were laughing at her! Mr. Black broke a genuine smile that showed a rack of brilliant white teeth. Somebody had had a great orthodontist. He shrugged. "Be my guest. You won't be the first to try and fail, and you won't be the last."

Angela sat back in the chair. She was headstrong, she was impetuous, she was emotional and she was scared out of her brains, but she was not stupid. "There is nothing emotionally wrong with me."

Brinks snorted.

She wheeled on him. "Fuck you!"

When several other men cracked smiles, she had the overwhelming urge to beat the crap out of every one of them. "I don't need to speak to anyone about what happened to me. I'm over it."

"Prove it," Brinks challenged.

Angela smirked at him, then turned and stared down the big bad boss man. "Do you know how I got to Montes?"

"Why don't you tell us," he invited.

Angela smiled, her lips tight. "When I found out that slime bag was a fed untouchable, I tracked down an old buddy of mine in D.C. Special Agent Wayne Rios. Ol' Wayne knew exactly where the safe house was. You know the rest of the story."

"Why don't you elaborate and tell us how you extracted that sensitive information from Special Agent Rios?"

Angela's smile loosened. She shook her head and tossed her hair back. Her gaze locked onto the boss man's. She saw fire there, behind the ice. Angela knew exactly how to work her assets. "I fucked it out of him."

Her remark was met with stone silence.

Angela stood and sauntered toward Mr. Black. "So you see, *boss* man," she softly said, "I've processed the assault, dealt with it, and filed it away. Done. Finito. *Gone.*" She snapped her fingers. "Just like that."

His gaze bore into her as if he could see past her soul. His intensity tipped her off balance. "Since you have dealt so succinctly with your trauma, tell us what Montes did to you," Mr. Black pushed.

Angela balked. *That* she would not do. Telling them about Rios was one thing. Seducing him had been her decision, her rules, and she'd controlled every second of the interlude. But she would not relive the shame and pain of Montes in public. She stared harshly at the boss and stepped back, shaking her head.

"You can't even talk about it," Mr. Black said. The bully leaned forward, his pale blue eyes narrowing to slits. "Well, you're going to. We're your team now. You need to trust us. Talk to us. Tell us everything."

"I have nothing to say to any of you!" she screamed.

Brinks stood and came around the table, intent, she was sure, on touching her. Angela took a defensive stance. "Stay the hell way from me."

He stopped before he crossed into her space and looked hard at her. His eyes softened just enough so that she could see his own pain hiding deep behind his cool exterior. "Officer," he softly said, "we all have our demons. Barbara Martin, the therapist here, is the best in the business. Talk to her, and you might find you have something in common."

The sudden sting of tears bit at Angela's eyes. She had not cried once since her attack. Not even when she'd received word that her mother had died. Why now? Why here in front of these strangers? She despised her weakness.

"I doubt I have anything in common with your shrink."

"You're not leaving this room until you tell us what happened," Mr. Black said.

Angela moved into his space, daring him to touch her, daring him to push her, daring him to cross her clearly drawn line. "Then I guess we're going to have a long night." She turned and plunked down on the chair she had been tied to. Crossed her legs and her arms and tipped her head back and closed her eyes.

She wondered how long it would take him. She wondered if he'd lose control and force the truth from her. Every muscle in her body tensed hard, anticipating an attack. Long minutes passed. Silence, save for the soft breaths of the men that echoed around her. She could feel Mr. Black's presence. He had not moved. She guessed he was staring down at her with that sharp scowl. Let him.

More minutes passed. Now she was bored. Slowly Angela opened her eyes and stared directly into Mr. Black's icy gaze.

"You will discover, Giacomelli, that as part of this team, you will have no secrets." He stepped closer. "You will also discover that cowards are not allowed."

His baiting worked. She stiffened but still kept her appendages crossed, closing all of them out.

"Cowards get other people killed. I value each and every life in this room above all others. I will not allow you to jeopardize any of them."

Angela looked up and said, "Well, I guess maybe you

should have done a little more homework before you *recruited* me. I have nothing to say to you."

Mr. Black moved in closer. Angela unwrapped and stood up. When he chest-butted her, she caught her breath. He lowered his head and spoke so softly that she barely heard his words: "Tell us what happened, now, or I send you back to Jessup."

Angela swallowed hard. For spite alone, she wanted to tell him to fuck off. Tell him she didn't need him, his little group of elite operatives, or his pity. But she didn't.

"We are not the enemy," he said with just enough sincerity that she felt herself crumble a little inside.

It wasn't his words, she realized, that struck something deep inside of her; it was the compassion in his tone. Angela fisted her hands at her sides, wrestling with the nightmare of what had happened to her and speaking about it to these strangers. They had no idea that for her to talk about it aloud was to relive it. And she was not strong enough to go there. Not yet. Not here.

Tilting her head back, Angela glared at each man in the room, and instead of arrogance, she saw in each one of them pain, buried and endured. Had they purged as she was being asked—no, forced—to do? She turned her attention back to Brinks, who had not moved and stood quietly waiting for her to speak. Swallowing hard, she opened her mouth to speak, but only a hoarse grunt emerged. She swallowed again.

"You say me and your shrink might have something in common?"

Brinks nodded.

Angela laughed, the sound harsh. "Was your Doctor Martin raped by a piece of shit pimp while her team, the team that was supposed to make sure that didn't happen, sat on their asses?" Angela demanded. "Was she tied up and beaten while the little girls he smuggled in from Mexico sat and watched, knowing if they didn't do exactly what he told them to do, they'd be next?" She trembled violently, unable to control the outburst. The faces in the room blurred as she was sucked back in time to Montes's filthy hovel. She could smell him. Sweat, cigarettes and tequila. His skin was soft and clammy, his arms furry, his breath putrid, his dick small. When she'd laughed at his midget hard-on, he'd lost it. She flinched, feeling the smash of his ham-sized fist on her face, the sound of crunching cartilage so close. The warm spray of blood on her face. *Her* broken nose, *her* blood, *her* body being violated. The screams of the children, their desperation as they were forced to witness her attack.

Angela jerked her head back and glared up at Brinks. "Did Doctor Martin's rapist break her nose and shatter her jaw?" Hot tears stung her eyes. She ripped open her prison jumpsuit, exposing her belly and the long pink scar there. "Did a lunatic butcher her belly, making sure she could never have a child?" The tears erupted as her rage and shame spewed like a geyser. She looked past Brinks to Mr. Black. "Tell me, big, bad-ass-mother-fucking King Arthur, did her partner sidestep her with a half-assed apology, blaming the screwup of the sting on her that night? And did her team turn their backs on her when that prick who raped, beat, and mutilated her was whisked away by the feds, who said he was an untouchable witness? Did the love of her life, the guy who promised to stand by her no matter what, dump her like she was a used-up piece of furniture because he couldn't bear to touch her?"

Angela stopped. The room was tomb silent and just as cold. Evenly she looked around at each one of them, and for the first time their arrogance was gone. She looked up at the man in charge. "Satisfied?"

He nodded and said, "Yes. I think we can be of help to each other."

She didn't want to help anyone, not even herself.

"Now," Mr. Black softly said, "tell me. What can we do for you right now?"

FOUR

ι

When the door closed behind the newest addition to L.O.S.T., Godfather forced back a scowl, doing his best to keep his face expressionless. Looking around the table, he saw uncertainty reflected in his fellow operatives' eyes. Silence weighed heavy in the tense air. Who would voice their opposition first?

Dominic Satriano cracked. "She's too unstable."

Godfather said nothing but walked to the mainframe housed in the massive black console in the corner of the large room. He pulled the keyboard out, grabbed the remote and hit a button. Light flickered across the screens surrounding them. Immediately, an image of Angela Giacomelli, beaten, bruised and broken, wrapped in a hospital gown, sprang up. "She is now," Godfather admitted. With a press of his finger, a slide-show began. Shots taken at the hospital. Obviously after that piece of shit Montes had destroyed her. But L.O.S.T. would rebuild her. Make her stronger, smarter, more lethal. The ultimate weapon against a man.

Very little caused Godfather to feel more than his normal dogged determination to put pricks like Montes away. But something about Angela Giacomelli moved him beyond his usual sober awareness. She was damaged, flawed, and hurting badly, but beneath all that pain was a woman who still had more than a little fight left in her. A woman who had the nerve and drive to clean up Dodge, one piece of crap at a time. He'd known when he'd read about her arrest last year that she was marked for L.O.S.T. Now he had her, and he was not going to allow L.O.S.T. to slip from his grasp. She was perfect for what he had in mind, but he worried that it might take too long to bring her up to speed. There were two ops right now he could use her on, but she was in no shape to be turned loose. He cursed under his breath. Time was not a commodity he had right now. But he had no choice. He was a patient man. And he knew that Angela Giacomelli would deliver in spades if she was handled correctly.

"The bastard deserved what she did to him and more," Brinks, aka Gage Stone, sneered. A chorus of agreement rang out. Godfather nodded and continued to watch the flat screen.

Images from Angela's life flickered up one after another, cataloging her from birth to her police academy graduation. A chubby baby held in her proud grandfather's arms. An eight-year-old riding a dirt bike, flying a mile high into the air as she challenged fate with a brilliant, exuberant smile. Her receiving first communion, looking annoyed in a prissy white dress. Sitting ramrod stiff on a horse as a judge pinned the blue ribbon to her mount's bridle. Nailing the winning goal in the women's NCAA Division One lacrosse championship. Then, finally, the chief of police pinning her badge on her chest when she graduated valedictorian of her class.

Something foreign kicked him in the gut. Powerful but poignant. Making his chest burn in a way it hadn't in a very long time.

Satriano cleared his throat. "Okay, yeah. She's something. She didn't deserve what was done to her. But I'll say it again, she's unstable."

Godfather nodded again, deep in thought.

"What are you thinking?" Stone asked.

Godfather threw the remote on the table with a casual flick of his wrist. "I'm thinking she's perfect for at least two ops on the table right now."

"She's too volatile!" Satriano shouted.

Godfather let out a long breath and looked at Dom. "Satriano, there wasn't a more pissed-off unstable operative than you the day we dragged your sorry ass through those doors. You were back on the street in less than a month."

Dante, another operative and one who had no room to talk, snorted, smacking Satriano on the chest but quieting when Godfather turned on him. "And you, I remember the day you were hauled in here, telling us all to go fuck yourselves and swinging those ham fists of yours." He looked past Dom to Slade and Dylan. "Don't shake your heads, you both were as bad." He turned to Gage. "And you, Stone? No one could get near you." Godfather stared down every one of them. "You were all fuckups when you got here. That's why you were chosen. Because of the hell you'd been through. Because you weren't willing to take it lying down. Because you wanted payback." He pointed to the frozen frame of a stunning, smiling woman. "Jax is no different."

The room grew uncomfortably silent, and suddenly Godfather knew what was bugging them. He grunted. No one was willing to say it. Yes, they'd all been screwed up, but they were all screwed-up *men*. They weren't ruled by hormones or the urge to nurture. Save for Naomi, his assistant, they were an all-male squad. That was about to change.

"I respect your hesitation, men. But just in case none of you happened to notice, Jax Cassidy has some serious assets none of us have. We need a woman for the operations where a dick just won't make the cut. We need a woman like Jax, who is trained, who is fearless and who won't hesitate to use what she must to close a mission."

"Calculating," Cruz muttered.

Godfather smiled. "Exactly."

He turned and stared at the static images left on the screen. At every turn, Jax had challenged life—no fear, no hesitation, no regrets. The woman who'd left the room less than twenty minutes ago was hard as nails on the outside, but terrified on the inside. He'd seen it in her eyes. And he'd seen it magnify each time she'd thought someone had been about to touch her. Sighing, he rubbed the back of his neck.

When he had chest-butted her, he'd honestly had no clue what she would do. But when she hadn't attacked, he'd known then he had her. He liked that despite her instinct to fight, she had the self-control to do what was in her best interest.

"She does a good job hiding behind that mouth of hers," Stone said. "But she's not just unstable. She's scared, and fear causes mistakes."

Godfather nodded. The future of the team hung on every member's being in top form, mentally and physically. "Fear can be turned around and used to one's advantage," he said.

"It can also make you second-guess yourself," Cruz said from beside him.

"In Jax Cassidy's case, her fear will keep her focused," Godfather rejoined.

"I know we all agreed to recruit a female operative," Stone started, "but . . . she makes me nervous. Our motto has always been no rules. We do the job and we do whatever it takes. Stealing. Killing. Fu—" Stone hesitated.

Godfather shook his head. "She's too smart to use her body as a first assault."

Cruz coughed. "Didn't she just tell us she seduced the information she needed out of that fed?"

Godfather nodded again, trying very hard not to get pissed at his men. Didn't they see the potential in her that he did?

"Different set of circumstances. When I'm done with her, she won't have to use her body in a sexual way to gain the upper hand. Her brain will do all the work. It's why I recruited her."

Stone swiped his hand across his face in frustration. Godfather knew what bugged Gage. He didn't attempt to quell his concerns. It would go down as it always did. When the team had reservations, they hashed it out, then came to an agreeable, mutual resolution. The last thing he wanted was for there to be dissension among his operatives. Each one of their lives depended on complete trust in the other.

"Did any of you notice how she practically jumped out of her skin when she thought I was going to touch her?" Stone asked, then directed his next question at

Godfather. "And when you chest-butted her, she about caved on the spot."

Godfather nodded. "Normal behavior in a perceived hostile environment. She'll be desensitized soon enough. She'll go through the same assimilation you all went through, but the accelerated version."

"I don't think—" Stone started.

Godfather flashed. "You don't think what? Or do you suddenly have a problem with my authority, Stone? Or is it something personal?"

Stone met the stares of his teammates. Leaning back in his chair, hands behind his head, he looked squarely at Godfather and said, "Nothing personal, sir. She's just damned distracting."

Godfather smiled. "I know. Another reason she was handpicked. I'm counting on every man we set her up against to be blindsided."

"How much time do we have before she needs to be up to speed?" Cruz asked.

Godfather stood, thoughtful, then said, "As much time as she needs."

Every man in the room stood, slack-jawed. Godfather shook his head in bewilderment. "Do I have to explain the differences between the sexes again?"

"How long is as long as it takes?" Cruz demanded. "And why?"

"Because, Cruz, she's a female! And a traumatized one at that. She needs to heal." He glared at each man in the room. "Do you want her discharged before she's emotionally stable? Do you want her as your cover and take the chance she's going to nut up, or do you want to give her the time she needs to work things out?"

"What if she doesn't?" Stone said.

"She will," Godfather flatly answered, then exited the room.

Godfather stalked from the war room and down the hall to the office area. He nodded at the petite blonde who turned from one of her four computer screens in her chair. Her dark brown eyes shone bright with intelligence and, he could see, concern.

He frowned and put his hand up in the stop position. "Not you too, Naomi."

He watched her set her jaw. Always a prelude to an argument. "I might be just your paper pusher, sir, but I have a stake here too. That woman is half cocked, loaded and about to go on a killing spree."

There was not much that got past Godfather's right arm. Naomi Sullivan was the one who facilitated the details. While he was lord and master of the team and ops, she was mistress of the internal working of L.O.S.T.—reports, dossiers, procurement of official dummy docs, fact finder, travel agent, realtor, shopper of all things necessary for survival, and, ultimately, backup. She even hired the housekeeper. *And* the cleaners who took care of messes they left behind. She was the glue that held them all together. Rarely did she work in the field. They were all better served by her doing what she did best—keeping them alive and making them disappear, all from a stroke on the keyboard. She was to Godfather what Miss Moneypenny and M combined were to 007.

"Did something happen between here and the assimilation chamber?"

She shook her head, her short blonde bob brushing her cheeks. "To the naked eye, no. But she's as jumpy as a rabbit and has serious people issues. She looked haunted. Unstable. She scares me."

"We all have people issues, Naomi, that's why we're here."

"She'll run the first chance she gets."

"While she was out we implanted a GPS chip in her scalp."

Naomi gasped, her big brown eyes widening before narrowing. "You are a bad, bad man, Mr. Black."

His smile retracted. "Don't forget it." As he strode past her to the observation room that gave him complete access to the assimilation chamber, Godfather scowled again. He stopped at the door to the observation room. As he opened the door, his frustration mounted. Did Angela Giacomelli have too much crap in her head to be of use to him? Would she be the downfall of L.O.S.T.? Had he made a mistake? He would never jeopardize what they had all worked so hard for. His gut told him she would work out. Yes, she was a head case right now. Unpredictable and too damaged to use. But he knew that with time and training he would have the perfect foil for getting to criminal masterminds.

He stepped into the dimly lit room. Though she wouldn't be able to hear or see him, Godfather was still careful when he entered. He was surprised to see Cruz and Stone inside, both intently watching the lone figure on the other side of the mirror.

Wrapped in a thick white robe, her dark hair hanging damp around her shoulders from her shower, Jax sat at a table, facing them, with a feast of Italian food spread out before her. He knew she hadn't eaten that day, and probably not much the day before. From his extensive file on her, he knew Italian was her favorite. He'd hoped to entice her with it, but her head hung from her shoulders as she picked at the meatballs in front of her.

"Dr. Martin is on her way," Stone said.

Godfather nodded.

"It's going to take more than a shrink, even one as good as Barb, to fix that," Cruz said, inclining his head toward Jax.

"Yeah, but I'm going to make her into a lethal weapon. Better than all you assholes combined," Godfather mused out loud.

"What's wrong with us?" Cruz asked, indignant.

"Not a damn thing. She's just going to be more."

Gage snorted. "I've got a hundred bucks that says Doc Martin won't be able to crack her."

"You're on," Godfather said.

They all knew firsthand what Barbara Martin was capable of extracting from someone who wanted to keep their pain buried. They had all been at her mercy at one time or another. She was ruthless and relentless. Godfather always had the feeling she had lost someone close to her, and maybe felt like she had something to prove to the rest of the world. When he'd voiced his thoughts, she'd shut him down, curtly reminding him he'd not been there to discuss her private life but to let her get into his head and make him healthy enough to bring in the bad guys the regular cops couldn't.

Godfather let out a long breath and looked back at Jax, who now twirled the spaghetti on her plate until she had a huge glob of it on her fork. She flung it down and absently started to twirl another glob.

"I liked her better full of piss and vinegar, not like this. Beaten," Cruz grunted.

"Don't underestimate her," Stone said. "Underneath that wet hair is a sleeping tiger."

"You're right, Stone. I don't think she has it in her to quit anything. Our problem, once she buys into her new life, is going to be keeping her leashed."

"You should have seen her all bristly and hissing in the sally port at the courthouse—and even on the bus. I think it's just part of her nature."

Godfather watched her intently as Stone's words penetrated his brain. She'd fallen hard, but it *was* in her nature to fight. But not quite yet. She wasn't done crashing and burning.

He knew from experience that it could take years just to be able to function on a most basic level. The hardest part was reaching out and asking for help, then accepting it. Because accepting help meant you had to be honest, and being honest meant exposing the ugly rawness inside. He still had his own demons that lurked deep inside him. Every day he wrestled with them, and every once in a while they got the upper hand. Yeah, he knew exactly where she was coming from.

He looked back at Jax through the two-way and stopped breathing. She stared at him as if nothing but air separated them. Her green eyes sparkled dangerously. But it wasn't her glacial glare that had him holding his breath, it was the way her fingertips probed the area behind her right ear. He knew the moment she figured it out. He cringed when she took the fork and bent back one of the tines on the edge of the table.

"Holy shit," Cruz whispered.

She dug the tine into her scalp and probed with her left hand. Godfather watched her face. Her eyes glittered in fury, not once wavering from the two-way mirror. Bloodied fingers lowered from her head. She raised them. There in her fingertips was the flat GPS chip, no larger in circumference than half the size of a small eraser head. She dropped it onto her plate, where it made a slight *ting* sound. Never once did she break her stare.

Unhurriedly, she stood and made her way around the small table. As she did, the sash on her robe loosened. She didn't bother to tighten it. She stopped when she stood directly in front of them. An excited twitter skipped along his spine. Not sexual excitement but the excitement of knowing he had hit the jackpot. All three men stood silent, watched and waited.

She leaned toward the mirror and breathed heavily onto it, fogging it up. With a bloody finger, she wrote A-S-S-H-O-L-E-S in the fog, then flipped them the bird.

Stone laughed.

Godfather nodded, his lips quirking as relief poured through him. "I think, boys, she's going to do just fine." He knew as he said the words that his initial instincts had been spot-on. She would become a prime operative.

FIVE

July 7, 8:32 a.m.
Washington, D.C.

It was already eighty-two degrees with the promise of hitting the century mark by noon. The dog days of summer held the nation's capital in a choke hold. But despite the heat and the oppressive humidity, tourists swarmed the city. Like the flocks of birds spanning the rich, velvety green carpet of the mall, they took advantage of the cooler temperatures of the morning before flocking to the cooler interiors of the numerous monuments and museums.

Senator William Rowland did not pause to behold the wonder of nature or observe the multitude of tourists that swarmed around him. Instead, he drew a deep, nervous breath and scanned the crowds who mulled around the steps of the Lincoln Memorial. He looked up at the solemn stare of Lincoln, then past the marble statue in search of the man he'd seen only a handful of times over the last two years. Always clandestinely. Always at night. Always beneath the Gettysburg Address. The symbolism of their meeting spot was not lost on Rowland.

Today, Rowland had insisted on a daylight meeting.

His lips drew into a tight line as he glanced at his watch. The man was late. But it didn't matter. Today would be their last meeting. Rowland was not a coward by any stretch of the imagination. There was no room for a queasy stomach in politics, but there was something about the man he was meeting that unnerved him on a very primal level. Even when he'd been desperate and, like an angel of mercy, the man had materialized, his instincts had told him to turn and run, that nothing but trouble would come from even the slightest association. But he hadn't run. Lives had been at stake, all because the American government had not done what had needed to be done. The man, however, had delivered, and the tentative alliance they had formed had blossomed into a full-fledged codependency. Unfortunately, while Rowland had known that codependent relationships always benefited one party over the other, he'd only just realized that he was the person at the losing end of the equation.

Feeling like a target standing out in the open, Rowland walked through the groups of awe-inspired tourists, the strolling couples holding hands, and the man reading a newspaper on a park bench.

Startled by the sudden pressure of a firm grip on his right shoulder, Rowland flinched and spun around.

"Senator Rowland, good morning," the man the senator knew as Colonel Lazarus said from behind him.

"Jesus, I hate when you do that!" A man always in complete control, the senator did not like surprises. Yet all this man did was surprise him. Rowland turned, facing Lazarus. He was dressed completely in black, not one inch of his pale skin showing except the lower part of his face. The guy was just plain odd. Reluctantly, Rowland shook the colonel's gloved hand even as he struggled to meet what he knew were pale, frosty eyes shadowed by a wide-brimmed black felt hat and thick sunglasses. The colonel's lips pulled back from very long teeth. At that moment, the senator knew how it felt to look down a shark's throat. The fine hairs on his body rose, and his skin chilled beneath his ample clothing. The colonel's grip increased. The senator scowled and yanked his hand away.

"Just staying on top of my game, Senator."

The senator's scowl deepened. Nervously, feeling like he was in the colonel's crosshairs, he glanced around, half expecting to see the glint of a scope. "This isn't a game," Rowland bit off, still unable to shake the feeling he was a target.

The colonel smiled wider and slid down the large pair of black sunglasses as he too scanned the peripheral area. Unlike Rowland's rigid stance, the colonel's body was relaxed in a defiant, I-dare-you-to-try-something kind of way. Apprehension settled with a thud in Rowland's gut.

"C'mon now, Bill, you're a sitting U.S. senator. No one would dare take out a U.S. senator." A short pause emphasized the colonel's next words. "Would they?"

Rowland narrowed his eyes, not missing the threat. It was a habit the colonel had fallen into, and one he was going to cut short, here and now. "*You* talk about audacity?"

The colonel raised a black umbrella he had been holding in his left hand and pressed a button. With a short, sharp snap, it popped open, casting a dark shadow over both men. Rowland jumped back at the abrupt sound.

The colonel smiled. "I have a slight sensitivity to the sun." He inclined his head forward. "Shall we walk, Senator?" he asked, inclining his head away from the thickening crowds. "I feel too much like a target standing still out here in the open."

"Talk about a target? You've painted one on both our backs." They walked toward the Vietnam Memorial. "This latest business in Venezuela? Too high-profile. Too damn high-profile."

"The job was completed," the colonel said.

"Damn it, man!" Rowland shouted, then lowered his voice when several passersby gawked. He grasped the colonel's beefy arm and steered him over to the far edge of the promenade. "The lunatic running that country already despises us as it is. And what do you do? Leave one of his oil ministers cut from balls to gullet—and on a public road, no less!"

The colonel abruptly stopped and jerked his arm from Rowland's grasp. Low and level he said, "He *needed* to be found. It *needed* to be public. It made the correct statement! And, might I remind you, we also left enough dope and evidence of dummied bank accounts to suggest cartel involvement."

Rowland moved to the edge of the grass and softly said, "It was in the papers for Christ's sake. If it ever leaked out that we, that *I*, was involved—"

The colonel quickly cut him off. "That's never going to happen because *I'll* never let it happen." The colonel laid a hand on his shoulder. "Senator, you contracted The Solution to do the things our government can't or won't do." The colonel leaned in until they were almost nose-to-nose. "*Why*? Because if it comes down to it, we'll take the fall instead of you. And believe me, that won't happen."

"And Turkey? Explain Turkey to me."

The colonel stepped back, dropped his hand and shrugged. "What's to explain? The Iranian consulate was harboring a known terrorist. That SOB Say-Ed and that extremist he was protecting had to go. Making it look like a homo love-murder-suicide was genius and not my idea, I might add, but that of a very good operative. The same one who handled Venezuela, in fact." The colonel softened his tone and said, "Look, Senator, we're on the same side here, and with all due respect, everything is fine. Could not be better, in fact. We're cleaning up a lot of the bottom-feeders out there." He looked pointedly at the senator. "That which needs handling is getting handled, and no one, *no one* is going to be the wiser."

He's patronizing me, Rowland thought. But he'd called this meeting for one reason and one reason only, and he'd be damned if he'd allow the colonel to bully him out of what he knew he had to do. Without his intelligence and his funding, the colonel was soon going to find himself and The Solution out of work. "I'm shutting it down, Colonel. It's over."

The colonel yanked off his glasses. His pale eyes narrowed, and he moved in closer. Rowland actually felt the outline of the man's .45 against his chest, and his pulse began to hammer even before the colonel whispered, "You'll shut down nothing. Do you understand?"

Fear curled in Rowland's belly, and he felt like a coward for it. He pushed through it. This was his mess to clean up, and as much as he would have liked to pass this along to his chief of staff, Rowland stood his ground. "Stand down, Colonel. This is not your decision."

"Bullshit! *This* country needs The Solution. It needs patriots like you and me, and the men who serve me. Men willing to not ask questions. Men of blind faith and dedication to a greater cause, a higher purpose. *For the greater good.* Men who make presidents and, yes, even senators greater men than they alone can be."

Rowland did not waver in his purpose. What had begun with noble intentions had turned into an enormous disaster, with this half-crazed colonel acting like God Almighty. "My mind is made up. I will no longer pass along classified information to The Solution. I'm withdrawing the earmark that would continue to fund your preferred government contractor status. It's finished, Colonel. I suggest you take stock of your employees and decide what, if anything, may need to be done with them. Whatever you decide in that regard, I don't wish to be a party to it." Rowland stepped past the colonel, wanting to get away from him. Afraid if he did not the colonel would take his wrath out on him personally.

Colonel Lazarus grabbed his arm and spun Rowland, all six foot two and two hundred forty pounds of him, around.

"My employees?" the colonel demanded incredulously. "Decide what might need to be done with them? They're heroes! Patriots! And you speak as if I'm just supposed to give them a company watch and say thanks for the memories."

"Remember your position, Colonel," the senator warned. "For that matter, remember mine. It's *over!*"

The colonel stepped back, but the senator knew he was regrouping to attack from another angle. "No, sir, *you* remember *my* position, and my position only, because right now that's the only one you need to concern yourself with." The colonel leaned in close and personal, now eyeball to eyeball. "Remember what I'm capable of, and that I will do anything to protect this country from her enemies, *especially* those from within."

"Your threats are falling on deaf ears, Colonel. We're through here." Rowland made to move past him, but the colonel grabbed his arm and jerked him back.

"How dare you threaten the security The Solution provides this country?"

Rowland dug in and harshly said, "This is exactly what I'm talking about. I've seen it coming, like a goddamn train wreck! You've gotten too damn big for your own britches. It's a checks-and-balances game, and you have tipped the scale one too many times into the mud. There is no debating here. I'm pulling the plug."

"No, Senator, you are not." The colonel slid his hand inside his sleek black jacket. Rowland nodded ever so slightly. Within seconds, two large sunglassed gorillas flanked The Solution's CEO. Sharp teeth glittered in the sunlight, and the colonel slowly pulled his hand from his jacket. His pale eyes lasered into Rowland. He swallowed hard.

"So the trust has been broken, Senator." Lazarus nodded, acknowledging the security detail. "And now, it will be what it will be."

He turned slowly and disappeared into the onslaught

of sun-starved tourists. "Sir?" Rowland's bodyguard asked, inclining his head toward the colonel.

Rowland slowly shook his head. "Leave it be." And knew as he said the words that one did not leave a man like Colonel Lazarus be and stay clean. But he had no choice. This was an election year, and he could not have his bodyguard take out the man in front of the Lincoln Memorial, no matter how much he deserved it.

SIX

Two weeks later
Las Vegas

The bright, flamboyant lights of the Vegas strip oscillated across the car windows like an electric kaleidoscope, beckoning gamblers from every walk of life with the promise of instant fortune but rarely delivering.

Jax was on her way to a party she wasn't invited to. Although the party's host would deliver on his promise of fortune, she knew that for most guests it would come at a far higher cost than monies lost at the gaming tables.

L.O.S.T. operative Shane Donovan chauffeured the sleek limo. Jax glanced over at Gage, her partner in what should be a simple extraction op. The lights of the strip flickered across his handsome face. "Why am I nervous?" she asked.

He reached over and squeezed her hand, a gesture that would have cost him a few digits several months ago. Now, it merely caused her a ripple of nerves, which she quickly willed away. A hint of a smile tipped her lips.

In just six months, she'd traveled thousands of emotional miles, learning to overcome her past and accept her future. She was fortunate and more than grateful for her second chance at life and to be a part of something

so big and so powerful as Last Option Special Team.
L.O.S.T.

Briefly, she closed her eyes.

She could do this. She could do this and more.

Angela Giacomelli was a ghost and Jax Cassidy was,
as Godfather liked to remind anyone who would listen, a force of nature to be reckoned with. He believed
it. Promoted it. And Jax had bought it, hook, line and
sinker.

Most of the time, anyway.

She opened her eyes when Gage squeezed her hand
again.

"First-time jitters. Once you step out of this car, it's
showtime, and when it's showtime, all you'll see is the
bad guy with a target on his forehead."

She squeezed his hand back and released it. Their mission was simple: walk into arms dealer Andre Kozovic's
private club as if they'd owned it, get past the goons
guarding his office, tap into his hard drive, and down-
load the arming codes for the Scuds he'd just sold to a
Sudanese terrorist. While they were at it, they'd get hold
of Kozovic's Zurich bank account numbers and pass
codes, then, as a parting gift, fry his server, which would
effectively shut down his operation.

A cinch.

The stretch rolled·to a slow, easy stop outside a mini
Sung Dynasty–style castle. Out in front, two valets and
several "doormen" dressed in black-and-red satin wushu
uniforms managed the comings and goings of all guests.
Each one of them looked like a Dallas Cowboy line-
backer stuffed in satin pj's.

Jax shook her head as she looked up at the "castle." Everything was possible in Vegas. The structure was only three stories, but it was long and wide. From the blueprints she'd studied, she knew that Kozovic's office was on the third floor at the very back of the right wing.

"It's showtime," Gage said as Donovan opened his door. Gage slid out of the limo and straightened his two-thousand-dollar Armani suit. It was the perfect complement to her own attire.

She was dressed to thrill in a skintight hot pink leather sheath dress that barely covered her ass. The sleeves were long, concealing all kinds of nifty little tools of her trade. Her long, tanned legs were bare, with just enough of a glow to make a man long to feel them wrapped around him. Peeking from her shoes were perfectly pedicured toes. Her deep-auburn wig was cut blunt in the back but framed her face in a long A-cut point. Her makeup was subtle but dark, highlighting her naturally high cheekbones, full, pouty lips and big contacted brown eyes. She looked hot, and despite her flashy colors and micro-mini hem, she looked classy as hell.

Beside Gage, Donovan stood as erect as a sentry. Gage extended his hand to Jax.

As planned, she slapped it away. As fluid as liquid silver, she slipped out of the idling Cadillac, her deadly gold Versace spiked heels contrasting nicely with the red carpet.

"How dare you set a limit!" Jax snapped in a pseudo-whisper. By the valet's raised brow, she knew he'd heard.

So far so good.

"Meine liebe," Gage said in a slight German accent

as he grasped her elbow, "I am not in za mood to write anoza million-dollar-check zis evening."

She yanked her elbow from his grasp. "Then, *meine liebe,* I'll write *mein* own check."

Jax strode past him, raising several more sets of eyebrows. Knowing the security cameras were on them, she let them take a long look. As soon as the security team identified them as the philanthropic and high-rolling German power couple Dieter and Sabrina Clausen Kozovic would authorize their entry, eager to take their money via stacked decks and loaded dice. They, like most of Kozovic's clients, would tolerate the scam for the privilege of trading in information and black market goods.

Jax touched the huge bouncer guarding the threshold on the forearm and smiled up into his suspicious eyes. "Make him stay out here." She pouted prettily. "He is so cheap!"

Gage gently took her hand from the bouncer's arm and tucked it into the crook of his. "Bri, *liebling,* let us not discuss zees things in front of strangers."

Jax smiled and leaned into Gage, "Didi, *bitte.*" She looked up into his eyes and silently pleaded for him to relent.

He sighed heavily, then dug into his jacket pocket for his wallet and presented his credentials. He didn't have to. The powers monitoring from inside had already granted them entry. The bouncer stepped back and opened the heavy vermillion trimmed golden doors. He made a short bow and said, "Welcome to Shangri-La, Herr Clausen, Frau Clausen." And allowed them to step over the threshold and into an opulent wonderland.

Several people milled around, staff dressed in the same black-and-red satin wushu uniforms lurking innocuously in the shadows. Murmurs and glasses tinkling were tempered with the soothing sound of several wall waterfalls.

"We have fifteen minutes before Kozovic excuses himself and returns to his office for his hourly count," Gage softly said. They entered a sleek Chinese-themed gaming room. Jax knew that farther down the halls they would find private gaming rooms, where private deals were being negotiated.

"Herr Clausen," came a voice to their left. Andre Kozovic himself walked up to meet them. An escaped Milosevic puppet, he was a small, wiry man with dark, sharp features. His small nose twitched like a sewer rat as he inhaled her perfume. He did an admirable job hiding his Serbian accent, but it stuck to him like stink stuck on a turd.

"Mr. Kozovic, my apologies for our impromptu visit—" Gage began.

Kozovic shook his head and directed his sharp gaze on Jax. "No apology is needed when you bring such a lovely lady with you." He ignored Gage's extended hand and took Jax's instead. He brought it to his lips and bowed slightly, then kissed it. His lips were warm, as were his hands, but his empty eyes were cold.

"Frau Clausen," he said, then straightened. Jax smiled into his eyes.

"Mister Kozovic, Didi loves his *habanos* and Glenfiddich, please see that he has both and show me to your craps table."

Kozovic smiled. "A woman who is direct and knows

what she wants." He waved his hand, and instantly a server appeared. "Have Petar bring my private humidor down, and bring Herr Clausen a bottle of Glenfiddich and a glass of ice." His smile deepened as he looked at Jax. "Madam, your pleasure?"

Jax smiled back. "Hot dice, the unloaded kind."

Kozovic's brows shot up into his hairline. Jax chuckled, the sound low and seductive. "Come, come now, Mr. Kozovic, I came here to vin. Legitimately." Jax turned to Gage and hugged his arm to her bosom. Kozovic's eyes dropped to them. "My husband came for his own reasons, and, while I powder my nose, he will be most happy to share them with you."

Jax inclined her head questioningly, and Kozovic pointed toward the west wing. "You will find all that you need down this hall, behind the door with the plum blossom."

Jax stood up on her tiptoes and kissed Gage full on the lips. She almost laughed when she felt his initial stiffening before he masked it and smiled lovingly down at her. Jax brushed her fingertips across his cheek. *"Meine liebe,"* she whispered, "zeh sky is my limit tonight." She turned and left them both. As she sauntered through the main gaming room, every eye at one time or another found her. She made it to the hallway and, as a female server walked by, said, "Excuse me, but could you please help me with my zipper in the ladies' room?"

The woman smiled and followed Jax into the vast power room. It was a lovely atrium, with the sound of subtle waterfalls in the background of the oriental flora. If she'd had the time, she would have admired it, but she didn't. Quickly clearing the room, Jax opened her purse, grabbed the small aerosol can from inside, turned and sprayed the server in the face. The woman immediately slumped unconscious to the floor. Jax dragged her into the large stall at the far end of the room and quickly undressed and exchanged clothes with her, then left her sitting on the toilet in the stall. Before exiting the bathroom, Jax pressed a button on her watch, scrambling the security cameras for two minutes. Just enough time to get to Kozovic's office. She had less than ten minutes to get in and out. The clock was ticking.

"I'm on my way up," Jax softly said into the mic on her necklace.

Quickly rounding the last flight of stairs to the third floor, Jax strode toward the gorilla in a suit guarding the outer door to Kozovic's office. "You're not allowed up here," he growled, striding toward her.

"I'm new, I—" Jax got in as close as she could. His massive paw grabbed her by the throat. Not missing one single beat, Jax bent her right leg at the knee. With a sharp twist, she freed her spiked heel from the sole, exposing the tip of a spring-loaded needle inside. She went limp in the goon's arms, dropping to the floor when he released her. As he bent down to gather her, she stabbed him in the neck, instantly releasing the poison into his bloodstream and dropping him to the floor.

Gage was right. Her nerves had disappeared the instant she'd stepped out of the limo. Now, she was all calm, cool, resolve.

Replacing her heel, Jax removed the other to reveal a small surgical scalpel. She grabbed the big guy's right hand, singled out his index finger, and, cutting around the knuckle, she snapped it back. She cut through the exposed joint, then lopped the digit off. Jumping over the body, she pressed the finger to the biometric scanner. The air-locked doors released. She entered the hallway leading to the office, tossing the finger aside.

"Entering office hallway now," she softly said.

She now had less than twenty seconds to get into Kozovic's office before the cameras unscrambled, then seven minutes to do what she had come to do.

She hurried to the opulent gold, glass and teak double doors, pressing her watch to the door. She rotated the outer ring of the watch face clockwise and scrambled the tumblers in the lock, then pressed a magnet to them. With a soft pop, the doors unlocked. She pushed the doors open and hurried in, closing the doors behind her.

"I'm in."

Ten seconds and the cameras would unscramble. She grabbed off her wig and tossed it onto the solitary camera in Kozovic's office, covering the lens. By the time they figured it out, she'd be gone. She moved quickly. She pressed the magnetic flash drive to the CPU of Kozovic's laptop and clicked it on, then moved to the double closet doors and opened them. His server. She pressed another magnetic key card, setting a three-minute timer that would trip the power surge protector and fry every digital imprint in Kozovic's server.

"Kozovic has just been alerted, Jax, get out of there," Gage said in her earpiece.

"One more minute!"

"You don't have a minute. Get out."

Jax dragged several heavy chairs from in front of the desk and wedged them under the ornate office door handles. The room had one high window. She was on the third floor.

The sharp *twap-twap-twap* sound of bullets shattered the glass panels of the office door. Jax hurried to the laptop, removed the magnetic flash drive and shoved it down her bra. She hopped up into the high window-sill, kicked out the glass with her feet, did a chin-up for advantage and somersaulted out the window just as the office doors crashed open. She felt for the narrow ledge below with her feet but found only air. She had to release one hand to allow her body to drop lower. Ah, the ledge. She let go of the building with her other hand.

"I'm coming out the back window," she said to Gage.

As she worked her way along the narrow ledge to the edge of the wall, she turned and leapt onto a swaying palm tree, then grabbed a thickly fronded branch and rappelled down against the narrow trunk just as the stretch came rolling into view. Jax sprinted toward her ride as the men in Kozovic's office opened fire on her.

As the limo reached her, a door flew open, and Jax dove in as Gage grabbed her arm, pulling her inside. The door slammed shut behind her.

Jax laughed as she tried to talk, but she could not utter a coherent word. Her heart was beating so fast and so furiously that she thought it would explode. Finally, catching her breath, she grinned. "Holy crap, we did it!"

Gage grinned in return as they high-fived. Donavan smiled at them in the rearview mirror.

"Nice job, Cassidy," he said.

SEVEN

i

Two weeks later
Washington, D.C.

From his secured place among the night shadows, Marcus watched Jason Blalock, hunched down in a dark trench coat, walk toward the dilapidated apartment building. Only one of the three streetlights on the right-hand side of the building was lit, and it sputtered a tobacco-stained orange, barely useful. Like a rabbit that knew the wolves were watching, Blalock shot his nervous gaze up and down the street—first right, then left, then right again—before he jerked open the graffiti-sprayed front door and disappeared through it.

Even from across the street, Marcus could smell Blalock's excitement; it was almost as potent as his fear. Excitement for what awaited him on the tenth floor and the fear of what his transgression would cost him, should he be caught.

And he would be caught.

Marcus curbed a sneer. Since his change seven years ago as he lay dying in the hills of Afghanistan, his natural predatory senses had become so acute, so fine tuned, so accurate, his vision rivaled that of a hawk, his sense of smell was as keen as a wolf's, and his reflexes and strength were that of a cobra. No living thing could stop him. He was a vampire of the highest order.

His kryptonite was his thrill of the chase, then his lust for the blood. Fresh, warm, human blood. It was what sustained him.

He raised his head toward the sliver of moon, and inhaled the heavy air. It stank of squalor and hopelessness. The people who lived here in the bowels of the nation's capital, had long ago given up on themselves, as had the people who ran the world's most powerful government, less than two miles away. The cops didn't bother coming down here, and neither did the social workers or the charities. There wasn't a church for blocks in any direction.

Senator William Rowland's press secretary was seriously slumming, but it was Wednesday night, after all. Even if it meant walking among the dredges of the nation's capital, Blalock never missed his Wednesday night boxing sessions: roughing up D.C.'s endless supply of prostitutes before he returned to the swank Chevy Chase town house he shared with his trust fund trophy wife.

Blalock probably considered himself lucky that the streets were so dark and deserted. Usually the pushers hung out with the hypes and the street whores who couldn't turn a trick that night. But not tonight. It was as if they knew Marcus was there and they had to stay away if they wanted to live another day.

They were right.

Marcus smiled tightly. Tonight, Blalock would come to an end, and his demise would send a strong message.

He pulled out a pair of black neoprene gloves and slowly put them on, never once breaking his stare from the building. A moment later, a shiny black Escalade skidded to a stop in front of the building. Marcus watched Don "Mageek Wan" Jackson, Blalock's oversized and over-ornate pimp, drag two girls from the backseat. Like those before them, they were scared and they were young. Marcus's temper spiked. Nothing pissed him off more than the exploitation of innocence. And they were innocent. Once. Quickly he leashed his anger. No sense getting heated over something he had no control over.

Life was a bitch. And then? He smiled tightly and watched Mageek shove the hesitating girls through the doors. And then Blalock dies.

Marcus watched, and waited. Two ghostlike shadows rose eerily from behind the Dumpster. Marcus knew why they were there. He'd smelled the stench of death clinging to their unwashed bodies like rotten trash the moment he'd taken his position over an hour ago. They were career criminals, and the stench of their many kills still clung to them long after the deeds were done. And, like him, they were patient. And it was only because he knew they were there for Mageek and not Blalock that he allowed them to live.

Several moments later, the pimp returned empty-handed. Marcus watched the two shadows that had been lurking behind the Dumpster leap from their spot and pounce.

Mageek cursed.

Twap-twap-twap. Twap-twap.

In less then thirty seconds, the shadowed thugs

pumped the pimp with lead and took off with his ride. Marcus stood for a long minute watching the motionless heap on the street.

How was that for poetic justice?

A slight impediment to his plans, but one that would play out in his favor. With Mageek now fresh roadkill, Marcus would have to accelerate his game plan. He'd missed his window of opportunity last week when a bunch of dopers had taken over the stairwell leading to the tenth floor, forcing Blalock to change his plans and preventing Marcus from doing his job. He never made his hits look like hits unless he wanted to send a message. And while tonight's mark was a message to be sent, he was simply going to cap the guy as he walked out of the apartment and lift his wallet, making it look like a simple mugging and setting D.C.'s tongues speculating over what a high-profile senator's press secretary was doing in the slums of southeast D.C. He still could, but not if someone discovered Mageek first.

Improvise, adapt and overcome. Marcus lived for this kind of shit.

He glanced up at the dimly lit windows of the tenement, watching for looky-loos, but no one had the balls to look out the window. Out of sight . . . out of mind. That was good for him tonight.

Slowly, he pulled the black neoprene mask down over his face. He gave the street one more sweep. Then, with a stealth and grace that came as naturally to him as his black hair and blue eyes, Marcus moved across the street to the man on the ground. Beneath the sputtering glow of the streetlight, the asphalt glittered with slow rivulets of blood. The coppery scent hung heavy in the air. Marcus's nostrils twitched at the blood scent. His adrenaline surged, but he kept his focus on what he was there to do. He grabbed the thug by his four-hundred-dollar Nikes and dragged the lifeless form to the curb. Then tossed him into the Dumpster.

Silently, he walked around to the back of the building and took the stairwell up to the tenth floor.

He had already familiarized himself with the other apartments, all of them empty. Blalock had made sure there would be no witnesses to what he did here every Wednesday night. Another plus for Marcus.

Even before he opened the heavy metal door leading from the stairwell to Blalock's floor, he heard the shrill screams. Noiselessly he moved down the hall, stopping several feet from Blalock's apartment door. When the screams escalated in volume, Marcus remained motionless.

He'd watched and listened to Blalock for almost a month. He knew the creep paid a pretty price to rough up the girls. As the minutes dragged on, Marcus continued to stand silent outside the door, the screams only white noise. He'd learned a long time ago to tune out the peripheral shit of his job. It had seeped into his everyday existence as well. Autopilot was safe, no room for emotions to cloud his judgment. In his line of work, there was no room for error, not even a fraction. If he failed, more lives were lost. And failure was never an option.

But tonight the screams set his nerves and ultra-heightened senses on edge. The scent of fear blasting from the apartment was so thick that it clogged his nostrils. The hard, fast staccato of heartbeats and the thick swish of blood as the heart pumped at capacity reverberated against his chest. Yes, he felt the fear, smelled it as if it had been something tangible. But he did not allow it to sway him from his course. He moved closer to the door, itching to get in and get out. His plan had been to wait for Blalock to come out after the girls had been collected, but Mageek wasn't coming back for his girls, and if his body was discovered, someone might call the cops.

He glanced at his Swiss-made chronometer. The screams coming from the apartment changed.

A little girl's scream for her life. Her life force cried out for help, then, like a candle being snuffed, it was gone.

He felt a pull to the apartment that had nothing to do with his mark. He closed his eyes and gritted his teeth, shutting out the fragmented images of a girl, naked and dirty, being pulled off her dead mother, who had just been raped by soldiers. American soldiers. As the images flashed in his brain like a slideshow on fast forward, he continued toward the stairwell. This was not his battle, damn it! His war was with the boss of the man inside the apartment. A long wail made the hair on his arms stand straight up.

"Fuck!" He whirled around. As he strode to the door he grabbed the doorknob and twisted it so hard that the tumblers snapped. He pushed open the door and stepped in. The dim apartment smelled of sweat, sex and fear. The wailing had turned to a low whimper.

"You killed her!" a girl's voice gasped. "You killed Amy!"

A sharp slap followed by a low moan of pain prefaced Blalock's denial. "That wasn't supposed to happen! She didn't do what I told her."

"B-but she's dead," the girl whimpered.

"Shut up and let me think!" Blalock's voice edged on hysteria.

"If you let me go, I won't tell anyone. I swear!" the girl pleaded.

"I said, shut up!" Blalock hissed.

Marcus cleared the rusty and mold-infested bathroom to his immediate left, then proceeded to the end of the short hall to the only other room in the closet-sized flat. And there the entire ugly scene played out before him. In the right corner, beneath a broken lamp and on a stained threadbare mattress, lay the limp, naked body of a girl not more than twelve or thirteen. Marcus knew from the unnatural angle of her head that her neck was broken. Her life finished.

To the left, near the cutout kitchen and the sliding glass door, there was another girl, about the same age, half dressed. A very naked Blalock towered over her with his hands wrapped around her neck.

Marcus's gaze narrowed on Blalock. His instinct was to take the piece of shit out at that precise moment and let the girl live, but another part of him knew that to do so would expose him.

"Plu—eezz," the girl begged, barely able to breathe. Her small hands clutched her attacker's. Blalock laughed and shoved her down to her knees. He grabbed the cord from the floor lamp next to him, yanked it from the socket, then wound it around her neck.

Anger galvanized in Marcus's heart. His own heart rate escalated, he could hear his blood swish hot and harsh through his veins. His body warmed, his neck corded, his teeth . . . He forced himself to focus.

"No—" the girl gasped. Blalock grasped the cord with

both hands, then twisted and pulled. He watched her eyes close and her body still, then lose consciousness.

Something inside Marcus snapped. He roared furiously. In two long strides, he moved into the room and grabbed Blalock around the neck from behind, catching him in a carotid choke hold. He applied pressure—not enough to choke Blalock out, but enough for it to hurt. Marcus wanted the prick fully conscious. He wanted him to feel the same terror he'd exacted on the girls. Marcus hauled him off the girl, who crumpled to the floor.

"What the hell?" Blalock choked, taking a swing at Marcus.

Marcus did not break the cadence of his step. He shoved open the sliding glass door, dragging Blalock with him onto the small patio. The chill of the night air hit him like a glass wall.

"What the *hell*?" Blalock cried again, continuing to try to wrestle free. Marcus didn't stop. One step away from the edge of the balcony, he shoved the pedophile over it, his pasty white ass up in the air, his eyes staring straight down to the concrete alley ten floors below.

Marcus dug his elbow into Blalock's back and kept his right arm locked around his neck. He could feel the thick cord of his jugular. The hot stream of blood as it flowed to his brain. Marcus fought the urge to show Blalock the monster he was. Maybe after he had the information he needed, he would. Though he sometimes hated what he was, there were times when he enjoyed the shock value of it just before he killed. It was the little things.

He leaned closer, and in the press secretary's ear softly asked, "Does Senator Rowland know what you do here every Wednesday night, you sick fuck?"

Vehemently, Blalock shook his head. Though Marcus could not out and out read a person's thoughts, he was highly intuitive. He knew when someone was lying, when they were telling the truth, and with the ladies? He could smell their lust before they even realized they wanted him.

Marcus ground his elbow into Blalock's kidney. "Don't lie to me! Does he look the other way?"

"No!" Blalock screamed. "No one knows except me and my pimp."

Marcus growled. "I guess the dead girl won't be telling anyone."

"That was an accident, I didn't mean to . . . I—it wasn't supposed to happen."

"Bullshit. Word on the street has it that isn't the first girl to fall victim to your rough play." Marcus dug his elbow in harder. "Now, before I toss your sick ass over this railing, tell me where Senator Rowland keeps the file with The Solution's intel."

"The S-Solution? I don't know what you're talking about!"

Marcus tipped him forward. Blalock flayed and tried to grasp at the concrete patio wall to keep from falling.

"Yes, you do. Tell me now, or I'm tossing you."

"Senator Rowland is tight-lipped when it comes to The Solution. He doesn't tell me anything!"

"Then how do you know it exists?"

"I—I just do the necessary paperwork to keep it on the preferred contractor list. But he instructed me three weeks ago to remove it. He said The Solution went belly up."

Marcus laughed. "My dear Mr. Blalock, I assure you The Solution is alive and well. Who do you think sent me?"

When Blalock shoved back, Marcus dug his elbow deeper into his back and tightened his choke hold. Blalock gagged and Marcus felt his body go limp. Like a pressure valve, he let up on his choke hold, and Blalock immediately revived. He coughed but hung limply over the railing. He gasped several breaths before he said, "The senator said The Solution went rogue. He was adamant we shut it down."

Marcus kept a firm hold on the naked man. "There you are very wrong. We still clean up what the CIA can't. It's your boy Rowland who has gone rogue." He dug his elbow deeper. "Now, tell me where I can find the file."

There was a long hesitation before Blalock said, "His district office. But—"

"Where in his district office?"

"If you let me go, I'll get it for you," Blalock mewled.

Marcus slowly shook his head. "I work alone. Now tell me exactly where the file is."

"Please! Let me go, I'll get it for you!" Blalock screamed as he struggled to free himself.

"Last chance, Blalock." Marcus tipped him forward so that he had to stretch his long arms to keep him from falling completely over the rail.

"Fuck you and that crazy bastard you work for!" Blalock screeched.

Marcus smiled and pulled the black mask from his head before standing back, bringing Blalock with him.

He turned the naked press secretary around and with one hand clamped around his neck, lifted him a foot off the patio floor. Blalock screamed harshly as he looked at Marcus. "What *are* you?"

"Your worst nightmare."

With one harsh shove, he sent Blalock flying over the rail, the press secretary's fading screams just more white noise. Marcus didn't bother to see where he landed. He was dead. Mission accomplished.

He pulled his mask back over his head, strode back into the apartment, and quickly took stock of the situation. There was nothing anyone could do for the girl in the corner. On the plus side, there was one less witness. He scowled, not liking the benefits tonight. He bent over the other girl, but as he did, she gasped, then coughed, fighting for air. Her eyes flew open and she hoarsely screamed.

Marcus slammed his hand over her mouth and shook his head. With his free hand, he put his finger to his lips, hidden behind the mask. Immediately, the terrorized girl quieted.

"I won't hurt you," Marcus roughly whispered and cursed himself for the words. Despite his personal code not to 86 children, he was a ghost, and if he was to remain a ghost, there could be no witnesses to his existence.

Wide-eyed, she stared up at him. Her fear tugged at his gut. When the cops questioned her, the only detail she'd be able to give was an estimate of his six-foot-four-inch height and his two-hundred-and-forty-five-pound body. He was dressed completely in black, his skin was completely obscured by gloves and mask, and his unusual blue eyes were camouflaged behind brown contacts. He was sure she hadn't heard anything that had been said on the balcony, or even that Blalock was splatter. Hell, until this moment she hadn't known of his existence in the apartment.

Marcus carefully unwound the cord from around her neck, then grabbed her shirt from the floor and placed what little there was of it over her bare chest. He growled when he picked her up. She didn't weigh more than ninety pounds soaking wet. He stepped into the bathroom on the way out, grabbed a grimy towel, then wrapped her in it. Once she was secured, he yanked open the door and headed for the stairwell.

She shivered hard in his arms. He didn't want to look down at her, but he couldn't help himself. Wide-eyed, blinking back tears, she stared at him. He felt like someone had kicked him in the balls.

"Wh-where are you taking me?" she croaked.

"Someplace safe," he said, knowing he would regret it.

EIGHT

Thirty minutes later

"Senator Rowland."

At the deep, arrogant voice, the senator stopped in his tracks. The colonel stood behind him, so close that he could feel the warmth of the man's breath and smell the rich tobacco on it. Rowland's skin chilled, and every hair on his body stood straight up.

"That's it," the colonel murmured. "Keep still and keep quiet. What I have to say will take only a moment of your valuable time."

Rowland slid his hands into his trouser pockets and fisted them. His gaze darted around the lightly populated private dining room in the ultraexclusive D.C. gentleman's club, Partisan.

"How did you get in here?" Rowland quietly demanded as he made to turn.

The hard nose of a pistol pressed against his back. "Ah, ah, follow orders, soldier, or pay the price."

Rowland stiffened but remained still.

"Now, listen to me very carefully. I'm guessing that in the not-too-distant future, you're going to get a call from DCPD informing you that your press secretary jumped out of a ghetto apartment building because he couldn't

live with himself after he killed the twelve-year-old pros-
titute he had delivered earlier tonight."

Icy foreboding dug into the senator's gut. "You bastard!"

The barrel of the gun dug deeper into his back. "Ah, ah."
When Rowland stilled, the colonel continued. "The reality
is, Blalock was thrown from the window. And the girl?"
The colonel *tsk*ed *tsk*ed. "Unfortunate collateral damage."

"You don't know who you're up against, Colonel," the
senator bit out.

The colonel chuckled. "No, my friend, it's you who
has no clue who you're *up* against." To accentuate his
point, the colonel shoved the pistol harder into Rowland's back.

Rowland moved to turn around, but the colonel dug
the barrel deeper.

"Don't turn around. I'm here to give you a friendly
heads-up so that when the cops call, you have the real
facts. And you know how those vultures at the *Post*
like to twist everyone's dirty laundry into a shit pile.
It's going to be very interesting to see how your PR
team spins this little, ah, sexcapade slash suicide. Especially since you're running such a tight race against that
incompetent Democrat."

Rowland remained still, too angry, too terrified to
breathe. This would topple him. It didn't matter that
Blalock liked young whores. Rowland was a California
conservative, a virtual unheard-of in that great state.
His opponent would pull out all the stops when they got
wind of this. "What good am I to The Solution if I lose
my seat?"

The colonel laughed low. "I like the way you're think-ing now, Senator." Colonel Lazarus relieved the pressure at his back. "It's simple, really. Reinstate our preferred contractor status, we go back to business as usual, and I'll make sure you not only retain your senate seat but you'll be hailed a hero as well."

Rowland spun around and faced his nemesis. The pacemaker in his chest was working overtime to keep his erratic heart rate from fibrillating. His gut gnarled in such a severe contortion that the Maryland crab cakes he'd eaten an hour ago rose in his throat. He was damned either way. Unless—unless he found a way to eliminate The Solution from the face of the earth.

"You forget, Colonel, I have records of every dirty deed you and your cohorts have carried out. All of it poised and ready to be delivered into the hands of the Joint Chiefs if I fall off the radar."

The colonel's smile widened. "Isn't your daughter, Grace, scheduled to begin Stanford in the fall? It would be a shame if she never made it."

Rowland's blood iced in his veins and the crab cakes rose higher, clogging his throat. "Touch one hair on her head, and I'll personally cut you up one piece at a time."

The colonel laughed. "Give me what I want, Sena-tor, and I'll leave your family out of it." He looked at his watch. "I'm giving you three weeks to reinstate The Solu-tion."

"I can't get it done that soon! My committee doesn't reconvene for eight weeks!"

The colonel's smile faded. "There *is* such a thing as an emergency." He backed away from Rowland. "I want an official certified letter delivered to the address on record for The Solution in three weeks or less. Once I have authenticated our reinstated status, we'll resume business as usual. I also suggest you call a cleaner ASAP. You'll be no good to me if you lose your Senate seat." The colonel smiled sadistically. "And, Senator? Between now and then if I discover you have made other plans or I feel you are not moving quickly enough? No one, especially your daughter, will be immune from my gentle reminders."

The colonel turned and disappeared into the darkened shadows of the room.

For a long time, Rowland stood silent, terrified and unsure of his next move. He was up against a terrible wall, but if he gave the colonel free rein to annihilate any person, group or organization he considered anti-American, he could bring about war with enemies the American government kept close to the vest.

One thing was for certain—The Solution's operatives were fueled by their blind faith in the colonel. Cut the head off the snake, and The Solution folded.

Rowland knew of only one man who could help him. A ghost. He pulled his cell phone from his pocket and made several quick inquiries. Armed with a phone number few knew existed, Senator Rowland exited the club and found a pay phone down the street. For a long moment, he held the phone in his hand, knowing that if he made the call, he put everyone he loved at risk. He also knew that if he walked away, the fate of the free world was just as much at risk. He dialed.

On the third ring, a deep voice answered, "Black."

The senator cleared his throat and slowly said, "Mr. Black, this is Senator William Rowland."

"Who referred you?"

"Attorney General Marks. He said to give you the code word Orion."

"Go ahead."

"I made a bargain with the devil and need you to eliminate him."

"I'm listening."

NINE

i

J ax woke with a start. Her skin was drenched in sweat
and her heart rate was through the roof. Even so, she
managed to feel a pinch of relief.

Six months ago, her night terrors had been about
Montes. Now they were about something else. She'd prefer to do without them altogether, but so long as Montes
stayed where he belonged—in her past—she'd take comfort in that.

"Latent performance pressure anxiety," Dr. Martin
had diagnosed right after the L.O.S.T. mission in Vegas.
It had pissed Jax off. The op had gone off perfectly, so
why the anxiety? She wasn't a nervous Nelly. Not by
nature. And not anymore.

Nonetheless, she couldn't deny it—something inside
her worried the next mission might not go so well. That
niggling something kept her up at night. Was it simply
the baggage of her past, or was it a premonition?

Shivering, Jax rolled on her side and mumbled,
"Don't get all woo-woo, Jax. Your past would give anyone nightmares."

But it didn't matter, she told herself. She'd left her old

life firmly behind. Angela Giacomelli was a stranger to her now.

For a long time she had felt less of a woman because of the internal and external scars left behind by Montes, her squad, and her boyfriend, Judd, a man she had trusted, loved and thought to spend the rest of her life with. She'd remember his horrified looks after the doctors had told him what Montes had done to her. He hadn't been horrified for her; he'd been horrified at the thought of touching her again. She'd also replay over and over again the way he'd walked away as she'd been wheeled into surgery. She'd understood perfectly: Her very public attack had very publicly disgraced him.

She'd understood, but she hadn't forgotten or forgiven. She still hadn't.

But she'd managed to put it behind her in order to move on with her life.

In time, with Doctor Martin's help and the help of every operative at L.O.S.T., Jax had shed all of her baggage and emerged clean and reborn. She was a survivor. She had a new life as a highly trained operative surrounded by other highly trained operatives. She worked for the real good guys and knew that this time she would not be left behind as collateral damage. Life was damn good, and she was damn grateful for it.

Suddenly, she realized what was behind her anxiety. She didn't want to lose this life. And she didn't want to disappoint the man who'd given it to her.

Godfather had created the ultimate weapon: Jax Cassidy. He had complete confidence in her not only as a woman but also as a prime operative. She *would not* let him down. Taking a deep breath, she rolled from the bed, dragging her fingers through her dark mahogany-highlighted hair. She'd colored it and had let it grow long. Longer than it had ever been. Maybe it was time to chop it off. She tossed the thick mass over her shoulder and headed for the bathroom.

As Jax got into the shower, she thought of the terror she'd experienced during her night sweats. She couldn't help it. She was like that. She wanted—no, *needed*—to know the whys of everything. Maybe it was her Catholic upbringing. Asking God why he did this or that. Mostly, she learned God did not have much to do with the whys. It was just life most times.

She focused on what Doc Barb had said—that once Jax got into the swing of regular missions, the anxiety would dissolve as her confidence increased.

She'd never thought confidence would be a problem for her.

Jax smiled as she turned off the harsh spray of hot water. She was cocky by nature and had become more so with her training. She knew she was good. Her fellow operatives knew it too.

Jax dried off. As she was dressing, her cell phone rang to the theme from *Godfather I*. Her heart rate leapt into high gear. There was only one reason Godfather would be calling this early in the morning.

Her next mission was at hand.

"Cassidy," she answered.

"War room, twenty minutes," Godfather said, then hung up.

Fifteen minutes later, still damp from her shower and dressed in desert fatigues, Jax sipped a hot cup of coffee as she entered the war room of L.O.S.T.'s ranch compound. As she strode deeper into the room, her fellow operatives stood up and clapped. They were all there. Stone, Cruz, Jackson, Satriano, Donovan and the others.

For the slightest nth of a millisecond, Jax felt a hard jolt of emotion wrack through her chest. She leashed it before it took on a life of its own.

"Nice work on the Vegas job, Cassidy," Jackson said, giving her a hearty slap on her back. She got another from Satriano, then Cruz. By the time Jax got to her seat and set her coffee cup down, half of it had sloshed onto the floor.

"Guys, guys!" she said, "enough, already. I want to drink the rest of my coffee!"

As she sat down, she wiped her hand on her cammie. The door behind her opened and she turned.

From the grim look on Godfather's face as he walked into the room, as always dressed in his I'm-a-badass black on black, she knew this was going to be a doozy.

She was ready. She was also eager to prove to these men that Vegas hadn't been an anomaly. She needed them to know, as much as she did herself, that she was a solid, dependable part of this team.

Jax looked up at her mentor, the man who had yanked her kicking and screaming from the black hole of life in prison and, in so many ways, had saved her. He had more confidence in her than she did herself. It was because she respected the hell out him that she'd allowed herself to even try. And in the end, Godfather had bet on a sure thing. He hadn't given up on her when she had given up on herself.

It felt good to be here. In the golden circle, the war

room, where the top secret details of each mission were presented, disseminated and strategized down to the smallest detail, ensuring mission success. The same place she'd been brought to six months ago, the same room where she'd agreed to join the Last Option Special Team, and the same room she'd been forbidden to reenter since her first mission two weeks ago.

Jax took a deep breath and attempted to look casual and relaxed, like this was old hat. Nearly impossible with the continued rush of adrenaline that flooded her system.

Godfather looked down at her, forced the grim lines from his face and actually cracked what might be called a smile. "Cassidy, I thought you might want to know the Sudanese bought the recalculated Scud codes the CIA mole gave them. Recalced to return home after launch, of course. That particular extremist group is enjoying their seventy-two virgins as we speak."

Jax smiled.

Godfather nodded and continued. "There was more valuable information encrypted in the files you downloaded than the Scud codes."

"Like what?" Cruz asked.

Godfather looked his way and answered, "Like a dozen secret locations of core plutonium."

A collective gasp rippled through the room. Godfather nodded. "Kozovic was dealing in atomic bomb parts."

Jax sat in stunned silence. A freaking atomic bomb? Suddenly shaking down prostitutes and chasing two-bit thieves didn't sound so important. She looked up at her mentor and knew that the reason he had called them together was not to congratulate her on the success of her last op.

"We get very few missions that directly threaten world peace," Godfather began, his tone grim, his handsome face taut with tension. "But as it is, we have a guy who thinks he's God. His henchmen do his bidding without question. 'Patriots' they call themselves, operating on blind faith." He picked up the remote on the table next to where he stood and pressed a button.

A picture of Senator William Rowland flashed up on the surrounding screens. *Christ.* A rogue senator?

"Senator William Rowland. A conservative stronghold in left coast California. He heads up some very powerful committees, among them the Foreign Relations Appropriations Committee. He's also a sub chair for the top security clearance Intelligence Committee. He's the go-to man for money and, as is common in Washington, earmarks have a way of funding nonearmarked ventures."

"More fleecing of America," Cruz crumbled.

Godfather laughed harshly. "Don't knock it, Cruz. How do you think we're funded?"

That answered one of a million questions that had been on Jax's mind. Interesting.

Godfather turned back to the screen and pressed another button. The face that sprung up around them gave Jax a hard chill. He looked like an aged version of a nasty Mr. Clean. Pale eyes stared at them with such intensity that Jax pushed back in her seat.

"Colonel Joseph Trueheart Lazarus, retired Army, and a legend among his peers," Godfather started. "The guy has balls the size of Texas, and so did every man in his specialized unit. So specialized, the details of their missions are still top secret, and trying to get any information regarding them is as difficult as breaking into Fort Knox. We do know when the unit was actively deployed they were used mostly to extract, but were also used to eliminate. The top gun honors went to Sergeant Marcus Cross, who we will get to shortly.

"Lazarus is sixty-two, retired seven years ago, never been married, no family to speak of, and now heads up a dummy corporation, The Solution. The Solution looks like and acts like a general contracting company that has met all of the U.S. government's preferred status requirements. It's supposed to rebuild in Iraq and other parts of the world where big brother wants to look philanthropic. The only thing The Solution builds is business for the local mortuary. The Solution searches for, then eliminates, enemies of the State." Godfather stoically panned the room, allowing the information to sink in.

Confused, Jax asked, "So what's the problem?"

"His message is patriotism, his method is terrorism."

Jax nodded in understanding. "So it's Rowland who uses the earmarks to fund The Solution's ops, and now he wants us to end the relationship."

Godfather grinned, the gesture nearly bowling Jax over. The Grinch had a second dimension. Go figure.

"Very good, Cassidy. Until recently, the earmarks funded The Solution's operations. Rowland put the brakes on The Solution last month. For his efforts, the senator's press secretary, Jason Blalock, was tossed from a tenth-story balcony last night."

"No shit!" Stone said.

Godfather nodded and hit a button on the remote.

The picture that flashed up on the screen made Jax's stomach lurch. She had seen some grisly crime scenes, but this one ranked right up there with the worst. A body, Blalock, she assumed, his head split wide open, gray matter splattered everywhere and his body broken in pieces.

"Jesus," she murmured.

"An associate of ours cleaned up the mess in the wee hours of this morning. To the world, Blalock fell asleep on his way home from a late night at the office and took a dive off the beltway. His car exploded, and, well, our condolences to the family." He looked pointedly at his operatives and continued, "Lazarus has threatened the senator with more dire consequences, among them elimination of his only child should he not reinstate The Solution's preferred status." He looked up at the picture of a blood-spattered Blalock, and then back around the room. "Under no circumstance can that be allowed."

Godfather pressed another button. A collective gasp rent the air. The picture showed the naked, broken body of a girl lying on a threadbare mattress. "The girl, identified as twelve-year-old Amy Stover of Towson, Maryland, reported as a runaway three months ago, and who was Blalock's amusement for the night, was also eliminated," Godfather said grimly.

Anger washed in rolls through Jax. Along with it, however, came fear. Murder was bad enough. Maybe sick fucks like Blalock deserved it, but an exploited child? Never.

Suddenly, it wasn't the girl's body she saw. Rage, and the violent urge to lash out and inflict pain on those who deserved it, ate at her like acid on flesh. Most of the time,

Jax managed to quell her violent urges. When, thinking of Montes and the abandonment by her department, she hadn't been able to quell them, she'd beaten the crap out of the heavy bag in the gym to the point of raw-knuckled exhaustion. Those fits had become fewer and further between, but they still lurked. Ever since arriving at L.O.S.T., when she felt the violence erupt, she'd replay Doc Martin's repeating theme: "Give yourself a break, for God's sake! You beat yourself up more than Montes did."

She focused on those words now.

She hadn't taken too kindly to them that first time. She'd stalked from the good doctor's office that day and refused to go back. She hadn't wanted to face the truth. Later that night, when she'd awoken in a cold sweat, the doctor's words had hovered in her consciousness.

She'd let go of Angela then. Angela was dead, and if she was going to survive, she'd known she would have to survive in this world as Jax Cassidy. A calmness had settled over her that night, and for the first time since her attack, some of the demons had subsided inside of her.

Jax sucked in a deep breath and slowly let it out, the practice easing the tension in her muscles. Since there was no punching bag in the vicinity, she mustered all her control, focused on the picture in front of her, and asked, "What kind of bastard kills a little girl who was already exploited?"

Godfather pressed another button. Jax stared unblinking as the face burst into her senses.

"Marcus Cross, Lazarus's triggerman also known as the Coyote. Our boy is a piece of work. Born Daniel Marcus Killroy, he legally changed his name to Marcus Cross when he turned eighteen. He was raised by his Native American grandfather on a reservation near Clearlake, California."

Another picture flashed up on the screen, this one of an old Indian man and a small dark-haired boy who looked solemnly at the camera. It was followed by another picture, similar setting, the two of them sitting on the steps of a dilapidated house, the boy, younger, with a man who resembled the older one in the first picture. But this man's eyes were dead. "Cross's old man became a classic cliché. Drank himself to death by the time Marcus was six. He had a good reason. His wife, a trust fund baby and heiress to the Taylor conglomerate, took off two weeks after Cross was born."

Another photo flashed up on the screens. The woman was extraordinarily beautiful. She could have been Jean Harlow's twin.

"Sophia Scott Taylor. She ran off with 'that half-breed' Johnny Killroy to California when she was sixteen. She lasted long enough to get pregnant, have the baby, and run home to Las Vegas, where her marriage was annulled, and Johnny Killroy and her infant son were erased from her life. Daddy hurried up and married her off to husband number two, retired ambassador to Japan, Holby Philips."

"You say that like there are more husbands," Jax quipped.

Godfather nodded. "Philips died of a heart attack five years after they were married. By then, the lovely Sophia was imbedded in politics. She was patient and chose her next husband with great care. There's chatter about him becoming Calhoun's running mate. Could mean

the White House. That ups the stakes exponentially."
He clicked another picture. It showed an older but still
gorgeous Sophia Taylor smiling beside Senator William
Rowland.

"Cross's mother is married to Rowland?" Jax asked,
shocked by the connection. "Does he know?"

Godfather shook his head. "I thought it was an
odd coincidence, so we pulled the birth certificate. It
names Jane Doe as Cross's birth mother. But we dug a
little deeper and found the original at the reservation
archives. We have no idea what he was told as a child.
From our perspective, if you combine the circumstances
and the paperwork, I'm betting he doesn't know."

"Does the senator know Lazarus's top gun is his
wife's firstborn?"

Godfather slowly shook his head. "No, and for now
we're going to leave it that way."

"Does Lazarus know?"

"I'm not going to assume anything about Joseph
Lazarus. It would be too much of a coincidence for him
not to know. And I don't believe in coincidences. I'd bet
my retirement Lazarus recruited Cross solely for the
blood ties to the senator's wife. Lazarus is a manipula-
tor. He wants it all, and he'll use the mother/son card if
he has to."

Jax slowly shook her head, wondering who else Lazarus would use and how. Was anyone off limits to a man
like him? "I doubt Cross, if he knows or finds out about
Sophia Rowland, would do much to save her. Hell, Lazarus would have to save the mother from the son."

"That could end up working in our favor, Cassidy,"
Godfather said, then clicked another frame. A picture of

an angry boy flashed up on the screen. "This was right after Cross was caught coming back onto the reservation. He was twelve. He'd taken off to parts unknown for over a month. No one knew where he went. He refused to talk about it. After that, the shit really started to hit the fan."

Jax held her breath for a short second, then exhaled. The expression on young Marcus's face defied description. If she had to give it words, they would be a subtle combination of hate, distrust and venom. The boy who stared at the camera held the entire world in contempt.

Jax sat in stunned silence as the assassin's pictures, one after another, flashed before her. Something deep and primal lurked behind his crystalline-colored eyes and the jagged scar that ran from just behind his right ear down his throat and across his collarbone.

"Marcus was a classic problem child," Godfather continued. "Antisocial. Acted out by setting fires, stealing from the local bullies, and swindling whites out of their cash. By the time he was fifteen, he'd been arrested for assault with a deadly weapon three times. The deadly weapon being his fists. He excelled at an early age in martial arts, kung fu specifically. Each charge was dropped for lack of witnesses, but there were notations in each case file that he was defending reservation kids against the white kids. Once Marcus hit his teens, he was regularly in trouble. Petty theft, alcohol, truancy and fighting. In and out of juvey. Lots of fighting, and he didn't discriminate. Delinquency seems to be a common thread with him."

Godfather pressed the button again. Another classy image of socialite Sophia Rowland flashed before them.

Marcus had his mother's light skin, which tempered the swarthy skin of his father, but his paternal ancestry was evident in his prominent cheekbones and square jaw. He was a complex compilation of angles and planes, punctuated by dark, hawklike features. He reminded her of something otherworldly in his intensity.

"His mother deserted him when he was two weeks old, his grandmother dropped dead in front of him when he was seven, his father was a drunk, and the grandfather had his own problems. The kid was screwed from conception. The day he graduated high school with a 1.5 GPA, his grandfather dragged him down to the Army recruiter and signed on the dotted line. Cross was seventeen."

Jax nodded. "That might draw a tear if he wasn't a child killer."

"Here's the kicker. He scored nearly perfect on every ASVAB he took. He went in as a private and was in the Ranger program in less than a year. Specialty sniper. He spent ten years in the military, mostly covert stuff, but suffered what should have been a fatal injury in the mountains of Afghanistan. He was immediately discharged."

"Why the discharge? Why not a desk job?" Satriano asked.

"He didn't want it. After his discharge, he drifted for a couple of years. There's sketchy intel about where he was and what he did. He's good at disappearing. He surfaced five years ago in D.C. and was recruited by Colonel Lazarus, who was his commanding officer when he was discharged. Something went wrong on Cross's last op. We think—but cannot confirm—his unit deserted him." Jax stiffened at the information and couldn't help but feel a tug of compassion for a man left behind by the unit he would have died for. They were bookends in that regard. Trust was something she held close to her vest now.

Godfather continued. "Yet someone was not willing to leave him behind as collateral damage. Personally? I suspect it was Lazarus, and because he came back for Cross, Cross owed him for his life."

Good for Cross. Somebody cared enough to come back for him. So maybe they didn't have much in common after all. "Boo-fucking-hoo. Sad, sad story. Still doesn't give him the right to kill a baby," Jax said.

Godfather looked long and hard at Jax, so long and so hard without speaking that she squirmed in her seat.

"Just remember that when you come face-to-face with him, Cassidy. He's your mark."

If her adrenaline had pumped before, now it shot through her system. "Take him out?"

Godfather nodded. "Eventually." He pressed another button and more images of Marcus Cross flashed before them. Most of them in regular army greens. But the one in his dress blues, his broad chest covered in medals, would have stilled most women's hearts.

Her suppressed rage surfaced.

He didn't fool her. He was a cold-blooded killer of children. He had no scruples, no code, no heart. And she would have none when she dealt with him.

Godfather freeze-framed a picture of Cross as a boy. "When this picture was taken, Cross had just shot and field-dressed his first deer. He's a killer. Don't forget it."

Jax nodded as the excitement she'd felt earlier heated her blood.

"Get into his head, Cassidy, get under his skin, get so deep he trusts you, then offer your services to The Solution. We need to know where Lazarus has gone to ground. Then we'll cut the head off the snake."

"What makes you think I can just waltz in and make him sing?"

Godfather grinned. "Cross has two weaknesses. Weaknesses we will exploit. He's a competitive bastard, and he likes women. Women like you, Jax, who are sleek and as intelligent as he is."

Despite herself, Jax warmed at the compliment. "So we invite him to a tennis match, I beat him and he's intrigued?"

"Cross does a little cleanup work on the side." Godfather pressed the button on the remote and another image popped up. "Salvador 'Chava' Tuturo. He runs the Vela cartel in Chicago. Our intel has it that he's recently contacted Cross to eliminate his brother Jaime."

"Sibling rivalry?"

"Not really. It's just business. Jaime is a loose cannon and has been bringing the heat down on Chava's operation. His latest screwup was turning one of the deputy superintendent of police's goddaughter into fish bait. Even though everyone knows Jaime is a ticking time bomb, big brother can't take out his blood brother, but he can pay someone to make it look like he had it coming, which by all accounts he does. He makes the Hussein boys look like lambs.

"Cross is scheduled to land at O'Hare at twenty-three thirty-eight under the name of Alan Matheson. We'll have a man on him. The DEA has a CI inside Jaime's circle. Gabriella Moncada. She's his amigo, Miguel

Vasquez's, flavor of the week. They're going out on the town tomorrow night. And so are you."

Jax smiled. "You think Cross will make his move then?"

"It's the way he operates. He's succinct, never staying in one place more than a day or two, tops. He has few habits, but that's one of them." Godfather set the remote down on the table and looked hard at Jax. "I want you to rain on Cross's parade. Do you know what that will entail?"

Jax swallowed hard and showed no fear. Indeed, fear was the last thing she felt. "Eliminate Jaime."

Godfather nodded. "Cross will come after you."

Jax stood and set her cup down. "And I'll be waiting."

TEN

(

Like a hammer to his chest, the hard beat of the music pulsed through him, reverberating all the way down to his toes. Glistening bodies gyrated on the dance floor to the hip-hop tune, noxious perfumes tangled with colognes, stifling his nostrils.

Keeping to the darkened fringes, Marcus scanned the throbbing club. It was here Jaime Tuturo trolled the waters like a bottom-feeder. His prey? Impressionable women. The kind most guys wouldn't give a second look. The kind that were so desperate for attention they'd go anywhere with anyone.

The kind that never came back.

Marcus curbed a primal growl, sensing his mark was near. He could feel the man's arrogance. It taunted him like a waving red flag at a bull.

On so many levels it would be his pleasure to end the cocky bastard's life. It wasn't because Jaime Tuturo was a predator—that Marcus understood; it was what Tuturo did to his prey that provoked Marcus's sense of right and wrong. The last girl he'd seduced from this club had ended up floating in Lake Michigan, naked, violated and mutilated, cut up like bait. Jaimito had picked the wrong girl that night. The heat had been turned on. And Jaime's eldest brother Chava had had enough. Tuturo senior's instructions had been simple: *"Make it look like he had it coming. Make it public. Make it permanent."*

Hell, even if Chava hadn't contracted him to take out his little brother, Marcus would have done this job pro bono. As it was, Chava had already paid him a fat down payment, and once the job was complete he'd swing by the downtown gym he'd joined last week and walk out with the two-hundred large Chava would deliver to his locker there.

Marcus scanned the dance floor again, watching, making mental notes. Through the gyrating haze of bodies, his focus narrowed on a short, fat, sweaty gangbanger dressed in a thousand-dollar suit. He could be wearing custom Versace and Jaime Tuturo would still smell like the turd he was. Marcus shook his head. The slick threads were working. Jaime was swaying on the dance floor with a chubby, innocent-looking blonde. She smiled adoringly up at him, her triumph of finally being noticed as transparent as Jaime's sweaty leer. Marcus could see it in Jaime's face, the way he licked his thick lips. He probably had a boner already and was visualizing all the ways he was going to hurt that girl. Anger pricked Marcus's gut. He never had liked bullies.

Marcus planned something special for Jaimito. He'd given his death careful consideration and settled on a garrote. Quick but excruciating. While he was slicing Tuturo's neck from front to back, he'd tell little brother it was big brother who'd hired him, and why. If he couldn't get him alone, he'd single out one of the types Tuturo liked to prey on, give her a whirl on the dance floor, get close to Jaime, and puncture his heart with one precise jab of his custom ice pick switchblade. He'd disappear before his mark fell dead to the floor. Neither the crowd nor Tuturo's friends worried Marcus. The adrenaline junkie in him liked a little public display of affection once in a while. But only if he had no other choice. He hadn't survived as long as he had by being arrogant. He was cautious. Always.

Tonight he would blend in. When the cops showed up, no one would be able to describe the person standing next to them, much less Marcus, who, though taller than most men, had dressed to bore.

"Excuse me," a deep, sultry voice said from behind him. Instantly Marcus's acute senses went on alert, and his focus went from his mark to his dick. The full swell of breasts pressed against his back and a soft hand trailed across his shoulders. He stiffened, fighting the primal reaction to the voice, the tits and her musky perfume. She smelled exciting. Like a wild roller-coaster ride. He turned as she passed to his left, and looked down into two liquid, dark-chocolate-colored eyes. Full red lips smiled, showing straight, pearly white teeth. She moved past him toward the bar and his gaze followed. His cock thickened. She was one long drink of water. Her languid gait called to him to follow, and he automatically took another step forward.

He caught himself after two steps.

What the hell was he doing?

He was here to do a job, not get laid. Still, as he watched the slow roll of her hips and the way tendrils of thick crimson-colored hair slipped from her topknot to tease the back of her neck, he imagined coming up behind her, slipping his hands around her hips to her belly and losing himself in her heat.

And she was hot, from her shiny red hair, to the short, fiery-as-hell red dress that hugged her J-Lo ass, to her shapely legs accentuated by strappy stilettos. He'd give his right arm to have those heels digging into his back.

As if she'd read his mind, the woman in red half turned and looked over her shoulder at him, giving him enough of a view of her chest that his dick lurched against his slacks. *Damn.* He had to hand it to her— unlike the low-cut back, the front of her dress clung to but covered every inch of her tits, making him and every other man in the place fantasize about licking and sucking them.

Son of a bitch! The last time he'd been this affected by a woman, he'd been thirteen and had lost his virginity to Ramona Steele, a cougar by today's standards, but to a thirteen-year-old horn dog of a kid, she'd been a goddess. He would have stood on his head, naked in the middle of the rez, if she'd asked him to. He scoffed at the memory. Mona wasn't his first lesson in manipulative women. Suspiciously, he eyed the woman in red.

He shook off the heat. He wasn't here to score, and he wasn't a dumb kid to be led around by his hormones. He was here to reduce Chicago's population by one. Dragging his gaze from the siren's retreating backside, he cursed when he lost sight of his mark. Spinning, he scanned the dance floor again for Jaime Tuturo. He stiffened when he saw the punk, the little blonde struggling to keep up behind him, strutting up to the bar, his ever-present entourage flitting around him like flies on turd. Every one of them flying their colors with a black-and-red silk shirt. Even with his flashy threads, his slicked-back hair, and the flash of gold on his thick fingers and thicker neck, Jaime Tuturo still looked like the gang banger he was.

Marcus smiled. He fingered the yellow bandana in his trouser pocket. All hell would break lose when he left it on Jaimito's body. The Reza cartel boys would get the blame for what he was going to do to Jaimito, and what happened after that was none of his business. He watched Jaimito stop in his tracks, and his gaze fix and hold. The lady in red strutted across the dance floor toward the bar as if she'd been Cleopatra and everyone else in the room had been mere slaves to do her bidding.

Although this chick was way out of Jaime's league, the gangster was arrogant enough to think all he had to do was snap his fingers and she'd roll right over. Marcus was not surprised to see Jaime send one of his lackeys over to the lady in red. Marcus smiled. Coward. For all of Tuturo's bravado, he was afraid of being shot down in front of his posse.

Marcus grinned as the lackey stopped in his tracks, then turned back to Jaime when she snubbed him with an imperious air of disdain. A few minutes later, he watched another gangbanger attempt to plead Tuturo's case to the lady in red.

Cold as an icicle, she reached for her drink and casually let it tip and pour on the guy's snazzy suit. Marcus growled when the prick raised a hand to her. She stood her ground, daring him with narrowed eyes to touch her. Slowly he lowered his hand, and as he did, she turned her lovely back on him. The dude stood for a long time, rigid, angry, insulted, his machismo squashed. Finally, the guy backed off. Marcus had to hand it to her. She had balls of steel. Most chicks would have scampered away happy to have been spared. But not this one. He liked that. He bet she was a tiger in bed.

Before he could further contemplate her sexual prowess, the music changed abruptly from the one-two punch of hip-hop to a spicy salsa. Intrigued, Marcus moved around to the other side of the bar. She stepped onto the dance floor. And she did not disappoint.

Marcus stood rooted to the floor and watched, mesmerized by the slow, seductive sway of her hips and the way the little fringes on the hem of her dress rocked back and forth. The crowded dance floor thinned as those around her stopped and watched her one-woman show.

Her lush body swayed, offering illicit promises, then taking them back. Jaime materialized beside her, watching, his beady eyes blazing in lust. Turning toward him, she backed away from him. He stepped deeper onto the dance floor. Like a starved puppy, he followed. Away from his posse, away from the pouting blonde and into Marcus's territory. Incrementally, Marcus moved closer.

Marcus scoffed at the man's macho attempt to look suave on the dance floor. His stubby body bucked and shimmied while he tried to look tough. Did women really dig that shit? To Marcus, Tuturo looked like the fool he was.

But damn, he could not blame Jaime for putting on the struts for the redhead. She was prime. He sucked in a harsh breath when she dug her hands up into her hair, threw her head back and closed her eyes. Her long, smooth neck beckoned. He had the inscrutable urge to grab her to his chest and sink his teeth into her creamy skin. To feel her surrender that luscious body of hers to him, right here, right now.

Since his change from mortal to immortal, his primal male had on several occasions wrestled for control of his rigid discipline. Much as it did now. By nature he was a hunter; he lived for the chase. As a vampire, he could quickly eliminate his mark. As a man, he would relentlessly persue the woman who taunted him from the dance floor.

When she opened her eyes halfway and came to a slow, agonizing stop, then reversed the direction of her swaying hips, Marcus swore aloud. He sucked in another harsh breath when she turned and faced Tuturo. Suspicion sliced through the cloud of lust that held him hostage. What would a woman like that want with a piece of crap like Jaime Tuturo? Marcus stepped closer, sensing he was watching an act, a very good act, an act that, if played out, might blow his window of opportunity. When she shimmied again, this time dipping low, Tuturo sidled up behind her as she slowly stood. When she didn't move away, Marcus knew something was up. He stepped onto the dance floor. She continued to sway her hips, pressing her ass, oh, so subtly up against Jaime's crotch. As she did, she looked straight up at Marcus. A slow, seductive smile curved her full lips. She winked at him, then turned away.

What the hell was she up to? And who the hell was getting played? Marcus's lust ebbed.

Refocused on why he was there, Marcus had eyes only for Tuturo now. He moved in. Two steps away, the woman abruptly grabbed Jaime's hand and pulled him down the hall to what Marcus knew were the bathrooms. Jaime's posse closed in behind them, effectively making it impossible for Marcus to get close. The door to the ladies' room opened. The lady in red disappeared inside with a panting Jaime hot on her heels. Ten seconds later, the door opened again as two indignant women came rushing out.

Marcus halted in the long hallway. He had no recourse but to wait; there was no other way in or out of the restroom save for the one door. Leaning casually against the wall, he pulled his throwaway cell phone from his pocket and pretended to be texting. He was far enough away from the bathroom doors that Jaime's boys ignored him. As he let one minute, then two, pass, his mind worked fast, flipping through the possibility that the woman had spotted him and was acting as Jamie's shield. Did little brother suspect big brother had had enough? That would explain the way she'd played with him. And no way in hell was he going to let her get away with it.

When three stacked bottle blondes came stumbling down the hall looking to use the restroom, just as many of Jaime's men told them they would have to wait. The women postured, pouted and used their wiles on the men. When one of the blondes pulled down her spandex sequined top and two impressive tits popped out, Marcus said a silent thank-you. A minute later only one of the thugs remained guarding the door. Marcus knew this would be his only chance. He also knew he'd have to take care of the lady in red. A fleeting stab of remorse needled his gut. He rushed toward the lone *Vela*, shouting, *"Reza! Reza!"* The guy started, looked up from his phone, then took off past him toward the club. When he did, the door to the ladies' room opened. Marcus stopped, surprised to see a petite blonde emerge.

She smiled up at him, and he could have sworn she

winked before she hurried past. A harsh wave of cheap perfume followed her. Marcus moved quickly. He shoved the door open. Dead silence met his ears. The thick scent of blood hung in the air. As Marcus moved toward the end stall, he pulled the wire garrote from the inside of his jacket pocket and wound the thick plastic coated ends around his fists. He shoved the last stall door open and stopped dead in his tracks.

"Son of a bitch!"

Jaime lay in a crumpled heap on the floor, blood running in thick rivulets from the wide slice across his jugular. His pants and underwear were bunched around his ankles with a note pinned to his dick. Shoving the wire back into his jacket pocket, Marcus grabbed the paper.

You don't get paid for what you didn't earn

xo

There was an imprint of red lipstick lips.

"Shit!" He noticed the crumpled heap of clothing on the floor. He shoved the note in his pocket, then grabbed the red material from the floor. *Her* dress. He brought it to his nose and inhaled the musky scent. It smelled like her. He grabbed the stilettos and the red wig. As he shoved them under his jacket, realization struck him dumb. The blonde that just exited. It was *her.* Impulsively he grabbed the yellow bandana from his trouser pocket, tossed it down onto Jaime's blood-soaked chest, then ran from the bathroom, knocking over several people as he rushed in a blur to the outside of the club.

When he got his hands on that little bitch, he was going to strangle her! He came to a skidding halt outside the club. The sidewalk was unusually empty. He looked up the quiet street, then down. Nothing. Not one vehicle. No one walking on either side.

Gone.

Raising his head, Marcus inhaled. Despite the heavy perfume she'd worn, he could, in the cooling night air, smell her natural scent. He walked south on the sidewalk, following her scent to where it stopped. Other scents, dominant male scents, intruded. Then they were all gone. Slowly he exhaled. A car, waiting for her. It was here she got in and here it took off.

For a long minute, Marcus stared down the brightly lit street. He moved past his anger and his frustration to the calm that would give him the clarity to reason. There would be DNA on her shoes, in the wig, on her dress and, most likely, the lipstick kiss. All he needed was a hair or a scraping of skin, or a microscopic drop of saliva. Then he'd know who she was, and knowing who she was would lead him to where she was.

A sudden thrill zinged through him. A thrill he had never experienced either in his former life as a human or his current soulless life. He hugged the clothing beneath his jacket and smiled, then hurried to his rental just as the club exploded with screams and a rush of patrons out the front door.

Jaime's body had been discovered.

At least they'd be looking for the redhead and not him.

And he'd be doing more than looking for his mysterious lady in red. He'd be closing in on her. Starting right now.

ELEVEN

Sitting back and waiting for something to come to her wasn't Jax's style. She was a dive-in-and-get-her-hands-dirty kind of gal. Fortunately, she also did what needed doing, and in this case, she was going to do Marcus Cross one way or another. She nearly smiled at the thought when Gage's voice came through the small audio device in her left ear.

"Target turned right on Michigan and is now approaching plant car at approximately twenty mph. Prepare to engage in less than thirty."

From where she sat in the long shadows of the encroaching evening outside a small café, Jax savored the intoxicating rush of satisfaction even as nervous energy filled her. She felt a brief tinge of doubt but quickly pushed it away.

Round two was about to begin. She'd bested Cross once. She could do it again. The man was good, but she was better.

Even if he had made her sweat for a brief time.

For the past week, he'd been more elusive than a white tiger in Africa.

They'd lost track of him for a full three days, from the time he'd dumped her clothes in a blacked-out studio apartment overlooking Lake Michigan, to the time he'd reclaimed them. He must like the scent of her dress, she thought viciously, because he'd gone back for it. He'd carried it with him when he'd retrieved the Tuturo pay-off, and he carried it now.

Perv.

But it was all good, she assured herself. The hidden GPS chips had bought them enough time to set up. Whether he was headed back to his apartment or to O'Hare didn't matter; he wasn't going to make it with the money.

And once more, she was going to make damn sure he knew she was the one who'd taken it from him.

"He's almost there," Gage murmured.

Holding her breath, Jax watched from behind dark shades as Marcus Cross came into view. Driving a sleek black Mercedes, he slowed to avoid the stalled car planted to stop him exactly twenty feet from her. As he did, he scanned the area, like a hawk wary of a bigger, badder prey animal lurking in the shadows.

"Now! Make contact, Jax," Gage instructed.

She slid the shades from her face just as Cross's gaze swept right, and their eyes locked. Her body jolted as if a live wire had been let loose and she gasped, almost involuntarily looking away. His penetrating eyes, how-ever, refused to release hers as he slowed to a complete stop in the heavy traffic. She knew the exact moment recognition dawned. Under the glow of the streetlamp, his eyes sparked in fury.

Suddenly the hunter became the hunted.

Even as he was hit from behind by Shane's truck, his black Mercedes slamming into the jalopy in front of him—even as his body lurched and the air bag deployed—he didn't flinch. No, he just shoved the air bag out of his face and stepped from the car.

Slowly, she stood, a small smile twisting her lips as she backed into the empty café. As planned, Dante jumped from the car in front of Cross and started railing obscenities while Shane angrily lunged from the truck buried in the Mercedes' trunk. In the confusion, Gage slipped along the passenger side of the car and waited for an opportune time to lift the black briefcase with Cross's blood money inside. Or rather, with hers. If he wanted it back, he'd have to make a deal for it. A deal to allow her into his world.

She was inside the café now, but at no time had Cross broken visual contact. In long, unhurried strides, he moved around the front of the wreck, ignoring her team's attempts to engage him. He maintained one single focus.

Her.

And that's exactly what she wanted.

Come to mama, baby.

She backed up, one slow step at a time, enough to keep him intrigued while her team continued to play the scenario out. Then, with a wicked grin, she ducked behind a wall and listened for the jingle of the bell on the café door.

Timing was paramount. The minute he strode through the threshold, she'd dart to the back of the café while the boys wrapped up. She'd hop in the waiting car and be off. Again.

But he never came through the front door.

Several long, silent minutes ticked by. In the lengthening shadows of twilight, Jax straightened and stood, confused, as she caught the puzzled eyes of her team through the window.

Cross was nowhere in sight.

"What happened out there?" she softly demanded. What should have been a finessed sleight of hand had quickly turned into a major FUBAR.

"I don't know," Shane responded. "He . . . just vanished into thin air."

"Impossible!" Jax hissed.

"The briefcase was empty—" Dante said from his position outside.

"Stone—any contact with the target?" she asked, knowing by now that he was in the alley behind the café.

"Nothing," Stone answered.

"Jesus," said Shane, exasperated as he looked at the damage to the pickup truck and shook his head. "How could he just disappear into thin air?" Dante walked up behind him and handed him a card. Shane nodded, dug into his back pocket and pulled his wallet out. He dug through it and pulled out a card. Dante handed him a pen. They acted as if they'd been exchanging insurance information.

"I don't know where he is, but we're going to wait," Jax said. "He saw me. He'll be here."

"A firm," Dante said and continued to play his part with Shane.

"I'm pulling my earpiece," Jax said as she moved deeper back into the quiet café and watched for Cross. "Do not engage unless I give the signal." She removed the small device from her ear and dropped it down her bra. Cross was smart. Smart enough to guess he'd been set up. He'd look for an earpiece and probably pat her down for a wire. No way was she going to give him a reason to keep walking.

She felt oddly exposed without the device. With it intact, all she had to do was gasp and the calvary would charge in. But in reality, she didn't need them. Jax Cassidy was more than capable of handling any man, even one as dangerous and as highly trained as Marcus Cross.

As the minutes ticked by with still no sign of Cross, Jax struggled with conflicting emotions. She had seriously misjudged him. Apparently, he wasn't willing to walk away from a pile of cash, but he was quite willing to walk away from her.

Damn it all to hell. A crashing sense of failure hit her hard, but she immediately pushed it away. So fine, she could accept he wasn't interested in her as a woman—screw him. But she didn't buy him walking away from information or revenge. He'd want to question her and demand to know what she wanted from him. Even if he hadn't wanted to play right now, he'd be back and she'd be ready for him. As she was about to signal the boys to shut it down, she stopped.

Her skin pebbled as if a draft had cruised across her naked skin.

Then she froze, all her senses flaring out of control.

Her nostrils flickered, a powerful, dusky scent engulfing her like a thick shroud. It called to her, thickening her blood. She could almost feel her veins expanding to allow the extra flow to every part of her body, preparing her for . . . what? Part of her shivered, not in fear but . . . something else.

She was not alone. How the hell had he slipped in?

"Once bitten, my lovely, twice shy," a low, husky voice said only inches from behind her.

Without skipping a beat, Jax drove a hard elbow into Cross's solar plexus, ducked and turned. Keeping close to his body, she took a shot at his throat with the heel of her palm, but he caught her hand just as it made contact. Dropping, allowing the velocity of her weight to pull her down, Jax twisted, giving him a hard kick to his shin, then brought her hand up to break his band-of-steel grip on her wrist. One-handed, Cross yanked her up, lifting her feet clear off the floor.

She gasped, shocked by his strength. Bringing her knees to her chest, she kicked him hard in the gut. Air woofed from his chest, but he maintained his grip. Jax pulled up to kick him again, but he anticipated her move. With his forearm, he easily batted her feet away.

"Tell me when you've had enough and I'll stop," Cross said, lowering her to the floor. Grabbing her other hand, he yanked her up by both wrists. For a brief second, their gazes locked. She shook the hair from her face and glared at him. His ebony-rimmed crystalline eyes were hard, unrelenting. For a split second, his gaze dropped to her lips, causing them to part. Then, unceremoniously, he shoved her away from him. Her back hit the wall, and this time it was her air that rushed from her lungs at the impact.

"Come at me again, I'm going to hurt you," he growled low.

Collecting herself and her thoughts, Jax considered her current tactics. They weren't working. She was strong. He was stronger. She eyed him covertly from beneath her long dark lashes. Power radiated off him in waves. He reminded her of a big, sleek, predatory panther. The photos in his dossier did him little justice. Even the angry scar that ran the length of the right side of his face didn't detract from his animal good looks. She hadn't gotten that good a look at him at the nightclub, but here, in the low light of the café, she didn't miss a thing about him. From his stylishly cut jet-black hair, his arresting face and full, mocking lips to his impeccable black suit and the way it hung effortlessly from his big, muscular body down to his custom black-leather Italian shoes, she didn't miss a thing. Most especially the harsh glint of his unusual blue eyes.

She nodded, mentally shifting gears, then pushed off the wall.

In total op mode, Jax slowly stalked her nemesis. She smiled slightly. His eyes burned with anger, but he couldn't hide the heat flickering behind them. She shook her head and was rewarded with his gaze raking her from her naturally thick, mahogany-colored hair, to her fitted black turtleneck to her short black-leather skirt down to the tips of her black, thigh-high stiletto jackboots that clicked on the hardwood floor.

She stopped two steps from him, planted her feet wide, and set her hands on her hips. "What if I like it to hurt?"

He took a bold step into her space. She didn't expect anything less, but what she didn't expect was the hard rush of desire that hit her body like a wave crashing on the beach. She tried unsuccessfully to deflect his arm as he grabbed a hunk of her hair and yanked, causing her to lose balance and fall into him.

In tandem, they caught their breath. Tension snapped and popped between them.

His smile widened, his white teeth glittered under the café lights. Jax's heart rate accelerated. Her skin heated, her nerves pulsated, and to her horror she felt a tightening between her thighs, a primal response she thought had died the night Montes had attacked her. She gasped at the unexpected vision of Montes's fat, odious body panting above her.

Frowning, Cross released her and stood back. She raised her chin and glared at the man standing a foot away from her. He was just as much of a monster as Montes.

Cross nodded toward the crash scene outside the window. The low wail of a siren cut through the absolute quiet of the café. "What's that all about?"

She shrugged and followed his gaze. Dante and Shane were talking to a uniform. Jax laughed low, the husky sexiness of it surprising her. She'd practiced what came natural to her, had honed it with razor-sharp precision, but still, hearing it now, it surprised her. It had its effect. His eyes swung from the building commotion outside to her. "I don't know what you're talking about."

"Liar."

She smiled and stepped closer. "Maybe." Then slowly stepped to circle around him, but he countered in what was becoming a tense dance. "I want in on your action."

He smiled again, his white teeth flashing as he savored her with his eyes. The close-up shots she'd seen hadn't done them justice, nor had the darkness in the nightclub where they'd first met. She was seeing them up close for the first time. They were an unusual blue, like a wolf's, but thick black circles and black striations humanized them, giving them a depth she had never seen in another's eyes.

"Maybe I don't share," he softly returned.

"You saw my work. I'm a pro. I can take what you don't want."

"I want it all."

Jax thought of little Amy Stover and got angry, but she forced herself to keep cool. "That's what I hear."

He scowled. "What else do you hear?"

"That you work for a guy who has connections all over the world. That he pays well." She cocked her head and said, "I like expensive things."

"So do I."

"Then make the introduction. I won't let you or him down."

Cross smiled and slowly shook his head. "Do I have moron stamped on my forehead?"

Jax pursed her lips. "So, you won't share?"

"I told you, I *don't* share."

"Then I'll take what's mine." She extended her open hand, palm up. "Hand over the cash." When he didn't move, she shoved her hand closer. "For the Tuturo hit. Hand it over."

His eyes narrowed to slits before widening. "How did you know about the contract on Tuturo?"

Jax smiled and trailed her fingers across his chest as the dance continued, but he grabbed her wrist, his fingers punishing. Showing no pain, Jax smiled up into his cautious eyes and shrugged, as if he'd been asking her for a pie recipe. "I have friends."

"Friends, huh?" He reached out with his free hand

and traced a finger along her jawline. The initial chill followed by the warmth of his touch did strange things to her. Unhurried, he ran his fingertip to her chin, then slowly along her full bottom lip. "Tell me who your friends are."

Jax slowly shook her head, then retrieved her wrist from his grasp. "I don't kiss and tell."

He slid a long muscular arm around her waist and pulled her hard against him, bringing an abrupt halt to their waltz. It suddenly occurred to Jax that she was no longer in control.

His harsh hiss of breath when her hips pressed to his hard thighs caught high in her own throat. He was warm. No. Hot. But cool. Like marble. Smooth and hard all at once. His power swirled around her, thick, heavy, hazardous. Seductive and terrifying in its intensity, she felt his imprint on every inch of her body.

It was too much, too soon.

She made to turn and pull away, but he stayed her. His hands suddenly felt like vises around her. She squeezed her eyes shut and fought the urge to give her team the signal for intervention. She could do this, she told herself. What was the worst thing that could happen? He'd get a few good shots in before the cavalry arrived? That she could handle. She opened her eyes and allowed her muscles to loosen.

"No, no," he breathed and lowered his lips to her cheek, "you, my bloodthirsty little minx, are going to kiss me, then tell me who your contact is."

Jax jerked her head back and opened her mouth to tell him to go to hell, but she didn't get the chance. His lips, hard, demanding, and warm, stifled her. His arm locked around her waist. She tried to bring her knee up, but he just pressed his big body more tightly to hers, making any advance impossible. She could feel each indelible inch of him against her body. She fisted her hands, intent on one-two jabbing him under the chin. He released her and caught both of her hands in one big one, yanking her straight up against him.

Immobilized as she was, she attacked with a different weapon. Her teeth. She bit him. Hard. On the lip. He flinched, then groaned. His blood, warm and thick, blended with her saliva. The thick, coppery taste of it didn't gross her out. Just the opposite. It felt like what the initial rush of cocaine must feel like. Exhilarating. Wildly freeing. She hated responding to him.

She sucked his bottom lip. He made a sound half between a groan of pain and moan of pleasure and retaliated by biting her back. He bit her! So hard he broke her skin. And despite the shock of his action, her body snapped, her eyelids suddenly felt heavy, her body thrummed. He moaned as he laved her bottom lip with his tongue. His chest expanded as if he'd taken a deep breath and his body hardened even more against hers. She licked him back and felt the prick of his teeth against her tongue. He made a sound so basic and so primal that Jax's body spontaneously responded with a warm flood of moistness between her thighs. Violently, she wrenched her head back.

"Jesus!" she gasped. What was happening to her?

He pushed her away and turned from her. His wide shoulders moved up and down as he tried to catch his runaway breath. She was glad she wasn't the only one affected by what had just happened.

"Who the hell are you?" Jax demanded, striding toward him.

Without turning around, he thrust his arm out toward her, his long fingers splayed, his palm halting her.

"Don't," he softly threatened.

"Don't what?" she demanded.

"Don't play games with me." He turned around then, and Jax nearly passed out. *Holy mother of God.* He looked as if he was about to tear her apart limb by limb.

Never had she been so terrified or sexually stimulated as she was at that moment. He stood before her, dark, hungry and so dangerous that she had to tell herself to breathe. Her blood on his lips made them darker than their natural tone. He looked like a panther that, once released, could and would do terrible things. His full lips parted, revealing strong white teeth, the incisors just slightly longer than normal. His crystal blue eyes mesmerized, his aura pulling her in. She felt like she had no control over her body.

He took a menacing step toward her. "You know who I am. And knowing who I am, you also know I don't play nice. If you get any closer, I will destroy you."

"Like you destroyed Amy Stover?" Jax blurted. He frowned. He knew exactly who she was referring to. Jax choked back her contempt. "No witness to you tossing Blalock off that tenth-story balcony, was she?"

His eyes flashed dangerously. "That girl was dead before I entered the apartment."

"You expect me to believe that?"

"You don't know what I am or what I stand for. I don't kill children." He turned toward the door.

Jax touched her swollen lip, then licked their mingled

blood. A sharp jolt of electricity speared straight to her womb. "What *are* you?" she whispered.

Cross turned. "I'm your worst nightmare. Stay away from me."

Jax took a tentative step toward him. "Or what?"

Cross wiped a drop of blood from the corner of his mouth with the back of his hand. For a long moment he stared at the crimson smudge on his skin before looking at her. The intensity of his gaze stopped her cold. "Or die." He turned on his heel, and just as he touched the doorknob, she saw Dante and Shane striding toward the threshold on the other side.

Cross laughed and opened the door. Just as she thought the three men would collide, Dante and Shane walked into the café. As if Cross had never been there!

"What the hell?" Jax said, rushing at them. "Did you see him?"

"Yes!" they said in unison. Jax jerked open the door and ran out onto the busy street. She looked up and down the sidewalk. Though there were several pedestrians, Cross's broad shoulders were nowhere to be seen.

Dante and Shane came up behind her. "We saw him through the glass. He was there!"

Jax stood stupefied. "He disappeared into thin air."

"How do we search for a ghost?" Shane asked.

Jax stood silent for a long minute, unable to comprehend what had just happened, and not wanting to believe what she thought she'd seen. One thing was for sure. He'd be back. She slid her hand into the long, shallow pocket of her leather skirt and pulled out a wad of one-hundred-dollar bills.

"He's going to want his money back."

◆ ◆ ◆

Marcus. Come to me, now.

The order ricocheted inside his head, angry and ominous, just as it had since he'd left his car to confront the woman. As blind rage and bloodlust fought a colossal battle inside him, Marcus continued to ignore Lazarus. Even worse, he hesitated and glanced behind him, tempted to finish what he and the woman had started.

With a curse, he strode away.

He'd chosen retreat because he'd been afraid of losing control.

It didn't set easily with him, but he had greater matters to attend to. That meant keeping his sights on the big picture and forgetting what was trivial.

Forget that little minx had bested him!

Forget that she had his money and that she had made him look like an amateur when it had come to taking Tuturo out.

Forget his own foolishness for leaving his car and walking into her little trap just as she'd planned. And it had been foolishness. He'd ignored Lazarus's call in a vain attempt to get answers.

Who was she?

Why did she make his blood boil?

What the hell did she want with him?

'Cause he sure as hell knew what he wanted from her.

He touched his lip even as his dick throbbed. Jesus Christ, her blood was more addictive than heroin. Worse, when she'd bitten him, he'd crossed a self-imposed line. He had sex because it made him feel human, but he'd never exchanged blood with a human and allowed them to live. Until her.

He had tasted her, wanted her and let her go. But God help him, he wanted more.

That had settled it for him.

She could have his money. She could keep her contacts. No way was he going back to that pond. She'd bring him to his knees. He knew it as instinctively as he knew he was going to kill that night. He continued his mad stride down Michigan Avenue knowing that if he didn't indulge his hunger soon, he'd lose all control. And when he lost control nothing good ever came of it. He turned down an alley. As he rounded the corner, he slammed shoulders with a local hood.

"Motherfucker!" the piece of trash yelled and pulled a semiauto pistol from his duster. Just as he leveled it at Marcus's chest, Marcus snapped. He grabbed the thug by the throat and shook him so violently that bones snapped. The pistol clattered to the ground. Marcus raised his arm over his shoulders, lifting the criminal off the ground. Violently, he slammed the thug against the brick wall of the building. Rage, spurred by passion for a woman he could not have, viciously ate at him.

Ignoring the thug's screams for mercy, Marcus let the beast inside of him take over. He sunk his teeth into the pulsing jugular of the man who'd had the misfortune of tangling with Marcus Cross. It would be his last tango.

Minutes later, he dropped the carcass to the ground, swiped the back of his hand across his mouth, licked the last vestiges of blood from his lips, and stepped over the dead man. He was sated, for the moment.

As the night turned to black, Marcus prowled the treacherous streets of south Chicago. No one dared cross his path. Tonight he was death to anyone who dared to look him in the eye.

And still, the vision, the scent, the taste of the woman permeated every part of him, reminding him of the promise he'd made her. Despite his best intentions, he knew they weren't through with each other.

Not by a long shot. Not for long.

i

"Godfather, we have a problem," Jax said when his face materialized on the computer screen. Behind her, Dante, Shane and Gage shifted, and one of them bumped into her. She threw an annoyed glance over her shoulder, but it was more out of habit than anything else. Nonetheless, they backed off.

She and her team had beat it back to their hotel room to figure out whether what they'd thought had happened had actually happened. All they'd confirmed was that they all thought the same thing but none of them was willing to verbalize what Marcus Cross was.

Perhaps Godfather could help them out here.

"Go ahead, Cassidy," he said. She knew by the sharp, tight lines on his face that he was not happy. She swallowed hard.

"It seems Cross is more than we believed."

When she didn't continue, Godfather frowned. "And by that you mean what exactly?"

Jax swallowed again and looked to Gage, Dante and Shane for help. Each of them looked away. They weren't going to voice the absurd. They were all too happy to make her look the fool. Fine.

"He's not human, sir." There, she'd said it.

The silence was so deafening that Jax struggled to

breathe. Godfather stared at her as if she had just asked him to cut off his right nut.

"I mean, he's human, of course he's human! But some kind of superhuman."

"Cassidy," Godfather said in a warning tone. "Keep it real."

Jax smoothed her hands along her leather skirt and took a deep breath, then slowly exhaled. Every instinct she possessed told her there was something very different about Cross. Something that she refused to admit scared her in that she knew he possessed power she had no clue of, but was keenly aware that it lurked dark and deadly just beneath the surface. "After the initial contact on the street, he disappeared. Like a vapor into thin air. Then just as we're about to give up and regroup, he turns up all dark and sinister right behind me in the café. Creeped me the hell out."

"It was nighttime; with all the commotion, he could have slipped in," Godfather countered.

"He didn't," Dante staunchly said. "After the initial impact of the collision, he exited the car with the sole intent of following Cassidy into the café. He never entered through the front door or the back door. He just materialized inside."

"So he got past you and found another way in," Godfather insisted.

Gage moved to stand behind Dante and Jax. He leaned over her back and added his support. "I was at the back door—only way in or out except the front door, sir. He never came or went."

"Sir," Shane started, "when Cross was done with Cassidy and headed for the front door of the café we were on our way in. I saw him coming at us through the glass of the door. When I opened the door, fully expecting to collide into him, he was gone."

"And he didn't come back past me," Jax injected.

"Okay, let's for the sake of argument say he found a way past you. I hardly think that is reason—"

"He bit me, sir!" Jax pointed to her ravaged lip. "He sucked my blood and then he picked me up by *one* hand and held me a foot off the floor for almost five minutes! Who does that?"

Godfather's face grew darker as blood infused his face. He did not blink. "So he likes rough play and he works out," Godfather finally commented, but he seemed more hesitant now.

Jax rubbed the heels of her hands into her eyes and rubbed hard. Dante was so close to her she could feel the rumble in his chest. She put her hand on his and looked directly into the screen.

"Sir, with all due respect, Marcus Cross is different. He's superhuman strong, can disappear into thin air and likes blood." Godfather began to speak, but Jax held up her hand. "You weren't there. I was. He's different. He's on a whole other playing field. Which makes him a lot more dangerous than we were led to believe." She sat back. "And that's a lot. Cuz he was pretty badass already without being a fucking superhuman on steroids or whatever crazy ass dope the army has him hooked on!"

Godfather steepled his fingers and pursed his lips. As he contemplated her words, Jax realized he was trying to find a way out of her absurd conclusion. When he couldn't, he asked, "So what now?"

Now they needed more intel. On The Solution. On Lazarus. And on Cross. They also needed to know exactly who Rowland had been talking to.

"Sir, everything went according to plan. He was easy. Too easy in fact to jack up. I'm wondering now who was set up, us or him?"

The implication of her words weighed heavily in the air. She waited, but when Godfather finally spoke, the words weren't what she'd expected.

"I'm pulling the four of you off this mission," Godfather slowly said.

Jax blanched, the force of his statement startling her like a slap to the face. How could he do this to her, to all of them now when they had made progress? "The hell you are!" Jax erupted.

"I take full responsibility for this, Cassidy. Perhaps I pushed you too far too fast," Godfather started to explained.

"That's a bullshit excuse if I ever heard one, and you know it! I got to him whatever *he* is. If you pull us, me specifically, you'll never see him again."

"We have other ways of infiltrating The Solution."

"What if they're all like Cross? The colonel looks like a poster child for a freak show!"

Godfather shook his head, then looked pointedly at her. "What if what you say is true? What if they are all hyped up army experiments? How the hell are we supposed to fight them?"

"With fire, sir. Look, Cross might be some kind of science experiment, but he's still a man. And he wants me." She held up the wad of hundred-dollar bills she'd stolen from him. "And he wants his money back. I'm the key to drawing him out. Let me do my job."

"What if he makes you what he is? Whatever that is. Would you risk your life to become his science experiment?"

Jax shivered at the thought but sat back and considered it. "I guess then L.O.S.T. will have a superoperative," she flippantly said. The thought of being like Cross terrified and sickened her.

"I'm not willing to jeopardize your life, Cassidy. We'll find another way."

Jax stood. "No. The clock is ticking. I'm the only one to get close enough to him to find out what the hell is going on, and I'm also the only one who has a chance of getting to Lazarus."

"Too risky."

"She's right, sir," Dante said, stepping into camera view. Grudgingly, Gage and Shane nodded in agreement. "Cassidy has her hooks in him. Let her reel him in. We'll be close by in case she needs help."

"What if you can't help her?" Godfather tersely bit off.

"Then I die and you send in the next round," Jax said. And she meant it. "Too much is at stake here to pick up our toys and go home. I'm in. All the way."

"I'm in," Shane said.

"I'm in," Dante dittoed.

Jax looked up to Gage who eyed her with more than professional concern. "I'm in," he softly said.

The next evening, Marcus casually strolled into Lazarus's richly appointed Lake Avenue penthouse. It swam with the seductive aroma of blood, fine tobacco and the scents of recent visitors. Marcus stopped halfway into the room. He raised his nose and sniffed the air. A distinct scent, one he felt some sense of familiarity with but could not recall to whom it belonged, toyed with his senses.

"Is there something wrong, Marcus?" Lazarus casually asked.

Marcus shook his head and dismissed the scent. It could belong to someone he'd passed on the street. "Looks like there are new players in town," he said to his commanding officer, who was also his maker. Not only was Lazarus Marcus's maker but the colonel was also the undisputed leader of *Ny Verden*, or New World coven, the most powerful vampire coven on Earth. As a member of the governing Grand Counsel, Lazarus answered only to Rurik, his creator and father of all vampires.

Joseph Lazarus nodded and handed Marcus a cigar. Marcus took it, put it to his nose and inhaled deeply. The scent of the fragrant *habana* reminded him that while he might have lost his mortal life in the hills of Afghanistan, he still desired the creature comforts of a man. Heat flared in his loins as his thoughts once more focused on the dark-haired beauty who had pushed him to the brink of his iron self-control.

His fingers flexed, snapping the *robusto* in half.

"I see the thought of them bothers you," Lazarus said, handing Marcus another *robusto*. He took it, cut the end and this time took his time lighting it.

Marcus blew deep blue smoke rings as he relaxed back into the overstuffed wingback chair. "They're pros. Lots of money behind them. And buried deep."

"I'm aware. I suspect they are the ones or associated with the organization Rowland cried to after you eliminated Blalock."

Marcus looked sharply up at his maker. He should have known. Lazarus knew everything.

"Do not think this latest act of defiance will go unanswered. Find out who the new players are and if they are directly connected to Rowland's plan to thwart The Solution, eliminate them."

Of course. There was no other way for Joseph Lazarus. Track down the enemy and eliminate them. No gray areas.

Marcus blew several large smoke rings. He watched them intercept the others, breaking the fragile rings. "I've run prints and DNA. Nothing."

"Then you're going to have to work a little harder on that front *and* keep tabs on the senator. You are up to the task?" Lazarus asked.

Marcus grunted and blew several more smoke rings. Lazarus never asked, he ordered. "I'm insulted, sir, you imply I cannot multitask."

"Hardly. Eliminate Rowland's Hail Mary and we have him in our pocket." Lazarus took a long puff of his cigar. "I trust you to see to the matter however you see fit." Marcus gave a curt nod. "But do it promptly. My patience is at an all-time low. When I give an order, I expect it to be followed."

Marcus cocked a dark brow and looked pointedly at the man who had created him. Marcus held nothing but the utmost respect for Colonel Lazarus. The colonel was a true patriot. A man Marcus would follow into hell.

"Why did you ignore my request last night to come

to me?" the colonel softly asked. He poured a snifter of blood from a crystal decanter sitting on the Louis XIV bombe chest, then stared at Marcus pointedly.

Tension tightened Marcus's muscles and a faint sense of resentment prickled his skin, making him frown. He wasn't in the mood for explanations—not after spending last night and most of the current evening trying to rid himself of a woman's hold—but that was no reason to act like a petulant child.

He stood and stubbed out his cigar. "I was busy."

"Since when are you too busy to answer me?"

His anger increased and Marcus rolled his shoulders, willing it away. He stalked the richly furnished room. He'd been here before. A long time ago. His commander had places like this all over the country. Lairs, as they were. A place where Lazarus and Marcus and others like them could hole up when they needed to lay low. They all ran together. Looked the same. Felt the same. That's why, in the last few years, Marcus had declined most of his commander's offers of respite, opting instead to find his own shelter. Once he'd gained that independence, returning to Lazarus had become harder and harder. It had gotten to the point where Marcus had begun taking on more outside jobs, but lately, Lazarus had been demanding. Insistent that only Marcus carry out the high-risk missions.

"Are you losing interest in The Solution's cause?"

Marcus paused, wondering briefly if Lazarus was reading his mind. But even Lazarus wouldn't dare. . . . Marcus shook his head and strode to the window to look out on the glittering lights of Lake Michigan. His legs spread, he clasped his hands behind his back and stood gazing at the ships as they came and went across the choppy water. "No." And that was the truth. He'd always stand on the side of patriotism despite his conversion from mortal to immortal. Even as a vampire, he was still, and would always remain, a patriot. But a restlessness had infused him recently, a restlessness he couldn't put his finger on. Maybe some unfinished business from his mortal life?

"Always succinct, aren't you, Marcus?"

Marcus turned and looked calmly at his commander. "Why expel the energy for more when you can conserve?"

The colonel sipped from the snifter. Marcus's gaze dropped to the glass, then went back to the colonel. "I could ask you if you've lost the thrill of the hunt by taking your sustenance from a crystal glass."

The colonel smiled, showing off his brilliant fangs. They were long and, Marcus knew, razor-sharp. His maker was of the old world and more powerful than an army of special operatives. His strength and passion for protecting his country was something Marcus could and did prize.

"Even the most heavily armed human is an unworthy opponent, Marcus. You will come to realize that soon enough. I find my sport other ways."

Marcus nodded. The Solution was the colonel's passion, his *raison d'être*. Marcus understood that. It was his as well. Except for that, he and the colonel were different.

While Lazarus disdained humans, Marcus grieved his lost humanity.

While Lazarus thought as much of humans as the crystal glass he drank from, Marcus hungered not just for human blood but the closeness of a human woman as well.

And while Lazarus commanded those who killed, Marcus was the one who did it. For his beliefs, yes, but also for the chase. The excitement. The exhilaration of knowing that he would ultimately conquer. But even that had lost its luster.

Everything had become too easy for him these last seven years. He was stronger and faster. He could see in the night, smell scents from long distances and even take the form of the victims he had drained dry. He was the six-million-dollar man except that he had no soul. He was the perfect killing machine. Isolated from humanity even while being in the thick of it.

So why did it bother him? Why now, when his human life had been unmarked by relationships?

Was it because he at least had hope then? The possibility, whereas now there was none? Not even when he found a woman who could affect him the way the one last night had?

"What's eating at you, son?" the colonel asked.

Marcus swiped his hand across his face as he thought of the woman who thwarted him. He didn't speak of her to the colonel. Instinctively he knew the colonel would eliminate her solely for the purpose of no distractions. Life, any life, was expendable to the colonel. Even The Solution's operatives.

"Are you bothered I had you eliminate Simon?"

"No," Marcus answered too quickly. Simon Roche, Marcus's spotter when he'd needed one, and the closest thing to a friend he'd had, was now his *ex*-spotter. He'd breached the code.

"Simon became vulnerable because of a woman," the colonel explained unnecessarily. "He broke a cardinal rule: He shared arterial blood with her. As such he could no longer be trusted and became a threat not only to The Solution's security but by being a threat to us he was a threat to the nation."

"I had no issue with your order, sir."

"Good, because I have another one for you."

Marcus looked up and the colonel expounded, "As we know, Senator Rowland has made no effort to reinstate The Solution. He has contacted an unknown organization to protect him and his family. Such blatant acts of defiance cannot and will not be tolerated. Not only did he not take my initial threat and subsequent punishment seriously, the senator did not take my second threat seriously, and for that he must feel some pain."

"What exactly was your threat?"

Lazarus smiled and drained his glass. "His daughter."

Marcus began to pace. "I don't kill children."

"I believe she just turned eighteen."

Marcus's scowl deepened. "I don't kill innocents either."

"She's hardly innocent."

"She isn't a threat to us."

The colonel looked pointedly at Marcus. "No, but her father is. He's shut us down! Do you have any idea the time and effort it took for me to find someone with Rowland's power and connections? To find the one person who could not only give us the information we needed to eradicate threats to this country but to pay for the execution as well?"

Marcus set his jaw and remained silent.

The colonel slammed his snifter down on the sideboard so hard that it shattered to pieces in his hand.

Blood seeped through his fingers. Marcus met his icy glare. Rarely did the colonel lose control like this. "Eliminate her," Lazarus slowly said, "and if the senator still has issues with my authority, I'll skin him alive one inch of skin at a time."

Marcus stood still, digesting this latest kill order. He didn't like it. On several levels.

"I'm not asking you, Sergeant."

Marcus brushed past his commanding officer to once again gaze out the window. In all the years they had been together, always on the same side, never once had the colonel asked him to eliminate someone who didn't deserve it. Until now. It hit Marcus at that exact moment that he was not free. The promises the colonel had made to him that night he'd lain dying in the hills of Afghanistan had been lies. Yes, the colonel had given him life, but he controlled it.

"Sometimes innocents must fall if the greater good is to be achieved, soldier."

"I understand, sir," Marcus said softly.

A hard hand clasped him on the shoulder. "Remember, son. What we do is for the greater glory of our country, and, as in everything we do, there is collateral damage."

Marcus stood rigid, his eyes focused on the far-off blink of a buoy. The red light cautioned. He nodded.

"I do not like the tension between us, Marcus," the colonel softly said.

Marcus turned to his maker and said, "Nor do I."

"I am glad we agree on something tonight. Now, the Young Republicans are throwing a three-thousand-dollar-a-plate fund-raiser for the senator this Friday night in his home district of San Francisco. His family with be in attendance. As will you. I will leave the details of Grace Rowland's departure from this world in your capable hands."

Marcus fought another scowl. "Perhaps I can take the senator aside and convince him to call off his dogs."

The colonel shook his head and grinned so malevolently Marcus feared for any person, living or dead. "I don't care for your melancholy, Marcus." Lazarus wrapped a linen napkin around his bloody hand. "I created you to save lives. You are a vampire of the highest order. I gave you *my* blood as did the king's consort, Aelia. Combined, our blood is among the most powerful of our kind. You serve a purpose. Once you serve your purpose, you will get what you want most. Assuming you still want it." The colonel tilted his head inquisitively. "Do you? Do you still crave the mortal life you gave up that night seven years ago?"

Marcus kept his face blank and met the colonel's eyes. Then he answered truthfully. "I don't know."

"My son has grown into quite a formidable man."

Lazarus smiled and turned to the soft feline voice. "He has more of his mother in him than he knows."

Sophia Rowland laughed. She exited the opulent bedroom at the end of the long hall and sauntered across the room. Joseph had been concerned when Marcus had sensed her. The sergeant was, after all, his greatest creation. He would hate to destroy him so early in the game. The young man exceeded his wildest expectations. If Marcus had known half the power he possessed, Lazarus might have had cause for concern. But Marcus would never challenge his maker. He knew the consequences should he do so. But still, Lazarus was careful. He never assumed anything.

He turned up his smile for the lovely lady. Ah, Sophia Rowland had been a true treasure trove of information. What an incredible find!

While he was not a man who believed in coincidences, Sophia Rowland had made him a believer. Nearly eight years ago he had met the senator's wife at a memorial for California's veterans. He was inspired by her husband's impassioned speech for his country, her fallen heroes and his willingness to defend the American way of life at all costs. A man he could respect. A man Lazarus would need to see his own dreams come to fruition.

It took time, and maneuvering, and more patience than he had ever exacted in his thousand year life, but when he discovered the lovely Sophia's son, Marcus Cross, was a decorated war hero and her dirty little secret, and at the same time serving in Afghanistan under the command of one Colonel Lazarus, he knew he had to have him, not only as leverage but as part of his greatest achievement: The Solution. He made quick work of the real Lazarus, draining him dry there in the hills of that troubled country, taking his form and setting his sights on the lovely Mrs. Rowland's son. His opportunity to create Marcus into the ultimate weapon had come sooner than later.

Now, he not only had his prime operative in his pocket, but the mother he didn't know in his other pocket and he would use them both to get the senator back into his hip pocket. Without the senator's intel and funding, The Solution would crumble and America's enemies would destroy her. That he would never allow, under any circumstances.

He smiled at the conniving little minx. She knew what he was. She craved his bite almost as much as he craved her blood.

She pouted prettily and ran a manicured fingertip along the mending cuts on his finger. Remnants of blood lingered. She raised his finger to her lips and licked. Her blue eyes burned with desire. "Joseph, why do you drink from a glass when I am warm and willing in the next room?"

He slid his fingertip along the twin bows of her upper lip, then along her full bottom lip. Lowering his lips to hers, he whispered, "Because you like it too much." He bit her bottom lip, piercing the skin. Sophia gasped but clutched him to her, moaning as he sucked harshly. Instead of pushing her away, he pulled her closer and kissed her deeply. She sought to seduce him with her wiles. But he did not crave the erotic pleasures of the flesh. No, his craving was for power. For control. For total annihilation of his enemies.

When he tired of toying with her, Lazarus shoved her away. Her blue eyes blazed.

"I want the White House, Joseph."

And Lazarus wanted complete control of The Solution's destiny. He was tired of being dependent on others for money and resources.

"I want world peace."

Sophia laughed. "Really? Then what would you do?"

His lips thinned into a grim line. "Enforce it."

"You can have it all, Joseph, but you can't do it alone."

He moved away from her and looked down at the hand he had eviscerated when he'd shattered the snifter. It was healed. He turned slowly and said, "I don't need you, Sophia."

"Really?" she purred low. "Do I not deserve some credit where credit is due?" When he did not answer, she moved into him. "I handed you my husband. Gift wrapped! I maneuvered him right into your hands. The instant he has a second thought, I nudge him back into your corner. When he told me he had gone for help, I informed you."

"That information is useless if I don't know who I'm up against."

Her perfectly plucked brows knitted. "I have no clue to their identity. I have eavesdropped, read his emails, and even tried to seduce the information out of him. He has remained stubbornly tight-lipped. Saying only they are so top secret not even the CIA knows about them."

"Find out who they are."

She shrugged, trying to play it off. "Who they are is irrelevant. You will defeat them regardless and it will be a moot point."

"Time is of the essence, my love. You heard my conversation with Marcus. Once your precious daughter disappears, your Family Values candidate will buckle."

"Do you think, Joseph, I will allow you to harm my daughter?"

"When you refuse to make the ultimate sacrifice, Sophia, you have no say in the matter. So like your daughter, you simply became a means to an end."

"Really? Do I mean so little to you?"

His eyes narrowed. She looked too confident. "What value are you to me?"

She laughed and moved from him to the picture window, where she stared out, much like her son had done moments before. "If you allow me to handle my husband and leave my daughter out of this, you will have the entire U.S. military at your disposal."

He moved swiftly across the room and grabbed her before she finished her sentence. Sophia gasped at his sudden passion.

"You offer more than you can deliver."

Vehemently she shook her head. "No, I *can* deliver! We both want the same things, Joseph! Give me eternal life and I will give you the vice president of the United States!" She grabbed his arms. "And we can rule the free world!"

"Do you plan on seducing the vice president of the United States?"

"I will not have to. I will be married to him." Sophia smiled at his scowl. "Last week the GOP presidential front-runner, James Calhoun's people flew out to see Bill. They offered him the running mate slot. Do you know what that would mean for us, Joseph?"

"Did the senator accept?"

Sophia threw her hands dramatically up in the air. "No! The fool. He said he had more power as a senator, then sent them packing, but I will convince him. And once I do—"

"What power does the vice president have that I do not?"

Sophia smiled slyly. "*All* of the power once the president is dead."

For the first time in centuries, the flicker of sexual desire intrigued Lazarus. His gaze swept Sophia's long, lovely neck. Her jugular pulsed. He smelled her wanton quest for power. In that they were equals. He grinned wide. "Ah, Sophia, you are truly diabolical. What will we do with your son once he discovers you? On principal alone he will kill you."

Sophia pressed her warm, voluptuous body against his. His blood warmed. "I trust you will prevent my demise by his hand. And with that, I will leave my son and his untimely ending to you, Joseph." She tilted her head back and swept her blonde hair from her neck. "Now, darling, drink from me, my body hungers for you."

As his hungered for her.

THIRTEEN

J ax heard him in her sleep. His voice. Dark, low, husky, calling to her.

She moaned and rolled over, burying her head under the pillow. Her body ached, as if she'd had a fever. The cotton sheets felt rough on her skin. The air was thick with the scent of a man's cologne, someone who'd stayed there before her. It wasn't unpleasant, but it wasn't the dark, dusky scent with twists of exotic spices she wanted.

Hands touched her arms.

She woke up with a start, jackknifing up in the bed. The sheets fell from her feverish body. Instinct took over. She grabbed the arms that held her and shoved them hard.

"Cassidy!" a harsh male voice choked out, followed by a loud crash.

Jax leapt out of bed, disoriented but ready to fight. Frantically she looked around the room and locked gazes with Gage, who, clad only in gray boxers, lay sprawled against the small desk and shattered chair. His eyes were as wide as quarters. He swiped at the trickle of blood on his bottom lip. "What the hell did you do that for?"

Frowning, Jax grabbed a pillow and hurled it at him, still startled by his touch. "I—you touched me!"

He shoved the pillow aside and moved to get up but

halted, eyeing her angrily. "Yeah, and you nearly killed me."

"What the hell's going on?" Shane complained from the open door connecting their rooms. His sleepy eyes opened and focused on her clad only in a black wife beater and pink flannel boxers. He looked down at Stone, then snapped back to Jax.

"Nothing," Jax mumbled. She shook the cobwebs from her head. Her dream had been so vivid. She'd thought . . . she shook her head. Hell, she didn't know what she'd thought.

She reached down to give Gage a hand up. Slowly, he accepted it, and she hoisted him up with ease.

"You must be eating your Wheaties," he grumbled. When she released his hand, he rubbed the back of his neck, then cracked it.

Jax raised her eyes to Gage's deep green ones and smiled. Couldn't help it. She had a soft spot for him. He was big and bad, but underneath he had a heart as mushy as a roasted marshmallow. "Next time, keep your hands to yourself and you won't get hurt."

Shane scowled. So did Dante, who, drawn by the commotion, had also come into her room. Both men looked hard at Gage. He threw his hands up. "Are you kidding me?" He looked hard at Jax. "I heard you cry out. I thought something was wrong. I come in here and you're tossing and turning like you were having a nightmare or something. Next time I'll let you be miserable."

In a sudden flash of clarity Jax said, "Cross. I dreamed about him. Like I was in his head." She shivered and ran her hands up and down her goose-fleshed arms. "He's hyperaware. And he knows I know it."

"I don't like this, Cassidy," Gage said. "He's too dangerous."

Jax looked at him and tried to keep the surprise from her face. "You backed me on this. Did you lie to Godfather?"

"No, I've just had time to think about it more. The guy has skills we can only guess at. I'll bet you my right arm he won't go down like one of us."

Jax scowled. "So you're saying with his unknown skill set I'm not up for this? Is it because I'm a woman or because you or Shane or Dante aren't up for it either?"

Gage cursed and rubbed the back of his neck again. "No, damn it, I'm saying everything about the guy is an unknown. He'll kill you."

"As opposed to you?"

Gage stared at her. He didn't have to say it; she knew what the real problem was. The last thing she wanted was for any of her team to go all knight and shining armor on her. It could get all of them killed. "He could have killed me at any given time last night. He didn't. He didn't because he wants me."

Gage began to pace the floor. "So, what prevents him from taking what he wants?"

Jax looked at each one of the men in the room with her and let the question hang in the air like a heavy balloon. Gage, his green eyes narrowed in concern and anger. Dante's deep-aqua-colored eyes and rugged face lined with apprehension, and then Shane's. He was good looking. Painfully so. Deep-golden-colored hair, crystal blue eyes, and a crooked half smile coupled with that sexy Down Under accent made even an old woman's heart twist with want. "His ego."

Gage snorted. "Bullshit."

Jax sighed, exasperated. "Look, we've been over this already. Stop thinking with your emotions, Gage. Think about the reality of the man, not the supersoldier he has been made into, because while he is whatever he is, at his core he is still very much all male. A competitive male, and believe it or not, an honorable one in his distorted way. Rape isn't his style. He likes exerting his power in other ways. To a guy like him, rape is cowardly. Marcus Cross is not a coward, and raping me would give him no sense of accomplishment. He's a hunter. His excitement comes from the chase and the ultimate surrender of his prey. He wants me to come to him. And I will. But on my terms."

"And then what? He killed a twelve-year-old girl, for Christ's sake! You think he's going to let you walk away after you wheedle your way into his secret life?"

"He didn't kill that girl."

Gage nearly jumped out of his shorts. *"What?"*

"Cross told me he didn't kill the girl. Said he doesn't kill kids."

Gage slapped his hand over his forehead and laughed. "And you believed him? C'mon, Cassidy, you can't be serious."

"As a heart attack."

"Jesus," Gage pleaded, looking to his buddies for support. "Shane, Dante, would one of you please tell her she's lost her objectivity."

All three men looked at her as if she had grown a third head. Jax bristled. "You can all go to hell. I have not lost anything; if anything, I have some kind of weird connection to the guy. I knew in my gut he wasn't lying about the girl. And it has nothing to do with objectivity; it has to do with going with my instinct."

Jax leaned over and grabbed her iPhone from the nightstand, pressed a few buttons, then waited a few quick heartbeats. "I knew it!" she said half to herself. She looked up to her team and smiled. "He's going to San Francisco." She held up her iPhone and showed them the senator's schedule for the month. "Senator Rowland has a fund-raiser in San Francisco Friday night. We're going." Jax set the iPhone aside and looked pointedly at Gage. "And I knew before I checked that Cross was headed west, so don't tell me I've lost my objectivity."

"I'll call Naomi to make the necessary arrangements," Dante said.

"And so the plan stands," Jax said. She warmed to it. "In a finesse game of cat and mouse, no better place to continue on to the next phase than at the fund-raiser. Should be a hoot."

"Then what?" Gage asked, none too happy. "He forgets he's supposed to eliminate the senator's kid because of his lust-induced frenzy?" Gage scoffed. "Oh, wait, I forgot, he's got a code of ethics, he doesn't off kids."

Jax shook her head and kept the lid on her temper. "No asshole, not what we do. I've shown my hand. I flat out told him I want into his world. He's seen my work, now I want a piece of the action. He wants me, not in his world but in his bed, and he'll want his cash back on principle alone. I'll make him an offer he can't refuse. A trade."

"I hope you're right, Cassidy," Shane said, looking none too pleased. "For all of our sakes."

She plopped down on the edge of the bed. "I'm right. He's a man, after all."

Moments later Shane and Dante left the room, but Gage remained. His deep scowl told her he didn't like the plan.

"What, Stone?"

"You don't have to sleep with him."

"C'mon, Gage. It's just sex. I will only do that as a last resort." And she believed it. She had to, to survive.

"Screw him, Jax, and he'll kill you."

She snapped, standing up and pushing him with both hands. She pushed him hard. "It warms my heart that after all this time, after all my training and after the success of Vegas you don't think I have enough gray matter in my head not to jump in the sack with him the first chance I get!"

"It's not that," he defended. But she knew it was part of what was bugging him. And that pissed her off. She was a lethal weapon. A weapon that could and did strike with deadly precision.

"Then don't tell me how to do my job." She moved into his space to make her next point. "And don't imagine there's anything but a professional relationship between us, Gage. Don't romanticize me. We both do what we need to, to survive and to complete our mission. That's all."

She saw the raw pain in his eyes. She didn't know Stone's story, none of the guys were chatty Cathys, but she knew he had suffered a devastating loss in his life. And she was sorry for that, but she wasn't the one to save him. That he'd have to do on his own, just like she had. "Don't you ever want more than just to survive?" he asked softly.

She thought of Marcus. Of his background. Of how his past shaped his present. "Sure," she said flippantly. "I also want world peace and a parade, but I'm not gonna get it. Survival and purpose suit me just fine for now."

He didn't move, but instead looked down at her with eyes full of hurt, anger and disappointment. "Go to bed, Stone," she wearily said.

He stalked off into the other room, leaving the door cracked. Jax strode over to it and shut it, then loudly locked it. She sat down on the edge of her bed. Angrily she picked up her phone and sent a quick text message to the man with the magic wand.

call off stone

For a long time Jax lay on her back, staring at the ceiling. She fought sleep, afraid she'd have another erotic dream of Cross. She cursed herself for being so susceptible to him, but when she closed her eyes, she still heard him. Calling to her.

From the darkness of the patio of the woman's twelfth-floor hotel room, Marcus watched a man leave her room. He followed his departure with murderous eyes, amazed that he'd kept himself from breaking the man's neck when he'd felt his desire for the woman swell. The only thing that saved him was that the woman didn't reciprocate the desire.

Through the thick glass that separated them, Marcus

could smell her wild, sultry scent. She fidgeted in bed for several long minutes before falling into a restless sleep.

After leaving Lazarus, he hadn't been able to resist coming to her. He was in her blood, as she was in his. And as long as her blood was in him, he could find her anywhere. She couldn't hide.

He smiled, the gesture paining him down to his groin. Never, not even in human form, had he wanted anything as badly as he wanted to sink inside her. He pressed his hand to the glass. Her body arched.

He slid his hand down the glass. He could feel her skin. Smooth, warm, wanton. He watched her undulate, her full lips parted. Her hand pressed to where he imagined his to be upon her right breast. He hissed in a breath and jerked his hand away from the glass. He could feel the soft, warm imprint of her hand upon his.

Slowly he backed away, adding distance between them. He had come only to see her. What he got was alcohol on the open wound of his desire. He wanted her. It didn't matter what she wanted with him; she would not get it. He was stronger, faster, deadlier. He had no fear of death. He was already dead.

The only thing that gave his soulless life purpose was doing what he hadn't been able to do as a mortal. Effortlessly infiltrate and eliminate enemies of the state. He had cleaned out more terror cells in the last seven years than the U.S. government had cleaned up in the last three decades. But they were like roaches. When one nest was eradicated, three more sprang up. He had nothing but clear skies and time ahead of him. The thought didn't electrify him as it once did. Quite the opposite. He wanted something more. Something . . . honest.

He smiled bitterly. There were those who took issue with his end game. He maintained his personal code of ethics, but admittedly, there had been collateral damage along the way. Some of it he wasn't proud of. He wondered, at times, if he would rot in hell when death finally claimed his immortal life.

Maybe he should stay where he stood and await the sun, then perhaps his soul would be at peace. As it was, it clamored for something he knew he could not find in his current life. What it was he didn't know. His eyes narrowed and he put both hands against the glass. With slow, methodical care, Marcus strummed her body, much like one would a harp.

Her soft cries of desire pulled at him . . . almost to the edge.

Abruptly he turned from the glass door, hopped to the top of the concrete-and-steel patio wall, then jumped into the night.

FOURTEEN

The elegant Green Room in San Francisco's War Memorial Veterans Building was a bustle of activity. From behind a green and gold-trimmed Corinthian column, Jax watched the waitstaff move with the vigor of a beehive. China clinked, crystal chimed and silverware pinged, each sound combining to make an oddly soothing melody.

Jax checked her watch. In just a couple of hours, two hundred and fifty of the senator's closest friends and supporters would arrive. Each one had paid three thousand dollars for a twenty-dollar cut of beef or hunk of Pacific salmon, as well as the privilege to chatter and pump hands with the upper crust. Of course, those friends would also remind the senator whose hard-earned cash had funded his last three terms as California's only Republican senator.

Rowland was a rare breed in California—a conservative politician who'd prospered despite the "anything goes" attitude of young adults exercising the right to vote. His opponent, a Democrat whose charm and slick words had captivated the city for years, had an abundance of public peccadilloes. Rowland had exploited them mercilessly.

During a recent FOX interview, he'd very famously stated, "Family is the foundation of our country. If you erode that, we have nothing." Then he'd calmly informed the public why he'd been unconcerned when his opponent, San Francisco mayor Johnny Mercer, declared his intentions to run against him.

"You've trusted me for eighteen years—a man who served his country loyally in Vietnam, a man faithful to his wife, and a devoted dad who coaches his daughter's soccer games; how could you possibly trust a philandering mayor, an admitted louse who preyed on the wife of his own brother? What message would that send?"

When the interviewer had asked him about his opponent's allegation—that Rowland had used his political muscle to squash a grand jury investigation against his old college buddy Walter "Waldo" Cummings—Rowland had publicly sworn on his daughter's life that Waldo had had no idea when he'd recruited members for investment opportunities that he'd been intentionally debunking Californians out of their hard-earned money.

Rowland had gone even further, opening his own books and showing that he, too, had lost a chunk of change in the investment.

That had taken some balls. For that alone, Jax was looking forward to meeting Rowland.

Jax backed slowly out of the room and onto the long, columned loggia. Ornate potted palms, brought in specifically for this event, stood sentinel between the columns, giving the illusion of security. They filled in the gaps between the columns, breaking the stiff Pacific breeze. Despite the leafy barrier, the warm, sultry scents of summer wisped around her nostrils. Dressed in a short black sheath, she found the temperature perfect.

Though the function tonight was not black tie, it was formal. Nonetheless, she'd dismissed wearing a fuller-length dress. She wanted optimum mobility if she had to take off after anyone for any reason.

Jax smiled.

Besides, she thought, she had great legs, and the dress showed them off to their advantage in the classic black Jimmy Choo peek-a-boo pumps she wore. The only problem with the attire was the fact that there was no place to conceal a gun, so she'd strapped a short knife to the inside of her right thigh. But she had a few tricks up her sleeve. Literally. Her wide gold bracelets broke down into Chinese throwing stars, and the double finger starburst ring on her right hand clicked into razor-sharp brass knuckles. She could do a lot of up-close damage. Those little trinkets and her hands would have to do the job tonight if she found herself or any of the Rowlands in a bind.

Closing her eyes, she inhaled. She could almost smell the expensive smoke of imported cigars as the gentlemen excused themselves after dinner and hashed out deals in the dimly lit alcoves. She loved the smell of a good cigar; it reminded her of her maternal grandfather. He was one of the reasons she'd become a cop. She'd wanted to be just like Pappy when she grew up. She shook her head and cursed. He would have disowned her if he had lived to see her disgrace.

Jax slipped between a palm and a column and walked to the edge of the balustrade, where she gazed out at City Hall. Inhaling deeply, she slowly exhaled. But if Pappy saw her now, he'd be proud. He'd understand. Everything happened for a reason, her Nona used to say. She'd had to

endure Montes to be here, where she served a bigger purpose. She shifted her gaze to the vast open areas between
the labyrinths of buildings that made up the performing
arts center in San Francisco—the opera house, the sym-
phony hall and this one, the Veterans Building, which
encompassed its own group of impressive rooms. It was
the perfect place to throw a mega fund-raiser.

Security-wise it sucked.

Too many entrances and exits. Too many stairways
and back-room elevators. And out here on the loggia
with all the potted palms enclosing the space like a comforting glove, there were plenty of places to hide. But
the senator wanted the lavish event to give his guests a
sense of privacy and security. Yeah, Jax thought, a perfect sense of security for anyone who wanted to take a
potshot at the senator or snatch his daughter.

Despite the foliage, Jax made a perfect target. To a
halfway decent sniper, it would be like pointing a shotgun into a barrel of fish. Her gaze traversed the span of
space between where she stood and the rest of the city.
Was Cross out there at this moment, watching her? Was
she in his crosshairs? A slight shiver ran along her spine
up through her neck and along her arms. What if he
was? Her lips pulled back into a tight grin. Raising both
hands, she gave him the universal salute he would have
no problem deciphering.

But she wasn't worried about anyone taking a shot at
the senator. Tonight was not the night Senator Rowland
needed to worry about. At least not for his own safety.

His wife and daughter were another matter. Lazarus
needed the senator alive. Family was a different story.
They were leverage, and if taking out one did not do the

job, then there was always the spare. If she'd been Lazarus and had had to take out one or the other, she'd have taken the wife out first. Surviving the loss of a spouse was easier than surviving the death of a child. It made more sense for the wife to be the next target. Then, with the senator's most precious possession left, he would do what most parents would do: he would cave. Jax snorted. At least most dads would move heaven and earth to save their child from harm. Jax's sperm donor would not have done anything for her unless there had been something in it for him.

Yeah, "Fast" Eddie Giacomelli would not win any father of the year awards. The prick had taken off when she'd been a toddler, then drifted in and out of her life when he'd wanted something from her mother. Jax crossed herself when she thought of her mother. God rest her soul. There hadn't been a gentler, kinder, more loving woman on earth than Carolina Giacomelli. And every time Fast Eddie had shown his snake charmer face, the woman who'd refused to divorce him had given him what he'd wanted, whether it had been food, booze, money or . . .

Jax squeezed her eyes shut. She'd heard her mother's sobs the mornings she'd woken to an empty bed. He'd never stayed for breakfast. Twice, before Jax learned to hide it, she'd found her piggy bank empty after he'd skulked out in the middle of the night.

Jax shook her head and the bad times out of it. She had a job to do.

"This place is a security nightmare," she said.

"Tell me about it, mate; once this room fills up we'll be elbow to elbow," Shane said.

"Down here isn't much better," Dante said from his position downstairs in the main vestibule. Jax felt a fleeting pang of guilt. Gage had been gone when she'd woken. Neither Dante nor Shane mentioned his absence. For the tact she was thankful.

"We have our work cut out for us tonight," Jax grumbled. Returning to the balustrade, she took a deep breath and slowly exhaled. Tonight was going to be tricky. Rowland had refused to hire more security, insisting only on L.O.S.T. and his personal detail of three ex–Secret Service gorillas. They were good. But Jax felt they weren't enough. She and her team needed to be proactive, not huddled around the senator waiting for lightning to strike. So they had split up the detail: Dante would take Mother Goose duty, while Shane acted as eyes and ears and backup where needed, and she was given the task of keeping Cross occupied, and in so doing convince him to make an introduction to Lazarus.

Jax shook her head not liking the odds one bit. If Grace was her kid, she'd lock her up. But she understood the senator's point of view. He was a public official running for reelection and he had to be visible and so did his family. Despite the fact he had kept them out of the limelight for most of his career. Now he had no choice. Mercer was running a nasty campaign, and Rowland had no choice but to put his family out in the public eye and show himself as the family value candidate he proclaimed to be.

Mercer. Jax couldn't help grimacing in distaste as she thought of the man.

Even though Rowland had navigated the Where's Waldo scandal, his bid for reelection would be no slam dunk. Johnny Mercer was smart. He was slick. He was solidly plugged into the masses of liberal constituents, as well as the still popolar sitting but termed-out liberal president. Even if he didn't have political clout behind him, Johnny had other intangible assets. He could charm the panties off just about any female who came near him while at the same time garnering slaps on the back from every man who'd crossed or thought of crossing the adultery line.

Jax shook her head. So much for righteousness and justice. If Rowland lost his bid for his fourth term to a snake like Mercer, it would prove once again how imperfect the system was. Why did that surprise her? It had failed her, miserably. Somehow, she doubted the state of California would benefit as she had.

She glanced at her watch. An hour until showtime. She looked up at the pale waxing moon. By this time next month, Joseph Lazarus and Marcus Cross would be but names on a couple of headstones at Arlington.

Jax shivered when she thought of Cross and what he was: on the one hand, a superhuman with a blood fixation that repulsed her—but there was the adrenaline junkie in her that was beyond intrigued. What would it be like to work beside a man like that? Her mind wandered to taboo thoughts. Would he be as voracious in bed as he was when he killed? Would he execute a woman's body as precisely as he executed his marks? Instinctually Jax knew the answer to her unasked questions. He would be insatiable. He would wreck her, body and soul. And she'd beg him for more. *"Shit!"* she hissed. She didn't like where her thoughts were headed, and more than that she didn't like that she was intrigued by him. He was public enemy number one.

What concerned her as much was knowing they had some type of unspoken connection, and she was unsure what that meant or how it worked.

Her body tightened, and suddenly she felt cold.

She rubbed her hands up and down her bare arms and hurried back into the warmth of the room, trying to push away the evocative thoughts of Marcus Cross that bled into her brain.

You cannot hide from me.

Jax stumbled, then stopped in her tracks, nearly falling over in the five-inch heels. "Who said that?" she demanded of her team.

"Repeat, Cassidy," Shane said, his voice clear and distinct. Jax shook her head.

"I didn't hear anything," Dante piped up. Jax shook her head again. Not Dante. Not Shane.

"Must have been one of the staff. Never mind," Jax said, looking around her and still seeing no one close enough to have been heard so clearly.

"What's your 20?" Shane asked.

Jax quickly reset her bearings and answered, "North corner of the Green Room." Her gaze swept the room and she felt no small sense of relief when she caught Shane's concerned gaze.

He was hard to miss even though he was dressed in formal black and white like every other waiter. He nodded as he entered the room from the south door that led to the kitchens.

"Dante? You copy?" she softly asked.

"I copy."

"Your 20?"

"Main entrance."

As complicated as the game was, their plan was simple. Watch closely, stick close to their subjects and engage Cross at every opportunity. Keep him off his game. Keep Grace Rowland alive.

As much as Jax was anticipating playing cat and mouse with Marcus Cross, she was just as intrigued by Sophia Rowland. There was something compelling about an heiress who had run off with the baddest boy in town, then deserted her firstborn child, buried her second husband, and had managed despite her stigma as a wild child to land the ultraconservative William Stanton Rowland. How was it that a force of nature had taken a quiet backseat to the dynamic California senator?

But what intrigued Jax the most about Sophia Rowland was the question of how a mother abandoned her own flesh and blood. Did Cross know who she was? Jax couldn't help but feel a tinge of sympathy for Cross as a boy abandoned by the woman who'd given birth to him. But now? He'd become a lethal killing machine for a man who gave no consideration to anything or anyone but his own desires. Did that man know about Cross? Of his difference? Jax shook her head, still denying the undeniable. She'd look harder at Cross tonight. Watch for the slightest telltale sign of weakness, then exploit it.

Jax paced the numerous floors, killing time and familiarizing herself with the floor plan, just in case anything went to shit. The next time she glanced at her watch, it was almost time.

As she came up the service elevator to the Green Room, her skin shivered.

He was here.

She sensed his dark energy. It encompassed her with deadly allure. For a long moment she didn't move. Not because she was afraid but because she needed time to collect herself. To remind herself he was a cold-blooded killer and it would be her pleasure to end his life.

It was showtime.

The room seemed to play out in slow motion before her. She shook her long hair off her shoulders. All she saw was the encroaching guests and the glimpse of shadows swirling here and there, but no sign of Cross.

A warm breath along her bare shoulders startled her. She whirled around, eyes narrowed, hands positioned to shove him back, but the air behind her was empty. How could that be? She'd felt his breath.

"The senator and his entourage are coming up the back service elevator. We'll meet you in the south anteroom," Dante said into her earpiece. Jax nodded to Shane, who hustled a tray of champagne between the growing swell of glitzy guests.

Jax slid past the guests and back toward the elevator she had just come up on. The anteroom was twelve steps from the front of the elevator to the right. She'd checked out the room, and though there was window exposure, it was locked. There was no way to gain access unless you were a mountain goat.

Her first impression of Senator Rowland as he stepped from the elevator was that he looked older than his dossier photos. Deep stress lines dug into the corners of his tired gray eyes. Jax smiled, locking gazes with him and extending her hand. "Jax Cassidy, sir. It's my pleasure to meet you."

He smiled, and the gesture changed everything. The stress lines deepened, but they lifted his tired face, showing a glimpse of a handsomeness that had been marred by the strain of his public service. White teeth flashed in a practiced but genuine smile. "I've heard good things about you, Miss Cassidy. I appreciate your vigilance." He glanced at the gorgeous platinum blonde standing hauntingly beside him. "My wife, Sophia."

Jax extended her hand as she looked directly at Sophia Rowland. Her body jerked as the woman's icy blue eyes, so much like her son's, stared back at her. Jax took an immediate dislike to the woman.

"Tell me, Miss Cassidy, who do you work for?"

The question caught Jax by surprise. Hadn't the senator informed his wife? Or had he, like many men in positions of power, kept the ugly truth from his family? Either way she understood the choice. But her loyalty was to the senator.

Jax just smiled and left the explanation to the senator.

"Darling," the senator said, "I told you that was classified. Now leave it alone." His tone was final.

Sophia shrugged, as if she didn't really mind that her husband had slapped her down in front of a stranger. "I think my husband is afraid of ghosts."

More than a ghost, Jax thought.

Sophia Rowland raised one elegant brow and cocked her head. Her diamond earrings glittered beneath the harsh light in the room. They complemented the woman's smooth alabaster skin and her cool blonde hair.

"Do you believe in ghosts, Miss Cassidy?"

Jax smiled again. "I'm always open to the possibilities." *By the way, did you know your son is a souped-up killing machine?*

Sophia Rowland smiled. "I'm glad to hear that, Miss Cassidy. It's smart to keep one's mind open to all possibilities."

"Indeed, ma'am, it is," Jax agreed.

The senator cleared his throat, then reached over his wife to the blonde-haired girl partially hidden behind Mrs. Rowland, gently drawing her forth. "My daughter, Gracie."

Rowland's eyes beamed with love and pride.

Jax smiled in response to the girl's. Her blue eyes twinkled in innocent excitement. For a minute, Jax held her breath, unable to break her stare. Those eyes again. Instead of cold and emotionless like her mother's, the daughter's shone with the *joie de vivre* of a young woman about to embark on the exciting journey of the rest of her life. The vision of Marcus Cross destroying this beautiful life, his own flesh and blood, infused Jax with instant anger, but more than that, a fierce protectiveness consumed her. Gracie Rowland would not die on her watch. She'd make sure of it.

While Gracie Rowland was all golden and smiles, she was a beautiful young woman who, despite her conservative, high-collared navy blue dress, had a bit of a rebel in her. Jax noticed Gracie's right ear and the many piercings that went from the lobe up into the high cartilage. That must have really pissed off her father.

The small, warm hand on hers tightened, pulling Jax out of her thoughts. She smiled deeper and said, "I'm happy to meet you, Gracie. I'm Jax. I'll be hanging around all night. If you need anything, just let me or Mr. Jackson there know."

Jax met Dante's stony stare. He stood beside Rowland's private security. He nodded subtly, then looked beyond the small group to the closed door.

"Yes, well, thank you," Mrs. Rowland said as she turned to her husband. "Alex and Colin are waiting to have a few words with you and me before you make your grand entrance."

Senator Rowland nodded and said, "It was nice meeting you, Miss Cassidy. Thank you."

Jax nodded as the small family, preceded by the security detail and followed by Dante, made their way from the anteroom to another private room. Alone, Jax stared at the closed door. Beyond it was the Green Room. And Cross. Her body thrummed with excitement.

As she stepped out into the room, she immediately noticed all the smells. Perfumes, colognes and body odor combined in a heady scent. Amazing how powerful the combined scents were.

But one scent overrode them all. It pulled her into the room. Jax's heart thumped against her chest. Ghost-like, she skimmed across the floor, weaving in and out of the crowd until she stood in the middle of the room. She looked up and caught her breath. Across the room, directly in front of her, crystalline eyes glowed with power and passion. He was dressed entirely in black. The suit fit his muscular build as if the threads had been sewn onto him. He didn't move but stood like a statue, his gaze locked to hers. And God help her, she couldn't fight his pull.

FIFTEEN

;

"I've got Cross in sight," Jax softly said. "Southernmost wall of the Green Room."

"Roger that," Shane said.

Jax watched Cross from the other side of the room. In less than five minutes, the crowd had swelled exponentially. It didn't seem to bother Cross, however. He glided in and out of the throng of laughing guests, turning every female head in his path. When a voluptuous blonde smiled and touched his arm, he flashed her a disarming smile but kept walking past her.

"He's headed toward the loggia. I'm in pursuit." Jax hurried her step so she wouldn't lose sight of him. Even so, when she strode out onto the russet-colored tile, the loggia was, despite the crowd inside, empty. "Shit," she cursed.

"Do you need backup?" Shane asked.

"Negative," she snapped. Cross had made her look like a rookie at the café. She wasn't letting that happen again. "I'm removing my earpiece. I don't want him hearing any chatter. I'll signal if I need assistance. Now, stand by while I find him."

She took the small device from her ear and slipped it down into her bra, then stepped farther onto the tile. A sharp, sudden breeze whooshed around her ankles and worked its way up her bare legs and between her thighs, probing the juncture there. She gasped. The temperature rose to hot. She whirled around at the sound of deep male laughter, but there was no one behind her. Where was he? She'd heard him. *Felt* him, the tricky bastard.

He was playing with her. Her frustration rose. He obviously knew the rules to the game, while she had no clue.

"Okay, Cross," she softly said. "I know you're out here. Now come out and face me like a real man." She turned in a slow circle, eyes straining for any sign of him. "*If* you have the balls," she added, hoping the taunt would prick his ego.

Long minutes ticked by. Smoothing her skirt and licking lips that suddenly felt parched, Jax moved in a slow, sanguine stroll farther onto the loggia. "I know you're out here, Cross. I can smell you."

It wasn't a lie. Every sense was keen tonight, keener than she could remember. His earthy scent swirled around her, tickling her nostrils. Her sharp gaze darted along the perimeter, looking for shadow or movement between the slightly swaying palms and the columns. When she had traversed the entire length of the loggia, she slipped between the sentry of palms and a column, leaning over the balustrade to view the vast space below.

"I want my money," a deep, husky voice said from behind her.

Jax stiffened, immediately pissed she hadn't heard him. A deep, balmy flush quickly chased her anger away as he moved closer, his warm breath caressing her bare back. She shook her head and, with hands grasping the top of the balustrade, stepped backward into his space.

They were secluded, out of sight from her team. But she held her ground. She'd play it out.

She knew she got to him. His sharp hiss of breath as her hair swirled in the air and across his chest told her he was affected. A small, satisfied smile tipped her mouth. He had his talents, she had hers.

"I spent it," she breathed.

He traced a finger along her bare arm up to her elbow and across her shoulder to her neck. Just one damn finger and her body melted.

Jax closed her eyes and bit her bottom lip to keep from showing her hand. She needed one thing from Cross—a way in to Lazarus. To get it, she needed to arouse him to the point of pain; to the point where he'd be begging to get inside her. She just needed to find some way to stop begging for it herself.

"It's not polite to take things that don't belong to you," he crooned, an edge of amusement in his dark voice.

Jax gritted her teeth but refused to move or evade his touch. "I earned it."

"It was not yours to earn."

"That's debatable."

"What are you doing here?"

"I'm working." She turned around to fully face him and smiled slyly. "Why are you here?"

He smiled, like a big bad wolf. Jax felt body parts she had long ago forgotten about begin to liquefy. "I'm working tonight too."

"Oh." She hadn't expected him to admit it.

"As if you didn't know." He moved slightly into her space. The air caught on fire. "Who do you work for?" he softly demanded.

Jax met his stare. "I'm an independent who's down on her luck at the moment. So, I took on a little surveillance job. Info gathering on Senator Rowland."

"What kind of info gathering?"

She shrugged. Her breasts rose, then fell, lightly scraping his chest. The contact for her was lightning striking. It was so fast, so unexpected and so damn explosive she had to catch the sharp hiss rising in her throat before it escaped, exposing her arousal. When she spoke, she couldn't help that her voice had dropped several octaves. "The usual. Does he have a girlfriend, is his wife a closet lush, is his kid as sweet as she looks?"

"You're working for Mercer?"

Jax snorted and moved back against the balustrade where it was safe. "I'm not that desperate. Yet. This is private money. They want to make sure when they invest in Team Rowland they aren't going to lose their money because he couldn't keep his dick in his pants."

"Tell me about Tuturo."

"He's dead."

He chuckled softly, deadly, slowly shaking his head, but his eyes glittered in good humor.

"Who were the goons with you at the café?"

She shrugged. "A couple of guys I hired for some muscle."

Again he slowly shook his head. "Tsk, tsk," he chided, then moved closer into her space. "You are a beautiful liar. And a beautiful thief. I want my money. Now."

"You want *your* money?" she taunted.

"For starters," he said, his implication clear.

She leaned back against the balustrade and rubbed her right foot along the inside of his left leg. "Feel that?"

"Your shoe."

"Not just any shoe, a Jimmy Choo shoe. I told you, I spent the money."

He grasped her leg under her knee and jerked her hard against him. He slid his hand slowly up from her ankle to her knee, and then to her thigh, where he fingered the smooth leather sheath strapped there. She jerked hard to get away from him, but his strength was impregnable.

"Who gave you Tuturo's information? And why were you willing to kill him to get to me?"

When she hesitated, he slid his big hand farther up her thigh and cupped the warmth between her thighs.

"I'm not going to ask you again," he growled.

Her breath hitched high in her throat. Jesus. Christ.

"Good," she choked out. "Then I won't have to tell you no twice." She shimmied, shaking his hand down to a more modest place.

He laughed, genuinely amused. The sound disturbed her. It made her imagine him happy, when she knew, because of where he came from, where he had been, and, sadly, where he was going, that Marcus Cross had found little happiness in life.

"So you're not only a beautiful thief and assassin, but one with a sense of humor. It's not a trait most women possess, but one I admire."

"I have traits men like you only dream about."

One hand gripped her hip punishingly. "Really?" He lowered his nose to the bend of her jaw and softly inhaled her scent. His body stiffened. "You want to know what I've dreamed of these last nights?"

"Tell me," she whispered.

"Of taking you until I break you."

And he would, if she allowed him to.

Tilting her head, she spoke directly into his ear. "Do you get off hurting women?"

He chuckled again, the sound like warm brandy across the tongue. "Only the mouthy ones."

Feeling vulnerable to his charm, Jax turned the tables. "I'm your worst nightmare, Cross. I know what you are. I know who you work for."

"Tell me then. What do you think I am?"

She hesitated. "You're some kind of army experiment gone wrong with a fixation for blood."

His eyes narrowed, blasting her with such coldness that she involuntarily quivered. When he smiled, revealing brilliant white teeth with slightly elongated incisors, an unholy fear caught hold of Jax.

"My God," she whispered.

His smile deepened. "I'm what horror novels and nightmares are made of," he said as if he was proud of it.

Jax swallowed hard, forcing the lump in her throat down. "Are you telling me you're a . . . ?"

"Vampire?"

Jax nodded, for the first time in her life at a loss for words.

"'Vampire' is such a tawdry term. It conjures up such barbaric images." His face tightened. "I'm light-years beyond barbaric."

"You kill for profit!" she blurted.

He cocked a dark brow. "Look who's calling the kettle black."

Shocked, unbelieving, believing? A myriad of thoughts pummeled her brain. Jax's reasonable side scoffed at his admission, but in her gut? It sure as hell explained a lot. But *seriously*! A *vampire*? She mentally shook herself. She had seen— "How did you get to be what you are?"

"If I told you, I'd have to kill you, and," he smiled showing his teeth, "I really don't want to do that, if I don't have to."

"But—"

He raised a finger, pressing it to her lips. "Take the advance warning I'm offering you. Turn around and walk out of here."

Jax stiffened. She pushed away from his touch. Fear, skepticism, and determination wrestled for control.

The fear of what Cross proclaimed to be was real. But for all that was holy, how could it be true? The skeptic in her refused to believe any of it. Vampire? Really? Puleese. So he was some kind of superhuman. And maybe he had some psychological blood condition and he *thought* he was a vampire . . . but Cross didn't strike her as psychotic. Quite the opposite. He seemed perfectly in touch with reality. Which meant . . . he was telling her the truth?

Despite the balmy temperature, Jax fought off a severe shiver. She quickly processed her worst-case scenario. Cross was a deadly vampire. He was stronger and faster, and had God only knew what other hidden powers. And he's given her fair warning: does she turn and walk away? Or see her mission through?

Thick air pulsed between them. She swallowed hard and looked straight at him. Vampire or not, he and his friends were bad for business. Now, she'd see his hand, and hoped he didn't call her bluff. "My intel, which is very reliable by the way, tells me your boss, Colonel

Lazarus, for obvious reasons"—she nodded at Cross—
"doesn't like publicity. I have a friend or two at the *Post*. I
could drop one of them a line and blow up you and your
operation."

His laconic eyes never once wavered from hers. "And
why would you want to do that?"

"Leverage."

"For what?"

"I told you, I like nice things." She wiped all hesitancy
from her expression and stared at him. "I'm good at
what I do. I need a job. Bring me in."

He threw his head back and laughed, the sound dark,
angry and, at its very core, painful. "Vampire or not, I
could snap your neck right now."

Jax head-butted him. If the situation had not been so
terrifying, she'd have laughed at his stunned expression.
She shoved him hard with her right hand. With her left,
she pulled the switchblade from the thigh sheath and
pressed the razor-sharp tip to his throat. "You'd be dead
right now."

He smiled that slow, laconic smile that made her
think of very bad things. "Promise?"

Her eyes widened. In a lightning-flash move, he
knocked the knife from her hand and shoved her against
the balustrade. His lips hovered inches above hers.
"You're good. But I'm better, and unless you're as good
as me, there is no place for you in my world."

Instead of backing away, Jax pushed her face into his,
so close she could lick his nose if she'd wanted to. "I'm
your worst nightmare, Cross. I know all about you and
The Solution. Let me in, and I won't expose you."

Instead of replying, he inhaled her scent, sighing as if he could smell her emotions.

Jax fought for control. Not her sexual desire. That was not going to ebb. She fought her own self-control. She was losing ground on the dance floor. She was no longer leading.

Lips parted, her breath coming in short, warm puffs, Jax stared up at him. His dark face hovered above hers. His hooded eyes had darkened to deep sapphire. She could smell his desire too. Her senses were on fire. So much so, she realized he had inadvertently given her an opening. This was a test of control. Whoever blinked first lost.

She arched her back and raised up to capture his lips in a kiss. He stiffened but did not pull away. She smiled and pressed to him more intimately, forcing his lips apart. His body swelled against hers, but he did not reach out to touch her. Save for the kiss.

She took her time, savoring him in a way that she had never savored a man. Swirling her tongue along his bottom lip, she nibbled there, then slid it along his top lip, gently flickering across his teeth. She felt the prick of his incisors. Fear mixed then shaken with desire made for a heady cocktail. But she didn't stop. She didn't want to. She was in control, she had the upper hand and she would not be the first to blink.

But his body didn't lie. She could hear the hard thud of his heartbeat in her ears. Hear the blood swoosh in his veins, feel the quickening of his body. Jax moaned, fascinated by this new heightened awareness. And, God help her, her fascination with him as a man and a—vampire.

Her body grew impatient, wanting more. More she wasn't willing to reach out for, but more she was willing to take if freely given. She closed her eyes and sighed against his lips, then viciously sunk her teeth into his bottom lip.

He shuddered hard against her, and she felt his hands fist at her sides. Blood, warm and alive, touched her tongue, and like the first time she had tasted him, she felt an immediate high.

In a moment of clarity, Jax understood this was their connection. Blood.

What would happen to her if she took more of him? Would she become like him? Stronger? Deadlier?

Lost and alone?

She pulled away. He grabbed her face between his hands and hoarsely said against her lips, "Come with me. *Now.*"

It was what she'd been waiting to hear, but she recoiled at the thought. Where would he take her? And would she ever be able to find her way back? Suddenly, she knew that Godfather, her team members, maybe even God himself wouldn't be able to pull her from the dark place Marcus would take her.

"No," she breathed. Never.

"I won't hurt you."

"As if," she snorted, even as a part of her longed to believe him.

Fool, she mocked herself.

He laughed, the husky sound so sexy that it vibrated through her. He quirked a brow. "You don't trust me?"

Jax scoffed. "Are you kidding me? Do you really expect me to believe you'd leave your mark for a quickie?"

"I can fuck you here," he offered. Jax opened her mouth to tell him to take a hike. Before she could, his expression grew serious. "But it wasn't what I had in mind for our first time together."

Her heart slammed hard against her rib cage, making it momentarily difficult to breathe. Looking into his eyes, she pondered his words. He didn't strike her as the type of guy who thought out a first date. He was the kind that didn't date. He took what he wanted, then once the thrill of it was gone, he discarded it. "How long," she cautiously demanded, "has having sex with me been on your mind?"

"Since the second you touched me at that gangbanger club in Chicago."

He grabbed the hem of her dress and, in slow fistfuls, pulled it up. Sweltering air swirled around her sensitive flesh. Jax shoved his hands away. She looked straight into his eyes and said with as much conviction as she could, "Maybe *I* don't want you."

He grinned, but behind the smile was a dark edge. He dug his thick fingers into her hair, cupping the back of her head with his huge hand. He pulled her lips to him. His warm breath hovered between them. His crystalline eyes sparked in unfettered concupiscence. "You're very good at a lot of things, lovely, but lying isn't one of them."

Forcing his knee between her thighs, he pried her open. Jax stiffened. This had gone too far. Teasing Cross was one thing. Delivering was something altogether different.

She was no one's whore. Not even Godfather's.

Yet her body wanted to betray her.

She felt the sharpness of his teeth trace against her

tight lips. "Stop," she commanded. He nipped her bottom lip. She choked back a cry of pain. She would show no weakness, even as the warm, coppery taste of their mingled blood terrified her.

He broke his hold on her mouth. She hung limp in his arms, her resistance pushed to the max. His lips, warm and wet, traveled down her throat. His low moan as he dragged his teeth along the pulsing column of her throat made her want him inside her. Her body ached with exquisite pain. Her blood was hot—she could feel it, hear the loud whoosh of it course through her veins. His lips traveled lower to her breast.

"Dear God," she moaned, unable to stop him. Not wanting to.

His dark head lifted and their gazes clashed. A drop of blood—hers or his, she did not know—glittered on his bottom lip. She licked it. He hissed in a deep breath and shoved her harder against the column.

"Please," Jax gasped, "don't." She knew she wasn't making sense. That she was pushing him away with one hand while pulling him in with the other. She was doing her best to hold on to whatever vestige of control she had left. If he trespassed here, she knew she would not have the strength to stop him from going further.

His grip tightened. His eyes narrowed, and she knew he would take what he wanted from her.

"Let go of me," she demanded.

"You started this, now I'm going to finish it."

"There is no honor in your assault."

His fingers dug harshly into her skin, and he retreated, only enough to press his forehead to her forehead. "I have no honor left."

The harsh reality of his words would have sent a lesser woman screaming from him, but Jax wasn't a lesser woman. She allowed her tight muscles to loosen as a show of trust.

"You mistake my declaration as some form of a truce." He trailed his lips along her cheekbone, hovering just above her ear. "I have no intention of letting you go. You want this, too."

Slowly, she shook her head. "No, I don't. Not now."

"You lie!" he growled.

Jax broke his grip with a quick upward karate chop and moved away from him. With several feet separating them, Jax stared at him. "Stop means stop, Cross, and I said stop." She smiled when he scowled. "Besides, if I had my way with you out here, I'd lose interest in you. And right now, I'm enjoying the chase. That is, unless you're willing to let me in? Let me into your world and you can have me right here, right now."

Deliberately, she turned her back on him, then bent down and picked up her knife, sheathed it and walked back to the balustrade and gazed out over the grounds.

She waited for several silent heartbeats, wondering if he was actually going to leave.

When his big body pressed against hers, she breathed out a sigh of relief. When he planted his big hands on either side of her on the railing, trapping her, she imagined being pressed beneath his big sinewy body. The breeze whipped against her face, cooler now but unable to cool the heat of her body or his. "I just told you, I have no honor, but you would take my word if I gave it to you?"

She nodded. "There is honor among thieves. And we are both thieves of the highest order."

"You want into my world?" Cross asked. She nodded. He lowered his head and whispered against her ear. "Are you willing to sacrifice?"

She couldn't breathe. Couldn't think. She was perched on the edge of an uncertain precipice. If she jumped, it might kill her. If she backed away, it most certainly would. Jax had no other recourse but to close her eyes and take a leap of faith. "Yes."

"You will follow my orders to the letter."

Adrenaline surged into her system.

This was it. She'd done it. Or was this a trap?

She'd take the chance.

She nodded, not trusting her voice.

He pressed his thighs against her. She felt his erection against her back. "Say it."

"Yes, I'll follow your orders."

He ran his big hands slowly down her bare arms. They were warm and strong, but they left gooseflesh in their wake. He turned her around and pressed her into the column behind her and held her gaze.

"Then, my lovely, my mark is your mark tonight."

Jax stiffened. "Who?"

"Grace Rowland."

Shit! "I don't kill children."

"Then I guess all bets are off."

"Bullshit! You told me you don't kill children either! How can you demand from me what you yourself are not willing to do?"

He smiled cryptically. "There are many things I demand that I refuse to do myself."

Jax considered his order. She could pull it off, make it look like Grace was dead, but that could get messy for the senator. Cross would find out soon enough that the girl was alive. But maybe by then Jax could have taken care of him and Lazarus.

A sudden thought occurred to her. If he knew who Grace Rowland was to him, would he kill his own sister?

Jax took a deep breath and slowly exhaled. "Have you met the Rowlands?"

"Only the senator."

Jax nodded and extended her hand. "You've got yourself a deal, Mr. Cross. I take out Grace Rowland tonight, then you immediately set up a meeting with the colonel, and introduce me as the acquisition of the century."

Cross took her hand into his, and slowly wrapped his long fingers around hers. The frisson of the contact, just like every other time she had touched him, sizzled and snapped. He pulled her toward him, knocking her off balance. "I want proof of death. Tonight. Then you're coming with me."

Jax let go of his hand and pushed him off. "No can do. I have plans after work."

"Break them." He turned and stalked away from her, slipping between the thick foliage that had shielded them from the gathered guests.

‡

SIXTEEN

J ax resecured her earpiece. "Report," she said as she walked slowly back to the Green Room.

"Go ahead," Shane said.

"Cross and I made a deal. I take out his mark for the night and he makes an introduction to Lazarus." She didn't tell them what else Cross wanted. She'd find a way out.

"The mark?" Dante asked.

"Grace Rowland, and he wants proof of death."

"Jesus!" Shane hissed.

"I can't believe it!" Dante said. "Do you still believe he didn't 86 that girl in Blalock's apartment?"

Her answer was irrelevant. "For the record, I do."

"Let's meet in five," Shane said.

"Let's make it fifteen. Cross is back in the Green Room. As soon as the senator and his family make their appearance and he sees Sophia Rowland, if he knows who his mother is, he'll know it's her and put two and two together. I'm betting he isn't monster enough to eliminate his sister."

"That's a big gamble, Cassidy," Dante said. "I'm going to go ahead and formulate Plan B. We make it look like she's been hit, and go from there."

"Roger that," Jax said as she picked up her pace toward the Green Room.

◆ ◆ ◆

Marcus was coming apart at the seams.

He needed succor.

Now.

Her blood was like heroin. An immediate high. He was instantly addicted. He wanted more. He wanted to sink his fangs into her femoral artery and fuck her at the same time.

His body ached. His bones, his muscles, his heart, his groin pulsed with a need so violent that he teetered on the edge of sanity. He wanted to mate, to spend countless hours, days, weeks and months between her thighs as he drank his fill of her.

A thousand times would not be enough.

The ache in his body exploded into fury. Since his change, he had become a creature of instant gratification. If he wanted it, he took it.

Now, with this enigma of a woman, he could not. Because as much as he wanted inside of her body, he needed inside of her head more. He was no fool. He didn't buy for one minute she was doing background on Rowland and his family. His instincts screamed she was the product of a very specialized organization, and one that would not give up easily. One that could potentially harm The Solution's purpose.

Yeah, she was tied to Rowland all right. He needed to find out how tightly. It would be damn convenient if he could read her thoughts, but he could not, not unless he changed her. A thrill wracked through him at the thought. As her maker, he would own her. What they could do together boggled the mind. The thought quickly evaporated.

Her demand to become a Solution operative was laughable. The only way she could compete at his level was to be turned. Lazarus would destroy her. As coven leader, Lazarus decided who was made, who was destroyed and they all played by his rules. They had no choice. If any of them killed their maker, they would die for the effort.

Taking a deep breath, Marcus smiled grimly as he strode into the congested Green Room. He'd find out just how far she'd go to get an audience with Lazarus, an audience that no matter what she did she would never get. Because once she did Marcus's bidding, and once he extracted the information he wanted, he would have her his way, on his time, and for as long as he wanted. He wouldn't stop until his addiction had been sated and any drop of desire he felt for her had been obliterated.

His certainty calmed his savage mood.

Some.

His sharp gaze ran across the females in the room, processing each and every one of them for their desirability. There were several who had made their availability known. He could smell their want before they were even conscious of it. He might just grab one or two to take the edge off. That way he could concentrate with a more level head on the elusive brunette.

Why her, why now? What was so different about her? She had tits and ass just like any other woman.

He grunted in self-deprecation.

It wasn't her, he told himself. As personal as his desire for her seemed, it was just the growing effects of his change. He was nothing more than a dead man fucking. His isolation and the emptiness inside him drove him to the extremes. Before his change, his libido had been healthy. Since then, it had heightened. Now, it raged.

He slowed his angry stride into the room when he realized he was knocking people over and drawing undue attention. He caught several harsh glares among the men, but none of them was man enough to confront him. No mortal was. Except that conniving little minx he'd just left.

She was smart. He'd sent her hair samples to a private lab, paid a fortune to find out she was a Jane Doe. The prints he'd lifted off the hotel room next to her, same damn thing. They all turned up unknown. The people she worked for had gone to a lot of trouble to bury her. But even a corpse held secrets, and it was just a matter of time before those secrets were revealed.

His blood thrummed as he imagined what he was going to do to her when he got his hands on her. He would turn her inside out and upside down, and then he would fuck her until she screamed her throat raw with pleasure. He fought the animal urge to throw his head back and howl. He would mark her through and through, so thoroughly that no man would be able to touch her again. And then she would know what it felt like to live his flawed, empty existence.

Marcus swore vigorously. His thoughts had gone dangerously off course. Mentally, he shook himself and pushed her as far away from his mind as he could. His personal mission aside, he had work to do for The Solution. And that didn't involve sex.

Grace Rowland, he reminded himself. That was why he was here.

The thought of eliminating an innocent girl put the

kibosh on his raging libido. The thought of the brunette doing it turned his stomach.

"Our guest of honor," a high-pitched male voice said from the small podium on the north end of the room. "Senator William Rowland, his wife Sophia, and his daughter Grace."

Marcus moved to the edge of the room while keeping his eyes focused on the podium. Senator Rowland emerged, his politician's smile frozen on his face. At his side stood a platinum blonde who—every part of him went still.

He raised his nose. His nostrils flared. That scent. Buried deep in his past. But never forgotten. His eyes narrowed. He took several more steps toward the podium. The scent was stronger now, floral feminine. Marcus's world tilted, then righted as realization dawned. What was left of his heart thudded to his feet. Movement slowed. Air evaporated. Marcus could not take his eyes off the woman who had the same unusually colored eyes as his. It was the only thing good she ever gave him.

His mother.

He'd seen Sophia Rowland several times in the news, even pictures of her beside the senator. He hadn't seen the resemblance. Maybe because he wasn't looking for it. Until now. The last time he saw her he was twelve. She was a brunette then. Younger. Angry. She'd threatened to shoot him on the spot if he didn't leave. When he refused, she called the cops. That was the day he turned on the world.

Rage so consuming he could barely contain it infused every cell in his body. He hissed in a breath. Next to the smiling woman was her miniature. Grace. His mark.

Now the brunette's mark. He shook his head. His—
sister.

He had a sister? Something moved deep inside him.
Emotion he'd rejected even as a human clenched his gut
and twisted with such ferocity that he nearly screamed
out from the pain of it.

He pushed away from the column he'd ducked behind.
In the blink of an eye, he was out on the deserted loggia.
Grateful for the privacy, Marcus began to pace the worn
tile. How ironic was that? His next mark was his own
flesh and blood. He could snap his mother's neck without batting an eyelash. His sister? An innocent? She'd
had no hand in the shitty cards dealt her.

Out of nowhere, a feeling of betrayal flared within
him, focused exclusively on the woman who'd given him
human life. Why Grace and not him? some part of him
shouted. But even as he asked, he knew the answer.

Sophia was the daughter of American royalty. To her
he was a half-breed. As such, he was nothing to her but
a dirty little secret. But for how long? He could, with a
simple declaration, take everything she held dear away
from her.

Abruptly, Marcus threw his head back and laughed.
He relished a renewed sense of power. What would the
senator do if he knew his wife had screwed a drunk-ass
Indian and kicked the child she'd had with him to the
curb?

In a moment of clarity, he sobered. Lazarus! Did he
know? Such a rhetorical question. Lazarus knew everything. Why else would he have sent Marcus to kill the
girl? It was the ultimate test. He wanted to know whether
Marcus, for the greater good of The Solution, would kill

his own flesh and blood. If he would give up every last vestige of humanity that had once existed within him.

He turned on his heel and stalked back into the Green Room, where he took up his post beside a column no more than thirty feet from the cozy little family. There, among the paying guests, he watched his mother and sister stand beside the man who was the lifeblood of The Solution.

A part of him snapped. Setting his jaw, Marcus stalked closer to the podium, not hearing a word the senator said. Marcus's focus was solely on the bitch beside him. When he was no more than ten feet away from her, he stopped, and stared hard. He willed her to look at him. The beaming teenager beside her looked at him instead. Her face glowed with youth and exuberance, with the hope of all possibilities her idyllic future would provide.

Marcus narrowed his eyes. She had everything he'd never had. She was alive and he was dead. Privileged instead of just existing. Loved rather than scorned. But she wasn't stupid. She caught Marcus's venomous gaze and shrank into her mother's side for protection. Sophia barely paid attention, but she finally tilted her head in his direction. Her gaze slowly swept the room, not in obvious observation but casually, as if wanting to make eye contact with all of her husband's supporters. When her gaze drifted past him, he stiffened. So, she didn't recognize him? Why should she? The last time she'd seen him, his hair had been down to his waist, he'd been dirty and tired, and he could have used a few meals to fatten him up. The only thing they'd had in common had been their blue eyes. That and their utter hatred for each other.

Marcus caught the girl's gaze again. He nodded so

subtly that he wasn't sure if he really had. Then he moved back into the shadows of the columns and waited.

"He just figured it out," Jax said.

"Roger that, keep him in your sights, Cassidy," Dante said.

"He's not moving, just watching and listening to the speech from the fifth column down from the podium on the right," Shane said as he easily maneuvered around the throng of guests.

Jax had been too mesmerized by the cacophony of emotions playing out across Marcus Cross's face to hear a word of the senator's. His realization of who Sophia Rowland was had torn her apart. And with that realization had come the next one. Gracie. He had a sister. Each time a different emotion had flashed across his features, Jax had felt his anguish. His anger. His frustration. The depth of his emotion surprised her. He was a cold-blooded killer. Why the confusion? He didn't know Gracie. He was not the type to care. It didn't matter, she told herself. He'd carry out his mission if she didn't. It was what he did.

And if he could read her thoughts, he'd know she'd do everything in her power to stop him. Grace Rowland was not going to die tonight or anytime soon. Jax was, at her core, still a cop. But deeper than that, she was a woman with a deep-seated instinct to protect. In the end, it was what had driven her to ultimately kill Montes. Not revenge, not anger, not retribution. Just simply destroy him before he destroyed more innocent lives.

The senator's short speech ended. With his wife and daughter on either side of him, he made his rounds to each table, thanking each and every person for their support. Jax kept her eyes alert and debated on engaging Cross again, in effect giving him the opportunity to call her off. Ultimately, she decided against it. It would show indecision, and indecision equaled weakness. So she backed off.

The room had warmed to uncomfortable with the surge of movement among the bodies and the clash of copious scents. "I'm heading out to the loggia for some air, then we'll meet," Jax quietly said.

"Roger that," both Shane and Dante said.

As she stepped out into the cool air, her hair stood straight up on her neck.

"Eighty-six the hit—I have other plans for you," Cross said from behind her.

An immediate sense of relief hit her but was followed quickly with trepidation. What exactly were his "other plans"? She turned to ask him, but he was gone.

"Get in here, Cassidy," Shane said in her earpiece. "Something's going down."

"Copy." Jax sprinted into the Green Room to see the senator moving toward the anteroom fast, while his immovable circle of security and staffers surrounded him. Shane weaved his way around from the south end behind her.

"What's going on?" Jax questioned.

"Not sure," Dante said. "Stick with them, Cassidy. I'm staying close to Goldielocks. Not taking any chances this is a ruse to draw us out."

"Roger that," she softly said and hurried across the crowded space to catch up to the men. Just before the door was about to close, Jax called out, "Senator Row-land?"

Rowland jerked and turned to look at her. He was pale. Sweating. Abruptly, he motioned her inside the sanctum of the anteroom, then held up a manila envelope that was clearly marked **Family Values?** in big black bold letters.

She looked at the senator. "Where—"

"It was at one of the tables. On an empty seat. Right next to the governor's wife!"

Jax clenched her fists and thought of Cross. Damn bastard. "We didn't see—"

"Obviously you didn't see. With you and your team's sloppiness, I'm surprised he didn't step up to the podium and join me." Hands shaking, Rowland ripped open the envelope and removed a color eight-by-ten photo. As Jax watched, his face turned to ash. "Oh . . . God," he whispered.

Jax looked over his shoulder and saw what he held in his hands. Damn. Gracie Rowland was not so innocent after all. Even as she cringed, instinct drew her to the open window behind him. Sure enough, a rope was tied to the balustrade. Just hitting the ground two stories below was a man clad from head to toe in black. Her first thought was Cross, but she quickly nixed it. He wouldn't run; he'd stay and watch. Besides, this guy was half Cross's size. He took off without looking back.

"Stay here!" she ordered, then grabbed onto the rope and swung herself over the balustrade. Despite the hindrance of her dress and heels, she rappelled down the two stories and was on the ground in seconds. As she did so, she spoke into her mic. "Need backup at the ante-room. I'm in pursuit of a male who went out the back window. Secure the senator and the envelope he has."

Jax kicked off her Jimmy Choos and took off barefoot after the bad guy. She continued to call out her location, but as she ran down Van Ness, she lost sight of the guy. His scent lingered in the air, and amazingly, she was able to follow it. As she did, she was quite aware that with the exception of the knife strapped to her thigh and her deadly jewelry, she was unarmed and that with each step the neighborhood was getting less and less affluent. And darker.

Still, her vision was surprisingly keen. Scents swirled around her. Some good, most nasty. Garbage, sewage, unwashed bodies. The bad guy's scent began to fade. She wrinkled her nose and slowed her gait to a jog.

Her vision was sharp, her senses on overload. It felt like more than adrenaline. It felt like she was on some kind of supersensory drug. What the hell was going on?

"Cassidy?" Shane shouted in her ear, "where the hell are you?"

She looked up. She'd been so focused on the chase that she had not given out her location for some time. Bad cop. "I'm headed west. Alley off of Van Ness."

As she followed the fading scent of the bad guy down the quiet alley, the hair on the back of her neck stood up. She was not alone. She could feel eyes, everywhere, watching her. If she turned around, she'd be at their mercy; she could only go forward.

"Disengage, Cassidy. Return home," Dante commanded.

Jax slowed her pace and looked over her shoulder.

At least half a dozen gangbangers fanned out thirty feet behind her. "Ah, that's a negative. I have company at six o'clock and they look like they might want to party."

"I'm heading your way, Cassidy," Shane said. She could hear his heavy footsteps in her earpiece as he ran frantically to locate her.

She eyed her surroundings. It was dark. Dank. Dirty. A perfect place to kill. "The buildings are two- and three-story. They look like a mingling of commercial and apartment. It smells like rotted food, so I must be near a few restaurants."

"*Mamacita,* you gonna be in heaven in a minute," one of her admirers called out. He was closer. His cloying scent of cheap cologne, sweat and pot mixed in a noxious odor. Jax swallowed hard. Not because she was afraid but because he stunk to high heaven.

She cast a quick glance behind her. There were more of them now, and they were closing in. "I'm going to make a run for it, boys. I have too many unfriendlies gathering." She took off then. She was fast, but in bare feet, in a littered alley, her pace was stalled by broken glass and debris. Heavy footsteps thudded behind her. She broke at the end of the alley and came around to a street corner. She looked up at the sign to find it missing. Both ways. She darted across the street just as the blaring of a horn and headlights flooded her senses. Blinded by the light, Jax reacted instinctively and leapt over the swerving car.

No one was more surprised than her. What the hell? When had she become superwoman?

She didn't stop to ponder it. Her adrenaline was amped up so high that she felt she could do anything, even outrun the pack of hoods. She ran down the side-walk and turned left. She ate up the sidewalk and almost closed her eyes at the sheer power of her arms and legs carrying her away. But then she turned another corner and slammed into a hard wall of chests.

Hard, callused hands grabbed her. She flung them off, but a hard ring of bodies circled her. Panic set in fast and intense.

The last time she'd been surrounded like this, Montes had pushed his animals aside and, with them watching, he'd violated her in the most terrible of ways.

She felt faint for the slightest second. Her pulse raced out of control. Her chest heaved up and down so pain-fully that she thought her heart would explode. But somewhere in the deepest darkest reaches of her soul, a calmness overtook her.

Straightening from her crouching position, Jax snatched the knife from her thigh sheath and tossed it back and forth from hand to hand. They were straight up gangbangers. *Nortenos* by their red bandanas. *"Ven con mama,"* she taunted. In the air across her neck, she made a quick slicing motion with the knife. She had their attention. As she brought the blade across her jaw, she jabbed it at the guy to her immediate right. Jabbed it straight into his neck, yanked it out and kicked the thug closest to her with her right heel to the nuts. When he grabbed his groin, she stabbed the back of his neck. As she yanked out the blade, Jax whirled around in a crouched position and moved menacingly toward the five who remained standing.

It was enough to evoke bedlam.

"Who wants to go next?" she softly asked.

She didn't wait for an answer. Surprise and the unexpected were her biggest weapons. She grabbed the closest one with her left hand and yanked him right into her knife. He squealed like a pig. She shoved him backward and took two more out. The two left standing backed up. She tossed the knife back and forth and stepped toward them. "C'mon, boys, you aren't afraid of little ol' me, are you?"

"Cassidy?" Shane breathlessly asked. "What's your damn 20?"

Jax laughed. The two men who stood undecided in front of her looked confused. She tapped her right ear. "My partner's all worried about me. He wants to know my location. Should I tell him to just look for your carcasses?"

Inexplicably, Jax did not want to be found. She was high. High as Mount Everest. On top of the world. Undefeatable. She didn't want the adrenaline rush to end. She wanted to exact justice. She looked at the two thugs standing in front of her. Normally the gangsters carried.

"No heat?" she asked.

They looked at one another, then at her. "We were told no heat," the smaller of the two said, shaking his head.

"Shut the fuck up," his buddy warned.

So, this was no random meeting, was it? "Told? By whom?"

"No way, *puta*," the bigger one said, shaking his head and stepping back until he hit the wall of the building.

Jax moved in. "I really don't care for that word." In a lightning-quick move, she jabbed her left hand out and with the heel of her hand struck the bigger of the two in the throat. He dropped, gasping for breath, to the ground. That left the small one with the answers. She moved in on him, pushing him backward until his back hit the wall of a building. He did not try to fight her. He just stared wide-eyed at her. When his stare lifted past her right shoulder and he turned white, then crossed himself, mumbling, *"Dios mio,"* Jax crouched and turned.

Her own heart felt as if it had dropped twenty stories to the ground. She too crossed herself. "Holy mother of God," she mouthed. And wondered if this night could get any worse.

SEVENTEEN

Jax couldn't move. Terror grabbed ahold of her and shook hard. Marcus Cross stood behind her, his blue eyes blazing red and in full fang.

The gangster behind her hissed in a sharp breath, cursed a blue streak in Spanish, then shoved her toward Cross, who caught her in his arms, then protectively pushed her behind him. As the gangbanger moved past them he threw the knife he had threatened her with at Cross. It landed with a meaty thunk in his right biceps.

Jax flinched. Cross just growled. Not in pain but anger. He looked at the knife impaled to the hilt in his arm, then back at the gangbanger who stumbled all over himself to flee the scene. Cross grabbed the knife from his arm and hucked it at the gangster's back. He hit him right between the shoulder blades, stopping him in his tracks.

In another lightning-quick move, Cross snatched the flailing, screaming body up by his right arm and flung him against the brick wall he had just been standing against. He hit with a sickening thud, then slid down the wall, leaving a bloody trail of shattered bone fused with gray matter before he crumbled in a heap onto the dirty ground.

Speechless, Jax ignored Shane's desperate pleas for information, stood still, and watched what followed.

The original bad guys were pouring out of the alley toward them. Cross stood in front of her to the left. She inhaled a deep breath and slowly exhaled.

"Cross, I'm not armed," she said to his back.

"I have this. Get out of here."

"There's six of them and one of you!"

"I said I have this. Now get the hell out of here!"

Torn by whether to stay and fight beside Cross or take off and save her own skin, Jax stood rooted to the pavement.

Tat. Tat-tat-tat-tat.

"Down!" Cross yelled. Jax hit the ground. The gang memebers' bullets ricocheted off the wall behind her and the ground in front of her. Most of them, however, hit their mark. Cross's body jerked back and forth, as bullets tore into him.

Jax watched in fascinated horror as Cross continued forward. He'd been hit at least six times!

"Cassidy? What's going on?" Shane screamed in her ear.

"You wouldn't believe it," she said and watched Cross systematically reduce the gang from six to none.

He'd felt her fear, her distress. He'd heard the rampant beat of her heart as she'd run through the dark city streets. He'd watched her fight her way out of one group of gangsters even as she'd seen the other approaching. They'd carried guns. He'd known they would kill her. And for some reason, even though he'd known he'd probably end up having to kill her himself, Marcus hadn't been willing to let that happen.

He wasn't done with Jax Cassidy. He didn't like the

name. It was too abrupt, and it didn't do her justice. She was a complex melding of all things female and kick-ass bitch. So much more than three letters.

Despite the dozen bullets that hit him, many in his vital organs, Marcus felt only marginal pain. He grabbed the closest gangster. With the other hand, he yanked out the six-inch blade the prick had just stuck into his liver.

He stared down the last two standing. Marcus grabbed one by the throat and yanked so hard that his neck snapped. He dropped the corpse to the ground, then turned and heaved himself into the night air after the last one, who had taken off. He didn't get far.

Marcus landed effortlessly five steps in front of him. He grabbed the kicking, screaming *norteno* by the scruff of the neck and tossed him to the ground. He grabbed him up and tossed him to the ground again.

"*Madre de Dios!*" his victim screamed.

Marcus laughed. "Not even that great lady can save your sorry ass, *mijo.*"

"I got drugs, man, anything you want, I got it."

"Drugs kill," Marcus quipped.

"I got kids! My mother, she's dying, man. *Por favor!*"

With his forearm, Marcus pushed the unfortunate up against the wall of the building they stood next to.

"I might let you live."

"I'll do anything. *Anything.*"

"Who sent you?"

The man stilled. "Nobody, man, we were out looking for some action."

Marcus growled and dug his elbow into the man's throat. A fit of coughs wracked the guy. As he caught his breath, Marcus pressed into him again.

"Who sent you and why?"

"I—I didn't ask his name—" Marcus cursed and pressed harder. The guy squirmed.

"What did he want?"

"He said to watch the second-floor window at the Veterans Building for a man in black, but to follow the person who came after him. He didn't say it was gonna be a chick!"

"What were you supposed to do with this person once you followed them?"

"Rough them up some. Tell 'em to back off."

The distant wail of sirens infused the still night air. Marcus decided to save the taxpayers some serious cash and also give the overworked cops in San Francisco a little breather.

In one hard jab, he crushed the gangster's windpipe with his elbow. Marcus dropped the body he'd just broken in half and immediately turned his thoughts to Jax. Was she hurt? Had she been hit? His long stride picked up. His mind ran rampant with thoughts. He jumped into the night to find her.

As he flew down the alley, he slowed his frantic pace as he saw her running toward him. He dropped to the ground in front of her and slightly to the right.

"Jesus! Cross!" she screamed at him, then punched him in the chest.

"Are you hurt?" He resisted reaching out, touching every part of her to make sure for himself she was unharmed. She would kick his ass.

"No, damn it. What the hell was all of that?"

The distant wail of sirens infiltrated the tension

between them. "You'd better get out of here or you're going to have a lot of explaining to do to SFPD," he said.

Jax looked over her shoulder to the carnage behind her. "That's all your fault, Cross. Hell if I'm going to pay for it." She moved past him.

"You owe me," he called to her retreating back.

He laughed aloud when she flipped him off.

He stood and watched her until she had completely disappeared, then took off in the opposite direction. As he made his way across town, he wondered who Jax really worked for and who would want to put the brakes on Rowland's people.

The obvious answer was the man running a heated campaign against the senator. Mayor Mercer.

But why? And what was the point of chasing down Jax? There was only one way to find out. The next time Mercer tangled with Jax Cassidy she was going to give him straight answers.

EIGHTEEN

ı

Jax nearly collided at the end of the long alley with a frantic Shane. "Damn it, Cassidy!" he bellowed, grabbing her by the arms and practically shaking her. "I was worried sick. Why didn't you call out your location? And what the hell was Cross doing there?"

Jax shook her head and grabbed his arms. "Dante, do you copy?" she asked.

"I copy," he said. "What the hell happened?"

"Boys, you are not going to believe this," she said, shaking her head. Hell, if she hadn't seen it with her own eyes she wouldn't believe it either!

When she was done replaying the entire episode, they didn't believe her.

"A vampire?" Dante asked incredulously.

"He took how many rounds?" Shane demanded.

Jax shook her head. "I know, it sounds like a bad episode of *The Twilight Zone,* but I'm telling you, this guy is for real. If he hadn't arrived on-scene when he did, I'd hate to think of what would have happened to me. I owe the guy, and that really pisses me off."

"Godfather is never going to buy this," Shane said, shaking his head. They were almost back to the Vet Building.

"I'll talk to him," Jax said, wondering how the hell she

was going to convince Godfather when despite what she had witnessed tonight, she was still in denial.

"We'll discuss Cross later. Dante, what's going on, on your end?"

"I took immediate possession of the envelope and instructed the senator and his staffers to mingle and act as if all was well. But as the evening began to wind down, the senator began to wind up. Prepare yourself, Cassidy. He's pissed, scared and demanding answers."

She could handle Rowland.

As they came upon the Vet Building, Jax grabbed her pumps from the courtyard and slipped them on before they hurried to the anteroom. Half a dozen heads shot up, including the senator's. He looked as if he had seen a ghost.

"Sir," Jax said as she approached. "If you would excuse everyone but my team from the room, perhaps we can make some sense of what's going on."

He stood, his hands fisted, his lips drawn thin. "I trust every person in this room."

Jax smiled wanly. "I don't. Please, do as I asked. I can't help you if you refuse to follow my orders."

"Now look here!" he spouted, taking a step toward her.

Jax tossed her head back and stepped into the senator's space. "With all due respect, sir," she calmly began, "I just spent the last hour fighting for my life against the thugs who left you that lovely calling card. Please, empty the room now."

Anger and fear wreaked havoc with the senator's handsome features. Reluctantly, Rowland curtly nodded to his staffers as well as his security detail.

Where was Sophia Rowland? Jax wondered. Were there trust issues between the senator and his scheming other half?

Jax drew in a deep breath and slowly exhaled. "Dante, the envelope."

He pulled a plastic bag with the envelope in it from the back of his jacket. Carefully he handed it to her. Gingerly, Jax extracted the single photo from it. She cringed for the second time. Rowland made a sound reminiscent of an animal in pain.

The photo was of Grace Rowland, naked and snorting cocaine with a naked man three times her age.

"I'm sorry," Jax said softly.

Rowland's head snapped around and his eyes narrowed. "It's Photoshopped!" Rowland defended as he stood up and began to pace the room. "Gracie would never do drugs! Or have sex with a married man! She wouldn't do that to me!"

Jax understood his pain. Trust. Such an elusive animal.

"You said he's married. So you know the man?"

Rowland swiped his hand across his face and closed his eyes for several long minutes. "Alan LeVech, my daughter's high school counselor."

Jax nodded. Shane and Dante stood quietly by; when she looked at them, they evaded her gaze, almost making her smile. Apparently, this touchy-feely stuff was outside their scope of skills. Not that it was her forte, exactly, but they were happy to have her do the hard work.

"Either LeVech is in on this or—" Jax looked closer at the photo but could discern nothing in the background but a rumpled bed. "Do you recognize the setting?"

Rowland dragged his eyes from the floor to the photo. He swallowed hard and shook his head.

"Okay, so unless you want to confirm the authenticity of this picture with your daughter, Senator, I'm going to go on the assumption that someone, most likely Mercer or someone who really wants him to win the election, took this picture. It's obvious what they intend to do."

Rowland put a hand to his temple and shook his head. "Mercer is a smarmy piece of shit, but he's not this stupid. He knows that by circulating a picture of a minor this way, I could have the feds up his ass on a child porn charge so fast he wouldn't know which side was right or left."

Shane coughed. "Sir, hardly a child."

Rowland speared Shane with a daggered glare. "She just turned eighteen. Do you have children?"

"No, sir!" Shane vehemently denied.

"Then you don't understand a parent's desire to protect their child from every bad in the world."

Rowland turned dismissively away and looked at Jax. "Regardless of who is behind this, I don't believe this is authentic. I want my daughter brought in here to look at it. When she denies it, I'm—"

"Senator, I'm sorry to interrupt, but whether it's real or not isn't our primary concern right now."

Rowland's face turned red. "What could be more of a concern than—"

"You seem to be forgetting that there's someone else who might have delivered this photo."

"Who else?" Rowland asked. "Who else would want to drag my name through the mud and use my daughter to do it?"

"The same man who threatened to kill her," Jax offered.

Roland sat down and dropped his head in his hands. He moaned and rubbed his eyes, then looked up to the three of them. "This is something Lazarus is more than capable of, but I'm no use to him if I no longer hold my Senate seat. He would not jeopardize it at this stage. He knows there is no way I can recover from something like this if it goes public. Lazarus is a lot of things, but impatient is not one of them."

"He's up against a wall at the moment. He needs funds, funds that only you can provide. He's showing his entire hand, and if you still resist? If he can't have you, no one will," Jax said.

Rowland ran his fingers through his thinning blonde hair and stood. He looked as if he'd aged twenty years in the space of an hour. "Bring my daughter to me, but keep my wife out of this. This would kill her regardless of its authenticity."

It took some wrangling to get her away from the clutches of overzealous supporters, but after twenty minutes, Grace Rowland was finally brought into the anteroom. She knew immediately something was wrong. Her blue eyes darted from her father to Jax, then back to her father. "Daddy? What's wrong?" She flew into his outstretched arms. A hard lump formed in Jax's gut as she stepped toward the table with the plastic-enclosed envelope.

"Grace," Jax slowly began, "I'm going to show you something. But before I do, I need for you to understand the importance of your complete honesty with me."

"Oh, kaaay," Grace carefully said, looking to her father for support. He nodded imperceptibly. Shane and Dante had the forethought and common courtesy to move across the room so as not to look at the photo again. The senator looked away.

Jax slid the photo out of the envelope. Grace gasped. Rowland groaned and turned farther away from his daughter and the incriminating photo. "Is it legit?" Jax softly asked.

Grace's cheeks flared red, her head dropped and her blonde hair hung down, covering her face. Slowly she nodded.

"Damn it, Grace! Do you have any idea what you've done?" Rowland roared.

Silent tears stained her cheeks. Jax slid the photo back into the envelope. Rowland strode to the window.

"I love him!" Grace shouted at her father's back.

Jax groaned and rolled her eyes. Shane and Dante stood, stoic, on the other side of the room, but she read the same can-this-get-any-worse? look on their faces.

Rowland turned, barely containing his fury. As a father, he was outraged. As a U.S. senator, he saw his entire life's work slipping away because his teenage daughter had an infatuation with an older man.

"How long has this been going on?"

Grace stood straight as a sudden infusion of indignation filled her. "Long enough for us to make plans. He's leaving his wife."

"The hell he is! His ass is going to jail! Not only for sex with a minor but for the cocaine!"

"It's mine!"

Oh shit.

Rowland's face blanched. "Do I mean so little to you young lady that you would buy drugs and cavort with a married man?"

"Maybe, *Daddy*," Grace spat, "if you had been around more, I wouldn't have strayed! Here's a newsflash for you: Your perfect little girl is not so perfect after all!"

Jax inserted herself between the raging, heartbroken father and the defiant teenage daughter. "Sir, Grace. Please, this is not going to help clean this mess up."

"There *is* no mess to clean up! Alan and I are moving in together next month, just as soon as he leaves his wife. There won't be anything *anyone* can do," Grace defiantly stated as she moved past Jax for the door. She wheeled around and pointed an accusing finger at her father. "Not even a U.S. senator!"

Something inside Jax snapped. Maybe it was the devastated look on the senator's face as the daughter he cherished and loved above all others slapped him in the face for his dedication to life, liberty, and the pursuit of happiness. Maybe Jax was angry that this girl was throwing away something precious, something Jax had never had—a father who cared. Maybe it was none of the above, maybe she just didn't like the way the spoiled little brat spoke to her father.

"Sir," Jax softly said, "may I have a private word with your daughter?"

Rowland looked at her, still stunned.

"Sir?"

He nodded. Jax turned to the defiant teenager, gripped her by the elbow and steered her into the small room off the anteroom. She shut the door soundly behind her and took a deep breath.

"Grace, I understand what you're going through—"

"*No!* You don't!" Grace shouted, shaking her head. Jax was about to say she did, but Grace waved her off. "Do you have *any* idea how hard it is to be perfect 24/7? To have no friends? No boyfriends?"

Sadly, Jax could relate. "More than you know. But listen to me. You must end it with LeVech. Your father is a very important man, Grace. He *must* win this election. If he doesn't? There will be hell to pay on so many levels you can't even imagine."

Tears erupted on the girl's face. "I didn't mean to hurt my father. I just want a normal life."

Jax felt compassion for the girl. She moved closer and patted her shoulder. "I know, Grace. But you need to fix this. Let's get past the election and see what happens, OK?"

The girl nodded but said, "I'm not breaking it off with Alan, but I promise not to see him until after the election."

Jax let out a long breath. "Fair enough. Now let's get back in there and look for some answers."

As they came back into the room, Grace softly said, "I'm sorry, Daddy." But she made no move to him when he held out his hands. Slowly he lowered them.

"Grace," Jax asked, "were you aware you were being photographed?"

"No," she softly said, looking at the floor.

"So that leaves two conclusions. One, the love of your life planted a camera, took the pictures and is now black-mailing your father—"

"Alan would never do that!"

"Which brings me to conclusion number two: Someone knew about the two of you and planted the camera."

"It wasn't Alan," Grace defended.

"Who knew the two of you met—where is this place?"

"He has an apartment."

"Who aside from the two of you know about it?"

"I don't know, he said it was just for us."

"Well, someone else knew about it. We'll find out who it is." She glanced at the senator, then said to Grace, "Please do not contact your boyfriend until we've spoken with him."

Grace nodded.

"Grace, give me your word," Senator Rowland said.

Grace lifted her chin a notch and met her father's hurt gaze. "I promise."

Jax looked to Dante and said, "Have HQ give us the 411 on LeVech, maybe he'll listen to the true voice of reason."

Jax strode over to the table with the photo and slid it back into the envelope. She sealed the plastic bag and handed it to Shane, then looked up at the silent senator. "Dante will escort you home while my partner and I go to speak with Mr. LeVech. We'll be at your place by nine tomorrow morning for an update and a briefing on how we will proceed."

She strode out of the room knowing Shane would follow.

Jax flew down the marble stairways, her adrenaline pumping hard and fast, infusing her for the third time that night with energy she could barely contain. She held her breath all of the way down to the front entrance, where she expelled it in one long, harsh *woof.*

"What a clusterfuck this is turning out to be!" Shane, said, hurrying to keep up with her.

No kidding. "The implications to national security aside, Shane, the entire episode sickened me. I'll bet you my next round of hazard pay the only thing LeVech wants from Grace Rowland is a meal ticket."

NINETEEN

"I'm sure she texted him the moment we left the room," Shane said.

"That slimy bastard is going to wish he'd never met Grace Rowland when I get done with him."

"Cassidy—" Shane started. She ignored what she knew was coming.

Jax cut him off when she realized she didn't have her cell phone. "Would you call Naomi and get an address on LeVech?"

"Why don't you let me take care of LeVech?"

Vehemently she shook her head. "No way. I want a crack at him."

"I think it would be better for everyone if you chilled out."

Jax abruptly stopped and turned to face him. "I don't *need* to chill."

"Have you taken a look at yourself, Cassidy?" Shane asked. "You look like a hype who's seen better days. You can't go anywhere looking like you do. Not to mention you seem to have some personal agenda regarding LeVech."

"Personal agendas aside, Shane, I'm going." She turned on her heels and strode past him.

Shane grabbed her arm. The touch startled her. She

whirled around and shoved him away. The velocity of
her move sent him sprawling onto his ass.

"Jesus Christ, Cassidy!" Shane bellowed. He lay
spread-eagled a good ten feet away from her on the
asphalt. His stunned face looked up to her. What had she
just done?

She strode up and stood over him, so ramped up on
the continued surge of adrenaline that she could barely
keep her feet planted. "Don't touch me. Not when—not
when I'm unprepared for it. Not when you're angry."
Jesus. What was wrong with her? He wasn't Montes, he
was Shane, her partner.

She reached down to offer him a hand up, but he
shook his head and managed without her assistance. As
he brushed himself off, he gave her a sideways glance. "I
thought you were over that."

"I am!"

"Then what's gotten into you tonight, Cassidy?" he
softly demanded.

Jax shook her head. She knew, but she didn't want to
go there. Didn't want to think about it. For once, the least
threatening option to occupy her thoughts was Cross.

Cross. He was the reason she was so off balance.
She felt out of sorts, not herself, but better than herself. Supercharged. She ran her finger through her hair,
securing the errant locks behind her ear. And there was
the vampire thing.

"Cross has me rattled," she said, hoping to steer him
away from her behavior. It worked.

Shane smoothed down his suit jacket and said, "The
whole vampire thing is unbelievable."

"No shit." Jax struggled with the unbelievable factor herself and what she had witnessed with her own two eyes. This entire mission was taking on an entirely different dimension from what they had anticipated. Cross a vampire. She still could not believe it—what Cross did tonight. He had saved her life.

"You've been through a lot tonight. Go back to your hotel room, Cassidy," Shane said, looking over at her. "I'll pay LeVech a visit and find out who's been taking pictures of him and Grace Rowland."

Jax stopped abruptly and shook her head. "I want to kick his ass."

Shane laughed, easing some of the tension. "You can't just go kick everyone's ass, Cassidy. There's finesse that goes into this. Like the way you finessed Cross tonight. You must have gotten to him for him to come to your rescue like he did. And showing you his skills? That's huge. Better for us to prepare. Now stay the course."

"But LeVech's a smarmy bastard who deserves an ass kicking," Jax pushed, ignoring his compliment and acknowledging the job she'd done tonight. She *had* scored big-time.

"Yeah, he is," Shane countered, "and it's not the end of the world. That kind of thing happens. You can't save every little girl from every predator out there. You'll die trying. Go back to your room, take a hot shower and get some sleep. I'll brief you in the morning."

He turned and strode down Van Ness toward the rental car, leaving her standing alone on the curb. Why *couldn't* she save the world?

"Screw you!" Jax yelled at his retreating back, then hailed a cab.

She was so amped up that she could have sprinted across town to the hotel. The cab ride only took fifteen minutes, but it seemed like hours.

She tossed the cabby a wad of cash and bounded out of the smelly car, then hoofed it up to her room at the Hotel Sokko, just on the fringes of the infamous Tenderloin. She used her security card to enter the building and took the stairway all the way up to the twenty-third floor, where there was extra security. Finally, she entered the quiet sanctum.

Instead of flopping onto the thick comforter on her bed, Jax shucked the remnants of her dress and removed what was left of her weapon jewelry. She stood naked in front of the mirrored closet doors. For a long moment, she stared at the stranger peering back at her.

She'd aged. Stress lines accentuated the full curve of her lips. Cynical green eyes glittered in anxious tension. Her thick mahogany-black hair hung in unruly hanks around her pale skin. She looked like a zombie, with dark mascara smudges surrounding her deep-set eyes. Her red lipstick had been smeared off hours ago, revealing dry pink lips. She licked them. As she did, she shook her head, tossing her hair behind her shoulders. A small bruise on her bottom lip, barely noticeable, pulled her closer to the mirror. Lightly, she brushed her fingertips across the slightly swollen spot. A warm wave of pleasure flowed across her skin, causing her to jerk her fingers back.

"Cross," she whispered. The hair on the back of her neck rose, her nipples tightened and her womb clenched. The air grew warm around her. If she'd been in her right mind, she would have sworn she could smell him. She closed her eyes and pretended he was there. She gasped as a warm breath crossed her right shoulder blade. Her eyes flew open and she stared at the mirror, sure she would see him smug and arrogant behind her. But there was nothing.

Jax stared at her body. While she was toned and in the best physical shape of her life, the scar that marred her belly and trailed down to her pelvic bone was ragged and ugly, a constant reminder of what had happened to her and what she had done about it. Jax had always prided herself on her physical attributes. She was no fool. She knew men liked her open personality and sexy curves, and she had no problem using her assets to gain the upper hand, but now? Since her rape, she'd viewed her body as a last-resort weapon. A way to inflict pain, to gain and hold control. She wanted to believe she was capable of sleeping with Cross—or any man, for that matter—then walking away, feeling as if she had just done her job. But it was a hard pill to swallow. She wasn't a whore who used her body for gain. She was a lethal operative. Her body was her own to use as she saw fit, not a means to an end.

The adrenaline that had begun to subside kicked up again. What did Cross have in store for her? Just thinking about what was ahead excited her. However, what was behind her confounded her. The last ten hours had been off the hook, crazy exciting. So much had happened that she couldn't explain. Yet, if she allowed her imagination to take off, there were more possible explanations than she could count, and every one of them scared her.

Was Cross really a vampire? He'd been rather candid in light of their relationship. Had he admitted it because he knew no one would believe her if she told them? Or because he was going to eliminate her? Maybe both.

Jax was a practical woman who believed in ghosts, but that was about as far as her beliefs in the otherworld went. How was she supposed to swallow Dracula stuff? But she knew Cross was different. Something *not* mortal. He proved that tonight. No mortal could do what he had done. Then there was the other part. He invaded her dreams as if he was in reality, beside her; she felt him. Her senses were so heightened that she could smell, see and feel like a cat! And the blood thing. *His* blood. It was in her, it gave her those heightened senses. It was like a drug to her. Either he infused himself with high-octane vitamins or he was . . . what he said he was. A vampire.

Holy hell! Her adrenaline spiked. Shaky-kneed Jax made it into the big bathroom and turned the shower on hot. But no matter how long she stood under the pulsing water, her skin shivered. Her gut told her she was in way over her head. That Marcus Cross was stronger and smarter than all of L.O.S.T. combined and that she was on a suicide mission.

Jerking the knobs, she turned off the water and stood unmoving in the large tub. She rubbed her hands through her hair, squeezing the water from it. Stepping from the shower, she grabbed a thick velour towel and wrapped it around her body.

Loud pounding on the door drew Jax out of the steamy bathroom. Her body tingled.

Cross.

On impulse, Jax strode to the door, unlocked the double locks from the inside and yanked the heavy metal door open. Be still her heart.

He was so damn handsome. A far cry from the bloodied bullet-ridden Cross she had last seen. He had cleaned up. He cleaned up well. Really well. His hair was still damp from his shower. His face clean-shaven. His clean, dusky scent swirled around her. He stood with one hand braced against the outer doorjamb, his jacket thrown over his shoulders; his fitted black shirt hugged his broad chest and tapered down his narrow waist into black trousers.

Jax smiled smugly and assumed the same pose but from the inside of her room. "Did you come here to gloat?"

"I came to ascertain your well-being."

"Right." She backed away and grabbed the door handle. "I don't need you to fight my battles for me."

Cross put his right hand out against the door, stopping her from slamming it in his face. "Tonight, you did."

"Screw you, Cross! I didn't ask for a babysitter. I could have handled those guys by myself." She shoved the door harder. It didn't budge.

"Don't you want to know why they were after you?" he slyly asked.

Jax jerked her head back and narrowed her eyes. "What do you know?"

"Invite me in, and I'll tell you."

Jax contemplated his request. "How did you get up here? This is a secured floor."

He slid his hand into his trouser pocket and withdrew a security card. For some reason, Jax was relieved. If he hadn't had a card, he would have had to have turned into a bat to get in. She shook herself and realized she was damp and naked save for the towel clinging to her. She was also losing her mind. He grinned and she nearly melted onto the floor. His face, his scar, his eyes radiated when he genuinely smiled. She could get used to that smile. Too bad she had to kill him.

Knowing she was probably making the mistake of her life, Jaz stood back and said, "Come in."

Cross grinned, showing his bright white teeth. "Thank you," he said softly, stepping past her.

Jax closed the door behind him and locked it. Putting her hands behind her back, she leaned against the door and eyed him when he turned that dangerous smile on her. "So tell me."

He laid his jacket over the chair back by the desk. As if he were staying. "Tell you what?"

"Cross, stop being an evasive ass. Why were those guys after me?"

He shrugged. "They weren't after you per se. They were after the person who came after the guy you were chasing."

"That makes no sense."

He leaned up against the bathroom doorjamb and crossed his arms over his chest. "It could if you told me why you were chasing him."

Jax fought a smile. He was sly with his angle. "One of the guests was attacked. I was bored. So, I followed the bread crumbs." Jax pushed off the door and walked toward him. "How did you know I was here?"

Cross casually shrugged. "Like the organization you work for, the one I work for has eyes and ears everywhere."

Jax yanked the big fluffy bathrobe from the counter where she had left it. She slipped it on, then dropped the damp towel that still clung to her. She watched Cross's eyes dip for a look before she secured the velour sash around her waist.

Jax ignored his "organization" reference. She turned and asked over her shoulder, "Why did you call me off tonight?"

He moved behind her, his big body warm and inviting. His large hand brushed her hair from her shoulders. He bent down to where her arm met her shoulder. Gently he brushed his lips across her skin. Jax remained rigid. She was not going to get all gooey like she had earlier. This time she would control every move. "I changed my mind," he replied.

Jax turned slowly and looked up into his hooded eyes. "Did you come here to give me my alternative mission?"

"Maybe." He grinned that grin again. "Maybe not."

Jax eyed him for a long, long time. He was quite a specimen. Big. Broad. Muscular. His hands were the size of dinner plates. His fingers thick and long, his nails square and neatly trimmed. His face. His face was classic Greco-Roman in style and grace. Firm yet boldly sculpted. The scar that ran from his right eye down his face and into his shoulder only added to the dangerous air that swirled around him like his unique scent.

But it was his crystalline eyes, so blue, so clear, so hypnotic that gave her pause every time she looked into them. While he was a reticent, quiet man, a killer, assassin and lost soul in so many ways, his eyes spoke volumes. Pain, deep and angry, lingered in them, just below the surface.

"Who really killed that little girl in D.C.?" She wanted to know. *Had* to know.

He reached out a hand to her cheek. She stood rigidly. She watched those oh-so-expressive eyes harden. His jaw set. His dark brows pulled together over his aquiline nose. "Blalock strangled her."

"Would you have eliminated her if she'd witnessed what you did to Blalock?"

Cross remained silent for a long time, his eyes never once blinking or wavering from hers. "There was another girl in that room that night. She's home now, with her parents, where she should be."

His confession stunned her. "Why did you tell me that?"

"So that you would see your intel is off. Don't believe everything you're told in preop briefings."

Jax contemplated his statement. She did not deny the fact that intelligence could and did get certain facts wrong or overlooked other ones. But he hadn't come to her room to tell her that. "Why are you really here?" she asked.

He grinned a half grin. "Because we both want the same thing."

"Which is?"

"To blow off some steam. It's been quite a night."

"Yes, it has. But if I had wanted more action, I would have stayed out. I'm in for the night. I want to be alone."

"No—you don't."

"What, you're a mind reader now?"

"No, Jax Cassidy, I just know you. We're too much alike."

He knew her name now. "How so?"

"At our core we're both primal." He moved in closer.

"We both come alive when the chase begins." He traced his fingertips along the curve of her collarbone. "We are masters of our craft." His fingers dipped between her deep cleavage. "We are both sensualists." He slid his other arm around her waist and pulled her against him. "And we both want to connect on the most basic of levels." He brushed his nose across the top of her head and inhaled her. "I didn't lie when I told you I wanted to fuck you all night long."

Jax held her breath for a long moment and composed her swelling desire. He did things to her with only a fingertip that her ex hadn't been able to do with his entire body.

"I want to take you to the moon, then to the stars and to the sun. I want to fuck you so hard and so deep a part of me will stay inside you forever."

"You're such a romantic," Jax said, the sarcasm not lost on him.

He smiled. "I've never told a woman that before."

"I feel so special." She shook her head, feeling delirious with desire. "But understand, I don't want to keep any part of you."

"Yes, you do." He slid his hand down her belly, unknotting the sash. When it fell away, her robe opened and cool air rushed against her skin. She shivered. He sank to his knees and pulled her against his lips. His hands trailed up her bare legs to her ass. Jax bit back a moan. His skin was warm and smooth against hers. It felt good. Solid. Strong. But it was wrong. She wanted control. She wanted to lead, to decide if and when this would happen. Not him.

Jax raised her foot and planted it against his chest. His fingers clamped around her instep, his thumb caressed her skin. His other hand brushed the inside of her thigh. Jax clenched her jaw. "I want to know why you pulled the plug on tonight and what I have to do to get an audience with Lazarus."

"Give us both what we want and I'll tell you."

"You want sex, I want answers."

He pressed his lips to her instep and softly kissed her. Jax nearly swooned. When he dragged his tongue across the skin there, the leg she was standing on wavered. He looked up at her and said, "You say that like it's a bad thing."

"It is if you're me."

He nodded, let go of her foot and slowly stood. Cool air wafted between them doing nothing to cool her sultry body down. Jax wanted to scream at him to take her, just throw her on the bed and impale her. But she didn't.

They stood facing each other for long-drawn-out minutes. His hooded blue eyes waiting for her to just say the word. Her body screaming for her to just do it, ease the torturous ache that consumed her. Jax moved to the other side of the room, putting the king-sized bed between them.

"Are you going to bite me?" She had to know. The thought terrified her and, on a very basic level, thrilled her.

He cracked a smile. His eyes actually twinkled under the lamplight. "Only if you want me to."

Jax swallowed hard as their gazes locked. She was

going to burn in hell for what she was about to do. "My terms," she whispered.

Cross's eyes glittered like sapphires on a sunny beach. He nodded so slightly that she wasn't sure she had witnessed it.

"Strip," she hoarsely said, hoping that her plan would get her answers and keep her integrity intact.

TWENTY

(

Amazing. That was the word Marcus would use to describe Jax Cassidy at that moment. He'd told her what he was, *killed* in front of her. He'd fully expected her to run for the hills. Instead, she stood there and challenged him. Brave, brave girl. So why should her command to strip surprise him? Of course she would take charge. Of course she would try to handle him. Use him. Make him believe that the job was the only reason she would give him her body.

He didn't buy it.

He knew she was sexually excited. He could smell it on her. He could see it in the sharp flare of her nostrils, feel the heat of her want through her open pores. There was no way she could deny it. In truth, he couldn't imagine her doing so. She was all ballsy honesty, more likely to slap his face than lie to it. Yet, beneath it all, he detected fear. And he knew it was founded. Her blood did not lie. She had been brutalized by a man. He'd sensed it the first time he'd tasted her.

It was a wonder she could feel desire for him at all. But she did.

That fact not only increased his own desire, making blood pulse in his cock with the same thundering beat his heart played out against his chest, but it also told him their intense attraction was unprecedented. For them both. That in and of itself intrigued him. As a human, he had never felt such violent desire for a woman. To feel it now, when he was soulless, was virtually unbearable. She was a shot of adrenaline in his mundane life.

After he'd had her, would his want for her lesson, or would it burn as savagely in his veins as it did now? He hoped it flared brighter. At least for a while.

Unhurried, he silently watched her. Her eyes boldly held his. Sparks of excitement gave them a preternatural glint.

He knew she had motives other than sex on her mind, but so did he.

He had questions and only she had the answers. Oh, he could snag one of her cronies, but it would not be nearly as interesting wrestling the information from one of them as it would be her. Besides, men bled more than women, and he wasn't in the mood to get his hands dirty. Not that way. He understood her need for control, but he would not give it to her. Never. That was his to command.

He unbuttoned his fitted black shirt one button at a time. The slight tremble in his fingers surprised him. Then it angered him. While she was most definitely a cut above every other woman he had had, she was still just a woman. And a conniving one at that. In a few minutes, he would find out if his fire would be extinguished or burn hotter.

Taking a step forward, he pulled the tails of his shirt out from his trousers. To his surprise, Jax put her hand up. "Stop."

He hesitated for a heartbeat before he stopped. Her fear had spiked. He wasn't the man who'd brutalized her. Letting go of the fabric, he dropped his hands to his sides. "Come here," he softly commanded.

She shook her head but stepped toward him anyway. When she stopped an arm's length away, he nudged her chin up with his hand. He saw the reflection of his fiery gaze in her eyes. "I won't hurt you like the other one."

Her body stiffened. The color drained from her cheeks. Slapping his hand away, she stalked to the other side of the room. When she spun around to face him, her eyes blazed like emerald coals. "I don't know what you think you know, but give me enough respect by not pretending with me."

He cocked a brow. "Pretend? How so?"

"You tell me you want to fuck me from the inside out. How am I supposed to take that?"

"Exactly as it's intended." She shook her head and looked at him, incredulous. He explained, "You and me, we're driven by pure animal instinct. And while there may be some hurt involved, it's the good kind. The kind that makes you want more. That's how it will be between us, Jax." He stalked closer to her until only inches separated them. "Hard, furious, primal." He traced a finger along her bottom lip. "That's how you take it."

Her body trembled, and he felt her desire shift. While she was intrigued, her fear evolved into something more complex. She no longer feared just physical pain but emotional torment as well. He smiled to himself.

She had every right to fear his emotional attack. He didn't like to be played, and, though he was Jonesing hard for her, he would extract the information he needed one way or another. Either by seduction or . . . by torment.

He frowned for a moment at the thought of hurting her. Of extinguishing a light that burned so bright. But then he reminded himself of who he was. *What* he was.

He preferred seduction to pain and would not hesitate to use more extreme measures. But only if he had to.

"Why should I give you what you want?" she softly demanded.

"Because," he answered as softly, "it's what you want, too."

"Then the chase will end."

Ah, she sounded disappointed. He crooked a smile.

Marcus slid his arm around her waist and, with his free hand, slid the thick velour robe from her body. She caught her breath. Behind his trousers, his cock flared. He pressed her to his bare chest and fought the sublime feeling of her tits digging into him. "And then," he softly said as he lowered his lips to hers, "it will begin again. But with higher stakes." And although he had no choice but to destroy her when her usefulness ended, all the same, he'd make them both burn with pleasure first.

His body caught fire when she kissed him back. Her lips were so soft, like a newborn's skin. Her ardor was open, honest, and innocent in its humanness. Her tongue swirled across his lips, along the tips of his fangs, touching him more deeply than if he'd been inside of her. He swelled against her, tightening his hold. She did not pull away. No, to his surprise and pleasure, she melded more intimately into him.

His darkness threatened to overcome him. He wanted to sink his fangs into her, drink his fill of her as he fucked her. He squeezed his eyes shut as he envisioned doing just that.

Her heart beat frantically against his chest. The whoosh of her warm blood as it coursed recklessly through her veins called to him to take it. He fisted his hand into her hair and pulled her head back, exposing her long, creamy neck. He opened his eyes, and through the fire of his passion, he saw true fear in hers. Her wide eyes stared helplessly at him. Her breath pulsed in short, harsh puffs against his cheeks. Her muscles tightened. Yet her eyes, though terrified, did not say no. He released her anyway and carefully stepped to the other side of the room. Why he gave her quarter, he did not know.

Raking his fingers through his hair, he turned to face her. "Tell me who sent you and why," he hoarsely demanded, knowing damn well he should have begun this little tryst with an interrogation first.

"I told you, I'm an independent."

Despite his frustration, he almost smiled. Even when frightened, she gave as good as she got. The image of her taking out those gangbangers earlier burned bright in his memory. It had been all he'd been able to do not to come to her rescue—until the very end, when she'd needed it. Her moxy had been admirable then, it was admirable now.

But he wanted the truth.

He lowered his head, as if he was preparing to attack. Of course, she read his intent and did the same. "You have no idea who you're tangling with, Jax Cassidy."

She moved around in the small space. "I guess you didn't get the memo about who you were tangling with."

"I spent years learning the fine art of torture. Do you want me to extract the information I want that way?"

"I've spent years learning how not to give in to the most heinous of torturers."

He read a bluff when he saw one.

He grabbed her right arm and yanked her hard toward him, but not before she got in a solid kick to his groin. He grunted, but the pain was gone as soon as it registered. "You shouldn't have done that." He yanked her around and, with her back to his chest, he bear-hugged her. As she struggled against him in a vain attempt to free herself, her ass rubbed against his cock. The rage of his desire was unbearable. Damn her!

"Tell me, damn it!" he hissed against her ear. "Or I'll force it from you."

She shook her head.

"I'll make you wish you were never born."

"Do your worst then."

Marcus counted slowly to ten. As he did, his passion waged war with his control. If she didn't relent, he'd be forced to show her the true animal he was. Roughly, he picked her up and tossed her onto the bed. She landed spread-eagled on the comforter. Stunned, she stared at him.

He crawled over her and threatened her. "I'm not going to give you a second chance!"

"I don't want one!" she screamed.

He laughed harshly and shook his head. "Then, my lovely, I won't give you one."

He dug his fingers into her thick hair and brought her lips up to his. "Kiss me," he commanded. Her short, warm breaths pulsated against his lips. He could smell her fury mingled with her desire. He was on the verge of losing what little control he still possessed.

She stunned him when she grasped his head to her, and in a mad rush, lips against lips, teeth against teeth, and tongue against tongue, she kissed him.

Jax's body exploded with sensation. The overload was terrifyingly exhilarating. She felt as if she'd been free-falling. No fear. No anger at herself for giving in to what they both wanted. Her endorphins had shoved it all aside, and her instinct to mate took over. And that was what it boiled down to at its most basic. Forget her mission. She wanted Marcus Cross, a dominant male, to take her, Jax Cassidy, a dominant female, and do what came natural to every propagating mammal on the earth. Mate.

In a flash of movement, Marcus rid himself of his clothing, then his hands grabbed her ass and his knee parted her thighs. His swollen cock jutted against her hip. She wanted him to slow down, to savor this—this mad rush of need—to give her time. To adjust, to prepare. It had been so long. The image of Carlos Montes's sweaty, fat body undulating on top of her as he'd tried unsuccessfully to stick his little dick in her swirled in front of her.

God, she thought she had locked that part of her life firmly away.

Jax cried out as a wave of fear returned. Cross stilled above her. She opened her eyes to find his blazing blue ones quietly questioning her. Embarrassment engulfed her. She could do this. It was just sex!

He raised his hand to her. It took every bit of control Jax possessed not to flinch. Gently, he dug his fingers into her hair, cupped the back of her head with his big palm, raised up, and pressed her softly into the comforter. For a long minute, he peered at her. Giving her time to work through what she had to. His sudden patience, completely out of character for the hard-ass he was, softened her. Her body loosened.

When he moved and settled against her, Jax held her breath. But instead of taking her, he kissed her. He took her face into both of his hands, lowered his lips to hers, and, in a light, almost reverent, way, he kissed her. The gesture nearly did her in. Anger, embarrassment and a dawning sense of gratitude for his consideration overwhelmed her. She felt the hot sting of tears in her eyes. Desperately she tried to stay them, but they leaked out.

"Don't cry," he softy said against her lips. His kiss deepened. She could taste her tears on his tongue. His body swelled, yet he did not push, though she wanted him to.

When he dropped his lips to a turgid nipple and sucked, Jax closed her eyes and arched.

Damn.

He took his time, savoring her until she felt wet between the legs and a deep buzzing of desire inside of her. He released her nipple and licked it, then licked her neck and chin, then hovered above her lips. Jax panted like she had just run a marathon. When he slid his hand down her belly, she hissed in a sharp breath. Slowly, his fingers brushed across her soft, downy mound and found her clitoris.

"Jesus," she gasped. His fingertips slid languorously across her moist curls.

"Now, tell me, Jax, who do you work for?"

"I'm"—she gasped as his fingers dipped just slightly into her wet opening—"self-employed."

His hand cupped her mound. She nearly came. He increased the pressure. "Stop—" she gasped.

"Not until you tell me what I want to know."

"Nothing until you finish what you started."

He smiled against her skin and trailed his lips down her belly to the inside of her right thigh. His hot breath singed her. His teeth scraped along her skin. Her entire body quivered. She could feel the moisture between her legs pool.

"Tell me," he softly urged as his teeth scraped harder into her skin.

Jax moaned and arched. "I told you, I work alone. I'm gathering intel on Senator Rowland for an ultraconservative group of investors who want to keep a very low profile. The two guys with me work for them too."

He licked the crease of her thigh where it met her pubis. "What kind of information?"

She swallowed hard and bit her bottom lip. "Anything that can cost him the election."

He nipped her thigh. "You're lying."

"No—no lies," she swore and almost believed herself.

His body stiffened; he knew she was not being honest. Would he carry out his threats? He slid back up her body and lowered his lips to hers, deeply kissing her. The rush of sensation was dizzying. He pulled slightly away and said, "If we're going to work together, there must be trust, Jax."

His implication that they might work together, as well as his asking for her trust, startled her. "I trust you not to hurt me," she said. And at that moment she meant it.

His eyes softened. "Ah, Jax, you make me forget what I am."

She wrapped her arms around his neck and said, "You make me forget everything."

He parted her thighs with his knees and gently pushed against her. Slowly she opened up to him. Keenly he watched her. This was it, the point of no return. She ran her fingers down his back and arched her back. He entered her then. Slowly. Fully. Deliciously. Shock waves of pleasure crashed through her entire body.

Jax's eyes widened. Oh, God. Marcus smiled and lowered his lips to hers. "You're perfect."

Emotion she didn't know she possessed welled up inside her chest. He moved slowly, reverently, as if she would break if he pushed too hard. His gentleness cut the last vestige of hesitation from her soul, and she gave herself completely up to him.

TWENTY-ONE

"I won't break, Marcus," she whispered in his ear. His body stilled. Then, as if a switch had been tripped, his long arms wrapped tightly around her, bringing her as close to him as he could. She wrapped her arms around his neck and arched as he drove deeply into her. They hung suspended as one entity, each wide-eyed at the depth of sensation they extracted from the other. Jax closed her eyes and let him take her away to any place he wanted to go. In the mad rush of their union, they rolled onto the floor, Marcus buffering her fall with his big body.

Out of nowhere, a fierce orgasm caught hold of Jax. Then, in a wild race against her next breath, it crashed with such velocity inside her that she screamed and dug her nails into Marcus's shoulders. The waves were so intense, so deep and so long, that she thought she would die. He moved deep inside of her as she came, never once letting up with his wild pace.

When the last wave receded and her body lost most of its strength, he swelled thicker inside of her. Jax felt his quickening. He pressed his palm to her chin and pushed back her head, exposing her neck as she arched her back and took him deeper still inside of her. His touch sparked another harsh wave of desire. It caught immediately. Jax's eyes widened. Dear Lord, she didn't know if she could physically survive another orgasm.

"You can do it, Jax," he harshly said as he lowered his lips to her jugular. "Keep up with me," he whispered against her slick skin. He licked the thick artery and, as their bodies prepared for devastation, he urgently asked, "Allow me to drink from you."

"Yes," she breathed. *"Yes."*

His fangs sunk into her neck. Jax cried out and closed her eyes in sweet sublimity. Her body exploded from within. She clung to his body as he drank from her. She wanted him to take more.

As her body undulated, she pressed herself closer to him, reveling in the intimateness of his coming inside of her as she came with him, of him taking her blood into his body. If only she could take the same from him. As the thought swirled in her head, she felt his body swell. He jerked away from her neck and pressed her back into the twisted sheets, his body still inside of hers. His lips glistened with her blood. Jax arched, reached her lips to his and kissed him deeply, tasting herself on his lips.

The darkness nearly overcame him. Barely, Marcus controlled it, as well as the ridiculous urge to press her against his chest and give her his lifeblood. If that happened, they would forever be connected. It was so damn tempting.

She was everything he'd known she'd be. And more. And knowing it, he knew she could not live. She would be his end if he allowed it.

The agony of that realization hit him hard. He threw his head back and cried out as the final wave of his orgasm hit him. His body pounded into hers. His body needed the violent release. When it ended, he collapsed beside her on the floor.

Breathing heavily among the damp, wrinkled linens, it took only seconds for him to realize he wanted more—needed more. More sex. More blood. All of her. But if he took more, he would lose it all. He needed to leave. Now, and not look over his shoulder. She would get them both killed.

As winded as he was, it only took him a few minutes to recover. It took his partner much, much longer. As he pulled away from her, she lay with her eyes closed, gasping for breath. He closed his eyes and tried to probe her thoughts. He felt her fear, her excitement, and he was glad to know any thoughts of that pig who had violated her were far away. He wished he could erase them for her, but he didn't possess that power. At best, he could read her emotions and soothe her with his thoughts. He wondered if having taken his blood, though only a slight bit, she could read his emotions, as well. The idea bothered him.

He turned to his side and studied her, slick and breathless beside him. Her full breasts rose and fell with each harsh breath she took. Her pink nipples were hard, her breasts full, round. And soft. He resisted the urge to rub his cheek against them. His gaze traveled down her belly to the jagged scar there. He scowled.

Lightly he traced a finger along the raised skin.

"Don't," she commanded and grabbed his hand, halting his touch. She turned to face him, her eyes blazing angrily.

He didn't push it, but he didn't withdraw his touch, either. "What happened?"

She sat up, shook him off, and grabbed her knees to her chest. "Nothing that concerns you." Standing, she strolled to the open bathroom door, wrapping herself in feigned composure, as if it had been body armor. She paused and, without looking over her shoulder, said, "I want you to leave."

Marcus snorted and stood. He walked slowly up behind her. "Why?"

"Because I'm tired."

He lowered his lips to her right shoulder. "Me too." He kissed her, not wanting to leave and not buying her sudden show of bravado. "But I need to shower before I go."

Her body stiffened. "Go shower in your own room."

He slid his arm around her waist and brought her against him. He closed his eyes and inhaled her wild scent. God, he wanted to go back there with her again. "Jax, I'm afraid we have a problem."

She tried to face him, but he clamped his arm tighter around her. He felt her heartbeat accelerate and her blood whoosh in her veins. "What problem is that?"

He turned her slowly around, entwined his fingers through hers and raised her hands above her head, pressing her up against the wall. "I want you all over again." And God help him, he never wanted to stop. He lowered his lips to hers and kissed her. Her body sparked against his. The mad rush of her desire hit him broadside. His body swelled in response.

"Be gentle this time," she whispered as she gave herself over to him.

Hours later, just moments away from the first rays of the sun breaking through the night, Marcus stood

over the sleeping body in the big rumpled bed. Her hair
was still damp from their shower. The impression from
his body was still embedded in the sheets beside her.
Once had not been enough for him. He'd taken her in
the shower, then once more in this bed. He was insatiable. As he buttoned his shirt, his cock thickened. There
was so much more he wanted to do to her before he
had to stop. He cracked a small smile. She had begged
him to stop in the shower. Begged him for more in the
bed until, finally sated, he had relented and laid down
beside her as she'd tumbled into a deep sleep.

Her creamy skin had paled. Dark crescents framed
her eyes. Marcus sat down on the edge of the bed and
brushed her dark hair from her neck. Her skin was cool
to the touch. He traced his fingertips along the slight
bruise marks his fangs had made. In a few hours, they
would be barely visible, by tonight gone. He brushed his
thumb against the marks. Jax stirred slightly and softly
moaned.

Had he taken too much from her? He felt a hint of
something he'd not felt in a long time. Guilt. Guilt, even
though she'd given so freely of herself.

"Jax," he called as he gently shook her.

She moaned slightly and reached out for him in her
sleep.

"Are you all right?"

She smiled and nodded.

Marcus smiled in return. He gazed toward the sliding
glass door. The dark was beginning to gray. He had less
than an hour to go to ground.

As he shrugged on his jacket, Marcus contemplated
his next move with Jax Cassidy.

It was obvious she was not going to willingly give him the information he wanted. But what if she were telling him the truth? That she was an independent and not associated with the organization Rowland called in? Part of him wanted to believe her; part of him knew he shouldn't.

During his twenty-eight years as a human and the last seven as a soulless immortal, he had never felt more alive. She made him realize how much he wanted to live again. In an unexplainable way, she gave meaning to his lifeless existence. And until he had no choice, he would not give up the sensations she elicited from him. Not until he absolutely had to. He strode to the door and looked at her one last time. She looked sated, content. At least one of them was. He exhaled loudly. He still had a job to do. He'd just take a different approach. As he thought of her two cohorts down the hall, he smiled. Looked like he'd have to get his hands dirty after all.

TWENTY-TWO

Marcus softly closed the hotel room door behind him. Immediately, his head snapped back and his nostrils flared. He looked down the short hall to an alcove. A tall, muscular body appeared, followed by the words, "The colonel is looking for you."

Marcus scowled at Gideon Dimarco, the colonel's guard dog. "How did you find me?" The why didn't matter nearly as much as the how. Marcus took great care concealing his scent from those who were as cursed as he.

Dimarco strode out into the harsh light. "I could smell you fucking all the way out on Filmore." His sharp gaze went past Marcus to the door he had just exited. "Any left?"

Marcus strode toward him. Dimarco was blood-thirsty and lacked self-control. Although he was older than Marcus by a few decades, his maker, Gustav, was not nearly as powerful as Marcus's maker—Thorkeel Rus, aka Colonel Joseph Lazarus. That in and of itself made Dimarco of no consequence to Marcus, except for the fact that he didn't trust him.

Or like him.

Just as he passed Dimarco, Marcus reached out and grabbed him by the throat, shoving him so hard against the wall that the impact dented the drywall. A light fixture shattered, dimming the area. Gideon's eyes burned red in his fury. "Don't fucking go there." Marcus let go of him, then proceeded past him to the elevator.

A short time later, Marcus strolled nonchalantly into the colonel's Oakland lair. He didn't feel nonchalant, however; quite the opposite. He was pissed. Pissed because an underling like Dimarco had tracked him down and, in the process, inadvertently tracked down Jax. But Gideon he could handle, if he had to. He'd pay for it in the end, but he'd protect what he had to and deal with the consequences.

Marcus faltered for a split second. The thought of protecting the woman who had gotten under his skin unnerved him. It unnerved him almost as much as the unexpected warmth that had surfaced when he'd realized he had a sister. He had protected her too, by calling off Jax. And he knew Lazarus wasn't going to like that.

Through the wide eastern-exposed window in front of him, he glanced at the pinkening horizon. The tall, dark figure of his maker was illuminated against the pastel sunrise. Unlike most vampires, Lazarus was, with considerable precautions, able to venture into the sunlight, but only for a short time. Marcus had long envied that ability, but not anymore. Recently, Marcus had discovered that he, too, could withstand the sun's more tender rays, but only on the fringes of dusk and dawn, never at the height of the day. He was sure that by the time Lazarus was done with him, enough time would have passed that he'd be stuck here, forced to spend the day as the colonel's guest—something he never enjoyed.

"Sir?" Marcus asked as he stepped farther into the room.

Lazarus slowly turned. As he did, Marcus saw the slight flare of his nostrils. He knew Jax's blood scent was all over him. Hell, a damn rock could smell it.

"I see you had some good blood sport last night," the colonel murmured.

Marcus nodded. "Very good." And it was true. Being with Jax had infused him with a shot of mortality he had missed for so long.

As he approached the colonel, he too detected a new blood scent. It was pungent, floral, with a hint of perfume. Marcus halted in midstep. The scent. It was oddly familiar but distinctly different. Last night. In the Green Room. Eerily similar to his mother's scent. He shook off the absurdity of his thoughts. He was mistaken. Many blood scents were similar. Besides, Lazarus would never betray him like that. Marcus smiled. "It seems, sir, I'm not the only one."

Lazarus scowled, apparently not liking the fact that Marcus knew anything about his extracurricular activities. Before Marcus could consider the idea further, Lazarus spoke. "Why is the Rowland girl still alive?"

Marcus shrugged and walked toward the rising sunlight. He felt the warmth of the rays as they penetrated the glass. If felt good. Comforting. For the first time since he could remember, he wanted to wake up to the sun with a woman in his arms. One particular woman. While the image warmed him, the reality of his folly chilled his blood.

He shook the ridiculous longing off and turned to face the colonel, continuing to enjoy the warmth on his back. Gideon hissed in the darkened corner, envious of where he dared not step.

"She's still alive because I chose not to eliminate her last night." Marcus decided at that moment not to divulge to his maker the fact that he knew Grace Rowland was his sister. If Lazarus knew, then it was simply a test, a test Marcus could pass on his terms. If he didn't know, then things were certainly going to get more complicated.

Lazarus's scowl deepened. He glanced at Gideon, then back at Marcus. "And since when do you determine these things?"

"I have always determined them, sir. It took me three weeks to finally get the opening I needed to take out Blalock. The stars were not aligned last night to eliminate Grace Rowland."

"Maybe if you weren't so wrapped up in nailing that piece of fluff this morning, you could have taken out the mark," Gideon sneered from the shadows. Marcus raised his hand and shoved hard at the air. The centrifugal force sent Gideon flying into the corner. Gideon growled and came at him, but the colonel stopped him with one piercing glance. Marcus smirked.

"What I do on my time is no concern of yours, Dimarco."

The colonel stalked closer to Marcus. "Tell me of this blood sport."

"I suspect she's part of the organization Rowland hired."

The colonel smiled, his fangs glittering in the rising sunlight. "Ah, now I understand."

He turned back to Gideon, who was literally beginning to simmer. "Go to ground, Gideon, before you turn to a pile of ash."

Dimarco dashed past them both into the darkness of the hall and, Marcus assumed, to the blacked-out bedroom where he would spend the day untouched by the sun.

The colonel turned his attention back to Marcus and asked, "You've grown less sensitive to the sun, I see."

Marcus turned back to the window and raised his face to the golden glow. "It feels good." Then he turned back to his maker. "Before I could only handle the first blush of dawn; then I had to go to ground like Dimarco. Why is my resistance stronger now?"

The colonel stood silent for a long time. When he did not answer immediately, Marcus surmised there was only one reason. Marcus possessed some hidden or latent power the colonel didn't want him to know about. One the colonel was threatened by. For the second time, Marcus felt disappointed in Lazarus. And now, wary of him.

Lazarus moved to stand beside Marcus. He faced the rising of the sun himself. "My blood, the same blood that flows through your veins, is of the oldest and strongest of our kind. Combined with Aelia's, you have inherited great power. Be thankful."

"I am. But I have not always been able to tolerate the sun as I am now."

"The glass acts as a buffer. If you were to go out as you are now and stand beneath the sun, you would fry in seconds."

Marcus tried not to show his disappointment. "What other powers am I to come into with time?" *And why haven't you told me about them?* he thought.

Lazarus chuckled and shook his head. "There is time

for that, son, but not today. Today I want you to school me. Tell me about the woman," he softly said.

Marcus knew there was no way of getting around the subject of Jax. He could minimize her and, in so doing, pique Lazarus's interest, or he could throw her into the snake pit and be her champion. He chose the latter. "She's holding out, but with some more maneuvering, I'll get her right where I need her."

"Bring her in. I'd be happy to hone my extraction skills."

Marcus was surprised by the urge to strike out. He was well aware of the colonel's tactics. He'd witnessed countless inhumane torture sessions. He'd only stomached them because the ones being tortured had themselves acted more inhumanely to innocents. Even so, if Lazarus sensed Marcus's need to protect Jax, he would only push the point. "Bringing her in will not be a problem; she *wants* in, as a Solution operative."

Lazarus looked at Marcus in stunned silence. Marcus nodded. Jax Cassidy amazed him on so many levels. His next words reflected his respect for her. "She's got some balls too. I think we should bring her in, act like we're interested, even give her a mission. Make her prove herself. Then, if she really does have what it takes to operate to our standards, convert her to our way of life, then use her as a double agent for the organization she's working for."

Lazarus stood silent and contemplative for a long moment, then spoke. "We suspect she works for a covert organization, the same covert organization Rowland has retained to protect him from us, and you want to bring her into the fold?"

"Yes."

"What makes you so sure she will obey if I turn her?"

Marcus set his jaw. "You will not turn her. I will."

Lazarus smiled, his fangs glistening beneath the morning sunlight. "You know the rules, Marcus. Only district or coven leaders posses the power to turn a mortal, and only with the coven leader's approval."

Marcus smiled back, showing his own fangs. "Then promote me."

Lazarus shook his head. "You're not ready."

Immediately taking offense, Marcus clenched his jaw. "I'm more than ready. As a mortal, I was squad leader, and would have been promoted to captain, then unit leader, had I not been ambushed by that band of Pakistani drug smugglers. I've carried out every Solution mission successfully. I have your respect and that of my fellow operatives."

"I decide who is promoted, and I say you are not ready."

Marcus paused, then sneered, "Would Rurik think the same?"

Lazarus shoved Marcus so hard that he flew across the room and crashed into the mirrored bar in the dining room. Lazarus flew at him, but Marcus, furious at being treated like a mere minion, was ready. He dove headlong into his maker's path, and together they crashed to the floor, rolling over the furniture, breaking everything in their wake. Seconds later, they whirled up and hit the ceiling, landed with a crash against the wall in the living room, then crashed through the double-wide sliding glass door out onto the patio.

Sunlight hit Marcus's skin, warming it to hot, but not

so hot that he burned. Lazarus immediately moved into the darkness of the condominium, trying to pull Marcus with him. Marcus shook him off. Slowly, he stood and faced the rising sun. No glass separated him from the ultraviolet rays. He did not burn.

Lazarus had lied to him.

He turned to find his maker carefully watching him. This was not the first time they'd quarreled, but it was the first time they'd physically tangled. The first time Marcus had let his anger move him so that, unthinkingly, he'd challenged his maker. Now, it appeared, the student rivaled the teacher.

"There is no glass that separates me and the sun," Marcus taunted, "and yet I am intact." Even as he said the words, however, he felt a slight cramp of nausea in his gut.

Lazarus straightened his jacket and smoothed back his hair, then *tsk*ed. "You are stronger than I thought, Marcus. Do not let it go to your head."

Marcus tried to withstand the nausea but couldn't. He strode past Lazarus into the cool darkness of the abode. Immediately, his stomach quelled, but he was indisputably rattled. He might be gaining power, but he was still no match for Lazarus and his army of rabid vampires. It had been foolish for him to mention Rurik, knowing how Lazarus would react. Foolish to think he could best him. He couldn't forget that he still needed his maker. Or that he owed him his life, limited as it was. He wasn't going to ruin their relationship for a woman he didn't trust. What had he been thinking? He turned to his maker and made a slight bow. "My pardon for evoking Rurik's name. I won't do it again."

Lazarus placed his hand on Marcus's shoulder. "Take my chamber and go to ground. You will not be disturbed. We'll talk when you arise."

"About the woman—" Marcus insisted, not willing to let the matter go.

Lazarus sliced his hand in the air. "Enough. It will be as you wish," he snapped. "But only because I wish it."

Marcus nodded, then strode down the hall. Despite Lazarus's generosity, he knew things had irrevocably changed between him and his maker.

And not for the better.

Jax woke with a start, jackknifing straight up in the bed. Sunshine streamed through the windows, warming her naked body. She gazed about the room. Linens and pillows littered the floor and lay strewn across the furniture. Her robe lay in a heap by the bathroom door.

Sounds and scents reverberated with precise clarity. One scent overrode everything else—Cross's earthy scent. It swirled in the air, across her skin. She touched her fingertips to her neck and felt the harsh rush of her blood beneath her fingertips. His presence swirled in her blood. She rose from the bed, feeling light on her feet.

Where was he? Had he—?

She shook her head and cursed her stupidity. Of course he didn't do mornings. Vampires didn't like the sun and all that. And after last night, Jax had no doubts. A vampire was exactly what Marcus was.

Besides, she snorted to herself, vampire or not, she'd bet he was the kind of guy that skulked out in the wee hours of the morning.

She strode to the window and pushed the curtains

all the way open. Sunlight flooded the room, and she blinked at the brightness. The city bustled beneath her, oblivious to her and what had transpired in this room. Her heart rate hitched up a few notches. What *had* happened? It was like nothing she had ever experienced. It had been wild. Frenzied. Epic.

Marcus's initial gentleness had surprised her. Then it had turned her into a pile of malleable mush. Never in a million years would she have believed he was capable of such tenderness.

And never in a million years had she thought she could be so dumb!

She closed her eyes and summoned an image of Marcus. She felt his power, his passion . . . his seething anger at the world. The way he'd reverently trailed his fingertips across her skin. Jax dragged her fingers through her hair and shook the thick strands. Taking a deep breath, she silently cursed herself.

Shit!

What had she done?

Compromised the entire mission by allowing herself to become emotionally involved with her mark! Yeah, she had some power over him, she could push his buttons, but he had her number, too. *Shit! Shit! Shit!* She grabbed her robe from the floor and shrugged it on. Now, she had to make it right. While she waited for her laptop to boot up, she made quick use of the bathroom. When she returned, she video-Skyped Godfather.

"Go ahead, Freedom Fighter," Godfather said, using her code name.

There was no sense in beating around the bush. "I can

no longer do this," she said, feeling as if she had let the world down.

"Do what?"

"*This!* This mission!"

Godfather didn't so much as blink. "Why?"

"I slept with him."

"And?"

"Did you hear me? I fucked him!"

Not even a flash of anger or surprise in those cool blue eyes of his. "So."

"You don't care?" Jax demanded, incredulous.

Finally, a reaction. And not the one she thought she deserved. Godfather shrugged and looked earnestly at her. "You did what you had to do. I'm sorry it came to that."

He wasn't getting it. Frustrated, Jax swiped at her chin with her hand. "You're wrong. I didn't fuck him because I *had* to, I fucked him because I *wanted* to!"

Godfather regained his stoic demeanor. "Are you implying you have become emotionally involved with your mark and can no longer remain objective?"

"I . . . yes." Jax swiped her hand across her face again, more frustrated. "I mean, no. Look, I don't—" She forced herself to say the words. "I'm not emotionally involved with him. But I slept with him, damn it, because I wanted to, not because he forced me or because it was a means to an end."

"Has the fact that you had sex with Cross jeopardized mission success?"

Jax sat back and stared at Godfather, who looked as if he'd been discussing the weather with her. "He got to me. Made me flash when I should have remained calm."

"Then I suggest you get a grip on that temper of yours, Cassidy." Godfather leaned in and softly said, "You have what it takes to see this mission through to the end. Now stop crying like a girl and get the job done."

"There's more!" Jax said before he logged off.

"What more?"

"Cross is a fucking vampire." She held her hand up when Godfather scowled. "He not only told me, but I witnessed him destroy six gangbangers *after* they shot him full of lead. Had he not shown up, I would have been the one dead."

"Cassidy—"

Jax rubbed her neck, the bruise of Cross's bite throbbed. She close her eyes, swept her hair from her neck, and leaned toward the screen. "He bit me, sir. Drank my blood. Not pretend, but the real thing."

Long silence followed her confession. "Cassidy, I'm at a loss for words here. I find all of this unbelievable."

She opened her eyes and stared at her boss. "Me too, but I'm not crazy. This is real."

"How do we fight it?"

"I don't know. But I'll tell you this: Cross might be a vampire, which explains a lot, but he has all of the emotions and desires of a man. And *I* think I've made a connection. We have an advantage in that we can operate during the day, and he cannot. We can do a lot in a day."

"We are completely out of our element here, Cassidy. I don't like operating in the dark."

She nodded. "Neither do I, but I'll tell you this much.

Cross will be back. At the very least for sex, at the most to bring me in."

"All right, Cassidy," Godfather reluctantly said, "I'm going to get to work on the vampire angle. See what I come up with. Meet up with your team and report back to me before dusk."

"Yes, sir," Jax said before the screen went dark.

For long minutes, she sat in the chair and stared at the dark screen. What the hell had she gotten them into? What if there were an army of Crosses? How could they fight them? And win? She shivered hard. This was becoming epic. And for the first time since they began, Jax doubted not only the success of this mission, but L.O.S.T.'s survival.

Heavy footsteps approaching her room startled her. Shane. She could smell him. Jesus, her senses were on overload, and even though she knew what—who—was responsible, she still felt the thrill of excitement. A girl could get used to this.

Tightening the sash around her waist, she opened the door before he knocked. Startled, he took one look at her, then past her. "What the hell, Cassidy?" Shane asked as he stepped into the room. Jax shut the door behind him. "Looks like a bomb went off in this place."

"Yeah, one did," Jax said under her breath.

He turned to stare at her. His nostrils flared and his eyes narrowed. Suddenly she felt very self-conscious. The musky smell of sex and pheromones practically stifled the air. "What did the pedophile counselor have to say last night?" she asked, diverting his attention.

"No one home."

"How convenient," Jax muttered. "Have you checked in with Dante?"

"All Rowlands are present and accounted for, but Dante said to be prepared. The female Rowlands have been going round and round about the boyfriend."

Great. "Let me get cleaned up and we'll go see the Rowlands, then pay LeVech a visit."

She moved past him. Or tried to. Shane grabbed her arm. His gaze skittered to the bed, then back to her. "Jax, you can't—"

"Don't go there," she said quietly. "Don't tell me what I can or can't do, Shane. Understand?"

Grimly, he stared at her, then let her go. "He's using you."

She nodded, remembering Godfather's faith in her. It gave her the strength to answer him. "It goes both ways."

TWENTY-THREE

⸮

W hen Jax and Shane made it to the Rowlands' Pacific Heights estate, they drove straight into a hornet's nest.

"Now that's a sight," Shane murmured, throwing the car into Park just as Grace Rowland barreled across the manicured front lawn. Her mother was hot on her heels.

"Who would have thought Sophia Rowland could run with that stick up her butt," Jax mused aloud.

"As much as I like the kid," Shane laughed, "my money's on her mom."

Jax snorted, not about to disagree with him.

Sighing, she opened her door.

"I'm an adult. I'll see who I want!" Grace screamed, running past Jax, who'd exited the car.

"Grace, you come back here. I—"

Instinctively, in a quick, powerful move, Jax reached out and grabbed the girl by the arm, yanking her backward. The velocity of the movement caught Sophia Rowland, who was gaining ground on her daughter, by surprise. Grace and her mother collided, then hit the cobblestone driveway with a resounding thud.

Shane looked at Jax as if she had grown a third head, then immediately reached down to help the Rowland women up. Jax drew in a deep breath and stepped back. Sophia threw her a daggered look as she adjusted the scarf hanging askew around her neck. Seeing she was unharmed, Jax focused on Grace.

Shit.

Not only were Gracie's pants torn and dirty but the collision had also bloodied up her right hand. Tears filled the girl's eyes, and she refused to meet Jax's gaze.

Jax couldn't blame her. She would be a bit embarrassed too if Grace had seen photos of her in such a compromising position.

"Oh, Gracie," Sophia said when she saw the wound. Instantly, her standard I'll-eat-you-for-breakfast expression transformed into one of genuine distress. She yanked the scarf from around her neck and hurriedly wrapped it around her daughter's wound. Surprised by the show of maternal concern, Jax stepped closer and was rewarded with another heated glare. "Miss Cassidy, was that necessary? You could have killed us!" Sophia snapped.

Oh, good. The bitch was back. The bitch she could handle.

"Necessity isn't the—" Jax stopped and frowned, then subtly sniffed the air.

Sophia's scent . . . It was a complex blend of feminine flora, iron and dominant male. It caught Jax's attention until she realized everyone was staring at her.

Shaking away her odd thoughts, Jax said, "My apologies, Mrs. Rowland, Grace. I meant only to stop the runaway train." She turned sympathetic eyes to Grace. "I assume all this commotion is because you've told your mom"—Grace closed her eyes in obvious mortification—"about the picture and Mr. LeVech—"

"Not here, Miss Cassidy," Sophia snapped. "In the house."

Sophia wrapped her arms around her subdued daughter and led her into the sprawling Georgian-style mansion that was the Rowlands' abode, leaving Jax and Shane to follow like paid help. Which, Jax supposed, they were.

"You have an annoying habit of stunts like that," Shane said as they indeed followed behind the two limping women. "Do it again, Cassidy, and we can kiss this assignment good-bye."

She looked up and found his angry eyes on her. "I didn't mean for that to happen. I just wanted to stop Grace."

"Next time, let me do it," Shane groused. "You obviously don't know your own strength."

She narrowed her eyes. "Keep it up, and I'll give you another demonstration."

He held up his hands. "Easy. Save it for your boyfriend."

Now her eyes widened. "What the—?"

But he walked ahead of her without letting her finish. And it really pissed her off. Cross was the furthest thing from a love interest that a man could be with her. That Shane would even joke about it made her want to hurt him.

She shook off her vigilante feelings toward her teammate, knowing she had to let it go. He could think what he wanted. If she was brutally honest, she had no regrets.

And that admission bothered her more than Shane's insinuation.

As they entered the cavernous house, Jax didn't bother admiring the classic décor. She was already familiar with the full layout of the house, from the rug at her feet to the fixtures in the guest baths. All she wanted now—all she was going to focus on—were answers and strategic planning.

Dante strode angrily toward them. "Mrs. Rowland came unglued when the kid told her about the photograph and LeVech. When things appeared to have calmed down, I went to take a leak and the next thing I know the Rowland women are running and screaming out the door! I'm about done with this babysitting detail."

That answered a couple of big questions. Sophia Rowland knew about the photo and the lover boy, and Dante had been watching them, but, well, a boy had to go when a boy had to go. It wasn't like he could take them to the john with him. Jax slapped him on the shoulder and shook her head. "Thanks for taking one for the team, man."

"What's the word on LeVech?" Dante asked Shane.

"No one home. No one answering the phone this morning either. We're going to head back over there as soon as we wrap up here."

They followed the women deeper into the house until they finally stopped in a large study. They came face-to-face with a scowling Senator Rowland and Alex Maksim, his campaign manager. Rowland, however, seemed to be scowling at Jax's appearance, not because his wife had been chasing his daughter down the street or because his kid was injured. Maybe he was a derelict dad? Maybe he wasn't the kind to fuss over a kid.

Was all the fatherly concern just an act, then? Was

he like every other scumbag politician, more concerned with his career than with his own flesh and blood? No wonder Grace had rebelled.

Jax closed the double doors to what she figured was the senator's office behind her. She nodded to the senator, who looked none too pleased with her.

Grace sat in a chair while being tended to by her mother. The senator finally moved around and asked, "Are you all right, Gracie?"

"Just a few scrapes, Daddy," she murmured, not looking up at him.

"Sir," Jax said, inclining her head toward the girl. Jesus, did they really think they could talk openly with her present?

"Sophia," Rowland softly said, "take Grace upstairs and tend her."

Sophia turned angry eyes on Jax, then up to her husband. She helped Grace up and walked her to the door. "I'll be up shortly, Grace. Have Leti see to you until then."

Jax couldn't help but compare Grace with her big brother. Only their eyes linked them physically. Emotionally, they were both passionate beings, but in such different ways. Grace was all blind sunshine, while Marcus was dark moonlight. Grace was like an untrained puppy wearing her emotions on her sleeve. Marcus was like a Schutzen-trained rottweiler. Jax watched her walk slowly from the room, knowing by her expression that she wanted to argue her place among the adults but was smart enough to know she would lose. Marcus never would have asked. He would have refused to leave.

Sophia closed the doors behind Grace and turned to face the room. "I'm not leaving this room, Bill." She stalked past Jax and sat down in the chair her daughter had vacated. Imperiously, she crossed her arms and legs, then looked hard at Shane, Dante, then Jax. "Not until you tell me what's going on. I want full disclosure."

Jax looked to the senator. It was his call.

He nodded.

"Full disclosure it is then," Jax started. "Sir, if we may, I'd like to put the photograph and who's behind it aside for the moment."

"I think not," Maksim said. "That photograph has to be dealt with immediately."

Jax looked to Shane and Dante.

"I think you should hear Miss Cassidy out," Shane said. "It might change our approach."

"Go ahead, Miss Cassidy," the senator said.

"I was offered the contract on Grace last night," Jax stated.

A collective gasp went up in the room.

"By who?" Sophia demanded as she absently fingered her hair along her neck.

Jax wanted to smirk and say, *"Your son. Payback is a bitch, isn't it?"* Instead, she looked at the senator. When he nodded, she said, "An assassin who has connections to the organization who has threatened the senator. But at the last minute, I was called off."

Sophia stood and faced her husband. "What kind of threats against you, Bill? And why is this organization still in existence?"

"It's complicated, Sophia. I only allowed you to believe there was a mild threat so as not to worry you. As I see you are now."

"How can you *not* inform me of serious threats

against you?" She wrapped her arms around her husband's neck and hugged him to her. "Bill, please, let me in. I need to know what is happening so I can help."

He caught her in the circle of his arms and smiled sadly down at her. "It's much bigger than the both of us, darling. It's why I called in Miss Cassidy and her team. We're going to flush the bastards out and fight fire with fire."

"Did these bad people take that photograph of Grace?" she asked.

"We don't know," Shane said. "I went to speak with LeVech last night. He wasn't home. We're going back there when we wrap up here."

"My money is on Mercer," Maksim said, shaking his head in disgust. "He has the most to gain by this. And unless we find a way around this mess, he's going to be the next senator."

"I wouldn't be so sure of it, Alex. My money is on Lazarus," Rowland stated.

Sophia made a small sound, bringing Jax's gaze to her. Absently, the woman rubbed her hair again. Why the sudden nervousness?

"He said three weeks," Sophia softly said, interrupting Jax's thoughts.

Before she could respond, Rowland did.

"How do you know that, Sophia?" Rowland asked, startling Jax. Sophia looked like a deer caught in headlights. Her perfectly painted pink lips formed a perfect O. "How do you know about Lazarus?" Rowland asked his wife again.

Sophia closed her mouth and straightened to rigid. She looked hard at everyone in the room, except her husband. When she finally did meet his gaze, she had the grace to blush. Jax didn't buy the act. Delicately, Sophia cleared her throat. "I was worried about you, Bill. I overheard a conversation last month between you and a man you called Lazarus. Since that conversation, you have been walking around as if ghosts lurked around every corner." She looked to Jax and her team, then at Maksim and back to her husband. "When you became so secretive and hired these people for protection, I assumed the worst. I see I was right."

Rowland swiped his hand across his face. "You know how I feel about subterfuge, Sophia!"

"It's not like I'm the enemy here, Bill! I'm your wife, and as your wife I will do anything and everything to protect you. Even if that means snooping around."

Jax watched his face crumble. He was on the verge of complete collapse.

"Sir," Jax began, "I suggest you allow us to take Grace into protective custody. Not only for her safety, but for yours and Mrs. Rowland's peace of mind. Until this is over."

"I think that's a good idea," Maksim said. "Then we can concentrate on this campaign."

Rowland sat down behind his desk and looked solemnly around the room. "I'm not sure if I have the stomach for this anymore."

Sophia Rowland stood up, strode over to a carved mahogany sideboard and opened it. She deftly poured what looked like a healthy shot of whiskey into a crystal tumbler and threw it back. She then grabbed a pack of cigarettes off the table and lit up. Irritated, she blew a

long stream of blue smoke into the middle of the room.
Then she began to pace the Aubusson carpet. "Bill, jump
ship if you insist. But I'll be damned if I'm going to allow
Johnny Mercer to push you out this way. He is the lowest
of life-forms! How dare he use such underhanded methods?" Sophia turned on them all. "Has there been any
word from him? A demand?"

Rowland nodded. Jax cursed under her breath and
moved in closer. "You heard from him and didn't inform
us?"

"I was going to get to it. I received a cryptic email this
morning, simply telling me to back out."

"Let me see it," Jax said, moving in on his laptop. The
senator pulled up the email. The sender, JokzOnU@hot-
mail.com, was probably a dummy addy. As the senator
had indicated, the email simply read

back out now

Jax pulled her iPhone from her pocket. "Senator,
please forward the email to J_Cassidy@yahoo.com." He
did so. A moment later, she checked her account and
forwarded the email to Naomi with instructions to find
out where it had originated. Who knew? Maybe they'd
get lucky.

But she seriously doubted it.

"Could be anything, from anyone," Shane said.

"It's Mercer," Sophia said, stubbing out her cigarette.

"Why are you so sure?" Jax asked.

Sophia looked to her husband, then to Jax, then to the
ceiling.

"I've had a few unsettling encounters with the man."

"What kind of 'unsettling encounters'?" Jax asked.

"Sophia, why is this news to me?" Rowland asked.

Sophia inhaled a deep breath, then slowly exhaled. "This seems to be our day of reckoning, isn't it?" She lit another cigarette. "I, too, have kept secrets to protect you, Bill." She inhaled and slowly exhaled, then casually waved her hand. "He propositioned me last year. I rebuked him, of course. He didn't take too kindly to it. Especially when I told him a lowly mayor didn't interest me." She looked at her husband and smiled apologetically. "He made a few more vain attempts until, finally, I became stern with him and told him if he continued to pursue me, I'd expose him."

Sophia looked directly at Jax. "He, of course, warned me that he would do whatever it took to see Bill humiliated." She raised her glass, and in a rather dramatic salute said, "And so it has come to pass."

The senator and Maksim started speaking at once. Jax held up her hand. "Are you implying," she loudly said to be heard over all their voices, "that Johnny Mercer went to all of this trouble because you wouldn't have sex with him?"

Sophia looked indignant. "Men have waged war over sex since the beginning of time."

Jax gave the haughty socialite a quick up and down. She was fifty-two, a very well-preserved fifty-two at that, but Johnny Mercer struck Jax as the type who liked his women young, blonde and stupid.

Sophia was not young, and certainly not stupid.

Jax stared hard at Sophia. "What else are you not telling us?"

Sophia waved her manicured hand. "Why is it so hard to accept what I just told you?"

"You don't seem like Mercer's type to me," Jax said. "The motives you've given seem too petty for a man so driven."

"Sophia," Rowland sternly said, "what else?"

She shook her head and pursed her lips. "Last fall, before he declared he was running against you, I agreed to hostess a soiree for the Treasure Island Foundation. You were in D.C. and since it was for one of your pet causes. I didn't think you would mind, so I agreed."

"And the press leaked the night before he was running," Rowland said. "I remember now."

"Yes, well, I couldn't be his hostess. I backed out. He lost face and tens of thousands of dollars and the developer he was wooing to revitalize Treasure Island."

"So, it's more like straight tit for tat then?" Jax almost laughed at the pun.

"I assure you, if it is Mercer, he's not going to get away with this! None of it," Rowland said, pouring himself a glass of whiskey despite the morning hour. It hadn't taken long to relight a fire under Rowland. Jax was relieved. Despite what was happening, he did not strike her as a man who would quit anything, not while he still had a breath in his body.

"Maybe he already has, darling," Sophia said.

"What? You're changing your tune already? Are you suggesting I back out of this election?"

"I'm suggesting you take Calhoun up on his offer."

Rowland and Sophia stared at each other, while Jax processed Sophia's words. Was she saying? . . .

"He's made his choice," Rowland snapped.

"Only because you turned him down," his wife reminded him.

"I'm not rehashing this, Sophia. We settled this matter long ago. Don't—"

"No, *you* don't," Sophia snapped back at her husband. "We need this now. Give Mercer what he wants and you can have more."

Shane leaned forward and spoke in Jax's ear. "Richard Calhoun, the GOP presidential front-runner?"

Jax nodded, then asked, "That's who you are talking about, isn't it? Richard Calhoun?"

Sophia nodded. "The one and only."

"It would solve a lot of our problems, Bill," Maksim said.

"The choice has been made. There's no going back."

"Bill," Sophia pleaded. "There is still time. There won't be an announcement until next week. Please reconsider."

"What offer?" Jax asked.

"Vice president of the United States," Sophia Rowland declared triumphantly.

Holy shit.

Senator Rowland scowled. "I told them I wasn't interested. I'm still not."

"How could you *not* be interested in the veep job?" Jax asked.

Rowland sat down behind his desk. "I can do more as a senator than as a lame duck vice president." He rubbed the heels of his hands into his eyes, then looked at them with bleary eyes. "It's a moot point. Calhoun has chosen his running mate. My only concern now is to salvage my daughter's reputation, get reelected to a fourth term as

U.S. senator if it's still possible, and get Joseph Lazarus off my back. Now, tell me how we're going to do that?"

"For starters, we take Grace into protective custody." Jax looked to Dante. "Can you arrange that?" He nodded. "Good, then Shane and I will head over to speak with LeVech. If he's in this alone, we're golden. If not, we'll find out who he's sleeping with and go from there."

"What about Mercer?" Sophia asked.

"First things first, Mrs. Rowland. There's no sense in getting his antennae up if he has nothing to do with this. He's being watched. If he blows his nose, we'll know it."

"I agree," Rowland said.

"Then let's get to it," Jax said, heading for the door.

"He's dead," she whispered as they approached LeVech's front door.

"Who?" Shane asked.

"LeVech," Jax murmured.

The front door creaked open against the late morning breeze. Shane pulled his pistol. Jax shook her head. "You won't need that."

Shane looked at her like she was crazy and kept his weapon drawn. First Shane entered. Almost immediately, she heard him cursing.

The blood scent was so strong, so pungent, that it clogged her nostrils. As she stepped into the foyer, she nearly gagged. Blood splattered in high arches across the soft green walls. Lying naked in a pool of his blood was LeVech, his groin mutilated.

"Whoever did this was pissed," Jax said as she stepped to the fringes of the room where there was no blood.

Farther down in the short hallway was a woman lying facedown in her blood, her neck severed so severely that it lay at a ninety-degree angle from her shoulders.

Other than the two bodies and the blood, the house looked to be in perfect order. "From the lividity, it looks like maybe twelve hours. What time did you arrive last night?"

"Right after midnight," Shane said.

It was noon, so the couple must have arrived home shortly after Shane's visit. Whoever had done this to them hadn't been far behind.

"Jesus. This runs us straight into a wall," Jax said, walking the perimeter in order to stay out of the blood.

She squatted and looked closer at LeVech. Her skin crawled. "Look," she said, pointing to the groin injury. "It looks like claw marks. Like an animal did this."

"Or made to look like an animal did it," Shane said.

"Mercer or Lazarus?"

Shane looked pointedly at Jax. "One has a senatorial seat to gain, and the other stands to lose it."

"Let's go chat with Johnny Mercer."

"But first let's go through the place and make sure there is nothing that can link LeVech to any Rowland," Shane said.

Less than an hour later, with not one thread to tie to any one of the Rowlands, Jax called in the details to Naomi, who called the cops on a blocked number. When Jax hung up, she looked up at Shane. "Let's get out of here."

As they drove back to the city, Shane looked over from the steering wheel and asked, "How did you know they were dead before we got out of the car?"

She swallowed hard but didn't flinch away from the question. "I could smell them."

"How?" Shane asked, eyeing her cryptically.

"I-I got some of Cross's souped-up blood in me. Apparently, it makes me more aware."

"Jesus, Cassidy. What if he has AIDS or something?"

She looked over at him. "Trust me, that is the least of my worries."

He opened his mouth to ask her more, but she shook her head. "Shane, after last night, I'm pretty sure Cross is going to make an introduction. I need you to trust me when it comes to handling him."

"I trust you. It's him I don't trust."

"That makes two of us."

TWENTY-FOUR

i

When Jax rolled into her room at sunset, she was startled to find Cross sitting at the small desk, casually playing solitaire on her laptop. Lucky for her she didn't keep anything confidential on it.

She scowled.

Why wasn't she surprised?

"I invite you in once, and now you think you're welcome anytime?" She was hot, tired and, damn it, horny. Mercer hadn't been reachable; he was out on his yacht, *Foreplay*—she couldn't help her mental snort at the name—and due back later tonight. She and Shane would be waiting for him. First, however, she was taking a few hours to clean up and rest up. "What are you doing here?"

Cross turned those laconic eyes of his on her and smiled, showing just the barest hint of his fangs. Apparently, he wasn't even going to try and hide what he was any longer. Absently, she rubbed the spot on her neck where those fangs had spent so much time last night. Along with the desire that flooded her, however, part of her mind was on business. How many other vampires were there? What did it take to destroy them? Or love them. She was afraid if she asked, he'd close up, emotionally and physically.

That was the last thing she wanted him to do. His gaze traveled over her body; she couldn't have controlled the warmth that spread through her or the tightening of her skin even if her life had been at stake. He did things to her no other man ever had, and she doubted ever would.

"Angry because I didn't stay for breakfast?" he asked.

She shrugged and dropped her handbag on the bed. She needed a drink. "I didn't figure you for the type that did mornings."

He slowly stood. She moved past him to look out the window. The sun blazed a red glow over the city. When he moved behind her, Jax held her breath. He brushed her hair from her neck and lowered his lips to her ear. "I would if I could."

She steeled herself against him. Sex with him again, no matter how incredible, was not a good idea. More sex would just complicate things . . . even more. She moved away, yanked open the sliding glass door, and stepped out into the balmy San Francisco dusk.

He followed her.

"I have a proposition for you, Jax Cassidy," he said.

She didn't dare turn around. She didn't trust herself. "I'm listening."

"Me and you team up and take care of a little business down in L.A. tomorrow night."

His hands pressed against the back of her shoulders and slowly began to rub. She closed her eyes. The day's tension strained her muscles. What she needed was a good hot soak in the tub and a full body massage. And a glass of really nice merlot. Or . . .

She bit back a moan of pleasure. Or she needed more of what Cross was doing. His big hands dug into her skin, his fingers moving across her bunched muscles, loosening them.

"What kind of business?"

"Solution business."

Jax stiffened. And waited.

This was it.

His big hands massaged her forearms and her biceps, then moved once more to her shoulders, to her neck. He dug his fingers into her hair and massaged her scalp. She fought the urge to lean back into him and let him do that to her entire body. He pushed her head to the left, then the right, releasing more tension. But a different type of tension was building in her loins. His fingers moved around to her waist, then her hips. He pressed softly against her back.

"Are you saying—" She gulped when his hands cupped the cradle of her hips and pressed her against him. She felt the sharp ridge of his erection against the small of her back. "—what I think you're saying?"

His fingers splayed across her lower belly. "Yes," he whispered against her ear.

Jax squeezed her eyes shut and steeled herself. Suspicion immediately reared its head, mixing with desire. Unfortunately, the desire was winning.

She wanted him. She told herself it didn't mean anything except a stress releaser on a really shitty day.

His fingers swept lower to her mons. "Don't," she barely managed.

"Stop me."

She didn't.

"Have you ever made love on a balcony?" he asked.

Jax didn't trust her voice. She shook her head.

"Me either," he said as he unbuttoned the top button of her slacks. Slowly, he pulled the zipper down. "Do you have another pair of these?"

"Pants?"

"Yes."

"Yeah."

He grabbed the fabric on either side of the zipper and pulled. A rending tear, followed by the soft swishing sound of her slacks landing on the patio floor, startled her. "You'll need them. Eventually."

He hooked his thumbs into the sides of her panties and easily disposed of them. Excitement sizzled through her. Warm air brushed against her thighs. He pulled her against him and lowered his lips to her ear and nibbled her there. "Have you ever made love beneath a sunset?"

"No," she croaked.

He unzipped his pants and parted her thighs from behind with his knee. "Me either."

Jax grabbed ahold of the railing to keep her balance. He trailed his hands up her waist to her breasts, cupping them in his big hands, and pressed hotly against her bare bottom. She leaned back and held her breath when he kissed her on the neck behind her ear. His tongue was warm, wet, and when it swirled along the shell of her ear, Jax moaned. She let go of one hand on the railing and grabbed his right hand and trailed it down her belly to her heat.

When he dipped a finger into her, Jax caught her breath and stood on her toes. His breath tickled her ear. Anticipation of all of him inside of her was almost more than she could bear. She bit back words begging him to quench the fire in her blood.

Her body shuddered as his thick finger slid deeper into her waiting wantonness. Jax pressed her head against his chest and closed her eyes. He felt so good.

"You missed me?" he softly asked, sliding his finger deeper, hitting that soft sensitive spot that drove her wild. Waves of pleasure rippled through her.

"Yes," she hoarsely whispered. She had missed him.

He moved his fingertip slowly back and forth across the sensitive spot as he pressed his swollen groin against her bare bottom. The sensations it caused were deliciously unbearable. Jax bit her bottom lip to keep from crying out. As much as she detested her weakness for him, she loved how he made her feel.

"I missed you too," he said against her neck, his teeth grazing her skin. "I missed the scent of your skin, the taste of your sweat, the way your body responds to my slightest touch."

Her hips moved hotly against the slow rhythmic movements of his hand. Jax rose to her toes as the tide of her arousal began to curl into a maverick wave.

She moaned as her body began to liquefy. Her thighs tightened around his hand, her body drew taut, and just when she thought she could stand it no longer, she shattered.

Everything shattered. Her body, her will, her control, her resolve, all of it, gone. In that one blinding moment of pure pleasure, nothing else mattered. She rode out the orgasm in quick, jerky movements, her body contorting as all synapses flared. Marcus slowed his rhythm to compensate the overload of sensations.

Jax gulped for breath as her lungs worked overtime to get oxgyen into her system. Marcus held her tightly against his chest. Jax licked her dry lips. She wanted more.

As if reading her thoughts, Marcus slipped his finger from her wet body, replacing it with his straining erection. Jax moaned loudly as he entered her. Inch by inch he filled her. The feeling of him filling her as his slow, rhythmic fingers strummed her mons was almost too much for her to handle. She felt his imprint everywhere. Not just where he physically touched her. He was everywhere. The way her body accepted him was as if they were designed for each other. In sync. Receptive. Complete.

Once again, she closed her eyes, leaned back, and gave in to the wild wantonness that was him. And once again, she tumbled headlong into a tortuously wicked orgasm that left her gasping for air.

Marcus's powerful body pumped heatedly into her. Sweat slickened their bodies. Marcus's breath singed her neck. His teeth scraped along her jugular. But he did not bite her. Jax arched her neck offering herself to him. He growled low, digging his fingers into her hips, and in a wild primal rush, his body nearly lifted hers as he came.

Wide-eyed and breathless, Jax stared out across the city as her body jerked against the one behind her. And finally their wild ride slowed, and, still connected, they watched the final descent of the sun into the western horizon.

Marcus moved slightly, releasing her. If it had been up to him, they'd have stayed connected and watched the sun rise. Instead, he watched her body quiver as she reached down to pick up her destroyed clothing. He didn't miss her frown. "I owe you," he chuckled.

He expected her to turn those fierce green eyes on him and say he damn well owed her. But she moved past him without looking at him and went into the bathroom. He zipped up, pulled a chair from the room and onto the patio, and sat down. Perching his feet up on the railing to the balcony, he gazed across the concrete jungle. The city sounds were loud. The weather unseasonably warm. Rarely did it get into the eighties, much less the nineties, as it had today.

He liked the sultriness of the air. Almost as much as he liked the way Jax's body had slickened in excitement.

He smelled her when she returned, and he took a deep breath. Damn, he liked her. Too much. He reminded himself that didn't mean he could trust her.

"Tell me about L.A.," she said, perfectly composed and wearing the exact same style of black tailored trousers he'd ripped off her. Just like a Boy Scout, always prepared.

He stood and offered her the chair. She shook her head and leaned against the rail.

"Can we talk about you first?"

Jax looked at him, surprised. "Do I have to pass a personality test or something?"

Marcus smiled and nodded. "Something like that."

"You can ask, but I won't guarantee answers."

"Why do you do what you do?"

"As in hits?"

"Yes."

"I like the money."

He raised his brows, not wanting to hear that answer. "That's it?"

Jax let out a long, expressive breath and looked over the patio to the darkening sky. She crossed her arms over her chest. "I don't like bad guys. I especially don't like bad guys who prey on innocents. I think the devil has a special place in hell for them, and I like to be the one to send them there."

"What happened to you?" he carefully asked.

She shook her head and he watched her body stiffen.

"Jax," he softly said, "we all have our demons. What's yours?"

She turned around and faced him, her face expressionless. "I was brutally raped, then mutilated, by a human trafficker. The guys who were supposed to have my back never showed. I barely escaped with my life. When I healed, I went back for the bastard and killed him. I'm on the lam, Cross. A wanted woman. I work alone and prefer not to get involved on any level with any person, or," she smiled, "vampire."

Marcus uncrossed his legs and sat up. "You're going to have a partner in L.A."

She smiled a big, bright, disarming smile that seemed completely out of place, considering the subject matter. Regardless, it warmed his cold, cold heart. "I guess I can make an exception for you."

"Good, because this isn't a one-man job."

"Beside the fact that you'll want proof I can deliver."

It was his turn to smile. "Sweetheart, I *know* you can deliver."

She cocked her head slightly to the side and said, "Then let's talk business."

Marcus got serious. "Dimitri Skarskov. Russian dissident who is working his way up the ranks of L.A.'s up-and-coming Mirov cartel. They run the gamut. But Dimitri has a penchant for smuggling highly trained al-Qaeda operatives into Canada, then the U.S. He was responsible for building a cell in Fremont, a city just across the bay. He passed them off as Afghani refugees. They were responsible for the bank bombings in Oakland last year. Word on the street is he's working on constructing another group. The Solution wants him and his pipeline eliminated."

"How can you ensure the pipeline will die with him?"

"He's got all the connections. It's the reason he's managed to evade Mirov's fist. Mirov's not going to move on him for fear his Middle East connections will retaliate."

"But if he's a part of the cartel, why would Mirov want to eliminate him?"

"He pays for the cartel protection but operates outside of it. It pisses Mirov off that he doesn't have control of that very lucrative pipeline. But our intel tells us Skarskov is ready to share. There's just too much of a demand. He can't handle all of the traffic himself. We need to take him out now before he meets with Mirov two nights from now and hands over his intel."

"Why aren't the feds after this guy?"

"They don't know who he is. And even if they did, by the time they got around to nabbing him, more lives would be lost."

"OK."

"He's on his way out of Toronto as we speak. Tomorrow night, we take him out."

Jax nodded. "In L.A.?"

"Yes. He lives in the Hiramoto Towers. It's a tough nut to crack and we won't be able to go in from the bottom. So we're going in from the top."

"The rooftop?"

He nodded. "Have you jumped before?"

"Yeah."

"The tower is sixty-five stories high. He lives on the forty-eighth floor. I'll drop you on the roof, then you go in from the patio. Eliminate him and grab his laptop. We want his intel as well."

He watched her for the slightest bit of resistance. And saw none. He grinned, but his words were serious. "I'll catch you if you fall."

"I won't fall."

"Meet me at the SFO domestic VIP terminal tomorrow at this time. We'll fly down together and back in the same night."

"And when the mission is accomplished, you'll introduce me to Lazarus?"

Marcus nodded, questioning his own selfish reasons for bringing Jax in. It wasn't about Lazarus, it wasn't about her, it was about him. He wanted a way to be with her. She made him feel alive. He was being selfish with her life and with The Solution's future survival. But he told himself he had complete control. If Lazarus threatened her, he would let her go. "Be careful what you ask for, Jax. He's not an easy man."

"I can handle him."

Jax sat silent for a long time after Marcus left. Part of her had wanted him to stay, but the realistic part of her had known that would have been impossible. She had work to do. After a quick shower she called Shane, then called Godfather. She gave him the lowdown.

"How do you feel about this, Cassidy? Is it a setup?" Godfather asked.

"I think it's legit. This is classic Lazarus. Skarskov is a terrorist trainer. Terrorists he's assembled and trained who have killed Americans. So long as I perform, I'm in." She paused for a thoughtful moment. "But if Cross doesn't take me to Lazarus after the hit, then we'll have to find a way to draw Lazarus out and take him down."

"I'll work on Plan B. In the meantime, I haven't been sitting here twiddling my thumbs, Cassidy. I ran with your intel. And apparently there *is* such a thing as a vampire, and regular methods of extermination won't work."

"I'll make sure I sharpen my wooden stakes." It sounded ludicrous, but what the hell was she supposed to do?

"That might not be a bad idea. I have spoken at length with renowned parapsychologist Doctor Yuri Romanov. He assures me vampires walk among the living all over the world."

"So I'm not crazy?"

"No. One thing you cannot allow, Cassidy, is no more exchange of blood. The doc told me if a vampire takes blood and the source is left alive, the vampire can find the source anytime, anywhere. Did he offer his blood to you?"

"No. But I bit him. And yeah, I got some of his blood."

"How do you feel?"

"Stronger. Faster. My senses are on fire."

She heard Godfather's frustrated sigh before he said, "Do not, I repeat, *do not* exchange blood with him again."

"Okay."

"According to Dr. Romanov, there are several ways to kill a vampire or, at the very least, immobilize one for a short time. A wooden stake directly through the heart, a silver-tipped wooden bullet directly through the heart, and direct prolonged sunlight, which is more like five minutes. Then most are toast, except the very old ones or the very powerful ones; those types can withstand some sun exposure."

"How do we know old and powerful when we see one—ask him?"

"No, treat all of them as if they can withstand sunlight to a certain degree. Lazarus claims to have a sun sensitivity, and the one time Rowland met with him during the day he was covered from head to toe. No skin showing."

"Cross isn't old but he's powerful," Jax said, thinking of their tryst on the balcony as the sun had set. "He can withstand sunlight to a point."

"Silver can neutralize a vampire. It burns them. Throw a silver net over one and you have him. I have Foreman working on silver-tipped wooden bullets and stakes. As I said, it must go directly through the heart. Not to the left or the right, a direct hit, Cassidy. Or you'll only piss him off. You'll have everything you need with instructions by the time you leave tomorrow. I want you miked."

Jax shook her head. "No. Cross's sense of hearing is like sonar. I'll attach my GPS chip to my bra or something. You'll be able to follow me. I'll have my cell as well. I'm sure I'll be miked to Cross. He's taking me in, I get to do the dirty work."

"I'll have a dossier on Skarskov to you in an hour."

"I'll be looking for it."

As she hung up, Jax took a deep breath and looked up as Shane entered her room. "I could eat a horse," she said.

"Let's go," Shane said.

No sooner had their steaks been served than Jax's cell rang to the tune of *Godfather Part I*. Shane snorted and shook his head. "Go ahead," she said, eyeing her steak longingly.

"We've got a major problem," Godfather said.

Jax scowled and looked up at Shane.

"Shoot," Jax said.

"Skarskov is undercover FBI."

"No shit."

"He's been under for almost two years and is about to blow the lid off of the Mirov cartel."

"I guess we need to find a way to eliminate him and save him at the same time," Jax said, spearing a chunk of rare filet. She plunked it in her mouth and chewed. "Any ideas how we're going to do that?"

"I'll find a way and get back to you. When do you meet with Mercer?"

"As soon as we're done with dinner, Shane and I are heading down to the marina and waiting for him."

"Keep me posted," Godfather said before he hung up.

Jax looked across the table at Shane and voiced what had been on her mind since they'd left the Rowland estate. "I think Sophia Rowland is involved with a vampire."

Shane rolled his eyes. "Do you know how ridiculous that sounds?"

"How the hell do you think I feel saying it?"

"I'm still not convinced. This is all whoo-whoo stuff."

"Well, get convinced. Godfather spoke with a para-psychologist and there is truth to the urban legends. On top of that, don't forget I've experienced it firsthand. Cross *is* a vampire. He's souped-up strong, fast, he can disappear, he can smell me a mile away, and"—she shivered—"he drank my blood last night." She swept her hair from her neck and showed him her bruise.

"There's nothing there."

Jax hesitated. "So it healed. But I'm telling you, Sophia Rowland smelled weird. Like blood and dominant male, and not the senator's scent."

"How did you get Cross's blood?"

She cut off a chunk of rare beef, plopped it in her mouth and chewed. "I bit him. Twice."

"Jesus!"

"I didn't know what would happen. I was just try-ing to piss him off, egg him on. It worked. I feel differ-ent. Like he must feel but not nearly as strong. But I *am* stronger than I was. Faster. My sense of smell is better. I could smell that dog Maksim's hard-on for Grace. The perv."

Shane looked at her expectantly. "Do you think Maksim planted the picture?"

Jax chewed another piece of beef thoughtfully. "No. He's just hot for the senator's daughter and he really wants to win the election."

"I can't wait to take a crack at Mercer."

"We can't just ask him if he's behind the pictures," Jax said.

"No, but we can begin by asking him if he knows LeVech. We can ask him where he was last night. We can—"

Jax's cell phone rang. "Cassidy."

"It's Naomi. I have an IP addy for you."

Jax smiled. "Go ahead."

"San Francisco City Hall. I've narrowed the computer down to the second floor. Same floor as the mayor's office."

"Bingo! Thanks, Naomi."

Jax hung up. "Shit, I didn't think it was true, despite what Sophia said. But the email came from Mercer. Now, we ask why."

Shane shook his head. "What an idiot. But it still doesn't mean he sent the picture."

"No, but it means, just as you said, he's an idiot. Who knows what an idiot would do?"

As they drove to the marina, Shane updated Dante, who thankfully had no fires for them to put out.

After two hours, *Foreplay* motored leisurely into slip number forty-two.

Minus the mayor.

TWENTY-FIVE

{

High above the city, the chopper steadied as Jax prepared to jump. Spotting the exact rooftop from this height wouldn't be an easy task, and she had no room for error. Giving the aerial map one final glance, she peered through the darkness to the twinkling lights below, then back to the pilot.

"Your target is three hundred meters west. With the wind currents, you should land directly on it," he said.

Jax nodded and positioned herself on the edge of the chopper. Wind blasted her backward, but she hung on and waited for the count.

"Three, two, one, jump!" he called in her headset.

"Geronimo!" she screamed and jumped.

Adrenaline infused her. Cold air rushed up, smashing against her skin. Euphoria claimed her. She could freefall for hours but had less than a minute on the shorter descent.

The harsh rattle of her jumpsuit buffeted by the rush of air filled her ears.

Reaching for the rip cord, she gave it a hearty tug, releasing the black chute. Her armpits felt a mighty tug when the parachute opened and her neck whiplashed backward. Grabbing for the toggles, Jax took control and began to navigate toward the city below. Crosswinds fought to move her off course, but she battled back, steadily falling earthward.

Fixing on her landmarks to the north, east and west, Jax triangulated, focusing on three possible rooftops. She'd known prior to the jump that their similarity to one another would be an issue, but she also knew the closer she came to them, the more distinguished they would become. Circling above, she slowed her descent and picked her landing zone. Increasing her speed now, the rooftop rushed toward her until her final tug on the toggles almost brought her to a hover.

No sooner had her feet hit the gravel and tar surface than a burst of wind swooped her ten feet off the ground and carried her toward the edge of the building, sixty-five stories above the ground. Quickly tugging on the toggles, she sloppily gained control of the chute and was slammed into the roof while being dragged to its edge. Jax dug her heels in hard and pulled with everything she had to rein in the errant chute.

The small wall surrounding the outer edge of the building top was getting closer, and she could see herself being hurled over it. Frantically reaching for her outer right ankle, Jax felt for the sheathed knife strapped to it. The chute continued its pull, and yards were about to become feet. Grasping the knife, she violently slashed at the cords in front of her, the razor-sharp blade severing them upon contact. Freed from the right side, the chute quickly jerked her to the left and spun her backward with the remaining attachments. She slammed into the wall and, reaching overhead, slashed at the straining cords as she felt herself being lifted above the rooftop, her backpack scraping against the wall.

Suddenly, she crashed downward and onto her ass with a mighty thud. She balled up and stowed the freed chute in a tight corner of the roof. Shrugging off the chute container, then the backpack beneath, Jax quickly removed the headset, mic and small radio, and put it on.

"Nighthawk to Coyote, Nighthawk to Coyote, over," she spoke into the mic as she clipped the radio to her belt.

Laughter burst into her ears. "That was some landing," Marcus said from his vantage point in the building across from her.

"Yeah, well, fuck you very much."

"Do you have any idea how much money we could make if that landing were on film?" he asked.

If he'd been within reach, she'd have clobbered him. Granted, she hadn't jumped in a while, but she considered herself an expert. If she hadn't been, she'd have been hanging off the side of the building right now. "Glad you enjoyed the show. Do you have Rapunzel?"

"Wh-what?" he asked, still laughing.

"Rapunzel! Do you have him in sight?"

"Oh, yeah, Rapunzel is in the tower."

Making her way to the west side of the building, Jax got her bearings and looked over the edge to the balconies below.

"One more row north and you'll be right where you need to be," Marcus directed.

"Oh, you feel like working now?"

She crouched alongside the wall as she removed several items from the backpack. Quickly assembling a rope to its anchor and embedding it into the bottom edge of the wall, she prepared for her descent. Removing the

.45 semiautomatic from its shoulder holster, she sharply pulled back on the slide, forcing a round into the chamber. Placing the gun back into the holster, Jax snapped the back strap into place, and it was secure.

Removing a silencer from the backpack, she spilled it into a front cargo pocket on her night cammies. Finally, she removed the night vision goggles from the pack and placed them atop her head.

Standing now, Jax clipped onto the rope and mounted the wall. Adjusting her radio mic so that the wire was loose, she spoke. "You ready to do this?"

"Repeat. You're breaking up," Marcus instructed.

Jax smiled to herself. Loose wire worked perfectly. Or for Marcus, imperfectly. "I said," she shouted, "are you ready to do this?"

"Say again."

She tightened the wire. "Something must have happened to the radio when I hit the wall. Can you hear me now?"

"Yes, I've got you now."

"Are you ready to do this?"

"Are *you* ready, Jax? Once you step off that roof, there's no turning back."

For either one of them. "I know."

"Then fly, baby, fly."

Jax began to rappel down the side of the building. Seventeen stories below, unbeknownst to Cross, the undercover agent patiently awaited her arrival. Slowly, she made her way past one balcony after another until she hung precariously alongside the seventeenth one.

"Any movement inside?" Jax queried and adjusted the wire again.

"You're breaking up again. One more time." Marcus was becoming frustrated. She could hear it in his voice.

"Any movement inside, I asked?"

"Gotcha back now. No, haven't seen him in about thirty minutes," Marcus advised.

"Good, then I'm going in."

"Copy that."

Walking along the wall to her left, away from the balcony, Jax ran back toward the right to generate enough momentum to get her onto the balcony. Too short. Once again, she moved left to run right and this time gently landed on the balcony. Tying off the rope, she quickly removed the gun, crouched and waited for any movement from inside. Retrieving the silencer from her pocket, she screwed it onto the barrel of the gun. It was showtime.

The sliding glass door was open and the curtains fluttered into the living room from the night breeze. *Sure, down here it's a breeze, up on the roof it was a torrent,* she thought. Slowly and deliberately, she stepped through the door into the darkened apartment and out of view of Marcus's watchful eye.

"You're on your own now. I no longer have a visual," Marcus advised, but he got no response.

His frustration mounted.

He didn't like not having contact with Jax. If she needed him, he would not be able to aid her. He also would not be able to hear the hit go down. And Lazarus would want irrefutable proof of Skarskov's death. So did Marcus. Beause if she was playing them . . .

He set his jaw. For her sake, he hoped she wasn't.

Intently, he focused on the balcony of the apartment. Long moments passed, and then he saw it light up with two quick flashes.

"Do you have Rapunzel?"

No reply. More long minutes. "Nighthawk, do you have Rapunzel?" he called. "Damn radios!" he cursed. He didn't understand it. They'd been working fine before. He'd double and triple checked them. Why—

In the framework of the balcony sliding glass door, he could see a lone figure looking back at him. The radio suddenly chirped alive.

"Are you there, Coyote?" Jax's voice broke the silence.

"Affirm!" he responded, letting out a relieved breath.

"Thought I lost you there for a moment."

"You did, damn radios."

"All is well. Mission accomplished."

Marcus watched as Jax took the rope and prepared to make her way to the street below.

"All is not well. Your radio was out again and I wasn't able to hear it go down. Someone is not going to be pleased with this." Hell, he wasn't pleased either. Again suspicion hung like a black cloud around her. He wanted to trust her, damn it, but trust didn't come easily to him, especially with a woman as dangerous as Jax. If she was just posing, if this was all a game, she'd make him look like a fool and he'd have to handle her in a way he did not want to.

"I kind of figured that when I couldn't raise you after I was inside. Not to worry. Now, make your way to the car and pick me up, cuz I'm not gonna hang around this place for long." Jax chuckled. "Get it, hang around?"

"Yeah, you're a regular comedian. I'm on my way."

By the time Marcus came around to their rendezvous spot, Jax was waiting. She hurried and climbed in, and he took off. As he negotiated the city streets back toward the airport, he remained silent. Lazarus would require proof of death. He wouldn't take Jax's word for it. And neither would Marcus.

She looked over at him and smiled. Warmth infused his body. He felt a sense of relief he hadn't expected. He had been genuinely concerned for her welfare. Afraid she might have become the victim and not Skarskov.

"The colonel is going to want proof of death," Marcus said.

Jax's smile deepened. "I'll give it to him."

"What is it?" he asked.

She shook her head. "You're going to have to trust me on this. He gets proof of death when I meet him."

Marcus scowled. He'd been hoping to postpone that meeting as long as possible.

They boarded the private jet that Marcus had arranged for only hours before. When Marcus turned to guide Jax into the cabin, he stopped short.

"Good evening, Marcus," the colonel said from the cockpit doorway.

"Colonel," he said, stiffening and masking his surprise. He reached behind him and drew Jax forward, but he kept her close beside him.

He didn't like surprises, and he didn't trust Lazarus with her. Jax was too much of a prize whether she remained mortal or agreed to change. He felt her stiffen as she made eye contact with the colonel. He also felt the colonel's very primal reaction to her as he walked toward them into the jet's cabin.

"Jax, I'd like to introduce Colonel Joseph Lazarus."

Jax extended her hand. "So, you're the man," she said.

"And you are the woman who has turned my prime operative's head."

Jax smiled. "I feel like family already."

The colonel took her hand and brought it to his lips. He bowed chivalrously and brushed his lips across her skin. Marcus felt an uncontrollable urge to eviscerate his commander. When his lips lingered, Jax carefully withdrew her hand.

"Speaking of family, Miss Cassidy, Marcus tells me you wish to join ours," the colonel said, inviting her with an outstretched hand to sit down. He sat across from her, while Marcus was relegated to the seat in the row behind her.

He remained standing.

"That's right, although not full time. I like my space. I don't do the relationship thing very well, but my work is top-notch."

The colonel's features tightened at Jax's impudence. "Who is your current employer?"

"I just told you, I fly solo."

"How do you know William Rowland?"

"I know *of* him. I did some work for a group interested in seeing how watertight he was."

"What group?"

"I'm not in the habit, sir, of divulging my clients."

"In this case, you either divulge or"—Lazarus smiled,

showing his long yellow teeth—"you won't leave this plane . . . until you do."

Marcus watched Jax carefully, hoping she didn't do anything stupid. If she went for her gun, she'd be dead before she could touch the butt.

Jax shot Marcus a scowl. "You didn't tell me I'd have to give up my sources to this guy."

Marcus smiled tightly. "You didn't ask."

Jax turned her gaze back to Lazarus. "The California Coalition for Conservative Causes. They have money and muscle, and want to make sure the senator was as squeaky clean as he portrays."

"Is he?" Lazarus asked, raising a brow.

Jax nodded. "So far so good. I still have some digging to do, but I think he's on the up-and-up."

"Where do you get your intel?"

"I have sources. *Private*, expensive, reliable sources."

"If you like working on your own, and have such reliable intel, why do you need us? Why should I believe you want to work for The Solution and . . . not destroy it? Or me?"

Jax leaned in. "Look, like I told your boy, Cross, I have my own code. I don't care for scumbags. Neither do you guys. I like nice things. I'm good at what I do and it just so happens to pay for my indulgences. Right now, my pipelines have dried up a little and I'm playing spy instead of soldier. I like the action, the challenge. My work speaks for itself. If I wanted to bring you down, would I be bringing you this . . ."

She slid the backpack from her shoulders, reached in, and extracted a laptop. She handed it to the colonel.

"Skarskov is toast. Mission accomplished. That's really what it's all about, isn't it?"

The colonel opened it. While he waited for it to boot up, he cocked his head and looked closely at her. "I am a patriot, Miss Cassidy. Not a death dealer for profit."

"Like I said, I have my code. I only eliminate scumbags. Scumbags by even a scumbag's definition."

"Did you by chance get a video of the corpse?"

Jax shook her head. "No—"

"I thought audio would suffice, sir," Marcus interjected, "but her mic was damaged during the drop, and I wasn't able to hear the hit go down."

Lazarus looked to Jax. "The laptop is not sufficient evidence."

Jax nodded and dug into her backpack again. "I had a feeling you'd say that." She pulled out a bloody towel and set it on her lap. Carefully, she unwrapped it revealing a severed hand with Skarkov's trademark Grim Reaper tattoo in the palm. Jax picked it up by the thumb and handed it to Lazarus. "Dimitri's left hand. I'd have brought you his head, but I didn't have time, there was someone knocking hard on his door."

Lazarus inspected the hand, then looked over at Jax, then to Marcus, who stared, unblinking, at his commander. "Did you take a picture of his corpse?"

"No, sir. Like I said, he had company. I didn't have much time for the extras."

For several long moments, Lazarus contemplated the hand, the laptop and Jax. Marcus did not offer any support. Nothing he could say or do would sway Lazarus's mind.

"I accept your offering," the colonel said.

Marcus nodded, not admitting to himself how relieved he was.

"Good. Then do we have a deal?" Jax asked, all smiles.

The colonel stood and stepped to the door, tossing the hand out onto the tarmac. He turned and softly said, "I don't make deals, Miss Cassidy. Should I choose to procure your services, I'll contact you." He looked at Marcus. "I'll expect you at dusk." He turned and walked into the night.

Marcus stared after his maker, not liking his tone or his indifference.

Jax looked at Marcus and said, "That guy needs a serious chill pill."

"The colonel has built The Solution from the ground up. He is the best at what he does. We handle serious business. There's little time for shits and giggles."

"All work and no play will kill a person."

Marcus pulled the door shut and secured it as the engines began to rev. Jax's words unnerved him. The colonel did need a chill pill, but tonight he'd been too cool, too accepting. The introduction and dissemination of information had gone too smoothly. Too quickly. If Lazarus had had any intention of using Jax in her mortal form, he'd have vetted her more thoroughly.

That he didn't meant only one thing.

Jax's mortal death and her resurrection as a true Solution operative were imminent. Once turned, Lazarus could control her.

That was absolutely unacceptable.

Not just because Marcus wanted to be the one to control Jax but because he wanted to protect her.

From Lazarus.

And there was only one way a stubborn woman like her would walk away from what she wanted: convince her her services were no longer wanted.

"Prepare for takeoff," the pilot said from his seat in the cockpit.

Jax buckled up. Marcus moved to sit beside her and did the same.

Once they reached cruising altitude, Jax decided she wanted answers from Cross. "Since I bit you, some of your blood got into me," she started, looking over at him. "It made me faster, stronger, more receptive to smells and more intuitive."

Marcus nodded.

"Is that normal?"

Marcus nodded again.

"Is Colonel Lazarus like you?"

Marcus stared hard at her. "I'll take that as a yes," she replied and pushed onward. "Are there more like you?"

He nodded.

"Do you all work for the colonel?"

Marcus sighed and turned to completely face her. He took her face into his hands and looked pointedly at her. "I can't answer your questions, Jax. Not all of them."

"Then I'll ask the colonel."

Marcus scowled. "He's dangerous. For your health, stay away from him."

She pulled away. "It bothers you that he wants me." Jax had felt the colonel's interest when he'd kissed her hand. Not sexual in nature but primal just the same.

Marcus's jaw clenched. "Seek other employment."

Surprise made her eyes widen. Jealousy was one thing, but she'd just killed a man. Well, at least that's what Marcus thought. And now he expected her to just walk away? So he would not have to share her? She shook her head. "I executed the mission flawlessly. I held up my part of the bargain and you held up yours. We both got what we wanted."

Marcus grabbed her by the biceps and shook her. "Listen to me," he hissed. "The colonel is powerful, one of the most powerful of our kind. I can't protect you from him." He shoved her back in her seat.

"You like me," she breathed, and smiled despite the tension. "You *really* like me."

Marcus looked at her like she was crazy, but he shook his head. "You're the most unpredictable female I have ever met, Jax Cassidy."

She leaned in closer to him and said, "I appreciate your chivalry, Marcus, but I haven't survived as long as I have in this profession by being naïve. I can take care of myself when it comes to Lazarus."

"He can turn you against your will."

"Turn me into a *vampire*?"

"Yes."

"Then I guess you'll have to make sure that doesn't happen."

"I cannot challenge my maker."

Startled, she stared at him. First, because she'd never thought she'd hear him speak the word "can't." Second, because he'd revealed something so personal. "So Lazarus created you? How? Why? When?"

Marcus shook his head.

Grrr. "What would happen if you killed him?"

"I would die as well."

Jax sat back, confused. And disturbed. She'd known from the beginning that killing Marcus might be necessary. So why did the idea of him dying at Lazarus's hands—dying at all—make her stomach curl? "A vampire can't kill another vampire?"

"Yes, but one cannot destroy his maker without himself being destroyed. It's our law. It cannot be undone."

Jax nodded. "But if, say, by chance a mortal were to eliminate the colonel, you would survive?"

Marcus raised his brows and asked, "Is Colonel Lazarus on your hit list?"

She swallowed hard and laughed. "Hell, no, he's going to make me rich. Why would I want to eliminate my bread and butter? Just call me curious. But if I had to protect myself from him, I would. Tell me how."

"No mortal can hurt him."

"I don't believe it, there has to be a way for one of me to kill one of you."

"As if I would tell you that," he snorted.

"The sun doesn't affect you?" She remembered the times they'd been together, when the rays of the rising sun had filtered through the windows and illuminated his dark beauty.

Marcus smiled and looked out at the pink horizon. "Early sun and late sun don't affect me, but more than that . . ." He looked at her and cupped her face in his hand, smiling slightly. "I'm not sure why I'm telling you this. Any of this. You'd use it against me, just as you'd use it against the colonel. Would you stake me out and fry me, Jax, if you could?"

"I wouldn't," she whispered, knowing it was true, "but the colonel . . . how about the colonel?"

Marcus shrugged, dropping his hand. "He, too, can withstand the sun with protective measures."

"So let me get this straight. You guys are super-charged. Can do all kinds of things we mortals can't, you drink blood to survive, and only go out at night."

"Yes."

"Do you stay with The Solution because you have to?"

"I stay with The Solution because I believe in what The Solution stands for."

"But—"

He waved away her rebuttal. "In the last seven years, as a Solution operative, I have eliminated dozens of terrorists. Not the minions, but the chieftains. I have prevented two of our embassies in the Middle East from being destroyed, as well as the American School in Amman." He looked hard at her. "Who do you think it was who tipped off the American military about Saddam Hussein's whereabouts? I could have easily done the deed, but it was much more meaningful allowing it to play out the way it did. I work with and for The Solution because it is the only organization on this earth that understands and supports what I am and who I am, and it fights the good fight against those who would harm our country."

He made it sound so romantic, so right. So noble. And to him it was all of those things. She understood. "What's the flip side of all of that?"

Marcus stared out the window for a long time before he answered. "I cannot explain how lost I feel of late. How I—I long for my humanity, Jax."

Compassion for this man overwhelmed her. She slid her hand across his. He grasped it.

"Is there a way to get it back?"

He shrugged, then turned to her. "Lazarus says there is. He's promised it to me."

Ah. That made sense. Explained why a man like Marcus would be working for someone like Lazarus. "In return for . . . ?"

Marcus smiled. "Things."

"Can I help with these . . . things?"

He stared at her. "Why would you want to do that?"

"I think I'd really like you the way you were."

"As opposed to not liking me the way I am?"

She thought about her answer. "I like you just fine. But I don't like the uneven playing field."

Marcus cracked a smile. "I can change that."

Jax's eyes widened at his implication, and she vehemently shook her head. "No. Never."

Marcus's face tightened. Still, as cool as it was having the super skill set Marcus's blood provided, she could not imagine living life as he did, surviving on blood.

"I'm afraid then, Jax, there is nothing you can do to help me."

Jax looked down at their entwined fingers. The urge to protect this man from what he was infused her with such ferocity that she felt the heat of tears. "Can't you just walk away?" she softly asked.

He moved toward her and caught her lips in a soft kiss. "No," he said against her lips, "not if I want to survive."

"What if I told you no matter what, I wanted you to survive?" she asked him. She didn't expect the surprised look he didn't bother to conceal.

Then he smiled and brought her hand to his lips to brush a soft kiss across her knuckles. "You have given me back a piece of my humanity, Jax. For that I will be eternally thankful."

She squeezed his hand and smiled back. "You are eternally welcome."

TWENTY-SIX

Lazarus had not been at his lair for more than an hour before an insistent knock on his door disturbed him.

The whiff of female floral drifted beneath his nose. Sophia.

He'd been expecting her.

A jab of excitement pricked his belly. Sophia Rowland had managed somehow to wheedle herself into his waking thoughts. It had been centuries since he had been intrigued by a woman, and by such a scheming one, never. Perhaps, he mused as he strode slowly to the door, that was what he liked most about her. She was sly, with a steel-trap mind, and she looked ahead for the greater good and was willing to make the hard sacrifices. She was also the key to his wildest dream. Control of the White House.

He smiled. Of course, the greater good for Sophia was herself. That too he understood.

He was feeling a bit festive after meeting the lovely Jax Cassidy. She had delivered vital information to him. Information the U.S. government would go to great lengths to possess. For that alone he'd become a fan and set some of his doubts about her aside. But Skarkov's hand had sealed the deal. Most men he knew would not have had the forethought—or the stomach—to do such a thing. That she did set her apart. Yes, Jax Cassidy would do very nicely for what he had in mind. His initial concerns about her working for the organization Rowland had hired were dispelled. But did that mean Lazarus trusted the woman? No. Never. He trusted no one. She would be watched closely. Very closely.

Marcus was wrong thinking she was associated with the organization Rowland had hired. She could not have done what she'd done last night and work for Rowland. He was too Goody Two-shoes. It was why he was having problems with him now. Marcus and his obvious infatuation with the woman surprised him. He'd have to watch them, but through Jax, Lazarus would have leverage on his number one operative. And if Marcus got out of hand? Then he would be more than happy to take his little toy away.

The knocks became louder, more insistent. Lazarus laughed low. So impatient she was.

He drew the door open with great flourish. "Good morning," he purred.

Her cool blue eyes, so much like her son's, glared at him. She moved haughtily past him. He closed the door behind her and locked it. Then turned and pressed his back to it. He liked it when she was angry. He liked to rough her up. She liked it too. His blood warmed.

She spun around. "How dare you!" she hotly demanded.

Her fury was palpable. His excitement rose. She had never been so angry as she was now. Oh, how she would fight him. He pushed off the door and walked toward her. "How dare I *what*?"

"How dare you offer a contract on my daughter! She is *off* limits!" She slapped him across the face. Blood shot to his groin. He grabbed her hard against his chest, twisting her hands in his fists. "Do not *ever* strike me again if you wish to live," he threatened.

She yanked out of his grip only because he allowed her to.

Lazarus looked hard at her. "The contract was not up for grabs. It was given to a specific operator." He smiled. "You might know him, you gave birth to him thirty-five years ago."

"You are vile, Joseph. The vilest of vile!"

"That may be, darling, but you are a bitch. And you will never win mother of the year, for either of your children."

Sophia paced the carpeted floor of Lazarus's Oakland lair, rubbing her hands and throwing scorching glares his way. "It was not Marcus!"

Suddenly, his amusement and tolerance vanished. His suspicion spiked. A niggling of apprehension gnawed at his gut.

Of course, he couldn't let an iota of weakness show where Sophia was concerned.

Where anyone was concerned. Suspicion was the one thing that had kept Lazarus alive and thriving for a thousand years.

Casually, he opened the lid to his humidor and selected a cigar. As he lit it, he squinted through the blue smoke and asked, "How did you hear about the contract?"

Sophia turned murderous eyes on him. "One of the people Bill hired to take you down told us she was offered the contract. But you can't get to Grace now, Joseph. She's in protective custody."

Her high note of triumph angered him. If he wanted Grace Rowland, he would have her. But more than that, this news of a woman instantly had him thinking of Marcus. And Jax. *Had* she fooled the master?

Lazarus dropped his cigar into the crystal ashtray and approached Sophia.

"Describe this woman."

Sophia clammed up. Such a fool she was. Lazarus reached out and traced his fingers along her slender neck, then grasped her so quickly and so tightly that she could not draw a single breath. She clawed at his hands, her nails leaving bloody wakes. When her face began to turn blue, he released her. Gagging for breath, Sophia slid to the floor.

"Describe her."

After several long minutes, Sophia composed herself enough to stand. She glared at Lazarus but answered, her voice hoarse. "She's a smart-ass with dark hair and big green eyes. My husband thinks she's some kind of super-operative."

"Does this superoperative have a name?"

"Cassidy. Jax Cassidy."

Lazarus's blood steamed. Was Marcus a party to the conniving bitch's ploy? Fury filled him. He could not, *would* not, believe the man he thought of as a son would betray him this way!

"Does she have any accomplices?"

Sophia rubbed her throat and nodded. "Two men. Two very big, capable men."

Lazarus pulled Sophia close to him. She flinched but knew better than to resist this time. Slowly, he caressed her neck with his fingertips. Once again, his long nails scraped light bloody furrows in her creamy skin. She whimpered, trying unsuccessfully to resist him.

"Ah, Sophia, you are so predictable." He wrapped his fingers around her neck and squeezed. He smelled the abrupt release of her musk. "You are a whore." He closed his eyes and inhaled her call to him. He would have her.

They were too much alike, he and she. While he had never really entertained the possibility of turning her as she so desperately wished, he could not deny, despite her weakness for her daughter, that she would make a worthy partner. Perhaps he would reconsider her request, *if* she would make the ultimate sacrifice.

He smiled widely and said in a low, hypnotic voice, "Tell me everything, Sophia, tell me everything and I will reward you with my blood."

Her blue eyes darkened. He felt her body shudder in excitement and, he supposed, in fear. After all, what he offered was heady, exciting, and could be deadly if not dispensed in exact measures. "I saw Marcus at the fund-raiser. I know he recognized me," she breathlessly said. She looked up at him, her eyes widened, and Lazarus fought a smile as the truth dawned on her. "But you knew he would, didn't you? You sent him there. Why? To kill me? To kill Grace?" Sophia closed her eyes, then opened them. "What I don't understand is, if he was there to hurt my Gracie, why did the Cassidy woman say she was offered the contract? He knows Grace is his half sister. Is my son so heartless? Or maybe that's why he didn't have her—"

Lazarus laughed low. "What? You think he felt swayed by his DNA? Called off the hit? No, Marcus doesn't have that kind of softness in him, Sophia. You killed it long ago. More likely, this Jax Cassidy is lying about the hit. But why?"

Lazarus dug his thumbnail into Sophia's jugular. She gasped but did not pull away. Warm, sweet blood oozed from the small puncture. "I assure you, darling, she will divulge her reasons to me." Lazarus inhaled the scent of her blood. "And if your son . . ." He didn't have to finish the sentence. If Marcus was playing him, he was dead. Period.

He licked the column of her neck. Sophia moaned, melding her warm, soft body against his.

"Joseph," she begged, "please, take me, now, like you did last week."

"In good time, darling, in good time. Now, tell me more."

She shuddered and licked her lips, clearly struggling to speak. "I . . . tried to talk to Bill again about accepting Calhoun's running mate offer. But he refused to entertain the thought. So, I-, I did something I thought would nudge him."

Lazarus licked the slow stream of blood on Sophia's neck. "What did you do?"

"Something stupid. Something very bad."

He checked his frustration. "Darling, you are very good at doing very bad things."

"Grace, she—she was seeing her counselor. I knew about it. I know everything my daughter does. I set up a camera in their love nest."

He paused, then *tsk*ed. "Oh, Sophia, you didn't?" he laughed.

"I planted a picture of them at the fund-raiser. I made it look like it was Mercer blackmailing Bill. I thought if

Bill saw them and blamed Mercer, he would step down, knowing he would not want to humiliate Grace. Then he would have no choice but to take the VP position. Because Bill refused Senator Calhoun's repeated pleas, Calhoun has now chosen Missouri senator Nathanial Bond as his running mate."

"But there has been no announcement," he bit off, furious she would do such a thing, thereby compromising all he had worked for, and then not inform him.

"They won't make the announcement until right before the convention next week."

"So there is still time. Time to change Calhoun's mind."

Sophia drew away from him. "What are you saying, Joseph?"

"There is still time to convince William."

"But how," she said, eyes wide, "can he? When Bond has accepted the nomination."

Lazarus stared at her, knowing she knew the answer. And was counting on Lazarus to do what needed doing. And he would.

"I suppose, then, Bond will have to step down."

Sophia laughed caustically. "That power monger won't step down. He's all but flaunted it in our faces."

"Leave that to me, my dear." He smiled down at her. "Now, what are we to do about those nasty pictures?"

Smiling, Sophia kissed the edge of his mouth, then slowly licked his fangs, making him shudder. "Alan LeVech, the man Grace was seeing," she whispered. "He's dead. Murdered. His wife too."

"Such a tragedy, and just when they had had such a lovely dinner in the city, too."

Sophia stiffened. "You killed him? You already knew?"

Lazarus dipped his head to her neck and licked the blood there. "My darling, I know everything. I've known about your daughter and her dirty little secret for months. It's my job to know everything. Never doubt that." What he hadn't known, however, was that Marcus not only was sleeping with the enemy, but he'd fallen for her as well. Why else would he have instructed her to eliminate Grace before he'd talked to Lazarus about bringing Jax in?

"Why did you kill LeVech?"

"Because, as you know, I don't care for loose ends, and he had the potential of being a very costly loose end. Now those pictures you let slip, even if they leaked, portray nothing but a deviant taking advantage of a young, innocent girl. LeVech takes the fall, not Grace, and not your husband."

"But don't we—"

"We want Rowland to be VP, you fool," he snapped, "and what would be a smudge on a senator's career would destroy a VP candidate."

"What do we do now?" she asked, closing her eyes as his warm breath caressed her skin.

"Right now, I'm going to take what you so selflessly offer, and then I will return the favor."

And later he was going to pay the honorable Johnny Mercer a visit and make him an offer he couldn't refuse.

Several hours after leaving Marcus, Jax tried to fall asleep. She couldn't. Visions of Marcus and their last conversation kept her awake. They had crossed an emotional line, both of them. They were no longer pitted foes but champions of patriotism—just on different teams. But his team not only did damage to innocents but it also threatened the security of the government of the United States of America.

The Solution had to be destroyed. That meant Lazarus and his operatives.

Including Marcus. She rolled over and stared at the ceiling. Would Marcus have been so beholden to the colonel if he hadn't held Marcus's humanity in his hands? Was he really so much like Lazarus, or more like her? Could he be convinced to switch sides?

"Jesus!" When had this become so complicated? She rubbed the heels of her hands into her eyes, trying to blot out the image of Marcus lying dead at her feet. He wasn't the monster he wanted her to believe he was. He had a soul. She'd seen it! If he hadn't, he couldn't have felt the things he felt. He wouldn't have shared like he did. He would not have been capable of the tenderness he showed her.

He would have let her shoot his half sister and his witch of a mother, too.

Her cell phone vibrated. "Cassidy," she said as a yawn caught her.

"Hey," Shane said. "How'd it go?"

Jax smiled. "The cadaver hand was a brilliant idea. Lazarus bit. He bit at the altered intel on the laptop too. I'm in. Next time I see him, it's adios."

There was a slight pause, then he finally said, "Nice work, Jax."

She smiled, then realized why. He'd used her first name for the first time since she had met him.

Her smile deepened, and she felt as if she really had

arrived. She respected the hell out of Shane. She was pleased it was reciprocated.

"Did Godfather let you know the agent posing as Skarskov has been successfully extracted and the shit is hitting the fan all over Mirov's empire?" he asked.

"No, but he said they were working on it. I'm glad to hear they got him out of there. It's a win-win all around."

"I'm getting ready to head over to City Hall, then I'm going down to the San Mateo coroner's office. The autopsy should be done on the LeVechs. Get some sleep and call me when you wake up. We'll meet and compare notes."

"Sounds like a plan." Jax hung up, wanting to go with Shane to roll Mercer, but knowing she'd be better served resting up for her next encounter with Marcus and Lazarus. Besides, Shane could handle it.

As for Marcus . . .

She turned on her side and stared at the empty space beside her. Smoothing her hand against the sheet, she closed her eyes and imagined Marcus's hands stroking her body and his gentleness followed by his unbridled passion. She caught her breath. She wanted to go there again.

She opened her eyes. Perhaps something could be arranged. Perhaps if they found a way to help him out from under Lazarus's thumb, there could be hope for him. But until she knew that, until Lazarus was dead, she couldn't risk it.

Bottom line, her job was to eliminate Lazarus and anyone who got in her way. If the colonel didn't call in the next forty-eight hours, she'd find a way to get to him, and then end this.

Another mammoth yawn caught hold of her. Hours ticked by until, finally, Jax was able to quiet her brain and sleep.

The ringing phone woke her. She fumbled in the darkness for the handset, muttering about her damn wake-up call.

Whoa. Darkness? She shot out of bed and looked out the window. *Shit!* It was past sunset. She'd missed twleve calls on her cell. She yanked up the hotel phone.

"Cassidy."

She held her breath, waiting for the blowup that she instinctively knew was coming.

"Shane's missing," Dante said. "He hasn't checked in since he left for the mayor's office this morning."

The blood drained to her toes.

TWENTY-SEVEN

Lazarus was seated in a brand-new wingback chair, smoking a cigar, when Marcus entered his lair shortly after sunset. As they stared at each other, Lazarus failed for the very first time to offer Marcus a cigar. Warily, Marcus looked around.

The place was pristine, with no hint of the battle they'd waged days before. Marcus, however, wasn't sure it would stay that way for long. He knew immediately, based on the dark energy reverberating off the walls, that Lazarus was furious.

Furious at him.

"What's wrong?" Marcus asked, striding confidently into the room.

"You tell me, Marcus."

Marcus stopped short. There was that scent again. Female floral mixed with blood. His nostrils flared and he glanced down the hall, half expecting to see a woman standing there. Instead, the hall was empty.

"Answer me," Lazarus growled.

Marcus turned to look at him. His creator. Not the brilliant military mind or stalwart patriot he'd long thought him to be, but a male with basic needs. And flaws. Flaws Marcus knew were now growing more and more dangerous for him every day.

"You have me at a disadvantage, sir," Marcus said.

"Jax Cassidy."

Marcus's heart rate hitched up several notches. "What about her?"

"She's not an independent at all. She works for Rowland."

Marcus should not have been surprised. When it came to her, he'd thought with his dick from their first meeting. "In what capacity?"

"Your initial suspicions proved correct. She is part of the organization he hired to protect him and to infiltrate The Solution. She has succeeded in both. And now her mission is apparently to destroy us all. Including you."

Marcus moved over to the sliding glass door and pushed the heavy brocade curtains aside. Subtle pink strands of the receding sun filtered through the window. He stared at the halo of the sun as it made its final descent of the day. He felt like he'd just been kicked by a mule in the gut. He was her mark? Why hadn't she done the deed?

What a fool he'd been. He'd actually started to trust her. She was a lie. All of it, lies.

"I didn't know," Marcus said.

"How could you not?" Lazarus said from behind him. "Why did you offer her the contract on the Rowland girl?"

Marcus turned around and cocked his head. There was only one way Lazarus could know that: if Jax had told him. Heat filled his limbs. She'd gone behind his back? He felt sick to his stomach, refusing to believe that after what they had shared in the plane she would do it.

But Lazarus knew only what Marcus or Jax could tell him. And Marcus hadn't.

Betrayed again.

"A test, to see if she was what she said she was. I called her off, sir, *after* I realized Grace Rowland was my sister!" Marcus began to pace the room. "Her mother is the bitch who gave birth to me, then deserted me when I was less than a month old."

"I am well aware of your circumstance, Marcus."

Marcus pressed his fingers to the bridge of his nose and closed his eyes. He lowered his hands and inhaled the sultry air in the room. That scent. He'd smelled it in the Green Room at the fund-raiser. In a moment of clarity, he knew who it belonged to. His blood chilled to ice in his veins. More betrayal! This time by his maker. Marcus tamped down his skyrocketing temper.

He turned to stare at his creator. "Why, then, would you demand I destroy my own flesh and blood?"

"I suppose you could say it was my way of testing you. You have seemed . . . distant of late. I needed to know you are still focused on The Solution's cause."

"My focus has not wavered."

"I am glad to hear that, Marcus." Lazarus moved to his humidor and opened the lid. He took his time selecting a cigar. When he finally did, he handed it to Marcus. Marcus accepted it but did not move to clip it or light it.

"I've done a little bit of my own investigating recently, Marcus, and, along the way, discovered some rather useful facts." He took the cigar from Marcus and cut it, then handed it back to him.

"Apparently, the mayor who is running against Senator Rowland has some dirt on our man Rowland. Dirt that will make it impossible for the 'Family Values' candidate to secure another term."

He reached into a drawer and pulled out a photo, which he held up for Marcus to view. "You can see what your little sister has been up to."

Marcus growled.

"I told you she was not innocent. Apparently, the mayor knew it too. He's blackmailing the senator with these pictures and a few others. Needless to say, the senator will not continue this campaign."

"How will The Solution be funded?"

Lazarus smiled a devilish smile. "As vice president, Rowland will be able to pull a few strings."

Marcus scowled. "I don't follow."

"It's quite simple, really. The GOP candidate, Calhoun, wanted Rowland, who declined the offer. He then offered the position to Senator Bond of Missouri. They plan to make the announcement at the end of the week. But I'm afraid the senator from Missouri is going to find himself permanently incapacitated, courtesy of The Solution. Rowland will graciously accept the VP nomination, leaving the senate seat to Mercer."

"What prevents someone else from running against Mercer?"

"Nothing, but it won't matter. Mercer will have momentum on his side. He's already quite popular with his fellow Californians."

Marcus scowled deeper. "What has Senator Bond done to threaten this country?"

"As VP, he would impede our work. Therefore he must be eliminated."

Marcus didn't like it. "The Democratic presidential candidate is leading the polls by twenty-three percent."

"Not for long. He has a few dirty little secrets that will surface when the time is right. Calhoun will win in a landslide, with Senator Rowland by his side, and ultimately, with me at his side, as well."

Marcus hid his concern. The colonel was traversing a very slippery slope. "Why are you telling me all of this?"

"Because, Marcus, I need to know I can trust you."

"*I* have not broken our trust, sir." His implication was clear. His creator had broken Marcus's trust several times. When he'd sent him after his own sister. Now . . .

"Perhaps not. But you must understand, I cannot allow Miss Cassidy to survive."

Marcus's head snapped back. "Why not?"

"Because," Lazarus sighed, "she works for an organization that is financially backed and government-sanctioned. Her sole mission is to eliminate The Solution."

"How do you know this?"

"I have one of her fellow operatives in my possession at the moment. He's not very forthcoming with information, but I extracted enough from his cell phone to put two and two together."

Marcus set the unlit cigar aside. Despite his anger at Jax's double-dealing, he understood her principles. She believed The Solution was the enemy. He would do the same in her shoes. Because of his beliefs. But could he . . . ? Mentally, he braced himself.

"I'll turn her before I kill her," he said.

Lazarus smiled that nasty smile of his again. "You won't be able to control her. I want her eliminated. Tonight. Then I want you to fly to D.C. and make sure

Senator Bond has an unfortunate accident before the press conference on Friday."

Marcus wanted Jax alive, for purely selfish reasons. She had touched something profound in him that had died years ago. He wasn't ready to give it or her up. Not now. Marcus decided to light the cigar after all. As he did, he eyed the colonel. He could challenge him. He'd probably lose, but then again, he might beat him. And if he did, then what? Rurik would mete out his own punishment.

"I'm not going to eliminate Miss Cassidy, sir. She'd be an invaluable asset to The Solution."

"Do you defy me?"

Marcus locked gazes with his maker. "On this, yes."

"She may very well be invaluable to you—in terms of keeping your dick satisfied—but she could just as easily be our demise. I will not take a chance!"

"I will." Marcus held his hand up when Lazarus made to move toward him. "I have followed every order you have issued me, sir, not only as a mortal but as I am now. I gave my life over to you that night seven years ago. I have not asked you for one thing. As for this? Do not deny me."

Lazarus sat back, his expression stunned. "Marcus, don't you see she has weakened you?"

"You are wrong. She has empowered me. I will take full responsibility for her change, and for her, once she becomes one of us."

"If she betrays us?"

"Then I will destroy her."

Lazarus puffed on his cigar, contemplating Marcus's request. Finally, he nodded. "Turn her, Marcus. Then take her with you to D.C. Do not return until Senator Bond is no more."

"Thank you, sir." Marcus stubbed out his cigar. Euphoria flooded his veins. Not because he was going to turn Jax. She would hate him throughout eternity if he forced her to turn, and he couldn't live with that. Not anymore.

No, his euphoria was bittersweet. Because on this night, he would spare her life, even if it meant he would never see her again. Even if it meant defying Lazarus, his maker and the only one who could destroy him.

He smirked. Looked like he had retained some semblance of humanity after all.

As Marcus reached to open the door, he turned to Lazarus. "Before I do this, I need you to tell me one thing. Who told you I offered Jax the contract on Grace?"

Lazarus simply smiled.

"I did, darling," a voice from his past said.

Violent rage rushed up from the very depths of his being, cold, hard hatred infiltrated every cell in his body. Marcus turned and glared at the impeccably dressed woman. She wore a flowing white peignoir and was gliding effortlessly toward him.

The shock must have registered on his face. Oh, not that she was here. He'd suspected that. He was shocked because she was no longer as before.

Now she was like him.

Lazarus had turned her.

She laughed. The deep, confident laugh of a woman who thought she was invincible.

"Why?" Marcus demanded, turning to his maker.

Lazarus smiled and strode toward Sophia. "I could not resist. How could I when she made the ultimate sacrifice?"

Blind rage, so complete that Marcus could scarcely focus consumed him. She had manipulated everyone and was clearly willing to abandon another child—this time, Grace—for her own immortality!

"Marcus, you have grown into a man any mother would be proud of."

He set his jaw and spoke in slow, measured words. "And you have grown into a more remarkable bitch than when you deserted me."

She smiled a beautiful, tolerant smile. "I was young, Marcus. I thought I was in love."

"Save your spiel for my sister. Maybe she'll buy it."

"I'm afraid Gracie will become an unfortunate casualty."

Marcus moved closer to her. "Is anyone or anything sacred to you?"

She gazed at him with a clear conscience. He could see it behind the evil in her eyes. "Marcus, you of all people know emotions cloud judgment. I cannot afford to have a lapse of judgment." She turned and pressed her hand to the colonel's chest. "Joseph has promised me the world. The price is your sister."

"No, Mother, Grace will not be a pawn in your vicious power games."

"You cannot stop me," she said with such an air of confidence that Marcus felt the hair rise on the back of his neck. He believed her. And one day she would be more powerful than Lazarus. He looked to the colonel, who stood quietly beside her.

"Think twice," Marcus whispered. In a lightning-quick movement, he grabbed the crystal ashtray on the sideboard next to him and smashed it in half. Using the jagged edge of the piece in his hand as a knife, in a violent swipe, he severed Sophia's head from her shoulders.

Lazarus screamed furiously and grabbed at the crumbling body. As her head toppled to the floor and rolled several feet away, Lazarus's screams of despair turned to rage.

Marcus reached down and grabbed the head by its short blonde hair. As he stared at the wide eyes and gaping pink mouth, he felt nothing but contempt. How could he feel anything more than hatred? She'd been evil through and through. He tossed the head to the floor, where it rolled to a stop at Lazarus's feet. "I have just saved us both from a world of hurt."

Lazarus puffed up. His eyes glowed molten red, and his fangs descended. "You fool!"

Marcus cocked a brow, not caring he had just destroyed his maker's chosen one. "You cared for her that much?"

"I cared for the political positioning of her husband. As a widower, he's far less likely to be voted VP now."

Marcus shook his head. "So that's all there is to you. Power, not justice. Not what we've fought so hard for."

"You have exhausted all of my patience, Marcus." Lazarus straightened.

"Meaning?" Marcus asked.

Lazarus pointed a long finger at Marcus. "An eye for an eye!"

Realization dawned and Marcus cursed.

"By your own hand, sever Jax Cassidy's head and bring it to me. Fail and I will destroy you both!"

TWENTY-EIGHT

J ax ran up the steps to City Hall, hoping she could get in and, more importantly, that there would be someone there to help her. Lucky for her, the building was still open. She ran up to the mayor's second-floor offices. She half expected Mercer to be in, pretending he worked hard for the city and would do the same for all of California's residents.

Although the smarmy bastard wasn't there, his assistant was.

The buxom blonde was just pulling her purse out from her desk drawer.

Jax didn't waste a precious second. "Was a Mr. Shane Donavan here to see the mayor today?"

"I beg your pardon?" the woman breathed. She was so overtly sexy that it made Sophia's accusations of sexual harassment by Mercer even more ludicrous. This woman was most definitely more Mercer's type than Sophia Rowland.

Jax stepped threateningly closer. "Did Shane Donovan see the mayor here today? Big guy, about six four, blond-haired, Australian accent?"

The blonde pursed her lips stubbornly. Jax snapped.

She grabbed Blondie by the front of her shirt and shoved her against the wall. "Look, sister, this is a matter of life and death. Now answer me!"

"No, he didn't," the woman sputtered.

Not good. If Shane had at least been here, Jax could have gotten a handle on time, and where he might have gone from here. She thought for a moment, then returned her steely gaze to the blonde. "Did anyone show up who wasn't scheduled? And where is the mayor now?"

The woman's eyes bugged out of her head. She looked terrified, and not of Jax. "Tell me who was here," Jax shrieked, "or you'll have me to worry about on top of them!"

The blonde whimpered and licked her lips. "A man," she began softly. She cleared her throat. "H-he told me to forget I ever saw him."

"What time?"

She glanced at the clock on the wall. "About an hour ago."

"What did he look like?"

"Sixties, bald, I think. He was wearing black from head to toe, including a hat, gloves and dark glasses."

Jax cursed softly. Lazarus.

"And you didn't think that was odd? That he didn't want anyone to—"

"H-he was very convincing. When he left, the mayor was whistling Dixie. So no harm."

Yeah. No harm. Except for Shane. "Where is the mayor?"

"I don't know, honest. He canceled his last appointment. He said he would see me in the morning."

Jax released the woman. "Call him."

"Mayor Mercer?"

"Yes."

Blondie looked like she was going to refuse, but Jax got back in her face. *"Now."*

The woman picked up her cell and hit a speed-dial number.

"It's me," she said.

Jax grabbed the phone from her. "Mr. Mayor, my name is Jax Cassidy. I work for the FBI and I have a most urgent matter to discuss with you. I need to meet you ASAP."

He hung up on her.

Jax looked incredulously at the phone. She hit redial and got his voice mail. "Look, you smarmy bastard, national security is at stake here. Whatever Lazarus told you today—whatever he threatened you with—is not going to be half as bad as what I'll do to you. I work for an organization protecting Rowland from Lazarus. He is a killer, do you understand me? He will use you and spit you out. Call me at 877-550-9210. NOW. Or I swear to God, I will kill you myself."

She hung up and threw the phone down on the desk, then ran from the building, leaving Blondie to gape after her like a thirsty fish.

She hailed a cab and headed for the Rowland estate, hoping Shane was somehow there, and kept telling herself that Shane was a big boy and could handle himself. But Jax knew he would not be able to hold his own against Lazarus or any of his kind.

A sudden sobering thought occurred to her. What if Marcus was the one who'd taken Shane?

He'd once said he'd get information out of her team if she wouldn't cooperate.

She shook her head. No, Marcus and Lazarus believed

she was on their side. Unless. *Shit!* Unless they'd found out Skarskov was not dead.

But how? She remembered talking to Shane about it on the phone. Had his calling her by her first name been a clue, rather than a sign of affection? Had it even been Shane on the phone with her? *Shit!*

Jax called Dante. "Any word?"

"None," he said grimly.

"I'm on my way to the Rowlands'. Maybe the senator has something."

"No one there. Grace is in the safe house, the Mrs. took off early this morning to Carmel for a fund-raiser luncheon, and the senator is in Sac meeting with the governor."

Shit! Shit! Shit!

"Dante, I'm scared."

"I am, too," he said quietly.

"They have Shane," she gritted out. "I know it. He never showed up at the mayor's office, but Lazarus did, about an hour ago. I know he spoke with Mercer. When I called that prick, he hung up on me! I don't know what Lazarus said or threatened him with, but he wouldn't answer his phone when I called back."

"Shane never showed up at the San Mateo coroner's office either."

Jax set the phone aside, slapped on the glass partition, and yelled at the driver. "Take me to the Sokko on Filmore." She put the phone back to her ear. "I'm going to my hotel room and summoning Cross."

"How are you going to do that? And what the hell for? You really think he's going to help?"

She rubbed her temple. "Yes. No. I don't know. But he'll come." He had to!

"I'll be right there."

"No, Dante. He'll know you're there and might stay away. Stand by for my call."

"I don't like this, Cassidy."

"I don't either, but I don't know what else to do!"

"I'll get a ping on the cell towers and see if we can locate Mercer. I don't know how, but he's involved in this mess."

Jax took a big, deep breath. "Stand by, Dante. This ride is going to get wicked."

"It already has."

"Marcus Cross! Come here now!" Jax screamed from her balcony. Her throat was raw. For over an hour, she had called for Marcus. He hadn't come to her.

Damn bastard. This was all his fault. His fault for being involved with Lazarus. For making her let her guard down and believe she could trust him. What had she been thinking? He was the same, same as Lazarus—

Fairness demanded that she stop her foolish thoughts. She slammed her palm against a wall and took a deep breath. This wasn't Marcus's fault. Not that she knew of, but she was terrified for Shane. For herself.

For all of them.

"Please, God, let him be OK," she prayed.

But she knew he wasn't. There was only one reason he was gone: The Solution had him, and it was her fault, not Cross's.

Somehow, some way, she'd messed up. She'd been

too cocky. Sparring with Marcus and thinking she'd had them all fooled, when all along—

She squeezed her eyes shut when the images of Alan LeVech's bloody body flashed in her mind's eye. "No!" she shouted. She could not stand the image of Shane lying in his own blood, his throat ripped from his body.

No more messing up. No more.

Quickly, she dressed in a pair of black cargo pants, a black wife beater and an old pair of worn combat boots. She hauled the metal ammo box that had been delivered earlier onto the bathroom counter. It was chock-full of vampire killing ammunitions.

She picked up her pistol and loaded it with the silver-tipped wooden rounds, then grabbed the extra magazines of the same, stored them with the pistol in her holster, then, for good measure, shoved a few loose bullets in her pants pocket on instinct. Next she grabbed three silver-tipped wooden stakes and slid them into her thigh pockets. Lastly she grabbed a thick silver chain and dumped it in her hip pocket. She shoved several smaller ones in her back pockets.

She was armed to the teeth and dared any vampire, even one as powerful as Lazarus, to mess with her.

She strode into the bedroom and gasped. Marcus stood at the door.

She rushed him and began pummeling him. "Where is he? What have you done with Shane?"

Marcus grabbed her, holding her flaying fists away from him.

Jax wrenched away and reached for her Glock. Marcus knocked it from her hand and threw her onto the bed.

"Who are you really?" he demanded.

"Where is Shane?" she cried, coming at him again.

He tossed her back onto the bed and followed her there, pushing her back into the pillows. "Answer me."

Anger rolled off him in harsh waves. His eyes were red, his fangs drawn. It was time. Only the truth would suffice. If it would save Shane, then she would divulge all. "My name is Jax Cassidy. I work for a covert government-sanctioned operation. My mission isn't just to protect Rowland but to infiltrate The Solution, then destroy Lazarus, as well as his operatives."

"Including me?"

She nodded. "Including you."

He stared at her, then stiffly moved away, picking up the gun from the floor. He chambered a round and handed it to her. "Then do it."

Her heart stopped beating for a moment. She took the weapon and aimed it at his heart. "Tell me where Shane is and I'll let you live."

"I don't know where he is."

She moved the barrel a hair to the right and pulled the trigger. A bullet tore through his right shoulder. His body recoiled from the impact, but he didn't make a sound. Just remained standing. His eyes narrowed. His dark shirt dampened with blood. She aimed at him again. "I don't believe you."

"I don't care what you believe." He stepped toward her again. She pulled the trigger and hit his left shoulder. He barely recoiled. A twin bloodstain to the one on his right shoulder erupted.

"Another step and this one goes into your heart."

"Kill me and you kill yourself."

"I doubt it."

"Lazarus gave me the kill order on you tonight."

"Lucky me."

"I convinced him to allow me to turn you."

"Never!"

He smiled then, despite his wounds and the blood. "How did I know you'd say that?" He looked out into the darkness, then back to her. "You give me no choice then. You're coming with me." He grabbed at her, but she danced away.

"Is it that easy for you? Killing me?"

His eyes widened and he threw back his head and laughed. The sound wasn't pleasant. "You just shot me. Twice. I could ask the same of you."

"I didn't kill you. Yet." *I never wanted to kill you,* she thought. *Not after having you. Knowing you.*

"Nor will you, Jax."

"You don't think I can," she challenged.

"No," he said softly, "but more importantly, if you kill me tonight, Lazarus will come after you, and he will find you and kill you, but before he does, he will make you wish you had never been born."

She believed him. Even if she hadn't met Lazarus, she could see the honesty in Marcus's gaze. But she *had* met Lazarus. She knew perfectly well what he was capable of—sending his team member to kill his own sister being only the beginning. "So you're being all knight in shining armor by offering to kill me instead? Without the torture first?"

He hesitated. "Yes."

"Why would you even care?"

He set his jaw. "Because."

"Because isn't a reason."

"It's the only one you're going to get."

Jax changed her tactics. "Why work for Lazarus when you can work for the real good guys?"

He looked bored all of a sudden. "I do work for the real good guys."

"No, you don't. Lazarus is a terrorist with delusions of grandeur. The more he kills, the more trouble he makes for the U.S. government. It's men like him, blinded by what they think is right, who jeopardize the freedoms over a million Americans have died to protect." Jax looked hard at him, as if seeing him for the first time. "Did you lose your sense of humanity when you became like him?"

He snarled and moved so close to her that she felt his breath on her cheek. "Careful, girl. Talk about the pot and the kettle. Besides, you don't know me. You don't know how I think, how I feel. Don't pretend to."

"I know your type," she spat, still thinking of Shane. "Anything goes so long as it's in the name of patriotism. You're no different than those fanatic Jihadists."

He grabbed the gun from her hand, stunning her with his quickness and strength. Then he grabbed her, trying to drag her to the door. She twisted, and kicked him hard in the groin.

"Stop fighting me, damn it," he growled. "I'm not going to kill you. I'm going to give you something I have never given to any soul I have been sent to eliminate."

She stilled, then almost gasped when she remembered the silver chain in her pocket. "What?"

He spun her around and cupped her face in his hands. "Your life."

She gripped the chain in her pocket. "What about Shane?"

"If Lazarus has him, no one can help him now."

Jax felt as if the air had been knocked out of her chest. Her team meant everything to her, yet he would do nothing to help.

But why would he? she thought. Would she have given Lazarus quarter? Still, the betrayal burned almost hotter than her body had when he'd touched her intimately.

"I thought you would be different, Marcus. I thought—" She shook her head. She was a fool. "I thought what happened here—"

His eyes had turned a cold, frosty blue. "Don't let the sex muddy up the waters, Jax. I gave you what you wanted and you lost. Now move on."

She glared at him from watery eyes. "I already have."

Whipping out her hand, she lassoed the chain around his neck, cringing when she felt the heat of the contact and heard him groan in pain.

He released her, and she roped another foot of chain around his neck, pressing it into him until he was so weak that she knocked him unconscious. His skin burned where the silver touched. Call her crazy, but she felt—compassion. *Shit.* She reached down and unwound the chain, leaving it laying across his neck. There, he'd be down, but he would not asphyxiate. She owed him that much.

When he came around, she'd be long gone and Lazarus eliminated.

She ran out of the room, blinking back tears that clouded her vision. When she reached the lobby, she took a moment to think.

She grabbed her cell phone and called Godfather.

"Black," he said.

"Sir," Jax whispered.

"Cassidy?" he asked, anxious.

"Yes, sir. I have bad news."

"Go ahead."

"By all accounts, we've lost Donovan."

She told him everything then. When she was done, he called her home.

"No, sir. I have a mission to complete. Lazarus must be destroyed."

"Listen to me, Cassidy," he urgently said. "We need to regroup. We need to rethink this one."

"No, sir," she softly said. "I'm fully armed. There's nothing to rethink." She hung up then and moved.

She wouldn't return to L.O.S.T. until Joseph Lazarus was dead.

*

TWENTY-NINE

"Looking for me?" Lazarus asked from the shadows.

Jax smiled to herself. Her tactic had worked: Feign vulnerability and the bad guy will reveal himself. Slowly she turned around and came face-to-face with evil incarnate.

"I applaud your tenacity, Miss Cassidy," he said. "But I must chide you on your stupidity."

Jax cocked a brow.

"Only an idiot would walk the streets of Oakland late at night and dare me to show myself."

"Ah." Jax smiled and slowly moved her hand across her chest. "Why don't you come closer. I double dare you."

The bastard actually snorted. "Bullets cannot hurt me."

Well, fuck, she thought. If that was true, she was in for a world of hurt. *If* it was true. "Let's find out, shall we?"

He was as fast as Marcus. Maybe faster. Before she was halfway to her pistol, he grabbed her hands and hoisted her a foot above the sidewalk. He threw her hard against the building wall behind her. She hit with a sickening thud. Pain flashed through her nervous system. It took her several moments to gain her wits and realize nothing vital was broken.

She looked up into his demonic stare. She slid her

right hand into her pants pocket and gripped the stake there.

He smiled, showing long yellow fangs. "Now, Miss Cassidy, we'll see what you're really made of." He squatted down to face her. In a quick, underhanded jab, she stabbed him in the chest with the stake. Lazarus hissed in shock. His eyes widened.

"Did you really think I was so naïve?" She grabbed the other stake and shoved it through his throat. Blood gurgled as he tried to breathe.

She kicked him away from her with her boot. As he tumbled backward, he yanked the stake from his throat, then the one from his chest. As he stood, he threw them to the ground. The blood flow immediately dried up.

"Did you really think I was so weak?" he sneered.

He backhanded her so hard that her body spun like a top out of control and she crashed into the wall again. This time her head hit first with a terrible thunk. Then her world went black.

Jax moaned as another violent wave of electricity ripped through her body. She screamed and the voltage amped up. Her body jerked as she hung, helpless, like the catch of the day. She dangled, a foot off the floor, from chains attached to large meat hooks in what smelled like an abandoned meat-packaging plant. Her torturer moved the cloth-covered shock paddles from her belly, then ran a sharp-tipped finger across the rise of her breast. Jax kicked at him. He laughed and moved away from her. He set the paddles on a table with a few other undesirable items, including a meat hook and cleaver.

Jax stared at her feet, her limp, sweaty hair hanging

in her face, trying not to whimper at the thought of that cleaver cutting through her skin. Tamping down on the overwhelming need to retch, she slowly lifted her chin and stared at the bastard in front of her. He made no effort to hide what he was. A vampire. Heartless.

If she'd met him on the street, she might have given him a second look. He was southern California handsome, a surfer with shaggy blonde hair. His red-rimmed brown eyes ruined the look.

"Who are you?" Jax hoarsely asked. He grinned. His fangs glowed under the harsh light.

"I'm Gideon."

"Where's Lazarus?"

Deep, blood-curling screams echoed into the room from somewhere down the corridor. Jax's skin chilled even more, and her heart pounded so hard that she almost passed out. Gideon smiled. "He's a little busy at the moment, but he asked me to soften you up for him."

Another round of harsh screams rent the air. They were followed by a familiar voice cursing Lazarus for the bastard he was.

"Shane," she whispered. Despite their predicament, hope washed over her.

He was still alive!

"A friend of yours?" Gideon asked, laughing. "Your relief is premature."

She narrowed her eyes at his arrogance, then closed them to shut him out. To gather her wits.

Jesus, help me, she prayed. *Help me think. Process.*

She opened her eyes, urging herself on. *Look, Jax. See where you are. Find what you can use to gain the advantage.*

The room they were in wasn't large. The bloodstained cinder-block wall to her back was as close as the ones at her sides. Maybe six feet deep. In front of her, about fifteen feet away, was a large gray metal door. She looked up at a concrete ceiling with thick steel rafters supporting large hooks; she hung from the middle of the three.

"Kill chamber," she muttered.

Gideon looked up from the tools he was perusing. "Yes, a kill chamber. But unlike the swine who bled out here in relative peace, you're going to bleed out slow and painful. Unless, of course, you cooperate." He picked up a thick orange hose from the floor and pulled back the lever behind the nozzle. "Please, don't," he grinned.

A harsh spray of cold water doused her. Jax held her breath and steeled herself against the hard stream. When she turned her face away, he followed her with the hose. She gasped, gulping for air, getting a mouthful of water. She coughed and gagged as more water slammed down her throat. Her body jerked wildly as spasms coursed through her. She twisted away and, finally, he stopped, leaving her to suffer in stubborn silence.

Her chest burned from swallowing water. The pain was unlike anything she'd felt before. She knew she was going to die. Almost wished for it. And for some crazy reason, that made her think of Marcus.

Marcus.

But that was foolish. Lazarus was his creator. His mentor. He actually believed that what they were doing was for the good of the American people.

After what seemed like an hour, she was able to breathe in a half-normal fashion. "What do you want?" she croaked, barely able to see him through the hair plastered to her face. She turned her head to move it away but only managed to smear more of it in her eyes.

Laughing, he turned the hose back on her, the force of the spray pushing the hair from her face. "Is that better?"

Jax shook her head as another fit of coughs wracked her entire body. Her throat was so raw that she could taste her own blood.

"How did you meet Marcus Cross?" he demanded.

She opened her mouth, but it took several tries for her to speak coherently. When she did, she put as much disdain into the words as she could. "We bumped into each other one night."

He looked up at her and smiled. It wasn't a pleasant gesture.

"Did you trade blood with him?"

"You're getting a little personal, aren't you?" Jax answered, knowing she was going to pay for it.

He picked up the cardiac panels. She steeled herself. Without a word, he pressed them to her belly and hit the switch. She screamed as the heat slashed through her organs. Her body jerked and jackknifed in agony. He stepped back. Her flailing body stilled. Jax closed her eyes and mentally tried to collect herself, but the electric impulses still ricocheting in her body would not allow her to concentrate.

Her strength waned.

She could not take much more. Her heart was beating so fast and so furiously that she thought it would explode. She felt the warm coppery blood well in her mouth. She had bitten her tongue.

He was getting off on torturing her, that was for sure,

but he wanted to get off another way too. She'd rather die than endure that. She glanced at the table, where her Glock lay beside her crushed cell phone, the last of her wooden stakes, the cleaver and the meat hook. If she could find a way—

"You can either be respectful and answer my questions without the sarcasm, or I can—" He tapped the paddles to her belly and gave her a hot shot. Jax bit her lip to keep from screaming. "—keep turning up the heat. Your choice."

Her choice would be to rip his head off and feed it to him, but she needed to change tactics here. Defiance wasn't working. Maybe cooperation would. Jax nodded.

"I knew you'd see it my way. Now, tell me how you met Marcus Cross."

Slowly, Jax opened her eyes. "I told you, we bumped into each other, at a club in Vegas."

He considered her, looking mildly surprised, but then shrugged. "Then what happened?"

Jax bit back a hoarse laugh, unable to help herself. "What happens in Veg—"

He cursed and shoved her so hard that her back hit the cinder-block wall with a bone-crushing thud. "Do you have a death wish?" he hissed. "Who are you really? Who do you work for?"

Jax's body twisted and came flying back toward him from the velocity of the hit. He grabbed her legs with one hand and grabbed the cleaver with the other. He pressed it to the crease of her right thigh and groin. "Tell me what I want to know or I start chopping off limbs."

Jax nodded. "I'm an indepen—" She screamed when

he slashed her with the cleaver. The burn was so excruciating that she nearly passed out from the pain.

She closed her eyes and tried valiantly to gather her wits, but the only thing that came to mind was Marcus. Only he could save her from this torture.

She opened her eyes and, through the haze of blood and tears, watched the man beneath her literally foam at the mouth with excitement.

He grinned, flashing his fangs. Stepping away and setting the cleaver down on the table, he looked back up at her and licked his lips. His tongue was long and thin, reminding her of a snake. "The colonel bade me soften you up." He grabbed her foot and yanked her boot and sock off, flinging them to the wet floor. "I think you're sufficiently soft. Now, I want a taste." He brought her foot to his lips and, before she could react, he sunk his teeth into her instep.

Jax screamed and jerked against the chains. If she didn't get out of this now he would tear her apart piece by piece. Summoning what strength she had left, not really expecting it to make a difference, she twisted and kicked him in the head with the heel of her other boot. To her surprise, he cursed, releasing her and spurring her on.

She twisted again and tightened the chains, raising herself up higher. This time, she kicked him in the teeth.

He screeched, grabbing his face. Blood oozed through his fingers.

The adrenaline pumped hard through her. She suddenly remembered whose blood she had in her. Without hesitating, Jax did a gymnast's move and swung her lower body up to where the chain hung over the large meat hook. She grabbed it, lifted the chain, and let gravity bring her down. As she came down, she threw the chain out, catching Gideon around the neck, and as she fell to the ground, he fell, too.

"No—" he gasped, making her grin.

"Oh, yeah," she muttered. "It's on now, you rabid bat."

Like a constrictor, she twined her legs and the chain around him as she grabbed for one of the high-voltage paddles. She pressed it to his face and hit the switch. His body flinched as he screamed. Jax let go and jumped up. She grabbed her pistol from the table and leveled it directly at his heart. "Move another muscle and I'll kill you."

He rallied, grinned a macabre grin, yanked the chains off his neck, and threw them at her. She ducked and pulled the trigger.

Stunned, Gideon stood motionless, then looked down. A bloodstain mushroomed dead center from his heart out. He looked up at her and Jax tried to smile, but it came out as a grimace. "Silver-tipped wooden bullet through the heart. Sayonara, Sunshine," she hoarsely said.

Gideon dropped to his knees and began to smoke. The smell was disgusting. Jax coughed and put her hand over her nose and mouth, watching in horrified fascination as he turned into a piece of human toast.

She shoved the pistol in between the small of her back and pants, then slipped the stake into her right thigh pocket. Grabbing the cleaver, she shoved it down the front thigh pocket of her pants and hung the meat hook from one of her back pockets, then took her pistol out again. Holding it before her, she tried to keep her hands from shaking and moved as fast as her ravaged body would allow her to.

The screams from down the hall had subsided. Carefully, she pushed the metal door open and peeked out into the corridor. Clear. There was only one door to the right and across the corridor. The screams had to have come from there. She made her way to the door, then carefully opened it.

Jax caught her breath. Tears sprang to her eyes. She fought back the bile in her throat. "Oh, my God," she whispered. "Shane."

He hung naked and crucified from a metal cross. She closed the door behind her, shoved the gun down the small of her back again, and hurried to him.

"Shane," she whispered as she came to stand before him. She nearly slipped and fell in the pooling blood at his feet. His head was tied back with constantine wire. Blood covered his face, but she could see a socket where his left eye had been.

Her stomach roiled. Thick meat hooks pierced through his shoulders and thighs, pinning him to the structure. His stomach had been savagely hacked; part of his intestines hung out. "Shane," she croaked.

He moaned, barely audible, but he moaned. He was still alive!

For a crazy, hysterical moment, all she could think was that Lazarus was far better at his job than Gideon had been.

Finally, she retched.

The air in the room became too heavy, too thick for her to breathe. "It's OK," she forced herself to murmur. "I'm here now. You'll be OK, Shane."

What could she do for him? Her cell was destroyed. She didn't know where she was. . . . But wait . . .

The GPS chip! The one in her bra.

She hurried and took her shirt off. Yanking her bra off, she tied it around his right ankle. Eventually they would find him, and if God was on their side today, he'd still be alive.

"Please, God," she prayed, marveling that she'd done it several times in the past few days. "Let Dante find us."

But she had to do her part too. Fearfully, she looked over her shoulder. Any second now, Lazarus would return. Then no one would be able to help them.

She needed to get Shane out of here.

She put her shirt back on and looked behind Shane, careful not to slip in the blood.

So much blood.

The cross was suspended by chains connected to a manual pulley. Jax grabbed the lever and unlocked the mechanism. Then, with every bit of strength she had left, she slowly turned the wheel and lowered Shane to the ground. He moaned as the hooks in his shoulders and thighs moved when their backs hit the floor.

"Geth ah—" he croaked.

"Shane," she said, going down on her knees beside his head. "I'm going to get you out of here. But first I have to get all this shit out of you. It's going to hurt."

He turned his head slightly and opened his one good eye. "Geth ah—" he said again, and she realized he was telling her to get out. To save herself. She fought back tears and used the tail of her shirt to gently wipe the blood from his face. "I'm so sorry."

He closed his eye, making a small sound before seeming to pass out.

Jax got busy. After several heart-stopping moments, she freed him of the hooks. Jax crossed herself and said a Hail Mary. She needed to get him out of there. Now. Bending over him, she prepared to haul him over her shoulder. Before she could, she heard him.

"You are a very enterprising woman, Jax Cassidy," a deep, dark voice said from behind her.

Lazarus.

Rage reared its head, and with it came a surge of adrenaline.

Jax turned, leveled her Glock at him, and pulled the trigger. Lazarus's body flinched. He looked down at the hole in his belly, then looked back at her. "You missed."

She pulled the trigger again, but her target had disappeared.

"You cannot kill me," he said from behind her.

Jax whirled around.

He inclined his head to her pistol. "Silver-tipped wooden bullets? I'll give credit where credit is due." The colonel moved closer to her. "Too bad it won't help you."

The room seemed to sway beneath her. Her insides burned and she was suddenly cold. She raised the gun. Her hands shook. Not from nerves, but from shock. She was on the verge of total collapse.

Lazarus seemed to easily take the gun from her numb fingers.

The room spun. Her chest became heavy. She couldn't breathe.

He grabbed her to his chest and shoved her head

back. He ran a finger down her jugular. "I can see what Marcus finds so fascinating about you. You are truly extraordinary. But I'm afraid he will have to find some other form of entertainment. I cannot permit you to live as you are—or as one of us."

Jax swallowed and summoned the strength to speak. "Why didn't you just kill me on the street?"

"You, my lovely assassin, are my insurance policy."

"For what?"

He smiled. It gave her the creeps. "Marcus has become quite independent these last few months. I have something very important for him to do, and since he refused my order to eliminate you, perhaps he will do my bidding if he thinks it will save you."

Lazarus chuckled demonically. "He's avoiding me, you know. But no more. He knows where to find me. He knows where to find you. Why do you think he isn't here?" He laughed low. "Perhaps I overestimated his fondness for you?"

No, asshole, he's tied up in a silver chain. But she wasn't going to tell him that.

"He's very territorial, you know. Maybe we should test that. I know what will bring him to me. To you." He brushed her damp hair from her neck. "You have lovely skin," he whispered.

Jax closed her eyes and went limp in his arms. Her right hand dangled next to the pocket with the stake in it. Trying to control her erratic heartbeat, she slipped her fingers into the pocket and clasped the blunt end of the stake, then gathered it in her fist.

His fangs hovered over her neck. Jax arched, offering herself to him. Just as his fangs pierced her skin, she brought her hand up and drove the stake into his back.

Lazarus screamed and dropped her.

Jax fell to the floor and scurried back toward Shane. She reached for her pistol, but her bloody hands could not grip it.

Lazarus twisted and hissed in terrible pain, but he didn't go down. After what seemed like an eternity but was only a few seconds, he straightened, reached around, and yanked the stake from his back.

His eyes burned molten red. "You missed again." He threw the stake to the floor.

Shit.

Lazarus reached down and yanked her up.

"Release her."

Oh my God, Marcus.

She tried to jerk around to see him, but Lazarus shook her like a rag doll. Her head rattled. Her vision blurred. Then she could not see. She went limp, her strength draining.

The pain was lessening now.

"Do not interfere here," Lazarus warned.

"She belongs to me," Marcus said.

"Do not defy me!" Lazarus mandated.

"Our laws permit me to claim a mate. I choose her."

"An eye for an eye, Marcus. You will pay for destroying *my* chosen one!"

Jax tried to comprehend their words. Her body was on the verge of total collapse.

Lazarus's body shuddered, as if he had been hit. His grip loosened. The warmth called to her. She let herself go to it.

She felt herself falling.

Angry words reverberated around her.

Strong arms caught her.

Warmth.

Marcus.

"Put the girl down," Lazarus commanded.

Marcus shook his head. "Not a chance."

Lazarus moved slowly around the bloody body of Jax's partner. Marcus detected the barest hint of a heartbeat. The man would bleed out in the next few minutes. "I'm not interested in her, Marcus. She's nothing but a means to an end." He held out his hands palms up in a show of trust. "You are my end."

Marcus considered the fatally wounded figure draped across his arms. She was losing body heat. Her organs had begun to shut down to sustain what life was left in her. He felt as if his world was crumbling around him with each shallow breath she took. The pain of his emotions tore him up inside. There was nothing undead about him. For the first time since he could remember, there was an aching inside him, a yearning for something other than himself. This broken creature had struck a nerve, and it numbed him to Lazarus's will.

"Our time is growing short, Marcus. Put her down," Lazarus commanded, his voice darkening to thunder.

Raising his eyes, Marcus returned his master's gaze. "There is no measure of bargaining here. No hold you possess any longer."

"I gave you life! Have you forgotten? I could have left you for the sand fleas and the vultures, but I breathed life into your dying body!"

"And now I return the favor by exacting no vengeance for the liberties you've taken today."

"You *return* the favor?" Lazarus demanded, incredulous. "Who the hell are you? You're no one without me!"

Not breaking with Lazarus's eyes, Marcus slowly moved toward the door as the conversation accelerated. If he could keep Lazarus engaged and enraged, there was a chance.

"You've been like a son and I your father!" Lazarus raged.

"No, Lazarus. More like the chattel to do your bidding! Am I to repay the deed for a lifetime?"

Lazarus shook his head and moved toward him. "One more request, Marcus. One more simple request and I will set you free!"

He would never be free so long as Lazarus lived. Inching closer to the hallway, Marcus could feel the slight breeze of the corridor wafting into the room. Jax's heartbeat had slowed to halting. Shane was closer to his end than Jax but not by much. If he could save them both, he would, but there was only so much he could do. First things first, and nothing, not even Lazarus, was going to interfere with his getting Jax out of there.

"And Jax?" Marcus asked in false sincerity.

"She stays here with me. I won't harm her further. I give you my word, Marcus." Lazarus stretched out his hands again in a gesture of friendship, but Marcus read through his façade. "I was only using her to reach you."

"What of him?" Marcus nodded toward the heap of bloody flesh that was Shane's dying body.

Lazarus stopped and turned to consider the figure

upon the floor. "His time is over, Marcus. He's beyond even my powers now."

With Lazarus's attention turned even for a brief second, Marcus seized the opportunity and made his break out of the room and down the corridor so fast that his body was only a dark blur. He cleared the exit into the sultry night air. He felt a sudden rush of air go past him. Lazarus.

Everything slowed to a grinding halt. Marcus saw the master vampire settling to stand just ahead of him. Gathering Jax tighter to his chest, Marcus cut right and accelerated toward the dilapidated packaging plant at the edge of the parking lot, but Lazarus was there again. Marcus could not fight his maker with Jax in his arms. If he set her down, she would be dead before he returned to claim her. Marcus bit down hard on his lower lip until his blood flowed down his chin. He pressed his lips to Jax's and with his tongue gave her as much of his life-saving blood as he could in the few short seconds he had.

Almost immediately, her heart rate stabilized, but it was still weak and much too slow. But— He looked up to see Lazarus coming straight at him. Marcus set Jax down on the asphalt and hurled his body straight at Lazarus. They crashed with a sickening thud in midair. He grabbed his maker by the shoulders and swung him in a high arch, then tossed him into the broken row of third-story windows on the plant. Marcus went crashing in after him. While the outside world was hurtling by, he and Lazarus appeared to be in a time warp of slow motion, movement matched by equal movement. Speed matched by equal speed.

The building was dark, dusty and full of broken pallets. None of it slowed Marcus down. Cutting back and forth in a fury of speed, Marcus rose to the fifth floor and met his maker, who stood atop a pile of stacked cardboard.

"Now what, Marcus?" Lazarus softly demanded. "We do battle?"

"That's up to you. You could just let us go."

"You, I might be able to trust not to divulge our secret, but not her. She has a separate agenda that I cannot allow."

"Then we really have no other choice." Marcus leapt and dove into Lazarus, hurtling him into the concrete wall behind him. The impact shook the glass from the windows. Shards rained down on Lazarus. But the old vampire kicked Marcus away, the velocity sending him nearly thirty feet away. He landed on a wooden pallet, shattering it. Marcus struggled to his feet, grabbing a two-by-four-foot piece of the pallet.

Lazarus hovered several yards in the air in front of him. "You've gained strength through your growth, Marcus. Still, I will kill you if you leave me no option." Lazarus stood above him, delaying his rise. Dropping onto his back, Marcus made a quick roll right and shot his legs into Lazarus, knocking him to the ground. Spinning away, Marcus leapt to his feet and darted deeper into the building. Lazarus was in hot pursuit.

"This can only end one way, Marcus!" Lazarus called from behind him.

Marcus flew through the air from behind and planted both feet into Lazarus's back. Any mortal man would have been dead from the whiplash caused by the impact, but Lazarus was no mortal; his neck remained intact.

Marcus·stabbed Lazarus in the back with the two-by-four, impaling him to the floor. Lazarus screamed, not in pain but in fury. Marcus leapt up and moved into the depths of the building.

"I grow weary of your game!" Lazarus called. "The girl will be mine again and you will have to come to me on my terms!"

Marcus watched from his perch as Lazarus yanked the wood from his shoulder and stood, tossing it aside. Then he stood still and scanned the darkness. When he could not detect Marcus behind the stack of pallets, Lazarus turned and turned and turned, forcing the air to rise up around him. With it, the littered pieces of wood from the old pallets flew through the air like missiles. Marcus braced himself, then deflected each piece of wood launched at him, sending it directly back to its point of origin.

Like the true master he was, Lazarus blocked them with forearm blows. The faster they came, the faster he defended his position. Marcus leapt from his spot and down to the floor beneath Lazarus. He grabbed a bundle of copper piping and hurled it backward toward the colonel.

"Destroy me and you destroy yourself!" Lazarus screamed. Marcus leapt toward his maker and grinned. A short piece of pipe had impaled Lazarus's left thigh. Marcus reached down, grabbed another piece of pipe, and shoved it into Lazarus's gut. Blood spewed from the wound. Lazarus looked up in complete shock. Marcus ran it through.

"Leave us be!" Marcus yelled at Lazarus. "I have

claimed her as my mate! It is my right, and I will defend it to the death if I must!"

Silence. Lazarus did not move. His eyed glared red. His skin had paled to white. He dropped to one knee. Reaching with his left arm, he grasped the pipe, slowly pulled it from his gut and flung it aside. Grasping with both hands the other pipe protruding from his thigh, Lazarus gave it a hard tug. As he pulled it clear, blood poured from the wound. Marcus had hit his femoral artery. Lazarus cursed and flung the pipe aside. He would survive, but it would take more than a few minutes to recover from the blood loss.

Marcus did not wait; he turned and jumped up through the broken windows to the asphalt parking lot and then to Jax.

She lay where he had left her. He gathered her into his arms and moved toward the dark streets for a car to hot-wire.

THIRTY

*

J ax was dying.

Without hesitation, Marcus took her north to Clearlake, where he'd spent his troubled childhood. After he had come home from Afghanistan, he'd purchased a small cottage on the lake. It was where he went to decompress. No one, not even Lazarus, knew of its existence.

It was just before daybreak when he pulled up in front of the lake house.

He gathered her into his arms and carried her to the house, kicking in the thick oak front door and striding to his room. Carefully, he laid her down on the bed.

"Jax," he called as he gently shook her. Her head listed to the right. Her skin had blanched white, and her breath was barely discernable.

After rolling up his right shirtsleeve, he sunk his fangs into the thick vein in his forearm. Life-saving blood sprang up. Giving the damning consequences of his action no thought, Marcus pressed his arm to her lips. "Drink, lovely," he softly said. Her eyes fluttered open and, in their depths, he saw clear to her soul.

His skin chilled. She was in a place he could not reach, a place she chose to retreat to, a place she might never return from. Her eyelids fluttered closed. Urgency gripped him. "Drink," he commanded.

She moaned, turning away from him. He grasped her head in the palm of his free hand and forced her lips to his blood. Still, she did not drink. "You're a coward, Jax Cassidy," he hissed. He forced open her mouth, then squeezed the bite on his arm. Blood dripped in a thick stream into her mouth. She gagged. He forced her to swallow. She gagged more and he forced her to swallow again.

Her fingers brushed against his arm, then she clutched him to her and drank herself. Her need for his life-saving blood and, even more so, her acceptance of it filled him with a crazy sense of elation. It didn't matter that he'd damned himself.

It was forbidden to willingly give a mortal this amount of immortal blood. The penalty? Death. Or, if his creator was feeling generous, perpetual torture.

He growled low. Damn Lazarus! Damn them all! Seeing what they'd done to Jax's friend—seeing what he'd planned to do with her—had broken the chains that had bound him to his creator forever. He would never succumb to another's command again.

Not even Rurik's.

Marcus looked down at Jax, who was still drinking from his vein. His heart, as much as he still had one, swelled with emotion. He hadn't realized until she'd come into his life how dead he had been. Knowing her, wanting her, and having her only to lose her would be the worst form of eternal existence. She was worth his life or an eternity of torture. Gently, he brushed her matted hair from her now sleeping face. Color had returned to her cheeks. Her chest rose and fell in deep, even breaths. He hoped his blood would be enough to sustain her ravaged body. Had she not had even the small amount she'd taken when she'd bitten him days ago, there would have been nothing he could have done for her. Now, he could save her, the way he hadn't been able to save her fellow operative. Shane's life was out of his hands now.

Tenderness for this tiny warrior filled him. Never had he felt such an urge to protect. Smiling, he imagined her reaction if he voiced his thoughts. Those huge green eyes would widen in surprise and she'd probably punch him.

She'd been a handful before she'd taken his blood. Now, with his blood surging through her veins, she'd be unmanageable. But, he let out a long, exhausted breath, she would be alive.

Her hands fell from his arm as she went completely under, falling into a deeper sleep than she'd probably know again. Good. She would need it.

Marcus rose, moved to the window, and pulled back the heavy drapes. The dark film on the glass buffeted by the thick plantation shutters on the outside kept the slightest rays of sun from the room. The rest of the house was exposed, but this one place, with the exception of an unused lamp, remained black.

It was unfortunate. The bedroom had complete lake exposure. The sunsets were one of his few fond memories of his boyhood here.

He gathered towels and warm water, then stripped Jax, growling at the harsh red and purple bruises on her belly. Several spots were raw. He cursed when he saw the slice to her upper thigh. Her upper lip was split, and she had a cut over her right eyebrow.

He shook his head. She was something else. And having taken out Gideon . . . Marcus cracked a smile. Good girl, Jax. But what amazed him more than the fact that she'd tended to Shane in this shape was the fact that she'd taken on Lazarus and survived. Twice. As if she'd really believed she could take down the North American coven leader with her special bullets and a stake to his back.

Marcus shook his head in disbelief. It would take more than her paltry armory to eliminate a vampire as old and as powerful as Lazarus.

Her naked body shivered in the cool morning air. He wrung a towel out and gently wiped the blood and dirt from her face, then the rest of her body. The cut to her thigh had stopped bleeding. He could not help but press his lips to it.

He closed his eyes as her essence filled his senses.

She moaned softly and moved. Marcus moved away and finished bathing her. When he was done, he pulled a sheet over her naked body.

Striding to the front of the house, he closed the door. The lock was destroyed, but he wasn't worried about intruders. He'd smell them within one hundred yards.

He showered fast. When he came out, toweling himself dry, he smiled. She had not budged. He climbed into the large custom-made bed with her, gathered her into his arms, and closed his eyes. Taking deep breaths, he soaked her in, reveling in the fact that she lived.

Her smooth warmth felt good against his skin. Her soft breath fluttered against his chest. He closed his eyes and just experienced her in this quiet state. Even as the euphoria of having her in his arms surged, he accepted it couldn't last.

He would die bringing Lazarus down, but he would do it. Only he could. There was too much at stake if he didn't.

Marcus kissed the top of her head. She snuggled more intimately against him. His blood flared in his loins. His fingers tightened on her skin. He closed his eyes, drew in a deep breath and slowly exhaled.

It was going to be a long night, but he would enjoy every second of it.

Jax woke to black.

Her first realization was that she was alive, but how? . . .

She tried to move but couldn't.

Where was she? Had Lazarus locked her up in a dungeon?

It took several minutes for her senses to adjust. She smelled Marcus before she heard his deep breaths. She was wrapped tightly in his arms.

Her heart rate picked up as her sense of security returned.

He had come for her. Fought Lazarus and saved her life.

She reached out and touched his hand. It was warm. It warmed her. He'd come for her. Despite everything, he'd come for her.

No one had ever come back for her before.

The blackness in the room diffused. She could see as if it were daybreak. The black curtains over the window, the oak nightstand, the lone lamp atop it. The large bed she lay upon. It was morning. She could smell the dew. She sat up, and the events of the last twenty-four hours flooded her system.

"Shane!" she whispered. Hot tears stung her eyes.

Strong arms once more wrapped around her naked body, drawing her close. "Shhhh," he soothed.

"Shane. Is he—?"

"I don't know."

Jax broke Marcus's hold, flinching at the pain in her belly. "You left him there?"

Marcus scowled and raised up on an elbow. "I was a little busy fighting my maker, who was pissed beyond description, *and* trying to save your life. Your buddy was the last thing on my mind." He reached up to her cheek and rubbed his knuckles across her skin. "But, because I'm not a complete monster, I called 9–1–1 and gave them his location. He's probably at Highland Hospital in Oakland."

She swallowed, trying not to remember the feel of Shane's blood on her hands. "What happened to Lazarus?"

Marcus shrugged. "I gave him a good ass kicking, he returned the favor, then I managed to buy a few minutes and get us both out of there."

She wrapped her arms around his neck, brought his lips to hers and kissed him. "Thank you," she murmured against his lips.

His body swelled and hardened. His arms tightened around her. "You're welcome," he breathed, then pressed her back into the pillows.

Jax's body responded, but her brain would not shut

down. "Marcus," she breathed, breaking their kiss. "How is it I'm not dead?"

He hesitated, then said, "I gave you my blood."

She stiffened. "Am I—?"

He shook his head and smiled a soft smile. "No, but once your body has absorbed all of my blood, you will feel like you did at twenty and have five times the strength." He kissed her nose, then said, "Don't let it go to your head."

She laughed. For a while, she snuggled in his arms, then looked up at him. "I need to know if Shane's alive."

He sighed. "The hospital won't give you that information. And besides, there is nothing you can do for him now."

Shaking her head, she urged him to understand. "I can call my people. They need to know where he is, they need to know I'm alive."

After staring at her for several long moments, Marcus nodded, then reached over to the nightstand to grab his cell phone and hand it to her.

"Thank you," she said and called Godfather.

"Black," Godfather said, his voice clipped.

"It's me," Jax said.

"Jesus Christ, where are you? We found your GPS in an abandoned meat packing plant in Oakland. Have you had contact with Donovan?"

"I'm safe. Lazarus got ahold of Shane. He . . . should be at Highland Hospital in Oakland. I don't know if he's dead or alive."

Godfather paused. When he spoke, his voice was even harsher. "Did you eliminate Cross? What's the status on Lazarus?"

"No, and I don't know."

"Cassidy, give me your location. I'm sending in a team."

Marcus took the phone from her hand and gently held her down when she tried to fight him for it.

"This is Cross. Jax won't be available until later this evening, at which time she will contact you." He hung up.

Openmouthed, she stared at him. "What did you do that for?"

"You're staying here. Where it's safe. No one knows of this place. Once you're at one hundred percent, you can give your people a full update. Until then, Jax Cassidy, you, are all mine."

Narrowing her eyes, she studied him. The worry in his eyes. She caught her breath. The raw burn mark around his neck. Gently she touched it with her fingertips. "I'm so sorry."

He grasped her fingers and kissed them. "I forgive you."

She reached up, pressed her lips to his wound and licked his skin. He stiffened. "I thought I was going to die, Marcus, and never see you again."

"As long as I have breath in my body, Jax, I will always protect you."

"Tell me everything is going to work out."

He smiled and gathered her into his arms. He kissed her eyelids, her cheeks, her nose and finally her lips. "Everything is going to work out."

She sank back into the smooth sheets, bringing him closer against her heart. "Make love to me, Marcus."

She gave herself up to him, inviting—no, demanding—his touch.

Somehow, though she'd never have thought it was possible, she let it all go. Lazarus. The pain. Even her worry over Shane. She reveled in the way his big hands stroked her skin to fire. The way he touched her as if she'd been fine china that, if handled too harshly, would crumble. The way he made her feel like the only woman on the planet.

His tenderness quickly turned to fiery passion. She responded with an appetite for him that she feared would never be sated. Their impatient bodies wanted to connect. To become one. Now, forever.

She arched into him as he entered her, oh so slowly, and oh so deeply. Jax closed her eyes, letting her head fall back and his hands catch her. Everything about him excited her.

His power, his passion, his smooth skin. And his eyes? His soulful eyes, so full of pain and glory. He made her feel things she had never felt in her life and instinctively knew she'd never feel again, no matter how long she lived.

He was her other side. The dark, demanding, passionate side. There were no words to describe what he was to her. Lover was so inadequate. She didn't love him. No, what she felt, what she knew, was beyond that. They hung suspended, connected, heart, blood and soul. She fought back tears as emotion overcame her.

She didn't know why it was him, a tortured and immortal soul, who'd given her back what she had lost so long ago—her hope, her willingness to open her heart again and to trust another being with it.

They were doomed, she knew it. He was dead and she was alive.

Still, it was perfect.

He moved slowly and tenderly in and out of her, and Jax gave herself up completely. "Marcus," she breathed. "Don't ever stop."

He pulled her tighter into his arms and kissed her so deeply, so profoundly, that tears leaked from her eyes. Her words and his actions were triggers for them both. The fire that he ignited within her exploded into a maelstrom. Jax cried out as she was overcome with sensation. As she came, she watched his beautiful, dark face. How it tightened in passion, how he fought his overwhelming desire to bite her. God, she wanted him to do it.

She arched, exposing her neck. "Take it, Marcus. Take my blood."

"No," he whispered against her sultry skin, "you have lost so much already."

"Do it," she breathed.

He moaned and scraped his fangs along her jugular. Her body spasmed with anticipation. The sensation was like an infusion of aphrodisiacs. Her muscles clamped around him, making him groan in pleasure.

"Jax," he hoarsely said, "I'm sorry." He sunk his fangs into her. Jax screamed, the erotic pain so profound that she nearly fainted from the overwhelming pleasure of it.

If it was possible, he held her tighter to him. His possession of every part of her was terrifying in its magnificence.

As he drank his fill of her, his body drove into hers. She felt his quickening, then, his release.

Long moments later, feeling as if she could run a marathon, Jax rolled over and propped her hands on Marcus's chest, her chin on her hands. "Tell me how it happened."

His hooded eyes closed.

"There is nothing romantic about it."

"I want to understand you, Marcus. How things are for you. Why it happened."

He opened his eyes and ran his fingers through her mussed hair, gently untangling the snarls. "I was in Afghanistan. My squad had one purpose there: Eliminate the Taliban chieftains one at a time. We were very good at our job. We'd rotate missions. It was mine and my spotter, Benny Melgoza's, turn. It took us three days of looking like rocks on a hillside to get to the caves, but once we got a lock on our target, mission accomplished. Then we hightailed it back. We were about three hundred meters from our DZ, but we had the misfortune to run straight into a camel train of opium smugglers." He closed his eyes and sighed. "They got Benny. I narrowly escaped. But they came after me. Eventually they got me. I was full of holes. I could hear the chopper coming in for me. They opened fire and it headed back to camp." He opened his eyes. "I was dying, Jax. And I was pissed off about it. My entire life had been a clusterfuck. I wasn't ready to go. The colonel showed up out of nowhere. Beside him was the most beautiful woman I had ever seen. She looked so exotic and smelled like flowers. I knew I had died and gone to heaven. But I was still alive, though barely, and on Earth."

He ran his fingers along her fingertips. "Lazarus offered me a different life. Aelia, the woman, explained I would walk among mortals. I would be limited in the mortal world but blessed with untold power in the immortal world. I was desperate to live, Jax. Lazarus cut open his chest and I drank from it, but for some reason my body rejected his blood. It was only after Aelia opened her vein that I was able to tolerate Lazarus's."

"Did you die?"

"Yes, and no. They waited until just before my last heartbeat. Only then would my body accept the transfusion of their blood. It took three days for my body to make the complete transition. It was torturous. I wanted to die. But I survived it, and thrived."

"Do you regret not dying as a mortal?"

"No."

Jax leaned up and kissed him. "Me either. Had you died that night, I would not be here in your arms."

"Jax, I'd do it all again to be here with you."

His words warmed her. She gazed into his eyes and asked the question she was afraid he would answer. "What's going to happen to us?"

"I can't promise you a future, Jax. It's not that I don't want a future with you. I want that more than anything, but right now there are complications, complications that cannot be ignored."

"What kind of complications?"

He smiled a slow, tired smile and kissed her nose. "Get some sleep and we'll talk later."

THIRTY-ONE

Jax woke to an empty bed. She jackknifed up, with newly acute senses impossible to miss, and sniffed the air. The rich scent of fresh coffee, scrambled eggs and toast filled the small place. Her belly growled. She was ravenous.

Naked, she slid from the sheets. Rising, she swayed for a moment, then blinked rapidly. Everything around her was brighter. Sharper. Her body fairly vibrated with a feeling of vitality and power.

And because Marcus was near.

She strode noiselessly in the dark, her instincts taking her down a short hall to a small living room.

In the kitchen, she took a moment to take him in. He was dressed in a pair of black boxer briefs. His muscles moved in perfect symmetry across his broad back. She resisted the urge to run her hands up his back and around to his hard belly, then lower. Not because she didn't want him again. There would never be enough of him for her, but she needed to eat. She was famished and she needed to think. Though they'd made love for hours, and he'd managed to take away her worry and despair over Shane, it had returned now with a vengeance. She had to know what had happened to him.

When Marcus turned to face her, she saw not the smile she'd expected but a guarded look.

"What?" she asked.

He set a loaded plate on the small kitchen table, then filled her coffee cup. "Shane was never admitted to Highland Hospital. I checked with the surrounding hospitals, and nothing."

Jax's appetite vanished. "He didn't make it." She sat down on a chair and stared at her plate. "Then he's . . ." She couldn't say it. Didn't want to believe it. "It's my fault. I should have been with him, Marcus."

He squatted down in front of her and nudged her chin up with his fingers. "Would it have been his fault if your positions had been reversed?"

She stared at him for a long time, knowing he was right.

"You both knew how dangerous Lazarus was. How dangerous I was. He went in with his eyes wide open, and it's no surprise he didn't win. No mortal should have survived. That you did will go down in the coven's history books."

He smiled and traced a finger across her nipple. It puckered beneath his touch. Jax hissed in a deep breath, but this time, her spiking desire couldn't override her despair over losing Shane or her determination to see Lazarus dead. Pulling away, she swore, "I'm going to kill Lazarus."

He stared at her, jaw clenching, then stood. "You're going to need my help."

His statement shocked her. "You'll help me?"

"Yes. Without my help there is no way you can win."

"But Marcus, if you do that, you die. You will never have a chance to regain your humanity."

"I have severed all ties with Lazarus. Any chance I had is gone."

He'd done that for her. Given up his life. A second time.

"Marcus, get me close to Lazarus. Close enough to kill him. You will live, and somehow we will find a way to give you back your life." He stared at her as if he did not comprehend her words. "Marcus, I would do anything for you, you *must* know that. I mean c'mon, I owe you a couple of lives."

He cracked a smile. "I suppose you do."

"So?"

"So, we'll do our best." He pushed the plate at her. "Eat. I'm getting you something to put on or we're never going to leave here."

As he strode down the hall she yelled, "We'll do our best? Is that it?"

"Yes," he called back. It occurred to her at that moment that he didn't know how to react to her offer and declaration. Knowing his story, she doubted she would either. But she would do more than her best. They would both come through this, and they would both be standing, together, at the end of the day.

In a moment, he was back with a soft blanket, which he wrapped around her. She smiled up at his thoughtfulness and shook her head.

"What?" he grunted.

"I never would have guessed that under those big bad vampire fangs there was such a marshmallow."

He smiled and traced a finger across her exposed collarbone. "Only for you."

Jax took the last bite of her meal, then sipped her coffee. "Where are we?"

"Clearlake."

She couldn't keep her brows from rising. "Really?" He'd brought her home. It touched her so much; he might as well have taken her home to meet his mother. Given who his mother was, this was better. Speaking of . . .

"Marcus, I think Sophia—"

With a dark look, he shook his head. "No one knows of this place. We're safe for now."

Okay, so obviously he wasn't feeling sated enough to talk about Sophia Rowland. Jax understood his need to protect himself and appreciated his need to protect her, as well. She couldn't stay, however. "I can't stay here, Marcus. I have to find Shane and I have to regroup with my people. We have to eliminate Lazarus."

"You have to find him first, and I know exactly where he's going next. He's going after Senator Bond."

She sucked in a breath. "The GOP VP running mate?" She remembered Sophia and Senator Rowland talking about the possibility of him replacing Bond. How coincidental was it that Lazarus was now targeting him? Uneasily, she stared at Marcus, who didn't appear to notice.

"Yes. Tomorrow Calhoun is holding a press conference to announce his pick. We need to get to Lazarus before he eliminates Bond."

"Why? So that Rowland will step in? I thought he wanted Rowland dead, not—" She closed her eyes as realization hit her. "Oh, shit."

"Exactly," Marcus said. "Why kill him when he can be so useful in the White House? Or rather, so useful in getting Lazarus to the White House. Lazarus has gotten power hungry, and that's not something I signed up for." He looked away, then back to her. "When the sun sets in a couple of hours, we need to leave."

"I know." She studied him and the faintly troubled look in his eyes. And suddenly, before he even spoke, she knew Sophia was involved in Lazarus's scandalous plan. Still, she certainly wasn't expecting what he said next.

He looked at her and softly said, "I killed Sophia Rowland."

Shock made her jaw drop. Horrified, she stood. *"What?"*

"Lazarus turned her. I had no choice." He sounded almost defensive. As if trying to make himself less culpable in her eyes.

There was no need. Sophia Rowland had been a monster before Lazarus had gotten hold of her. Still, Jax sat back, stunned. "Why would he do that? Turn her, I mean."

"They have been an item for some time now. I knew there was a woman. I could sense her. The colonel can be very charming when he chooses. Turning her was probably the only way she'd give up her husband. She wanted the power and immortality the colonel could give her."

"Even more than she wanted to be the first lady? Because I'm assuming that's where it would have gone, right? Only, as a vampire, she couldn't—?"

He shook his head. "No, not in the traditional sense. But with Lazarus as her maker, she'd have been strong as long as she limited her exposure. She could have claimed she had a sun allergy like solar urticaria. Lazarus often uses that excuse for protecting himself or limiting his exposure to the sun when in public."

Her mind could barely comprehend what he was telling her. "How did you kill her?"

He hesitated, then thrust his chin out. "The only way I could. I decapitated her."

Jax grimaced. "Shit, Marcus . . . did you ever love her?" Her voice trailed off as she thought of her own mother. How they'd fought sometimes, but had always been connected by an indestructible bond. . . .

"She gave birth to me, Jax, and deserted me when I was two weeks old. When I was twelve, I ran away to find her. I was so sure she was searching for me. When she saw me and realized who I was, I cannot describe the look of horror on her perfect face. She threatened to kill me if I ever showed my face to her or anyone she was associated with again." He looked at Jax. "She was a power-hungry, manipulative bitch. She would have eventually destroyed my sister. I wasn't going to let that happen."

Jax let out a long breath and shook her head. But she understood why he'd done what he had. Given Sophia's plans, Jax would have done the same thing. Slowly, wanting to comfort him but not knowing how such action would be received, she took his hand. "I knew that night at the Green Room. I watched your face as realization dawned on you. It was the first time I felt something other than lust and anger toward you."

He grinned and released her hand, only to push her back into the chair. "You lusted after me?"

She snorted. As if he could have missed it. She moved

into him, knowing somehow that he needed her touch now even more than she needed his. "Yeah, big-time."

"Good. Because you had me so hard, so fast, I could barely see straight." He stood up and cleared the table with one quick swipe of his hand, then laid her on top of it. The blanket fell away and he gazed at her body. "You're beautiful, Jax." Her nipples tightened and Jax felt overcome with desire. He traced his finger down her belly and softly said, "Your scar is gone."

Jax gasped and looked down to her smooth, flat belly. Shocked, she looked up at him. "How?"

He grinned like the cat that ate the canary. "My blood is potent. Not only did it repair the fresh damage to your body, it repaired the old damage as well."

Jax grabbed his hand and pressed it to her belly. "Marcus, when I was stabbed, my uterus was hacked up. It's full of scar tissue. The doctors said I would never have a child."

He splayed his big hand across her belly. "Like I said, my blood is potent. It's powerful, directly from Lazarus, who was created by Rurik, the father of our kind. Aelia, Rurik's consort, was a part of my creation as well. Her blood is as strong as Rurik's."

He moved her hands away and lowered his lips to her belly to kiss her there. "Jax, you will be a magnificent mother one day."

His words were bittersweet. She had always wanted children, but the only man she'd wanted them with was incapable of giving them to her. Or was he? "Marcus?" she moaned as his fingers stroked the inside of her thighs and his lips traveled lower.

"Hmm . . ."

"Can vampires have children?"

His head snapped up and his eyes caught hers. "I don't know." He lowered his lips back to her belly and kissed a warm, wet trail south. "Let's find out." He took her into his mouth. Jax nearly rose off the table. He slid a thick finger into her, gently moving it in and out of her while his lips trailed just down to the inside of her thigh. She felt his teeth scrape against her artery there. Heat swept her up into a firestorm. She opened wider for him and lay back, giving him all of her.

He took it.

His lips, his tongue, and his fingers whipped her into a fierce frenzy of desire. The orgasm rose high and, just as she was peaking, he sunk his fangs into the inside of her thigh. Jax screamed at the sublime mixture of pain and unadulterated pleasure.

He moaned as he drank from her. His fingers took her higher before she finally crashed back to earth. When he rose above her, his eyes were molten blue and her blood glittered on his lips. "I have wanted to do that to you from the moment I first laid eyes on you." His body swelled and his cock was rock hard. Jax felt an overwhelming urge to bite him back.

She blinked.

He smiled a devilish smile, understanding what impulse had taken hold of her. He reached over to the counter and grabbed a knife. Before she realized what he was doing, he made a small puncture in his chest right above his heart. Blood oozed out in a slow, thick stream.

He moved above her. She arched up and licked his chest. Marcus moaned and slid his hand around to the back of her head. "Drink from me, Jax, as I have from you. My blood will make you stronger. It will connect us in a way no human would understand."

Fear skated across her skin. "Will I be like you?"

"No, but this is the first step if you should ever want that." He spoke confidently, as if he knew what her desires would be more than she did.

Jax nodded, her craving for his blood overpowering her caution. She pressed her lips to his chest and drank. Like the first time she'd tasted him, she felt as if she'd been on a wild, drug-induced high. He was addictive. He filled her body with his, and Jax imploded. The sensation of taking him into her, body and blood at the same time, was euphoric.

He came in a wild burst. She clamped tighter to his chest as he undulated above her. Glorying in the intimacy of their blood union, Marcus's body shuddered as she licked the last vestiges of blood from his chest. He growled and stood, grabbing her into his arms, then carrying her back to the bedroom.

Almost an hour later, Marcus heard them over the wild beat of Jax's heart. So did she. A wild whoosh of wind and low, screechy growls. Her head jerked up and she looked at him. Her green eyes snapped with fire and her nostrils twitched. "What are they?"

"Furies."

"What the hell is a furie?"

"A mortal who was forced against their will to become a vampire. They are crazed with only one purpose. Blood."

"Holy shit. How did they find us? Lazarus?"

He nodded grimly. "He called upon his telepathy, a

forbidden act. It's the only way he could locate me. Get dressed," he whispered.

"Why did he send the furies and not come himself?" Jax asked as she pulled her pants on.

"Lazarus is strong, but he can't be in two places at the same time. He's going after Bond and sent the furies to slow me down."

As she finished dressing, Marcus handed her a black velvet bag. He withdrew two silver scythes no bigger than a dinner plate.

He handed them to her. "These are razor sharp. They're yours."

Jax took them. The weight and grip fit her perfectly. She smiled. She could do some serious damage with these. "Thank you."

Two minutes later, they were dressed and heading out the sliding glass door toward the lake. The sun had just sunk behind the western foothills.

The terrible, high-pitched screeching was closing in fast. "Drown them or decapitate them, Jax, it's the only way they will die."

They turned and faced the pack of—they resembled humans, each form retaining its own individuality, but their elongated heads and exaggerated fangs gave them away. There were five of them, all male and all at least two hundred and fifty pounds of pissed-off psycho vampire. Just as they reached the water, Marcus moved first. Turning, he faced them head-on. He leapt up in the air, and two furies jumped up after him. He grabbed each by their hair as they snarled and tore at his arms with their clawlike hands. He plunged them into the lake, the water swallowing them up.

Jax looked at the three remaining guys. They formed a wedge and slowly approached. "Nice vampires," she murmured. One broke and rushed her. She lowered her body and ran straight toward it. She gripped a scythe in each hand and, in a wide, powerful swipe, slashed at the vampire. It screamed when she cut its head off.

The two other vamps charged her. Jax jumped up in the air just as Marcus had, exhilarated at how easy it was. As she turned in a matrix move, both beasts attacked her. She slashed at one, catching part of it with her blade. As she came down to the ground, she turned and kicked one in the face and the other in the chest. The one closest to her rolled backward and Jax pressed on, slashing at it in wide, powerful strokes until it lay in a mutilated heap.

The other beast bit her hand, forcing her to drop the scythe. That pissed her off. Jax turned and landed a roundhouse kick. As the furie lunged toward her, Marcus emerged from the water. Jax grabbed it and, as Marcus had done, dove into the water with it.

She had always been able to hold her breath. She was an avid diver. Now? With her increased strength, she felt as if she could stay under for an hour. It only took a few minutes before the creature lost the battle. Jax emerged wet and ready to kick more ass. She let out a joyous battle cry.

Marcus was standing on the bank, grinning like a proud parent. "My blood agrees with you."

"I feel like the Queen of the World. Let's go kick some more ass!"

He grew serious. "We need to meet with your people.

Let's get back to your hotel room and computer and get this show on the road."

As they drove west toward the city, Jax called Godfather and gave him the complete lowdown. "You need to get people to Bond ASAP. Calhoun and Roland, too, and get them to a safe house." She looked at Marcus. "Like a freaking cathedral?" she asked.

Marcus shook his head. "The safest place for them during the day is out in public in the sun."

Jax repeated his words to Godfather. "Any more word on Shane?" Jax asked.

"No, he was not at the location you gave, but the GPS chip was. He has not been admitted to any hospital in the Bay Area."

She looked at Marcus and voiced her biggest fear. "Do you think Lazarus has him?"

"I don't know, Jax, but I promise you: if he's alive, I'll find him. And tell Cross, if he's holding out, he'll have me to deal with," Godfather said.

"Will do," Jax said and hung up.

"You and your team are amazing. That guy really thinks he can take me out?"

"I wouldn't put it past him. Godfather is slightly scary. He has the means to so many ends it's ridiculous."

"You have a crush on him?" Marcus growled, making her jerk in surprise.

Jax laughed. "Are you jealous?"

He shifted in his seat, looking like he wanted to disappear. All he said, however, was, "Maybe."

She pressed her lips together, refraining from teasing him more. With a sideways glance, she finally shrugged.

"Not a crush in the way you're thinking. He saved my life. I'll always be grateful to him for that. He believed in me when I didn't believe in myself."

Silence reigned for several long minutes before he spoke again. "What is your real name?"

Her eyes widened. "I'm Jax Cassidy," she replied without hesitation.

"Before Jax Cassidy. What name were you given when you were born?"

"Angela. Angela Giacomelli."

"Heavenly messenger. It suits you."

She shrugged again, pushing away painful memories. "Yeah, more like devil's deliverer."

Marcus laughed. "Never. You are an angel of mercy sent to save my soulless self." He reached over and squeezed her hand. "Thank you."

Emotion tugged at her heart. "You're welcome."

As they drove, Jax's mind raced with thoughts and scenarios. "Marcus, what will happen to you when this Rurik dude knows you were in on Lazarus's death?"

"Rurik is reasonable."

"Yeah, but don't you all have some kind of code that you can't kill each other?"

"Under certain circumstances, yes, but there are always exceptions."

Jax gave him a sideways glance, not buying his answer, but she didn't push it. They made good time to San Francisco. When they strode into Jax's hotel room, it was wall to wall testosterone—Godfather, Gage, Dante, Dominic and several others. None of them, not even the L.O.S.T. team members combined, could, in her mind, hold a candle to Marcus.

He would always be, for her, the male that would stand out in a roomful of others.

More importantly, she knew she'd never want another man again.

That's when she knew that Angela was truly gone and Jax was all that remained.

Marcus thought he was going to save her, but in a way he already had, as surely as Godfather had.

She'd be damned if she'd allow anything to happen to him. She'd kill Lazarus and she'd protect Marcus. And if she had to sacrifice herself in the process?

Well, she'd already died once. She'd do it again if she had to.

THIRTY-TWO

J ax held her breath as Godfather strode toward her.
His blue eyes snapped in anger, perfectly matching the
expression of every other man in the room. He looked at
her for several long, piercing seconds before turning to
Marcus, who faced them all with cool indifference.

Jax rolled her eyes and moved deeper into the room.
"OK, boys, let's move past the pissing match and get
to work, shall we?" When no one moved or spoke, Jax
planted her hands on her hips in disgust. "How much
time are we going to waste? Because last time I saw him,
Shane didn't look like he had much left."

Several hisses preceded movement and murmurs of
agreement. Gage shot Marcus a scathing look, as did
Dante. She let it slide. They didn't know him like she did.
He'd had no part in what Lazarus had done to Shane.

Godfather nodded. "Cross, I don't like the fact we
have to go on your intel on this. I'm giving you fair
warning, if this is a setup, I'll destroy you."

Marcus's jaw clenched, but he simply said, "I assure
you, that is the least of my worries at this point." Sideways, he looked at Jax, who nodded.

Marcus faced the entire group of men. "You will be
going up against an enemy who has the strength of ten
men. An enemy that can see, smell and hear like a wolf.

He can break a neck with a flick of his finger. He can be destroyed only one of three ways.

"First, with a wooden stake driven directly into his heart. Second, via decapitation. And third, full and prolonged exposure to the sun.

"Sound easy? It's not.

"He can evade you better than a ghost. Because of his strength and his age, even if you stake him, he can pull it out and survive. Therefore, the stakes must be barbed at the end and must run him completely through. I daresay that all of you combined could not accomplish Lazarus's demise. You need me."

For a moment, he paused and looked at Jax, and she sensed more in his words than the obvious. Before she could blink or flush, he turned back to the men.

Gage spoke first. "So what are you going to do? Invite us over to dinner?" Dante and Dominic laughed, but Marcus cut them off with a low growl.

"This isn't a joke, jackass. Lazarus and those like him can change bodies. It's how he's walked the earth the past twenty-eight years as the colonel, ever since he killed the man. When he tires of his present body or needs a new form, he simply drains another person of his blood and takes it. I'm going to guess he has already done this. There are only two people in this room who will be able to detect him for what he is. Myself and"—he looked at Jax—"Cassidy."

"Something he's sure to know," Godfather said. "So what do you propose?"

"We need to get to the two senators, keep them together, and wait for Lazarus to make his move. He will do it today, before sunrise. He will have help. *Furies.* They are vampire soldiers, similar to kamikazes in their purpose, as they are single-minded killers. Lazarus will do everything in his power to prevent the announcement of Bond. He wants Rowland in."

"Going after Bond and then trying to control Rowland seems a pretty indirect way to do things. Why wouldn't he just drain one of the senators and assume his body?" Godfather asked.

"Because he still has limitations with respect to the sun. Taking the human form of a public figure limits his mobility and maximizes his exposure. This way, he can be whoever he wants, move wherever he wants, and do whatever he wants while having complete control of the White House." Marcus shrugged. "Lazarus also has a keen sense of . . . gamesmanship. He'll take pride in beating you. Us."

Godfather scowled deeply and nodded.

Jax sensed Marcus subtly relax. "You must also keep in mind that Colonel Lazarus thinks he is the savior of this country. He's a fanatic and one of the strongest of our kind. I won't say what you endeavor to do is impossible, but understand this . . ." He stopped to look at each man in turn. "Some of you who stand in this room will not return."

"We understand the risks," Godfather said. "I have a plane waiting to fly us to D.C. We can formulate our plan of attack on the way."

Jax changed into clean clothes and packed her sparse bag. In less than an hour, they were in the air on their way east to D.C. It had taken permission from the Secretary of Homeland Security to allow L.O.S.T. to get their plan up and running.

The plan was simple. Simple and gory.

Bond, who traveled with a double because of a threat several years ago, would be the bait. Each of the operatives would be armed with the special bullets, wooden stakes and bulletproof vests. They would be protecting Bond in the guise of the Secret Service, who were more than pissed about that. The rest of the team would be protecting their backsides.

As they flew, summer thunderstorms beat up the small jet. Several times, Jax, who was usually a fearless flyer, doubted they would hit the ground alive. Each time her heart ended up in her throat she would find Marcus staring at her from across the aisle. He would give her a reassuring smile, then lean back and close his eyes.

His confidence gave her confidence, but she was too wired to close her eyes and rest. All of them except Marcus were bouncing around in the plane like the thunder and lightning outside.

Over and over, her thoughts returned to Shane. As much as she wanted him to be alive, she knew that even if he'd survived his wounds, he'd never be the same. And someone like Shane Donovan would rather be dead than be less than he was. Just like Marcus.

Once more, she looked at him. His confession about killing Sophia Rowland had stunned her and, in fact, still did. She wondered how the senator would react when he learned of his wife's death. How would Gracie handle it? She wouldn't be able to seek comfort from her older brother because she didn't even know he existed. He could die and she'd never know there had been someone who, even though he'd never met her, had cared enough about her to spare her life.

Marcus's big body was scrunched up in a captain's seat that would have been adequate for most men, but Marcus, like the others surrounding her, was not an average man. Her belly did a little somersault. He wasn't an average man, but he was a good man. Honorable and, he had proven repeatedly, gentle and caring.

Jax felt eyes on her and looked to her right to find Godfather's intent gaze upon her. How long had he been watching her? And did he know that Marcus had come to mean a great deal to her? Uneasiness rumbled deep inside her gut. She held Godfather's gaze until he looked away.

The plane landed just after 4:00 a.m. D.C. time. The jet skidded on the wet runway. Jax crossed herself and grabbed hold of her armrests. As the engines revved down, she felt the aircraft hydroplaning and begin to spin.

Shit.

She looked over and found that Marcus's seat was empty. The door to the cabin flapped back and forth. The plane jerked a hard right before it settled. The engines roared in defiance, but the vessel slowed. Jax let out a long, relieved breath. She didn't know what Marcus had done, but she had no doubt he'd done something imperative to their safety. As they taxied in, Godfather strode to the cabin.

With her enhanced hearing, it was easy to eavesdrop.

"What's wrong with the pilot?" Godfather asked.

"Aside from the fact he stinks at his job, nothing."

Jax laughed.

She watched Marcus stride out of the cramped cabin. He met her gaze, then extended his hand to help her up.

"You got us down?" she asked, amazed. He was a pilot too?

"It was either me or they'd be hosing down the runway."

They were met by Naomi, who pushed a rack of basic-black Secret Service–type suits. She'd also brought a trunk of earphones and an arsenal of vampire-destroying weaponry. The L.O.S.T. team quickly changed into standard Secret Service black suits, then piled into three black Suburbans. No one spoke. The plan was set. All there was to do now was execute.

The press conference was scheduled for ten o'clock that morning at the Marriott Wardman Park. On the way to the hotel, they were pounded by the torrential sheets of rain that dogged them. In less than twenty minutes, they arrived at the hotel. As they entered the hotel from one of the back service entrances, Godfather called Jax and Marcus over. "Senator Rowland has insisted on a briefing. He's concerned about his wife."

Jax looked at Marcus, then back at Godfather. She'd been planning on waiting to tell him about her, but—

"Sophia Rowland is dead," Marcus said.

"*What?*" Godfather asked incredulously. He didn't lose his cool often, but he did now. He moved in close to Marcus, who didn't back down one inch.

"Lazarus turned her. She would have become more deadly than him. I eliminated the threat."

Godfather swiped his hand across his chin and shook his head. "This is a clusterfuck straight out of the *Twilight Zone.*" He quickly composed himself. "Who knows?"

"Jax and Lazarus."

"Let's keep it that way. For now we'll let the senator think she's alive but under protective custody in Carmel."

As they headed into the bowels of the hotel, Jax familiarized herself with it. All of them had memorized the complicated floor plan on the way out, but seeing it was completely different. She needed to know every exit, every corner. The very texture of the place.

Senator Bond and his entourage were holed up in the old Wardman Tower. It had easier exit access than the newer part of the hotel. The press conference was to be held in the grand ballroom, where both Bond and Calhoun would give a speech. But Lazarus would strike before dawn.

"I don't like the proximity of the grand ballroom to the outside," Jax said to Marcus. "It's too deep, with absolutely no chance of getting the colonel out in the open sun."

"It doesn't matter. The storm clouds will protect him enough so he can move around outside. He'll get a little warm under the collar, but it will be tolerable."

"Damn weather," she muttered.

Marcus reached down and squeezed her hand. "We don't need the weather's cooperation. We'll get the colonel regardless."

Jax nodded. She refused to entertain the slightest thought of defeat. Lazarus *had to* die. He was more dangerous than a nuke. Fifteen minutes later, everyone assembled in a staff room for a briefing.

"We're going to divide into two teams," Godfather said. "Cross, you're in charge of Team One. Take half the men here." Godfather looked at Jax. "You're with me on Team Two."

"She's with me," Marcus said, his voice implacable.

Godfather didn't move a muscle. "I said she's with me."

"Not tonight. I know the target," Marcus reasoned. "If we have any chance at all, we'll need the combined forces of Jax and myself. Split us up and you dilute the alpha team."

Godfather was macho, he was stubborn and he was always the one in charge, but he wasn't stupid. Jax knew he wouldn't sacrifice a man for his ego. He nodded. "Point taken. Be sure you keep your com on. Now," he said, turning to encompass everyone, "Team One will go up and replace the posted Secret Service. Cassidy and Cross, I want both of you in the room with Bond and his decoy. Team Two, we'll take care of the perimeter and Calhoun. There's no sense in looking for trouble; trouble is going to find us. At the appropriate time, Team One will escort the decoy senator and his wife to the ball-room. When Lazarus makes his move, we'll be going out the back door with the real Bond."

"And if Team One fails to bring down the mark?" Gage asked.

"Then we take both senators and run like hell for sun-light." Godfather looked at Marcus. "Is there anything you'd like to add?"

"Trust no one. Lazarus has the ability to kill instantly and take his victim's form just as fast."

"Is there any way we can tell the difference?" Godfather asked.

"No. Only coven blood can detect coven blood." Marcus looked to Jax. "Ready?"

"I'm ready."

"Then let's go."

Marcus took point and Jax took up the rear. Between them, they had four highly trained armed men, including Gage. Jax's senses were on high alert. She didn't take one smell or sound for granted. As they approached the service elevator, Jax sensed a change in Marcus. And immediately knew why.

Furies.

The furies swarmed them from all sides, their lethal fangs and claws slashing through the air as they screamed their hair-raising battle cry.

"Down!" Jax ordered. The L.O.S.T. team formed a Roman turtle in the corner while Jax and Marcus protected the front. Standing back to back, Jax withdrew her double mini silver scythes while Marcus bared his hands.

They hit.

She kept her stand and, as one flew around Marcus, she crisscrossed her arms in a high slashing motion, hacking the furie into pieces. Its screeches sent shivers down her spine as her blade severed its jugular. It fell silent when its head hit the floor.

Another descended from the ceiling. She lunged upward to do it in but was pulled back by the quick strength of Marcus's hand. She returned to safety beside him.

"No separation, Jax," he said softly. Even so, she heard his voice above the din of the battle. As the creature dropped toward them, she thrust her swords into its belly, yanked them free, and made hash out of it.

Another one crawled along the ceiling. She waited a

heartbeat for it to drop, then reached high and cut it in half. She cursed when she saw two of them heading for her team. They battled back, shooting the vamps with their silver-tipped wooden bullets. They fell dead to the floor.

The three remaining furies bunched together and exited as quickly as they had materialized.

"We good?" Marcus asked, turning around to face Jax and her men. She watched as the body parts began to smoke, then catch fire and burn out.

"Jesus," Gage said.

"Jesus has nothing to do with them," Jax said. She hit the elevator button and the doors opened. Marcus allowed the L.O.S.T. operatives to enter first, followed by Jax. She turned to make room for Marcus just as the doors abruptly slammed shut. "Damn—"

"Jax!" Marcus yelled through the closed doors even as the elevator car rose unusually fast.

"What happened to Cross?" Gage asked as the car raced upward.

"Lazarus. He has control of the car." And Marcus was alone. And vulnerable.

The car abruptly stopped. Jax looked up to the escape hatch. She jumped and punched it open, then climbed onto the top of the car. They were between floors. She moved to the edge of the car, reached up to the doors and pulled. They didn't budge.

"Gage," she called. "Get up here."

He scrambled up. "Get the other side and pull." The door cracked open. She wedged her scythe in and pushed with her foot. Slowly, it opened enough for her to shimmy through.

As she stood, she froze. She didn't know if she should laugh with happiness or cry in despair.

Shane stood smiling in front of her.

She shook her head and he stepped closer.

"It's me, Jax."

"How?" No way could he be standing in front of her after the wounds he'd suffered. It would have taken months to recover.

"Aelia," he grinned. "She saved me."

He looked like Shane, sounded like Shane. *Had* Aelia saved him? Why? How? When?

He took her hand. "It's OK. I guess Lazarus called for her. She saw what he did and I don't know why, but she got really pissed off and she bit me. I'm like Marcus now, Jax. I'm here to help."

"A vampire?" His hand was cool, clammy. She pulled hers away, not sure. . . .

He smiled, his deep aqua-colored eyes shining bright. "Yes. It hurt like hell, but I'm healed."

"Jesus Christ," Gage said from behind her as he shimmied through the opening.

Shane's smile waned just a fraction, and Jax caught it. *Shit*, she thought, remembering Marcus's words. *Trust no one.*

"We thought you bought the farm," Gage said, moving closer.

"I'm doing just fine, mate, as you can see."

Marcus materialized from behind Gage. "Stand back," he said to Shane.

Shane did what he was told, even raising his hands in compliance. "I'm not here to hurt anyone. I'm here to help."

Marcus strode slowly toward them. He caught Jax's gaze and inclined his head for her to move away.

She took Gage's hand and drew him with her to the other side of the hall. A new scent began to assail her nose. Faint yet detectable.

"What is the name of the man who heads up your organization?" Marcus asked Shane.

When Shane hesitated one heartbeat too long, Marcus dove at him.

Lazarus! He'd taken Shane's form. And that could only mean one thing.

Shane was dead.

As Marcus and Lazarus tumbled down the hall, Jax charged after them. Lazarus leapt up to the ceiling, reached down and plucked Jax from the floor. He kicked Marcus hard in the chest, sending him tumbling backward. Jax pulled her scythe. Lazarus laughed and swatted it out of her hand.

"You are nothing compared to me," Lazarus growled, then hurled out the window with her clutched to his chest.

THIRTY-THREE

Marcus had thought he could never be more frantic than when the elevators had closed, separating him from Jax. He'd been wrong. Seeing Lazarus dive through the window with Jax was almost enough to paralyze him, but he shook it off.

His job was no longer to protect Bond but to eliminate Lazarus. Swiftly. Once and for all.

He gave immediate chase.

Marcus hurled himself down the elevator shaft, knowing Lazarus would go to the bowels of the building. In less than an hour, it would be dawn.

"Alpha leader," Godfather called in Marcus's earpiece. "What's going on?"

"Lazarus has taken Shane's form and he has Jax. I'm in pursuit."

"Jax," Marcus softly said, knowing that even though Lazarus had her she would still have her com on. "Can you hear me?"

"I can hear you loud and clear, Marcus," Lazarus sneered.

Marcus's heart skipped several beats. "A trade," he said. "Her for me."

"Why make a trade when I can have you both?"

"I'll hunt you down and stake you in the Sahara if you harm one hair on her head."

Lazarus laughed. "Fear not, my friend, it's the neck, not the head, I fancy." He laughed again and sighed in exaggerated contentment. "I never thought I'd live to see the day when you'd pine over a woman, and a mortal one to boot. A mortal until dawn, anyway. Then I will turn her or she will die in the process. And she will belong to me." Lazarus laughed demonically. "As a furie. How will it feel when I give her the kill command for you, Marcus? How will it feel when your enemy lover is stalking you to the death?"

"What do you want?" Marcus bit out.

"I want Bond. You have fifteen minutes to tell me you have him or I cut your girl's heart out."

"And when I have him?"

"You'll have to wait to find out."

Marcus turned off his mic and hurried back to the Wardman Tower and Godfather.

He strode angrily down the hall of the penthouse floor where the senators and Godfather were.

"I heard it all," Godfather said.

"I want Bond," Marcus demanded.

"I can't do that, Cross," Godfather said, stepping in front of the senator's door.

"If you don't move, I'll kill you and every one of your men here."

"Where is Lazarus?"

"Move aside."

"I want Jax as much as you do, Cross—" Godfather began.

Marcus grabbed him by the throat and shoved him hard against the door, lifting him off the floor. "No. You don't."

Marcus felt the press of Godfather's team behind him. He didn't want to hurt them, but he would. Godfather warned them off. He grabbed Marcus's hands and pushed them away, but only because Marcus let him. He set Godfather down.

Godfather cleared his throat. "Let's be smart about this, shall we?"

"We have less than ten minutes."

"We'll use the decoy, but only if he gives his permission."

"No decoy. Lazarus will know the difference. He'll kill Jax."

"Take a look at the decoy before you say no. He's a dead ringer," Godfather said, then turned and knocked on the door to the senator's room, where the decoy was also staying. He was gone for less than a minute.

The door opened and Godfather motioned Marcus in. He came face-to-face with two men who could pass for twins. Both tall, dark-haired, brown-eyed, almost nondescript. The kind of face that blended in. The only difference was two inches in height. From the dossier photos of Bond, Marcus guessed the one on the right was the real senator.

"Have either one of you met a Colonel Joseph Lazarus?" Marcus asked.

"I have not," the Bond on the left said. His voice carried the same deep cadences as the voice samples Marcus had listened to.

"Nor have I," the other Bond said. Remarkable. Virtually no difference. Since neither had ever met Lazarus, so much the better.

"Which one of you is the real senator?"

The man on the left stepped forward. Marcus looked to the decoy. "You fooled me." He pulled a wooden stake from his inside jacket pocket and handed it to the decoy. "Find a place for this." Then he handed him his Glock loaded with vampire-killing rounds. "Don't use these unless Lazarus makes a threatening move on you. Aim for the heart. Now let's go."

As he strode down the hall with the decoy Bond in tow, Marcus turned the mic back on. "I have him."

"Bring him to the ballroom. Come alone, Marcus. My friends don't play well with others, and it's my friends holding the girl."

"Let me talk to her."

"Not until I see Bond."

"No proof of life, no Bond."

"Marcus—" Jax cried out as Lazarus hit her.

Marcus cursed, knowing that if he didn't beat Lazarus to the draw, Bond or not, Jax was dead. He killed his mic and cursed.

"We'll be right behind you," Godfather said.

"No," Marcus growled. "He'll kill her." Lazarus was going to kill her regardless. "Let me get into the same room as him and then I'll eliminate him."

For a long minute, Godfather didn't say a word. Then he held out his hand. "I'm trusting you to bring my top operative home. Alive."

Marcus looked down at the proffered hand and took it. "I will, sir."

Then Marcus looked to the decoy. "Don't be a hero. Don't say a word, just follow my every command without hesitation. Do that and we'll all walk out of here alive."

"I'm a retired ranger, son. I can handle myself," the decoy said.

As they passed through the long glass corridor that connected the original tower to the newer hotel, Marcus noted that the rain had stopped. Between the clouds, the first blush of dawn began to rise.

That was good. More than good. It might give them the chance they'd need.

He walked purposefully through the main gathering area, then right toward the ballroom. The corridors were eerily quiet and the carpeted floors sucked up their footsteps. Only the far-off sound of vacuums disturbed the early morning hour. The doors to the grand ballroom were closed. Marcus selected the ones farthest to the right to enter. He paused for a moment and drew a deep breath through his nose. Jax was on the other side.

As they entered the dark room, Marcus could see it was already set up for the conference, with a stage at the far end, and rows upon rows of chairs and press stands.

The scent was becoming stronger. The lights flooded on with a harsh flash. The decoy blanched and pulled back. Marcus grabbed his shoulder and pulled him deeper into the room.

"That's far enough," Lazarus said from above him. Marcus looked up. Lazarus hung suspended from a light bar, Jax dangling from his right hand. Several furies stuck to the ceiling like bats around them.

Jax's hands and feet were tied behind her back. He had immobilized her. "I'm going to kill you, Lazarus," Marcus softly said.

His maker scoffed. "Then you kill yourself. You're willing to give up your life?"

"Yes."

"For a woman?"

"For the woman."

Lazarus sighed. "I can give you back your mortality, Marcus, and I will allow her to live."

Until two weeks ago Marcus had thought the only thing he'd wanted had been the return of his mortal life. Now, he didn't care about that. Only one life mattered to him at the moment. "In exchange for what?"

"You leave Bond and walk out of here and never look back."

Lazarus had just shown his cards. Making the offer meant that Lazarus knew Marcus's strength and knew it was enough to kill him. "No."

"Let me remind you. Rurik is not only my creator; in our mortal lives we were of the same bloodline. He considers me his son. If I should fall by another's hand, and you should survive this day, Rurik will make you beg for death."

"I'm willing to take that chance."

"There is no chance, Marcus! Betray your maker and pay with eternal torture. Destroy your maker and die the same death. It cannot be changed; it is our law, as well you know!" Lazarus shook Jax at him. "Why have you turned against me? Against The Solution?"

"Because you are no better than a crazed fanatic. You have lost your perspective. Too many innocent lives have been lost for your personal causes. I want no part of it."

"That is unfortunate, Marcus. I am on the precipice of my greatest triumph. The White House! I will rule the free world!" He threw Jax across the room, then swept down upon the decoy. Marcus leapt after her. She hit the wall with a sickening thud. Before he could reach out to her, the furies swarmed him like wasps on a mouse.

Marcus's fury was so intense that all he could see was red. He rose up against the mercenaries, who were slashing and stabbing him with their fangs and claws. He didn't feel any of it. Instead, he grabbed them and twisted them with his bare hands, tearing them apart limb by limb. Their blood splattered across his face and drenched his hands. In a wild frenzy, he destroyed them.

As they smoldered to dust on the carpet, he went to Jax. He pulled her into his arms. He felt her broken bones and damaged organs, but she breathed. "Jax," he said gently, smoothing her hair from her face. "You're going to be all right." He kissed her lips and rubbed his forehead against hers. He felt as if his heart was ripping in half. The overload of emotion he felt at that moment was indescribable. Never had he loved anything or anyone in his life. He was clueless to how that emotion was supposed to feel. But what he felt for Jax had to surpass even that. He could not bear her death and would gladly give up his life to preserve hers.

"If I were human, I would never let you go except to die for you. Again and again if I had to." He kissed her again and said against her lips, "Good-bye."

Then he turned on his mic and looked for Bond. Gone. Lazarus had him. "Godfather, I'm bringing Jax out, meet me in the main lobby."

Marcus held her close to his chest, trying not to move her. She had hit the wall hard. He knew she was broken inside. He prayed the blood he had given her the night before would sustain her life until she could get to a hospital.

Reluctantly, Marcus handed her over to Gage. Marcus scowled, not liking the way the man took possession of her as if he had some right to her. Marcus shook off the jealousy. Maybe he did have a right to her. She would be better off with her own kind than with him. Marcus inhaled, then focused on what needed to be done.

He followed Lazarus's scent. He was headed for the old tower. The decoy was still alive.

And the sun was rising.

Marcus took off after Lazarus, who was just leaving the glass corridor, dragging the decoy behind him. "Lazarus!" Marcus yelled. The colonel turned around, and Marcus sprung like a panther at him. At the same time, the decoy pulled the Glock and shot Lazarus at point-blank range in the face. Lazarus roared in fury and knocked the decoy aside, then turned and ran for the tower. Marcus flew after him, knocking him into the wall. Plaster crumbled around them. Lazarus shook Marcus off and bounded for the stairway. Marcus grabbed him by the leg and hauled him backward, then swung him up into the air. Lazarus crashed into the ceiling but grabbed onto the chandelier. He yanked it from its anchor and hurled it down at Marcus. He easily dodged it. As Lazarus descended, Marcus leapt up and hit him. Lazarus grabbed hold of Marcus, and they went crashing to the ground.

Rolling over and over from the impact of the hit, Marcus twisted with Lazarus, then, on the fly, yanked him up by the shoulders and hurled him hard toward the all-glass corridor. Lazarus rolled, but he was strong and was onto Marcus's game. He dug his feet into the carpet, slowing his velocity. The patterned carpet ripped in waves behind him. Finally, more than twenty feet deep into the glass corridor, he stopped. Then stood. Marcus moved toward him, keeping himself between Lazarus and the safety of the tower behind him. On the other side of the corridor, leading into the enclosed lobby, was L.O.S.T., waiting with enough firepower to destroy ten vampires.

"Will you force me to stay here? We'll both burn," Lazarus hissed even as he eyed the deepening rays of sunlight.

"Yes, we will."

"You cannot match my strength, Marcus."

"Then why am I still alive?" Marcus taunted.

"For the same reason I am. We are equals. You cannot kill me, nor I you."

A sharp ray of the rising sun caught an angle of glass. It beamed in on Lazarus's face, and he flinched. Marcus smiled and dove at him. Crashing through the glass wall, they rolled into a small courtyard beyond. They struggled for control of each other. They were evenly matched, but Marcus had an edge Lazarus didn't. Love. He'd die to save the woman the loved.

The struggle raged on. Just when Marcus gained the upper hand, Lazarus would twist out of his grip and turn the tables. Finally, Marcus pinned Lazarus to the ground, then swiftly flipped them both over as the sun rose higher.

Like an octopus, he wrapped his legs around Lazarus and restrained him from moving. Lazarus arched his back for separation, but Marcus narrowed his wrapped arms around his upper body and held his maker in a death grip. Now Marcus knew he had the advantage.

"Equal in strength, superior in mind," he whispered into Lazarus's ear. Marcus looked up and closed his eyes. The warmth of the dawning sun was all around him, and he could feel it. He could feel it like no time before, and it reminded him of his life before darkness. How he longed for that life again, except this time with Jax. But he would never have it.

Lazarus continued to struggle for his very existence. "You cannot escape me," Marcus said. "We will die together, Colonel. The maker and his creation."

"Marcus," Lazarus pleaded. "I will let her live! I will give you your mortality!"

"And then you will find a way to destroy us both."

Lazarus's struggles began to subside. His strength was waning in the morning sun. His flesh began to simmer, and he knew the end was near.

"Save us, my son!" Lazarus pleaded. "Now, before we are both ashes! You owe me your life!"

Like a constrictor, Marcus tightened his arms and legs around him.

Lazarus was beginning to really cook. He let out a small sound that steadily grew into an agonizing shrill. Marcus could feel the heat against himself. The stench of burning flesh assaulted his senses. It hissed and popped. He pulled his arms tighter around Lazarus and tucked his hands under his forearms for protection. He needed to hold on until it was finished. Lazarus stopping moving. A frozen prisoner to the sun. In a moment, he would combust into ash, and then Marcus would suffer the same fate.

Marcus.

The sweet tone of Jax's voice filled his ears. His end was near, yet he smiled.

"Marcus!" He opened his eyes to find Jax standing above him. His hands momentarily loosened, and Lazarus slid off. Blindly his nemesis reached toward the safety of the corridor, but his legs would not move. Jax turned from Marcus, reached into her jacket, and withdrew a silver scythe.

Lazarus looked up at her, his eyes aflame. He had reclaimed his original form as the Viking Thorkeel Rus. "Kill me and you will be hunted by my maker and destroyed."

"He'll have to catch me first, you son of a bitch," she sneered. She raised her scythe. As she brought it down, she cried, "This is for Shane!"

His head did not separate from his body. She brought the other one down and cried, "And this is for Marcus!"

Lazarus's head rolled from his body. He immediately burst into flames.

As Marcus watched his maker's death, he squeezed his eyes, fighting back the fire on his skin. His body quaked as it succumbed to the sunlight. Nausea overcame him. He struggled to reach out to Jax.

"Jax," he whispered, his strength nearly gone now. "You live."

Marcus smiled even as Jax cried out to him, "Marcus! You're burning!" She covered him with her body and screamed toward the corridor. "Someone bring me a blanket. Help me get him out of here!"

No one moved.

"Help me!" she pleaded.

Frantically, she pulled off her jacket and covered Marcus's face, then grabbed his hands and pulled him across the grass. But her strength was not what it had been. Her body had sustained damage. He tried to push at the earth with his heels to help her, but his strength was gone. She slipped on the wet grass. His heartbeat slowed, his eyes closed, his chest burned.

The sun was too much for him. Marcus felt himself being carried off to a dark, comfortable place. The last thing he remembered was Jax's hysterical screams. Then he heard nothing. He felt nothing.

He was . . . nothing.

Jax watched in horror and disbelief as what she could only describe as a demonic-looking angel emerged from the trees and landed beside Marcus. He was big. Long black hair swirled about his wide shoulders. A black tattoo she could not decipher crept up from beneath his black shirt, twisting around his neck to his jaw. Full red lips twisted in anger, and his furious red eyes looked as if they would spout fire. He was magnificently terrifying. He glanced at the burn spot where Lazarus had been, then he reached out and effortlessly took Marcus from her. She grabbed at Marcus, unwilling to let him go. "No! He belongs with me!" she challenged.

"He belongs to me," the dark one thundered. He took Marcus into his long, muscled arms. He looked up and, as enigmatically as he had descended, he rose with Marcus, disappearing into the morning sunlight.

Jax watched Marcus become one with the clouds as tears blurred her vision. Anguish twisted her heart.

He was gone! Sobs wracked her. Gage tried to console her. She shook him off and stood. "Don't," she said. She looked to the corridor and saw Godfather, Dante and the rest of her team watch her with a mixture of admiration, awe and compassion. She strode toward them and stopped several feet away. Emotion so painful that it felt like a knife in her chest made it hard for her to breathe. "You let him die! He saved my life and you let him die!"

She would never forgive them. She turned away from them all and started to walk.

THIRTY-FOUR

Three months later
Clearlake, California

Jax felt just as alone as she had the night Marcus had disappeared. Despite her begging and pleading for him to come to her, he remained only a heartbreaking memory. Yet she couldn't shake the feeling that he was out there. Somewhere. Alive. And today, as she sat in her rental car in front of his small lake house, and every day since she had last seen him alive, she daydreamed of him. In the night she'd awaken hot and breathless as he invaded her thoughts.

She sighed and sat back in the seat. The dreams were always so real. Like the first one in Chicago, even though Chicago seemed so long ago. So much had happened since then.

She closed her eyes and exhaled. "Marcus, where are you?"

Like always, a part of her hoped he would answer, but she knew he would not. Then the anger would surface, as it did now.

"You're a coward, Marcus Cross," she yelled at the cottage. He obviously didn't want to face her. But why? Had she meant nothing to him?

Then, quite predictably given how often it had happened in the past, her mood shifted and her emotions
ebbed and flowed like the tides. She reminded herself that
she *had* meant something to him. He had saved her life,
twice, only to leave her, but he hadn't left her on his own.
He'd been swept away by a dark demonic enigma.

The one called Rurik.

Had he punished Marcus for attempting to kill his
maker? Had he taken his life, just as Lazarus had pre-
dicted? Her eyes burned. He'd been willing to give his
life for hers. The only reason he wouldn't have returned,
she reasoned, was because he couldn't.

Yet, again, reason didn't match what she felt. That
faint though unreasonable feeling of hope had begun to
take its toll. Her anger at her L.O.S.T. team had not subsided. It had mushroomed.

"Cassidy, we had no idea what that thing was. I was
not willing to lose a man when it was obvious Cross was
on the way out," Godfather defended.

She'd told him and every other operative to fuck off.
She had not stepped back into the compound for nearly
three months. She wasn't going back. Not for a long
time. Maybe never. They could erase her, she didn't care.

The pull to this place, Marcus's only home, had been
too much. She had resisted, not wanting to feel more
miserable than she had, but she'd come. And now, as she
had for the last four hours, she sat in the car unable to
move. Unable to go in. To say good-bye.

"Go, Jax," she said out loud. "Go in."

Slowly, she got out of the car. The November air was
heavy with coming rain, but cool. She liked the rain. An

image of her snuggled up close to Marcus as the rain poured outside the window tugged at her emotions. She stood for a long time, looking at the place. It screamed neglect. The planters were overgrown with weeds. Several tumbleweeds clogged up the stone path to the small porch. It was as if he'd never existed. Her heart sank. She'd hoped that he had come home and she would find him here.

She walked down the stone path to the door. The lock was still broken. He had not returned to fix it. She pushed the door open and could not help a small smile. It was exactly as she remembered it. The sturdy oak table they had made love on was unmoved. Her empty plate, her coffee cup in pieces on the floor. The frying pan on the stove. She fingered the knife he had used to cut his chest so that she'd been able to feel what it was like to take from him.

Jax closed her eyes, remembering the sublimity of everything about him. As she opened her eyes, she exhaled and moved down the short hall to the bedroom. She pushed open the door. His scent wisped around her head. Faint but there. She reached down and picked up the sheet from the floor, exactly where they had left it, and brought it to her nose and inhaled.

Marcus's scent engulfed her. The hot sting of tears, tears she didn't bother to fight, welled in her eyes, blurring her vision. In slow, long streams, they tracked down her face. "Oh, Marcus," she breathed. "Come to me. Please." She lay down on the bed, wrapped herself in the sheets, and remembered how he had given her his blood and saved her life.

What she wouldn't give to have him back for one hour.

She closed her eyes and, once again, dreamed of Marcus.

He stood in the darkness and watched the shallow rise and fall of her chest. Her scent stirred his primal instincts. Mate, mark and protect. He longed to do all three, but he could do none. It broke what little piece of his heart he had left into crumbles.

Rurik had nearly destroyed him for turning on Lazarus. It had only been Aelia's influence that had allowed him to live, but perhaps that hadn't been so merciful, after all. Rurik had banished Marcus to an eternity of nothing. He could have no purpose, no reason to wake at dusk each day. He would walk the earth truly soulless. Alone.

His chest tightened.

Jax was all he wanted, yet he couldn't have her. He could watch her, but he'd never again know her love, for it was his very love for her that made him physically unable to get within ten feet of her. If he even tried, she would simply disappear, never to be seen again. He would not do that to her.

Take her, Marcus.

His body jerked in stunned surprise, and he spun around. "Aelia?"

Save for Jax, the room was empty, but he heard Aelia's voice just the same.

Take her, Marcus. Bring her to our side. Rurik is too stubborn to see we need you. And her.

Her statement immediately made Marcus suspicious.

Playing him was one thing, but get Jax involved? Aelia should take care. "Why?"

There is unrest amongst our kind, talk of civil war. Many are angry Rurik allowed you to live after what you did. I, too, am angry, but Thorkeel would have been the destruction of us all. He needed to be destroyed. She did that for us. She could do more.

Marcus looked at Jax. "She does not want the life we lead."

She does not now, Marcus, but given the chance to live eternally by your side, she will come to change her mind. Take her. Regain her trust and the trust of her people. They are powerful mortals whose help we may one day need. Live among them until I have need of your service.

Marcus was not so sure. The woman he knew would never choose to be turned, but Aelia's words? Aelia's words caused a flicker of hope to swell within his tattered heart, a hope he couldn't quash no matter how hard he tried.

Aelia laughed, the sound full and victorious, that of a confident woman. *I was a mortal princess in love with the king of vampires, Marcus. It was just a matter of time before I realized I could never live without Rurik. I have no regrets. Neither will your Jax.*

She left him then.

For long, drawn-out minutes, Marcus did not move. Fear, euphoria and more fear prevented him from doing anything, even breathing.

Testing, he moved forward until he was close. Closer. Standing within a foot of her.

He didn't implode or collapse in agony. Nor did she disappear. Which meant he really was free to love Jax, he realized. Free to stand beside his queen and fight for her cause. He was free, free of everything except his immortality.

He took a step closer to the bed.

If Jax would be at his side, he didn't care what he was. Mortal or immortal didn't matter anymore. Together, they were powerful and meaningful. They could work together and affect more than a small army of mortals.

He allowed himself to breathe. Then he smiled. Finally, he took her into his arms.

"Jax."

His voice was low and husky, full of . . . what?

It was a dream, but so very real.

Warm lips pressed to her lips, parting them.

She moaned and shook her head. Emotion overwhelmed her. She couldn't take waking from another dream. Those moments of realization were killing her with despair. With a whimper of denial, tears leaked from her closed eyes.

"I'm real, Jax," he whispered against her lips. "Open your eyes."

No. She shook her head. He was not real.

Big, warm hands stroked her body. His spicy, earthy scent swirled around her nostrils. She reached out a hand and touched warm skin. Her eyes fluttered open. He smiled above her in the darkness. His blood was still in her, and she was as strong as she had ever been.

Still not believing he was real, she reached her hand to his face and traced a fingertip along the scar there. "Marcus?" she asked in disbelief.

"It's me."

She cupped his face between her hands and kissed him with such fervor that she lost her breath.

He laughed and rolled over onto her.

"How? Where have you been?" A sudden spike of anger nipped at her. "What took you so damn long?"

"I was banned from everything that mattered to me, Jax. You, Grace, my cause. Everything."

"Because of Lazarus?"

"Yes. Rurik would have tortured me to death to set an example, but his consort, Aelia, stayed his hand. Instead, as punishment, he gave me eternal nothing. No love, no hate, no justice for those who cannot defend themselves. That Rurik did not eliminate me has created difficulty for our king. Lazarus was one of the most powerful vampires of the realm. There is a large, powerful faction who wants me dead for what I did."

Jax swallowed hard. *Just let them try,* she thought. Losing him before had been torture; losing him again once he'd found his way back to her? Not in her lifetime. As if reading her thoughts, he smiled deeply. "We have the rest of our lives together, Jax."

"What? You just said—"

"Once again, Aelia has interceded on my behalf. While she does not approve of my means, she was grateful for the end. Lazarus, or Thorkeel, as he is known to her, was jeopardizing all of us for his personal gain. She released me from my sentence of eternal doom."

"At what price?"

Marcus laughed. "Ah, Jax, always the suspicious one, aren't you?"

She snorted. "It's my nature. What does she want in return?"

"My help with the impending civil war, your help, and the help of L.O.S.T. if we should need it."

"What can L.O.S.T. do that you cannot?"

"Walk beneath the sun. Be our eyes and ears when we cannot."

"But—" she frowned. "Aren't your kind bloodsucking murderers?"

Unbelievably, Marcus looked hurt by her careless words. "Uh, present company excluded," she hurried to add.

He paused, then nodded. "Some are. But most of us are not interested in dominating humans. There is a whole Otherworld out there, Jax, one you have no idea exists. It's a dangerous world balanced on tenuous truces."

Jax soaked it all up. If what he was saying was true, then he would be in danger she would not even be aware of. Could she live like that?

Could she be like that herself? She'd heard his words well. Heard him use the word "we," not "I." Was he talking of turning her, because she didn't know—

"We'll take it slow, Jax."

Her eyes narrowed. "So what are you offering me?" she asked, chin tilted challengingly.

"Life with me. Whatever kind of life you want."

"As one of you?" she pressed.

"If that's what you want."

"And if I don't?"

He pressed his lips together, then shrugged, the casual gesture at odds with the fire in his eyes. "That choice is only yours to make, Jax. It will always be yours."

Her thoughts were racing. Her options tempting her. And scaring her. "What if I remain mortal? What happens in fifty years?"

He smiled. "You'll be old."

"And wrinkly, while you'll still be hot and studly."

He laughed. "I could make love to you if you were one hundred years old."

She slapped him. "That's gross."

"I'll change your mind. But Jax . . ." His face grew serious. "Jax, I cannot give you children."

She shrugged. "I can live without children. I can't live without you."

He smoothed his hands across her face. "Are you sure?"

"Positive. We'll work out the details later."

He smiled and let out a sigh of relief, then stood. Very slowly, he began to undress.

Jax sat back and, while she didn't want to ruin the moment, she needed to tell him. "Marcus?" she quietly said.

He looked up from unbuttoning his shirt.

"Senator Rowland retired from public service. He's taken Gracie on a world tour. They were both really torn up about Sophia."

Marcus pulled his shirt off. "If they knew the truth about her, they would be dancing in the streets with joy."

"She knows about you. Gracie knows she has a big brother."

His eyes widened in stunned disbelief, and she saw the uncertainty there. "How?"

"Sophia told her after the pictures surfaced. Told her

if anything happened to her and she needed help, to contact me and I would contact you."

Marcus's face froze to stone. "Why? She was a bitch of the highest order!"

Jax stood and walked to him. She rubbed her hands across the hard smoothness of his chest, then pressed her body against his. He wrapped his arms around her and held her tightly.

"Because, Marcus, I think despite everything bad about Sophia Rowland, at her core she loved her daughter. And she knew you wouldn't hurt her. That you would protect her. Even at her worst she trusted you with her most precious possession."

She felt the hard thump of his heart against her cheek. She looked up into his eyes and saw pain, regret and resignation in them.

"At least in that she was right."

Jax caressed his cheek. "I'm sorry."

"So am I." He kissed the top of her head.

Despite the weighty moment, euphoria fluttered like a wild mass of butterflies in Jax's belly. She had her man. There was nothing else that mattered. Nothing. She chuckled and lifted him clear off the floor, and in a one-handed heave she shucked him onto the bed. He hit the mattress and looked up at her, speechless, stunned.

She laughed so hard she nearly fell to the floor. Once she gained her breath, Jax stalked to the foot of the bed. "You're going to pay for the last three months, Marcus Cross. And I am not nearly as forgiving as Aelia." Jax stripped and leapt onto the bed and into Marcus's arms.

Marcus laughed, rolling over with her in his arms. The joy of his happy laughter was music to her ears. This was the Marcus she wanted. The one she knew lived inside of the dark, angry man she had come to love.

"Show me no quarter, Jax," he said, smiling as his lips captured hers in a long, passionate kiss.

And she didn't. Not then. Or the day after, or even the day after that.

Discover love's magic with

a paranormal romance from Pocket Books!

Nice Girls Don't Live Forever
MOLLY HARPER

For this librarian-turned-vampire, surviving a broken heart is suddenly becoming a matter of life and undeath.

Gentlemen Prefer Succubi
The Succubus Diaries
JILL MYLES

Maybe bad girls *do* have more fun.

A Highlander's Destiny
MELISSA MAYHUE

When the worlds of Mortal and Fae collide, true love is put to the test.

Available wherever books are sold or at
www.simonandschuster.com

Discover all the passion the nighttime can reveal . . .

GENA SHOWALTER
SEDUCE THE DARKNESS

An *Alien Huntress* Novel

She has a body made for temptation…and a kiss to die for.

Alexis Morgan
Dark Warrior
Unbroken

An eye for an eye is the Talion warrior's way of life—
but will he lose his heart and soul to a beautiful mortal?

SHARIE KOHLER
To Crave a Blood Moon

A *Moon Chasers* Novel

Hunting in the night has never been so deadly or so passionate.

MOLLY HARPER
NICE GIRLS DON'T DATE DEAD MEN

Forever a bridesmaid…Never an undead bride!

Available wherever books are sold or at www.simonandschuster.com

Passion
THAT'S OUT OF this world.

Don't miss THESE BESTSELLING PARANORMAL ROMANCES FROM Pocket Books!

Kiss of a Demon King
KRESLEY COLE
A fiery passion rages between a demon king fighting to reclaim his crown and the wicked sorceress who dares to use his most secret desires to thwart him.

Moonlight Warrior
JANET CHAPMAN
A powerful highland warrior is determined to win over a stubborn—and beautiful—small town woman. Will his ancient secret help him earn her trust…or will it push her away?

Darkness Unknown
ALEXIS MORGAN
A handsome stranger ignites a red-hot romance with an irresistible woman. Can his warrior's strength withstand the assault she launches on his heart?

A Highlander of Her Own
MELISSA MAYHUE
Ellie makes an innocent wish to find her true love—but Mortal schemes and Mortal dreams are no match for the power of Faerie Magic.

Available wherever books are sold or at www.simonandschuster.com

 POCKET BOOKS
A Division of Simon & Schuster
A CBS COMPANY

 POCKET STAR BOOKS
A Division of Simon & Schuster
A CBS COMPANY

20470